Advance Praise for *You Can't Be That.*

Susan Wright Beard has written a highly readable novel that shows a pastor and a church at its best, struggling with how the gospel is to be lived out and bravely witnessing to the life of Christ for *ALL*. That the pastor is a woman is a gift to the reader and to the church. She is a brave, vulnerable, and uncommonly wise young minister who lets us in on the secret of the unique and extraordinary gifts women bring to the practice of ministry.

The novel brought to mind Charles Sheldon's classic, *In His Steps,* a novel that shows Christian transformation at work as people try to follow Jesus. Beard's novel is all the more important as it shows *church* transformation as well as individual change. It can well be used for small group discussion and for church leaders who are grappling with the issues addressed in the book.

You Can't Be That gives us a glimpse of an under-appreciated phenomenon in American Christianity, those of progressive congregations who are just, thoughtful and inclusive and who are undergoing spiritual renewal as they seek to be faithful to the way of Jesus. It is the kind of congregation Diana Butler Bass describes in *Christianity for the Rest of Us.*

I commend Beard's book highly for ministers, church leaders, church study groups, and other Christians seeking to be faithful to their church tradition *AND* to Jesus.

H. Stephen Shoemaker, Former Senior Minister, Myers Park Baptist Church, Charlotte, NC.
Theologian in Residence at Queens University and Visiting Assistant Professor of Religion at Johnson C. Smith University, Charlotte, NC.

As more and more Christians recognize the many conflicts that exist in outdated and ill-informed teachings, books like *You Can't Be That* help people better understand themselves. More and more congregants disagree with their church's teachings on a variety of important issues, from women's roles in church leadership to marriage equality for gays and lesbians. Susan Beard's book gives a helpful lens into advancing society toward more inclusion, equality and ultimately, happiness.

Mitchell Gold
Founder, Faith in America
Co-Founder, CEO, Mitchell Gold + Bob Williams Home Furnishings

SUSAN WRIGHT BEARD

YOU CAN'T BE THAT

Patten-Miller House
Salisbury, NC

This is a work of fiction. Names, characters, places, and incidents either are the product of the author's imagination or are used fictitiously, and any resemblance to actual persons, living or dead, business establishments, events or locales is entirely coincidental.

Patten-Miller House, LLC
P.O. Box 1624
Salisbury, North Carolina 28145-1624
susanwrightbeard@gmail.com

Cover design by Maegen Worley

ISBN 978-0-9911079-0-2

LCCN 2014900639

Publisher's Cataloging-in-Publication
(Provided by Quality Books, Inc.)

Beard, Susan Wright.
You can't be that / Susan Wright Beard.
pages cm
LCCN 2014900639
ISBN 978-0-9911079-0-2
ISBN 978-0-9911079-1-9
ISBN 978-0-9911079-2-6

1. Baptists--Clergy--Fiction. 2. Women clergy--Fiction. 3. Southern States--Religion--Fiction. 4. Southern States--Rural conditions--Fiction. 5. Psychological fiction. 6. Christian fiction. I. Title.

PS3602.E2528Y68 2014 813'.6
QBI14-600014

This book is dedicated to my husband Jim, a wonderful Christian man who lives his faith on a daily basis and inspires me to be a better person.

Acknowledgments

As a first time author, I did not know how often I would have to ask others for assistance, and I was pleased that I found both friends and strangers to be helpful.

My early readers were Lynn Porter, Kathy Hagenow, and Kelly Berry, and they gave me just enough feedback to help me believe I should continue with this project.

There were several people who I contacted with various questions, and they were gracious and helpful along the way. They include Karen Knight at the Monroe, NC State Troopers Office, Lori Harris from UNC-Chapel Hill who let me know when Chinese was first taught there, Liz Carter who answered some of my questions about China, Uzma Panjwani who offered excellent advice about marketing, a volunteer at Willow Meadows Baptist Church who referred me to a church in Georgia with a woman minister, Phil and Susan Cooley who answered questions respectively about ordination and the VA Hospital, Denise Cannon at the Anson County Sheriff's Office who gave me information about jurisdiction, and Dicy McCullough who offered ideas on marketing.

I want to thank Tracy MacKay-Ratliff for the author's photo.

I want to offer a very special thanks to Samuel B. Johnson, an attorney from Greensboro, NC, who shared some Biblical interpretations with me.

Peggy Dekay lead a wonderful workshop in Charlotte on preparing and publishing a novel, and my husband and I were lucky enough to attend. During that workshop we also received a referral to Kyle Citrynell, an attorney in Louisville who graciously answered an important question for me.

My husband Jim has been my rock through all my insecurities and impatience. He believes in me and whatever else happens, that makes it all okay. My children David and Landon and daughter-in-law Ktlyn have cheered me on all the way and also helped me with technology.

Both my parents, Edgar and Louise Wright are deceased, but I want to acknowledge that they were my primary teachers about how to treat and respect all people, even those who are different from me.

There is no doubt in my mind that God led me to my editor, Peg Robarchek. Peg attends a church in Charlotte, Caldwell Presbyterian, that is inclusive to all, and she understood clearly what I was trying to say in this story. Her contributions and suggestions have been amazingly on target and timely, and without her help, this story would not be the same.

Chapter 1

Who knew it took forever for fried okra to get tender? The oil was sizzling, and I was trying to get it done without burning it. Frying anything was totally new to me, but I really believed I could do this. Darn it! Mike would be here any minute, and the okra was still way too tough. To hear him tell it, his mother was the perfect Southern cook, and all I was trying to do was be in the same ballpark with her.

The doorbell rang. I ran to the door, put a confident smile on my face, and greeted him with a very wet kiss. Let mother compete with that!

"Wow," Mike said, "That's quite a greeting, Annie. You know it's only been two days since I saw you."

"I know that, but I missed you."

I walked back toward my okra. "How was your trip?"

"Very nice. Mom and Dad send greetings to you, and Doug does as well. If I didn't know better, I'd swear my little brother had a big crush on you. He asked more questions about you than anyone else."

"Don't be silly, Mike. Doug is just a very sweet teenager who is just trying to show his approval of his big brother's choice of a girlfriend. Sit down and relax a minute. Dinner will be ready soon."

The timer for the baked chicken and the one for the corn on the cob went off just as I walked into the kitchen. The okra looked a little too brown, but it was certainly tender now. I had made cornbread, and I had another timer for that. Thirty-five seconds left on that, time to pour two big glasses of sweet iced tea, and dinner would be ready.

Now all I had to worry about was telling Mike my news.

I finished putting food out on the dining table. Mike joined me at the table, I said grace, and we started to eat.

"The chicken's great, and so is the cornbread. We had the same thing yesterday for lunch except Mom fried her chicken."

Of course she did.

We ate in silence for a few minutes, and then I gathered my courage and said, "Mike, I have some exciting news. I've been invited to preach a trial sermon this coming Sunday at a small church just outside of Charlotte."

There was an awkward silence, and then he looked at me and asked, "What does that mean?"

"It means they might ask me to serve as their interim pastor. That's a temporary position, but it could last up to a year."

Mike put his fork down and looked at me. His initial expressions were of disappointment and hurt. Then his look hardened.

"What are you talking about, Annie? You're Southern Baptist, and you've told me repeatedly that Southern Baptist churches are not usually going to call a woman as pastor."

"I know. But this congregation seems to be different."

"Different how?"

"Mike, it's hard to explain, but I think this church is courageous enough to look at issues in a different way from the Southern Baptist leadership. Obviously, they know I'm a woman, but they still want me to come and preach, at least this one time. Also, the woman who called told me they were looking to be more inclusive in their congregation, particularly with gay families, undocumented residents, and families of color."

Mike stood up and pushed his chair away from the table. "And you really want to get in the middle of that? I think you forgot to mention to me that you were still pursuing this idea of being a pastor."

"I didn't forget to mention it, but it's just been on the back burner for a while."

"Maybe you ought to keep it there, Annie. That is unless you want to move me to the back burner."

"Mike, that's not fair. And I don't want to do anything to hurt our relationship. I'm not trying to get into a controversial situation, but I'd like to think I could help bring some resolution to these issues."

"Bullshit. Annie, you can't wait to be right in the middle of a conflict. Tell me how you're going to change the minds of most Southern Baptist churches about women pastors?"

"I can't resolve that, Mike. You know that. It's just that I am still so sure that God is calling me to be a pastor of a church that I can't do like some of my friends and settle for something that's not right for me. I need to take a stand for what I believe. You've known that all along."

"Good God, Annie, grow up and be an adult. You have a job with the food bank that is rewarding and that helps people. What else do you need?"

"Mike, please. You have known for a long time that this is what I want, and yes, what I am called to do. I've wanted this since I was nine years old. I thought you understood a little more about me."

Mike took a deep breath and rubbed his forehead with his left hand. Then he just shook his head.

"You're right. I should have known better. All the time and energy I've put into this relationship, and all the time I sat and had to listen to you talk about this magical, supernatural 'call' you have from God. I really thought we were done with that and…"

"Stop it, Mike. That's a cheap shot about what I believe."

"Annie, we have a good thing going. I thought we had a future together. But I can't be second in your life. I have to come first, even before your God. Even before this 'call' you claim to have from God. If you were to become a pastor of a church, you would have to be available twenty-four hours a day. How could we have any kind of life? Is that all-consuming career what you really want?"

I sat quietly for a few seconds. First of all, God would always come first in my life, but I decided that I didn't have to remind Mike of that right now. Mike was right about the twenty-four hours a day on call. But I had known that all along, and it was something I thought I could handle. What could I say to Mike that would let him know we could still have a life together?

"Mike, most Protestant ministers are married and have families. What makes you think we couldn't handle the pressures of the ministry and those of a family as well as others do? What is it that scares you about that?"

Mike started pacing from the kitchen to the living room as he talked.

"I told you, Annie. I don't want to be number two or three on the list behind the congregation, your parents, or children.

That's what marriage means to me. You find someone who puts you above everybody and everything in the world. Otherwise, what's the point of getting married?"

I honestly did not know how to respond to that. It makes sense that your spouse should come first in your family life, but Mike implied there was no room for anyone else. It seemed to me that even if you try to put your spouse above everyone else, there will be occasions in your life where others have to come first. Your children will be small, and their needs can't wait. Your parents could become ill, and they might need more of your attention. Mike's view of marriage just did not seem realistic to me.

"Mike," I said, "there are just too many variables in relationships that cause that kind of commitment to be impossible to make. Be realistic."

"Really, Annie, you are telling me to be realistic. This is from someone who talks to a God she can't see, and oh yeah, He talks back to you, right?"

I stood up and glared at Mike.

"Mike! That's just hateful. We need to continue this conversation if we are going to work this out, but there is no need to get ugly."

"You know what, Annie. I don't have a need to continue this conversation. I am done talking to you about this. If you change your mind about this 'call' you say you have, let me know. And maybe, just maybe, I will consider talking to you again."

He stood up, grabbed his keys and stormed out the door.

My heart hurt. I told myself I was too young to be having a heart attack, but it physically hurt. I couldn't move, and I could barely catch my breath. How could I have misread him so completely? How could Mike be so ugly to me? How could he just leave before we finished our discussion?

How could I be so stupid about love? I was twenty-eight years old. I should know better.

And could I be wrong about God and my call? Was it really some supernatural fantasy that had nothing to do with reality? Was I a complete idiot to lose Mike over something I might be wrong about?

For me, everything was always such a struggle. Other people always seemed to see black and white, while I always saw gray. I had an amazing ability to see both sides of a story or situation, which is wonderful except when I have to decide what is right or wrong or the best decision for me. My faith and my religious beliefs are an integral part of who I am until the occasional doubt attacks me, and I wonder what is real and what is not.

Suddenly the tears came. I have always been what my dad called a crier. I just start crying whenever I am hurt, angry, or sad, and since I was all of the above, the tears did not surprise me.

Then came the sobs. I wanted to be married. I wanted a family. I wanted Mike. Why couldn't I have all this and the career I was called to? Other people did this all the time. I was feeling really sorry for myself and hopeless about ever getting what I wanted.

I knew I needed to just take a breath. Even though I felt like I was in some kind of shock, a part of me, albeit a very small part of me at this moment, knew first of all, that God was real in my life and second, my call was real. I had to pursue this opportunity to be something I had wanted for nineteen years. How could I stop now? How could Mike ask me to? Surely, we would be able to work this out. I just needed to give him some time to process my news.

The price I might pay for this opportunity was incredibly painful, but I wanted to do this. I wanted this dream to come true.

Finally, I got up and got ready for bed. I was pretty sure that the phone would ring, or that in a day or two, we would talk and it would be all better. But something had changed tonight, and I realized it might not be fixable. I had one last thought before I turned off the light. *I have a sermon to write, and right now, that is the most important concern in my life.*

Chapter 2

The next five days were a blur. Preaching a trial sermon for a congregation was kind of like an interview. First of all, I needed to make a good impression. Should I wear a suit or slacks and a blazer? I did not want to look like a nun, but I needed to look like a caring, serious professional who could take on the responsibility of running a small organization with members who have a variety of personalities, needs, and expectations.

I stood in front of my closet for five full minutes, and nothing jumped out at me. Everything was too black, too pink, too sexy, or too short. This problem was definitely going to require a shopping trip with my two best friends.

First I called Jane Wilson, a fellow seminarian from my days in Winston-Salem. She answered promptly, and I said, "Jane, help me. I've got a trial sermon, and I don't have a thing to wear. Do you have any time to go shopping this week?"

"Annie, you scared me to death. Don't start conversations with 'Jane, help me.' And yes, I do have some time Thursday late afternoon and evening. Does that work for you?"

"Yes, and thank you, thank you, thank you! I'm going to call Sheila, too, and see if she can go as well. I will text you details."

"Great. I can't wait to hear all about this church."

Next, I called Sheila Gray, another friend from seminary. She is a youth minister at a big Baptist church in Charlotte. I had to leave her a message. I told her about the trial sermon and the clothing crisis and begged her to go with us on Thursday.

I was at my computer later that evening trying to write a sermon when Sheila returned my call.

"I am so excited about this trial sermon you have. And I must confess, I think I'm a little jealous. I have arranged to be off Thursday and will be happy to shop with you and Jane. I'm eager to hear about this church."

"Thank you, Sheila. I am very excited about this possibility, but I am also a little anxious. I was beginning to wonder if my ordination was all in vain and if I would work at the food bank forever."

"Don't say that, Annie. Each of us was ordained for the ministry, and even though it may take different forms for us, I believe God's call to us is real. This may be exactly what you've been hoping for."

"I know that, and I guess that's why I'm so scared. I am working on my sermon right now, and it is a real challenge because it's so important. I don't want to screw this up."

"Annie, you'll do a great sermon. We can talk about that on Thursday as well. What time do you want to meet, and where do I need to be?"

"I will think about that and text you in the morning. See you soon."

The next couple of days passed quickly as I was working longer hours than usual at the food bank and had two night meetings. In my spare time, I was trying to complete my sermon. I was also trying diligently not to think about Mike.

❁❁❁

Jane, Sheila, and I agreed to meet at Southland Mall at 4:00 on Thursday afternoon. After quick hugs, we got down to serious shopping. I didn't know what I was looking for, but I knew I would recognize it when I saw it. We started at one end of the mall and dipped into each store that sold women's dress clothes.

"How did this church get your name?" Jane asked as we walked out of the fifth store we had looked in.

"I think one of the men on the Board of Trustees of the food bank is related to someone at Covenant Baptist, and my name and a recommendation were shared by him."

Sheila said, "Well, Annie, tell us what you are thinking. Is this the right time and place for you?"

"I wish I knew for sure. I'm praying for God's will to be done, but what I really want to say is 'Please, please, God, let this be the church for me.' We've been out of seminary for three years, and I am getting impatient for a place to serve. It is both exciting and terrifying for me right now."

In the next store we entered, I held up a red dress I found. It had a few sparkly things all over the front and the back was cut a little low.

Jane looked at it and said, "Not a chance," and Sheila went thumbs down. We moved on.

"Why does it frighten you that this might work out?" Jane asked.

"Mainly because I have so many questions about my own abilities. Take the sermon. I am trying so hard to make it perfect that I'm forgetting about letting God be a part of it. I worry about meeting the spiritual needs of a congregation. And what about their emotional concerns? Am I mature enough to help church members with their problems?"

"Annie, you're not going to know how to cope with everything that comes up in a congregation. That will only come with time and experience. But I know you are a compassionate and caring person, and the church members will see that."

"I hope so. I'm also concerned about the denominational fallout. My Southern Baptist male friends have always said to me that the service of women is valued highly in their churches, but that they believe the Bible teaches against women as pastors. What's going to happen to this church if they call a woman as pastor?"

Sheila asked, "Let me ask you this first. What do you know about the church?"

"There are somewhere between sixty and eighty members, most of whom attend fairly regularly. It's pretty 'gray,' but then what church isn't these days. It's about forty-five minutes out of Charlotte near a small town called Bakerstown. This church was very active during the civil rights movement and though they have continued to minister to the community, they now seem to want to focus on a new mission. And by the way, they have a parsonage where I can live, which will certainly help with expenses."

"I think you just answered your own question about what will happen to this church if they call a woman pastor. If they actively fought for civil rights in the sixties, then calling a woman pastor in this day and age will be a breeze for them. The church sounds very promising," Jane said.

We walked into the dress department, and suddenly I saw exactly what I was looking for. It was a medium blue, soft jersey knit dress with a waist length jacket that looked warm, feminine, and strong. I knew it would be perfect with my two-inch black heels.

I tried the dress on and stood in front of the mirror. I saw a young woman of medium height with shoulder-length brown hair and dark eyes looking back at me.

Jane was standing beside me and said, "The dress is great. You look very attractive in it."

"It even makes your cuteness more mature," said Sheila with a grin.

"Thanks a lot," I said. "I don't know if male ministers worry as much as I do about what to wear, but I am greatly relieved that I feel like I have the right 'look.'"

Dinner followed at a new bistro near Southland Mall. We were later than the dinner hour rush and were seated promptly. I didn't know about my friends, but after three hours in the mall, I was tired. Sheila ordered all of us a chef's salad, each with our favorite dressing and then said, "You're going to look great. Now what are you going to say to these lovely people?"

"I haven't decided. I'm looking over the five sermons I have written but none of them seem to be right for a first sermon."

"Annie, tell me this, what kind of sermons do you usually deliver?" asked Jane.

"I know I should have a style, but really I can't define what I do. I try really hard to say things that connect with the congregation on a deep spiritual level. I try to relate scripture to the present day, and I love to tell stories that make my points for me."

"Sounds familiar, Annie. Perhaps seminary taught us similar attitudes about sermons and their message," Jane responded.

Sheila spoke up and said, "I know you probably have already thought of this, but I would be careful not to make my first sermon on a controversial topic. A lot of those topics don't really belong in the pulpit anyway, in my opinion. The topics that do belong in the pulpit need to be researched and prayed about carefully and presented in a thoughtful manner."

Just then our food came, and we relaxed and let go of that topic. They brought up Mike's name. I didn't really want to talk about him, but I couldn't seem to stop myself.

"I've thought about calling him several times, but I never pushed the send button. I don't want to face what I might hear if the phone is answered."

"Annie, I don't want to be critical of Mike. He is a nice guy, but his intolerance of organized religion was sure to come up as an issue between you two," Jane said.

"I agree," said Sheila. "I think maybe you thought his ideas would change eventually, but these beliefs seemed awfully definite to Mike. He was quite verbal about that."

"I know. I think I wanted to believe our love could conquer all our problems. How stupid is that?"

"Hey, we've all been there," Sheila said. "Mike's not necessarily a bad guy because he didn't come around to your point of view."

"That's the problem. He really is not a bad guy at all."

Jane said, "I know, Annie, and I am sorry."

Sunday morning came. I guess I was shaky because I dropped my first cup of coffee, shattering the cup and splashing the coffee everywhere on the kitchen floor. Then I accidentally spread my mascara on too thick and left most of it under my eye when I tried to fix it.

I tried to be rational about this church opportunity and to say to myself, *There are plenty of fish in the Bible and you don't have to catch this one.* For some unknown reason, my stupid little joke made me smile and gave me comfort, and I relaxed just a little.

It seemed to take forever to get out of Charlotte. There was not much traffic, but close to town, there were lots of stop lights, and it seemed I always caught them on red. The farther I went out of town on Hwy. 74, the more rural the scenery became. There were few businesses to be seen, and some of those looked closed. There were lots of trees and shrubs along the side of the road, including the ever-growing Kudzu, and then there would be a few houses or mobile homes. Occasionally, there would be a farmer's field full of either soybeans or corn. I was using my GPS to find the church, and it was a good thing because there seemed to be a lot of two lane roads going in many different directions.

Finally, I drove up to the church, and I sat in my car for just a minute. It was really hot, as was usually the case in late July, but the humidity was lower than usual, and the sky was an amazing Carolina blue without a cloud to be seen. The church building was white brick, medium sized but not too small, with a beautiful stained glass design in the front window of the church overlooking the narthex. Three concrete steps led up to the entrance, and the doors looked as if they were solid oak. The steeple was silver and had a cross at the very top. Small shrubs along each side of the church were perfectly trimmed. It looked just the same as the pictures they had sent me. To be honest, because they had been without a pastor for some time, I expected the building to look neglected and uncared for, but this was not the case at all. Behind the sanctuary, there was an attached red brick building which I assumed held the church offices, classrooms, a fellowship hall, and probably a kitchen. Over to the right of the church, I could see a gravel driveway that led behind the church to what looked to be a very old cemetery.

Then I took a quick look at the house next to the church, the parsonage, my potential home. It was the same red brick as the educational building with black shutters in the front. The trim was white and it looked freshly painted. The same type of shrubs near the church also warmed the front of the parsonage, and in addition to them, there were a couple of rose bushes in the yard, both of which had several pink roses in bloom. It looked like somebody's home, and I couldn't help but wonder if it might become mine. I took a deep breath, said, "God please be with me," and got out of the car.

I walked confidently to the front of the church where a lovely older lady appeared to be waiting for me.

"Rev. Adams, I presume?" she asked.

“Yes, good morning.”

“I am Edna Allen, chairperson of the deacons here at Covenant. Welcome to our church.”

“Thank you. I am very happy to be here.”

“Walk with me to the offices. We are hoping for a good crowd today. We sent out a notice about your preaching here today to all our members. We are eager to find a pastor and to become more aggressive in our ministries.”

I swallowed hard and thought to myself, *Wow, she doesn’t waste much time on small talk.*

We walked into the education building, and several people greeted me warmly. I heard names, but none of them stuck with me, and I berated myself for not listening more closely to what they said. I think I was in kind of a zone.

One person I did take note of was an older gentleman who was the music coordinator for the church. I smiled warmly at him and got nothing in return. His name was Mr. Owens, and he looked to be in his sixties with silver wire-rimmed glasses, light brown hair, and blue eyes. He had a small frame, but he stood tall and came across as a confident gentleman. The most obvious thing about him was that he was not excited to meet me.

In just a few minutes, Mrs. Allen led me into the sanctuary for the worship service. The inside of the church was very nice with oak pews and dark blue carpet. The light coming through the stained glass window above the narthex gave a warm glow to the entire sanctuary. As I looked out over the congregation, I saw about sixty people. Most of them seemed to be older, but there were at least two younger couples who had school-aged children with them.

The service began, and the announcements, the music and the offering moved along quickly. Soon it was time for me to speak, and, as I walked up to the pulpit, I felt an amazing sense of being in the right place at the right time. I preached about God’s grace and the idea that we could all receive it. It wasn’t the sermon of the year, but it was solid, and, as I looked out into the sanctuary, everyone looked back at me warmly and seemed to be listening.

After the service, there was a great deal more handshaking and greetings. I met the two younger couples and their children. Then I met Pete Stoudemire, a retired minister who had recently lost his wife. An older couple also greeted me, and the husband told me to look out for the ghosts in the fellowship hall. My face registered surprise and disbelief, and then Joy, his wife said, "Please don't believe anything Thomas says. He is a big storyteller, and you can't trust him."

Thomas got a sheepish look on his face, and I just grinned at both of them.

Eventually, Mrs. Allen thanked me profusely for coming and said she would be in touch either today or tomorrow. I hoped her quick action was a good sign.

Chapter 3

Two weeks later, I moved into the parsonage. Mrs. Allen was extremely gracious when she called. Her comments were, "The church members voted overwhelmingly to issue you a call as our interim pastor. We are excited about you coming to lead this church."

I was absolutely thrilled and had been praying about my response to her. Therefore, when she asked, I knew my answer was "Yes."

Mrs. Allen's comments made me feel wanted and appreciated, and I was thrilled to be their pastor. I was sure I would sometimes feel as if I had no idea what I was doing, but I was still excited to be here.

I was ready for the next day, Sunday, with another new sermon, another new dress, and the new confidence that came with being wanted. I knew the church had been turned down by two other pastors, but I didn't care. They voted for me, and I wanted to be here.

I awoke early the next morning, and after I ate breakfast and got dressed. I decided to go on over to the church. It was early, but I wanted some time to get the feel of the place. I had just gotten my keys yesterday after I moved into the parsonage. I was headed to my office, but then I heard the organ playing softly, and I knew Mr. Owens, the man who directed the music for the church, must be practicing. As I listened, I was surprised to realize that he played beautifully, that he really had talent. He played with so much emotion that I was touched and listened quietly as he played "Rock of Ages." Wow! Who would have guessed? When he finished playing, I spoke up and said "That was beautiful, Mr. Owens."

"What are you doing in here?"

"Uhm, I was …uhm..I was just going to my office and heard you playing."

"Well this is my practice time, and I like to be left alone."

"I'm sorry. I wasn't aware of that."

That was met with silence. I stood there for a moment, but then I knew I had to say something. "Have a good practice, and we will talk more later."

I went to my office, sat down, and took a very deep breath. In fact, I took several.

Amazingly, the rest of the day and the service went beautifully. Everyone seemed warm and welcoming, although I knew now not to be naive about everything being perfect. There were going to be issues. After the service, I shook hands with everyone at the back door, and it felt comfortable and natural.

The woman who had greeted me when I gave my trial sermon and when I had moved into the parsonage was Mrs. Allen, a seventy-two-year-old woman who had grown up in this church and who had returned to it five years ago after her husband had died. They had lived in Charlotte for forty-four years and had reared two boys and two girls together. A little round, with hair a beautiful shade of white, she was dressed in a navy blue suit with matching shoes, pearl earrings, and a pearl necklace. She told me that three of her children had left Charlotte to make their lives elsewhere. Though one son had stayed in Charlotte, Mrs. Allen decided to make a change and return to Bakerstown after a couple of lost and lonely years following her husband's death. Her sister and brother still lived here, and she had two nieces in the area.

After the service, as I returned to my office to get my things and to reflect just a moment, Mrs. Allen knocked softly on my door. "I just wanted to see how things were going."

Suddenly I could not speak, because I knew if I did, I would burst into tears.

She looked at me for a few seconds, and then said, "Change is hard for everyone, the person who makes the change and also for the group who experiences the change. Give it some time, and you won't feel so lonely even when others are around. When schedules and names and places become familiar, you will feel more at home, and others will warm up to you."

She promised to call later in the week and left with a smile. I realized I had just been the recipient of ministry, and I wondered if I would ever be as sensitive to need and as comfortable as Mrs. Allen sharing support and caring for those around me.

❁❁❁

The next week, I spent a lot of time calling church members and setting up times to visit them in their homes. I wanted to get to know each of them.

One of the first families I visited was Erin and Danny O'Reilly and their two children, Bobby, aged six, and Kristin, aged seven. They were new members of the church compared to most of the older members, but seemed comfortable in the church and committed to it. Their house was a modest ranch style brick that reflected the chaos of living with two active young children. There were two small bicycles, one with training wheels, parked near the front door. A basketball was in the grass to the left of the sidewalk, and a rubber kickball was next to it.

I walked up the sidewalk and rang the doorbell at 7:00 in the evening. Danny opened the door and said, "Come in, Pastor Annie. It's good to have you in our home."

I liked the designation of "Pastor Annie" and hoped that would stick.

Erin walked in and said, "The kids go to bed in about an hour so they asked if they could come in and talk with you first."

"Of course," I said, wondering to myself what I was getting into.

"This is Bobby, and this is Kristin. They have a few questions they want to ask you."

"Okay. That will be fine."

Bobby spoke first and said, "Are you like a nun or a priest?"

Erin said quickly, "I'm sorry, Pastor Annie. Danny and I come from Catholic families, and our children are familiar with those titles."

"That's fine, Bobby. I am not really like either of those positions, but if I had to choose one of them to compare myself to, it would be the priest. I will be leading worship in your church and preaching sermons like a priest would do."

"Can you get married and have babies?"

That came from Kristin, and I laughed and said to her, "It is allowed for a pastor in the Baptist church, and I can only hope that will happen."

"Why did you become a preacher?"

"That is a great question, Bobby. Since I was nine years old, I knew I wanted to be the pastor of a Southern Baptist church. Instead of playing school with my younger sister, I played preacher. I made her sit down, and then I would stand up over our night stand, and I would preach to her. Sometimes I talked about how much God loved us, and usually I would emphasize that He really loved us when we did what our older sister said to do and when we let our older sister play with all our toys. Growing up Southern Baptist in Mississippi, I was told over and over again by everybody that I couldn't be that, that God did not want women to be pastors. But I kept praying and listening to God's direction, and I did feel called by God to be a pastor. That's why I am Pastor Annie today."

"Wow," said Kristin. "That's cool."

Danny spoke up and said, "That is enough questions for tonight. You two go get ready for bed, and we will come in for prayers in a little while."

Both children moaned and groaned about bedtime, but then as Kristin said, "Goodnight, Pastor Annie. Thanks for answering our questions," they both took off running for their bedrooms.

Erin spoke up and said, "I think you made a good impression, Annie. Most adults don't take enough time to answer children's questions. Our children are the most important people in our lives, and we notice when people are attentive to them. Thank you for that."

Erin then shared that they had been at Covenant for three years and really loved the church and its people. She was a stay-at-home mom, and Danny worked for the highway department. After a little more conversation, I asked if I could pray with them, and then after the prayer, I headed home.

❁❁❁

I met Pete Stoudemire for breakfast the next morning at a diner in Bakerstown. We were talking about the requirements of ministry when all of a sudden he said, "I can't believe I'm talking to you about the ministry."

"I don't understand, Pete. What's wrong with doing that?"

"Two years ago, I agreed completely with the idea that women should not be lead pastors in a church. I had no doubt about that point of view. Then my wife, the love of my life, got sick with cancer, and when we realized she wasn't going to make it, we talked about everything."

His eyes filled with tears, and his face contorted as if in pain.

I sat quietly and waited for him to compose himself.

"She told me that even though she had loved being my wife and serving in the role of minister's wife, that she actually had a secret desire to be a preacher herself, that she thought maybe she could've been a pretty good one. But she never pursued that idea because she had been taught that wasn't right, and she would never have gone against the Bible. When she told me that three weeks before she died, I have never been more shocked in my life. I was heartbroken for her. This was from the woman I'd been married to for forty-four years, the woman I thought I knew everything about. I had to walk away from her when she told me that 'cause it was such a shock. I really couldn't even think about what she said till after she died. But when I did think about it, my first thought was what a waste that my Belle didn't have the opportunity to fulfill her desire to preach, and I decided right then and there that no one else should be denied the right to serve God in the best way they could. That's why I'm in your corner now, Rev. Adams."

"I wish I could have met your Belle. I think I would have liked her. I'm glad that you understand that my being a pastor is not about rebellion or women's rights or anything other than I have accepted God's call to serve Him in the ministry. I'm looking forward to serving with you."

The only problem I had the entire week was finding where everyone lived. In rural areas, most people seemed to use landmarks instead of addresses. When getting directions, I would be told to go by the little gift shop with wooden rockers full of flower baskets in front of it and to then take the next left. When that road forked, take a right and go past two trailers and a barn to find the house I was looking for. Or else I would be directed to go past the old Sites home place and then go four miles beyond that and take a right turn. This, more than anything else the first week, made me feel like an outsider, but somehow even with numerous turnarounds and lots of deciphering directions, I found the homes I was looking for.

This time was actually a wonderful experience. I know as well as anyone that you cannot rush the development of a friendship or any other relationship, but I began to laugh with and talk with some of the people I visited, and it made me feel a little connected to them.

There was, of course, Mr. Owens to deal with. I found out he usually spent about fifteen hours per week at the church, practicing the organ and looking over the music for worship services. I knew we were going to run into each other soon, and I was trying to come up with a plan so that we could work together.

On Friday morning when I went into the office to copy the church bulletin, he was there, making copies of an old hymn he wanted the congregation to sing. I never have been good at letting things ride, so I took a deep breath and was just about to say something to him about how we should try to work together when he said, “I didn’t mean to be disrespectful the other day. It really was not personal. I am very uncomfortable with the idea of a woman minister, but I was in the minority in this church, and I have to work with you as pastor.”

“Thank you for being willing to work with me. I hope we can make our worship services meaningful for the congregation.”

I so wanted to say more, but I decided that time would help determine my relationship with Mr. Owens.

Chapter 4

The next few weeks went by quickly. I was having trouble completely letting go of my relationship with Mike even though I really did know it was over. I had not heard from him even though I had emailed him two times asking to meet so we could talk, so I finally broke down and called him. I knew I was being the clingy ex-girlfriend, but I just needed to hear Mike say there was no hope. He answered his phone, but his voice was very tentative and distant.

"Hello Annie. What's up?"

"Really? What's up?"

"That's better than 'What do you want,' isn't it?"

I couldn't say anything for a moment, but then I said, "I'm not sure it is, Mike. I just called because everything ended so abruptly, and I want to see if we might try to resolve some of our issues through talking about them."

"Did you change your mind about being pastor at Covenant Baptist?"

"I did not, and I don't intend to, but Mike, we had a pretty good thing going, and I just hate to see it end like this. Can we at least get together and talk about these issues?"

This time he hesitated for a moment, and hope shot up in me. Then he said, "Annie, I have moved on, and you should, too. I've been dating someone new, and it's going well."

I couldn't speak for a moment. Then I gathered myself and said to Mike, "Thank you for telling me that. I do think you owed me that much."

"Yeah, I guess, Annie." He hesitated just a moment and then said, "I wish you the best, and I hope you are happy with your choices."

"You, too, Mike."

I ended the call and just sat for a very long time. I knew I did the right thing for the sake of my future, but knowing that didn't keep me from having regrets and sorrow about the results of my decision. I knew I was going to have to allow myself some time and space for grieving the loss of my future with Mike as well as the loss of the Mike I thought I knew.

The next few days, I was very busy and was settling in to my routine of continuing to visit parishioners and their families and of preparing worship services. I had met with the deacons and with most of the church committees. The people of the church were welcoming and seemed eager to try to figure out how we could help the church to grow, how we could attract more people from the community.

At the first finance committee meeting I attended, I learned a lot about Covenant. The chairman of this committee was a gentleman named Jesse Akin. One of the first things he said to me was, "This church has been blessed with financial security. Edna Allen's husband left a pretty big endowment to the church in honor of Edna. This money can be used for operating expenses or special projects."

I was pleased to hear that but even more pleased when Jesse also said, "However, we do know that if Covenant does not grow both in membership and spirituality, just having enough money to operate will not keep it alive."

We had already talked about a church-wide meeting in September to discuss future plans and strategies. Everything was going well.

I was actually home on a rainy Thursday night with no meetings and no one to visit. About 9:00, I was already in my pajamas watching television when I realized I had not put up any curtains yet and that I had twelve to fifteen boxes sitting in my dining room that had not been opened. The parsonage was a charming little house, two bedrooms, a great kitchen, a dining room, two baths, and a large living room with a wood-burning fireplace. I had unpacked everything I needed for my daily life, but I had not done anything to make this house my home. It was time, and I promised myself I would do one project a day. In fact, I walked over, picked up one of the unopened boxes and carried it to the couch. I was going to unload it while I watched television. As I took my scissors and cut through the packing tape, the phone rang.

One of the two younger mothers in the church, Erin, was crying and saying "He has to go, my children are in danger, and we will not set foot in the church again unless the church kicks him out."

I had no idea what she was talking about, and my first goal was to clarify what she meant. "Erin, please slow down and tell me what's going on. Take a breath. Talk to me."

"I need to talk with you face to face. Can you come over here? My kids are already in bed, and Danny is bowling with some friends."

"Of course," I said. "I'll be right over."

I dressed quickly, grabbed my keys, locked up, stopped just long enough to say a quick prayer for guidance, and took off. The rain and the darkness made driving a little precarious, but it only took about fifteen minutes for me to get to their house. After I pulled in, I grabbed my umbrella, locked my car and ran quickly to the front door, taking a deep breath before I rang the doorbell. I was rather anxious about what the heck was going on, but I put on my pastor face and waited for Erin to come to the door. When Erin came to the door, she was a little calmer than she had been on the phone, but she was still breathing hard and had obviously been crying. She apologized for her tears, but began to cry again when she invited me in to talk. Erin, who had been impeccably dressed every other time I had seen her, was wearing shorts and a t-shirt with flip flops on her feet and her hair pulled back in a sloppy ponytail.

Always the gracious Southern hostess, Erin asked me if I would like some tea or coffee. I declined, and said to Erin, "What is going on?"

She looked at me with fear and grief in her voice and said, "I have a good friend who teaches at Bakerstown Middle School, and she says that Cliff Burnside, the sixth grade social studies teacher, has been arrested on suspicion of molesting a student."

I stared at Erin. "The same Cliff Burnside who is a deacon at our church?"

"Yes. Can you see why I am so upset? The story will be in the paper tomorrow, but Cliff teaches the children at church sometimes and helps with our once-a-month children's worship. How could I even think about leaving my children with him?"

I was speechless and shocked. Cliff and Sarah were a lovely couple, obviously in love, and wonderful parents to Justin, seven, and Robbie, eight. How could this have happened? Then I had an incredibly bizarre thought. Is this what happened in the Catholic church? Was it just so hard to believe that good men could do this? Could Cliff be guilty of this abuse, or was he being falsely charged? How could any of us know the answer to that question at this point, and in not knowing, how should we act?

"Do you have specifics about the charges or just that he was arrested?"

"I don't know all the details, Pastor Annie. All I know is what my friend said, but I do know she teaches at the same school. What should the church do?"

What a loaded question. I hesitated before I answered. What should the church do? I felt as if my being a newcomer to the community was such a handicap because I didn't have any idea how the church members would react.

I suddenly knew that my reaction to this situation and the church's reaction might define who we were as well as our future.

Finally, I gave Erin the only answer I could. "I am not sure. We certainly do not want to do what other denominations have been known to do and close our eyes to any behaviors like this, and I personally feel that protecting our children is one of the church's as well as any adult's highest responsibilities and priorities. However, I also keep thinking if Cliff is innocent, what should the church be doing for him and his family? Do you see what I mean?"

Her face hardened and she said, "No, I don't. And I am afraid it is obvious you don't have children because if you did, you would do anything to protect them and you would not even think about helping a child molester. That family needs to be kicked out of our church and banned from ever attending again, and if that does not happen, you will never see us in that church again."

"Erin, I do understand how you feel, and I believe that child molesters should be punished, but all I am saying is let's see what happens. I think you are right that we could no longer allow

Cliff to be around the children by himself, but to punish him and his family before we even know the facts might be a little premature. I would think Sarah, Clint's wife, might need some support right now as she tries to figure things out as well. Their children are old enough to understand what is going on, too. Someone needs to show them God's love right now."

Erin gave me a clear and meaningful look of disgust. "Do what you have to do, Reverend Adams, but keep him and his family away from me and don't expect any ' love' for that animal to come out of this house. We won't be seeing you again in church. Now if you will excuse me, I have some chores to complete."

I nodded to her and let myself out the front door.

What the hell! What a mess! I was shaking from all the emotion of the conversation with Erin, and I knew I had to get control of my feelings and my thoughts before I did anything else.

I drove away from Erin and Danny's house, but I honestly did not have anywhere to go for help. I realize that sounds very strange for a pastor, but sometimes in situations like this, I forget I am supposed to go to God for help. I do believe that God is involved in our daily lives. I believe God is so magnanimous that He can become involved in very small parts of our lives, that it does not threaten His sovereignty to relate to people in a personal way. I used to wonder why I believed God cared about me, because in the whole scheme of things, I am so insignificant, as are all of us humans. Even when I wonder why God is interested in me, I know that He is, and not only does God care about me, Annie Adams, He is also involved in my life – my choices, my worries, my loved ones. If He does that for me, He will do it for anyone else who asks Him to.

As I drove along Highway 218, I knew where I had to go. I was afraid. I really wanted to go home and bury my head in the pillow, but I knew I could not do that. This was one of those times when I believed God wanted me to do something, and even though I did not want to do it, the demand was too strong.

I drove directly to Cliff and Sarah's house. It was 10:15 p.m., but I knew Sarah would still be awake.

As I walked to the door, all I could say was, "God please help me."

I rang the doorbell and stood right in the center of the door. I wanted Sarah to see me clearly and decide for herself whether or not to answer the door. I waited just long enough to start wondering if the doorbell was working, and should I knock on the door when suddenly I heard the deadbolt turn. The door opened slowly, and Sarah stood there.

Never in my life have I ever seen a face so full of despair, and I instinctively took a step in the doorway and held out my arms. Sarah fell into my arms and began to sob uncontrollably. She held onto me for dear life as if I were her anchor. In reality, I was only a representative of her anchor, but for that time, I had to be strong enough to figuratively carry her.

After several minutes, I asked where the children were, and she said they had gone to bed. I asked her if she was strong enough to move into the kitchen. My fear was that these children would try to listen to most conversations in this house in the next few days, and I wanted ours to be private.

She nodded, and we walked slowly into the kitchen.

"How did you find out about this so quickly?" she asked.

I hesitated just a second and she said, "Of course. Someone heard about it and was concerned about Cliff working with the children at the church. Is that why you are here?"

"No it is not, Sarah. I am here as your family's pastor and all I came to do is remind you of God's love and to see if there is anything I can do to help."

"Thank you, Pastor Annie. I didn't mean to sound critical, but there have already been several phone hang-ups and a couple of calls I wish had been hang-ups."

With fire in her eyes, she said, "How can anyone who knows him believe this of Cliff? I have known him for seventeen years and lived with him for fifteen, and I can tell you that he did not do this. I am as sure of that as I am of my name. He has talked about the young man who accused him and was actually worried that he was being abused in some way at home. Cliff had just started asking him a few questions about his home life when these charges were made. They just came out of the blue, and I want them to go away."

She began to cry again, and I took her hand and gave it a good squeeze. I did that because I was at a loss for how to offer her any comfort. It would have been easy to acknowledge that I, too, thought Cliff was innocent and that I was sure all this would go away, but there was so much of this abuse in our society that I could not say for sure he was innocent. I hoped he was because of the pain it would bring to everyone involved if he were guilty, including the young man making the charges. The real tragedy I kept thinking about was that this would probably never go away, that Cliff and Sarah's lives would probably never be the same again even if he was proved to be not guilty. I don't use the word innocent because, in many cases, the person charged is never considered innocent again.

Finally, I said to Sarah, "You are right to believe in Cliff. No one knows him as well as you do, and you need to trust your heart. He needs you to be there for him, and your children need to see your faith in him. I just want you to know that you can call on me any time you need to. I will be here for you and Cliff and your children. I am your pastor."

"Thank you, Pastor Annie. I'll tell Cliff and the children that you said that. Would you be able to go by and see Cliff? I know he would appreciate that so much."

Oh God, I thought to myself. Could I handle seeing him declare his innocence when I just did not know that for sure? How will I interact with him? What I said, however, was, "Of course I will."

There was nothing else I could do tonight so, after giving Sarah another hug, I went home and crawled into bed and quickly fell asleep. I desperately needed to turn off my mind for some needed rest before I faced Cliff the next day.

Chapter 5

When I awoke the next morning, I felt a sense of dread, and I felt like I could not face Cliff. I wanted to make up an excuse why I could not visit him but then I thought of how he must feel, and I knew I had to force myself to go see him. I called the county jail, and they told me that, as his pastor, I could visit him between 10:00 and 11:30 that morning.

I arrived at the jail at 10:15. I wanted to look like a minister, so I had on a very plain dark blue suit, and I carried my Bible with me. I explained to the officer at the front desk who I was and who I had come to see. There was a flicker of disgust in his eyes, but he looked down quickly. I did not know if the disgust was for me or for Cliff, but either way, it was an unpleasant sensation. He had me sit for a few minutes on a long bench while he called for Cliff to be brought to the visitor's room. After fifteen minutes, another officer came to get me and escort me to where Cliff was waiting.

We went through one door, and it locked shut behind us. Then we walked down a hallway through another door which the officer opened with a key. After we passed through it, he turned and locked it behind us. I felt closed in and separated from the rest of the world. He explained that a female officer would have to search me for weapons or contraband, and I thought I would really have a complete breakdown over that. Is this what I went to seminary for? A female officer came through the door, and while the male officer stood there, she first waved a wand all around me. Then she took her hands, and in a very professional manner, "checked" me more personally. It was not as bad as I thought it might be because of her professionalism, but I got a small taste of what Cliff must have gone through last night. I wanted to scream "I'm a minister, not a criminal!"

Finally, the male officer opened one additional door, and I walked into a small, bare room with one table and two chairs in it. Cliff was sitting in the chair opposite the door, and he was handcuffed to a bar on the wall beside him.

The officer said "Do you want me to stay in here or just outside the door?"

I wanted to say, "Don't leave me here behind all these locked doors with this man I hardly know," but somehow I managed not to do that.

"Just outside the door is fine, officer. Thank you."

I looked at Cliff, and although I thought last night that Sarah had the most despair I had ever seen in anyone's face, I knew now it was nothing compared to what I saw in Cliff's face. When I smiled and said good morning, he burst into tears, and with his free hand covered his face. The sobs came freely, and I gave him a minute to try to compose himself.

Finally, I said, "Cliff, are you alright?"

He looked up at me and said "I don't think I will ever be alright again."

"Tell me what happened."

"They just showed up at my door and told me that I was under arrest for sexual molestation of a minor, Eddie Jamison. They handcuffed me in front of my wife and children and brought me here. The county magistrate read the charges to me and said I would not be eligible for a bail hearing until 1:00 this afternoon. It has been a nightmare, Pastor Annie, but one I can't seem to wake up from."

"I am so sorry this has happened to you. I saw Sarah last night and although she was upset, she said she was okay, and that she would arrange for bail first thing this morning."

"Thank God for that. I was so afraid I might have to spend the weekend in here, and to be honest, Pastor Annie, I'm scared. The only thing that gave me any hope at all was this morning at breakfast, I saw two of my former students, two kids that I really tried to help, and they told me not to worry, that they would look out for me. How can this be happening? How can I be in this position? I am a middle school social studies teacher who qualifies as the biggest nerd on campus, and I need two former students to look out for me in jail?"

Cliff began to cry again, and I knew I had to do something drastic to get his attention. I said something to Cliff I never thought I would say to anyone because it did not fit into my concept of ministry. I said to him, "Stop crying right now and sit up straight, Cliff. Feeling sorry for yourself is not going to help you. You have to get yourself together to save yourself and your family. First you regroup physically, and then you and I will work together to help you regain your mental and spiritual balance."

He looked up at me, and for just a moment, I saw a momentary flash of hope in the midst of his despair. He seemed to manage a modicum of control, and he pulled his shoulders back.

I asked if he had an attorney, and he said Sarah would know which attorney to contact, and she would call him. My brief time with Cliff was almost up, and I wanted to offer spiritual comfort without sounding trite. I asked Cliff if he would pray with me, and he nodded.

"God," I said, "where are you? Right now Cliff cannot see you in this mess, and he and Sarah both need you desperately. I know we can't solve this problem immediately, but at least let us feel your presence in this room, in Cliff's cell, in their home. Please let Cliff know that you love him and that you will be right by his side throughout this ordeal. In your name I pray, Amen."

Cliff managed a smile and thanked me for coming. "You will never know what it meant for you to visit me."

"I am sorry for what you are going through, Cliff, and I will continue to pray for you and your family."

Suddenly, the heavy metal door opened, and the officer said, "Your time is up."

I stood up and turned toward the door to leave, and Cliff said one last thing, "I think God's presence was here with me in this room."

I turned back to smile at him and then walked out the door.

I managed not to run out the front of the jail after they unlocked all the doors, but I did not manage not to cry. I made it to my car but then I just put my head on the steering wheel and cried, not for myself, although I was pretty shaken up, but for Cliff and his family and what they had already gone through and what they still had to face. I again asked God to let them feel his love in the coming days.

I learned later that day that bail had been granted and that Cliff was going to be able to go home. There were some pretty rigid restrictions on where he could go and who he could see, but at least he could be in his own home.

I had to get myself together for the Sunday service, and that took my mind off Cliff and his family for a while. I wondered how church members would react to him, but at least they would have some time to process the situation. Since I was not sure of how I should handle this information with church members, I called Mrs. Allen, the deacon chairperson, and shared my concerns with her. She already knew about the arrest, but thanked me for letting her know what else had happened.

Later that evening, I got a call from Sarah that answered the question of how church members would respond, at least partially. Edna Allen and three of the other ladies of the church had brought two meals for the family to have. I also got another call from Erin telling me again that we would not be seeing her family in our church again. She blasted me for visiting Cliff in jail saying, "What kind of minister loves a child molester?"

I am never sure how Christians will respond in a crisis. Sometimes it seems like it is an attack mode, like kill the bad guys. Other times they show great compassion and love, even to the alleged bad guys or to those they're just not sure about.

Cliff and his family did not come to church on Sunday, and I really didn't know if I would ever see them there again or not.

Chapter 6

I had been so totally focused on my professional responsibilities that I did not take much time to think about myself as a person with needs outside the role of minister. Mike had come to mind a couple of times, and I couldn't help but wonder why we didn't talk more about the breakup. Most couples I have known who broke up took several weeks to go through the "it's over" again and again. I began to think that maybe Mike was looking for a way out of our relationship, and I had handed it to him.

Being a pastor had been pretty stressful so far, and that, along with just wanting to talk to a friend, helped me to decide to call Jane for a lunch date on Monday.

Jane was waiting for me at a booth in the restaurant. I was so happy to see her. She jumped up and gave me a hug, and as usual, my eyes filled with tears. She noticed and laughed. "Still crying at the drop of the hat, I see. I thought your church members would have toughened you up by now."

"No, not yet."

She looked at me for a minute and then asked, "How's your new church treating their new pastor?"

I didn't really want to talk about my job and what had been going on with me, so I told her, "Actually, it's pretty good. The people are very nice and supportive of what I am doing. It is never-ending work, and I feel responsible for the world, but at this point I am still enjoying it."

"You look a little stressed. Any problems?"

I hesitated for just a second and said, "Nothing I can't handle. Now tell me about you and Sheila. And everyone else I know who lives in the big city."

"Is Mike one of those people you are curious about? Have you talked with him at all?"

"Yes, I'm afraid I have. He let me know pretty quickly that he had moved on and was dating someone new. Honestly, his telling me that has helped me move on, too. I never have wanted to be where I wasn't wanted, and he made things pretty clear. I am curious, though, if I know the person he is dating."

"Mike is dating the paralegal from his firm, and I hear it's becoming a regular thing. I'm sorry, Annie. I know this has been hard for you, and you deserve better."

"Thank you, Jane, for telling me that. Now I've started trying to figure out where I start looking for hope for a new relationship. Before I met Mike, I hadn't dated anyone seriously since college, and I'm slowly reaching the point where I don't see anybody else in my view."

"I understand, Annie, as you well know. Frankie and I have been dating for two years, but it still feels like high school. He seems perfectly happy still living at home and us just dating. He is a good guy, and I do love him, but he seems to be missing the gene that makes him a grownup."

"I know Frankie really cares for you. Hopefully, in time, he will find the best ways to express his love. You know what, I am grateful for one thing in regard to Mike. We were not sexually intimate. As you know, I can't claim to be a virgin, but I am happy that at the ripe old age of twenty-one, I decided that I would not have sex again until I was married or in a totally committed relationship that was leading to marriage."

"I actually wondered about you and Mike and sex."

"It was sometimes a difficult decision, as I thought Mike and I were heading for marriage, but it just did not turn out that way. You know, if Sheila had been able to come today, we would be doing some good old male bashing, wouldn't we? But somehow that doesn't seem to help. I know there are some wonderful guys out there somewhere, but when our careers take so much time and energy, how the hell are we supposed to find them?"

"If I had the answer to that question, I could make a lot of people very happy."

"And what about sex? Here I am, according to my sociology professor in Marriage and Family class, in the early stages of my sexual peak. I believe it because I seem to be horny all the time, and everything reminds me of sex. The meter reader at the church is about fifty, and before he comes in once a month, I make sure my hair is combed. I look at every male's hand to see if there is a wedding ring. I think about all the novels I have read where couples are swept away by passion, usually within a week of meeting each other, and I keep waiting for that to happen to me. What is God's plan for that? Believe me, I have asked him over and over, but so far I haven't had any answers. Why did he give us this wonderful thing called sex if he doesn't want us to participate in it? I want sex! And also, if I'm supposed to wait until marriage, that better happen soon because this sexual peak thing is driving me crazy."

I was beginning to get angry and was starting to rant just a little.

Suddenly, Jane giggled hysterically and could not seem to stop. I looked at her and said, "What's so funny?"

She couldn't even talk but just kept trying desperately to get her composure. She put her face in her hands and shook with laughter. I was about to get angry with her when she choked out, "The ladies sitting at the table behind us just called the waiter over and asked to be moved to another area of the restaurant. They discreetly pointed at us. I think your talk of your desperate need for sex was freaking them out."

She put her face in her hands again and started giggling, and suddenly I did the same thing. I was laughing so hard I really thought I might wet my pants. Naturally, we laughed so hard that we eventually cried, and it was the best therapy I could have had.

One of the first things I did the next morning was to call Cliff and Sarah. Sarah answered the phone on the fourth ring just as I was about to end the call.

"Annie, don't hang up. I'm sorry I took so long to answer. I am very careful to check the caller ID before I answer. We are still getting some very hateful calls."

"I'm sorry, Sarah. I just wanted to know if you guys needed anything."

"We need this to go away, but except for that, we are doing okay. Justin and Robbie have been hassled quite a bit at school, and I'm actually thinking about home schooling them until this is over. Cliff doesn't do or say anything hardly. He's not talking to me or the boys. It's like he has just zoned out."

"It sounds like you are handling a lot of this by yourself."
"I guess I am. Annie, please pray that this will be over soon for the sake of my family."
I only hope that someday this will be over.

Chapter 7

The more I got to know some of our members, the more impressed I was with the make-up of Covenant. Edna Allen invited me for lunch, and I was eager to talk more with her. When I arrived, she was wearing a long, mint green, oriental-looking dress. It had short sleeves and a long slit up one side.

"You look beautiful, Mrs. Allen," I said.

"Thank you. This is a traditional Chinese dress that I have had a long time and never seem to have occasion to wear. Today it just felt appropriate."

"It is a beautiful dress and such a unique design. May I ask where you got your dress?"

"You may. I actually bought it in Taiwan, and I will tell you about that. First, let's eat."

"Something smells wonderful," I said.

She smiled and said, "It is one of my favorite Chinese dishes that I learned to cook while living in Taiwan. It is called Ma La Chicken, and it was my husband's favorite dish. It is rather spicy. I hope that's okay."

She led me into the dining room where a beautiful mahogany table was set for two. There was a matching china hutch on one side of the room and a large matching buffet on the other. The wallpaper was a beautiful design of burgundy and pink flowers, and the bottom half of the walls were painted a matching deep burgundy.

The place settings consisted of beautiful porcelain cream-colored china, which was designed with pink flowers in the center of the plates and around the edges. The silverware glowed from being polished recently, and the glasses for tea were a heavy crystal. The napkins seemed way too delicate to use.

As I sat at the table, I said to Mrs. Allen, "Your home is beautiful."

"Thank you. When I was making plans to move back to Bakerstown, I heard about this house being auctioned off, and although it was much bigger than I needed, it was so lovely I really wanted it. Compared to prices in Charlotte, it was very reasonable, so I made an offer I could afford, and here I am. I have enjoyed being here, and when my children visit, I have plenty of room for them and the grandchildren. It's been great."

Mrs. Allen brought in two plates of steaming food. One was a dish with chicken, onions and mushrooms and the other dish contained white rice.

She spoke up and said, "Now when I say spicy, I mean hot as heck, so be prepared. But the flavor of the sauce does not get lost in the heat, and I think you will enjoy it."

We started to eat, and I said, "Mrs. Allen, tell me about living in Taiwan. I didn't know you had done that. Was your husband working there?"

"First of all, call me Edna and I will call you Annie. No, this was before I even met my husband, William. When I was a child, my hero was Lottie Moon, a Baptist missionary to China. I desperately wanted to be like her so when it came time for me to go to college I looked around until I found a school where I could study the Chinese language. I actually took every course in Chinese that I could at Berkeley, which is where I went to school, and I always hoped to go to China. The political timing was bad for that, and so I went to work for the biggest newspaper in Charlotte. After we had a visiting team from a newspaper in Hualien City in Taiwan, and I was the only staff person who could communicate with them, they contacted me and asked me to come teach their staff English."

"Exactly when was this?"

"This was early in 1959. My parents were very progressive, and my family had traveled extensively as my dad had been a diplomat to Italy for years. Even so, they were not thrilled with my going to Taiwan alone, but they knew this had been my dream and they could not stand in my way."

I had taken two bites of food while Edna was talking, and the food was delicious. All of a sudden, however, I realized my mouth was burning, and I grabbed my tea glass and downed it in one continuous gulp.

"Oh my," Edna said. "I should have warned you more. Put a small amount of the chicken with a large amount of the rice to begin with. Are you okay? Let me get you some more tea."

The food actually tasted very good, but I was not prepared for the heat of the chicken. My eyes were watering, and I definitely needed more tea.

Edna brought in an entire pitcher of tea and poured me another full glass. I gulped it down and felt much better.

"I am so sorry, Annie. I fix this dish at least once a week for myself and I forget how hot it is."

"I'm okay. Really. I did not mix any rice with my first two bites, but I definitely will do that now."

I giggled a little as I said that, and Edna laughed along with me. She thanked me for being a good sport about the food.

I wanted to continue the conversation and get the attention off of my burning mouth so I said, "How exciting that you were able to travel on your own so far away. I have always wanted to travel, but to be honest, I am not as brave as you were, and I have not pushed for the opportunity. Perhaps hearing your story will help me get more adventurous."

"You know, Annie, taking on a job as a pastor in a denomination that does not approve of your doing that is pretty adventurous. There are still lots of people who will condemn you in this position, so you may be braver than you think."

After lunch, she apologized for the hot and spicy dish and for monopolizing the conversation, but I thoroughly enjoyed hearing her story. I couldn't wait to get to know the "story" of the other church members.

Chapter 8

I'd been at the church for about six weeks when I began to realize that the hardest task of this job and maybe of any job, was to take time to reflect on what I was doing and where the church was going. Since I had been here, I almost felt as if I had not taken a day to think. It had only been a week since I had lunch with Jane, but I was feeling a need for contact with someone who was not involved with Covenant Baptist.

As much as it contributed to my feelings of inadequacy, I called Sheila from home one evening. She answered promptly and seemed excited to hear from me.

"How are you doing?" she asked.

I hesitated just a second, and she immediately said, "Annie, what's going on?"

"Oh Sheila, this is so much harder than I thought it would be."

"Tell me what's hard about it."

"Everything. I have committee meetings a couple of times a week, including the finance committee for which I have to prepare and oversee the budget. Can you believe that?"

"Oh my, and with you having no clue how to balance your checking account. What else?"

"The copier keeps breaking, people keep getting sick and going in the hospital, I have to have a new sermon every Sunday, and I'm still trying to visit all the church members and their families. That's not counting answering the phone a hundred times a day."

There was a few seconds of silence, and I immediately realized that I sounded like a whining child.

"Sheila, I am so sorry to have bothered you with this. I am really happy to be serving as a pastor. I don't know why all these responsibilities seem so overwhelming all of a sudden."

"Annie, my guess would be that you are not taking care of yourself. Fast food or healthy eating? Exercise or coming home and sitting on the couch? Prayer time and study of scripture or winging it spiritually?"

"I'm afraid it's all the wrong answers."

"Annie, expressing these concerns is going to help you grow as a pastor. I have a feeling most pastors struggle with these feelings of being overwhelmed at some time in their ministry, particularly early on. I think it would be helpful for you to find a local mentor who would help you with these concerns."

I said, "You are probably right. Thanks, Sheila." But I didn't mean it. I didn't know any ministers who had to have a mentor to help them do their job, and I wasn't going to be the first. I knew some of the changes I should make, and I was going to work on those right away.

First of all, there were no gyms nearby so I decided to start jogging three mornings a week. I hate having to wake up and quickly go do something, but I also knew if I didn't do it then, it would not get done. I actually kind of run-walk, but it works for me. I always feel energized after about thirty minutes. Second, I was going to have to take a little time and plan meals. Yuck! I had been eating fast food for lunch for weeks, and since the only food place close to my home was a pizza place, that was quickly becoming my answer to what's for dinner. I just needed to take an hour or two to plan some meals, go to the grocery store, actually cook these meals, and then they would be easy to heat up in the evening.

My greatest concern was how I could keep myself in a place where I could continue to be of service to others. It was the first time in my life that I wanted to slow down, think about what I was doing and saying that could impact others, and seek God's guidance. I believed God cares about our lives, but I didn't practice getting His input into my decisions, my words, or my actions, and that was something I wanted to change.

It occurred to me that I might not be alone in this frustration of not taking time to talk to and listen to God, and maybe I could invite others to join me for one meeting a week to do just that. It would have to be in the morning because by the end of the day, no one had any energy left. I wouldn't want it to turn into a gab session (at least not with each other), so it would have to be structured to be a lot of quiet time. That should be fun. Odds were against this turning into a popular meeting but at least if it was scheduled, I would have to be there and could find my quiet time. Wow. I actually felt as if I was taking control of my life. I wondered what would happen next to shake things up!

Chapter 9

One Friday night, I got a phone call that I really had dreaded. My mother called to say that she and my dad were coming to my church on Sunday. I loved my parents dearly and was very grateful for how they raised me and all the things they did for me, but I was aware that I was not exactly what they wanted in a daughter. My younger sister was exactly what they wanted so that should have taken care of things, but my mother wanted me, as she said, to "reach my full potential." What that meant was that she wanted me to be married and to have a "successful" and "acceptable" job. Kids were optional as my older brother and younger sister had already produced grandchildren for them.

When I was growing up, and I told people that I wanted to be a minister, they would smile at my mother and say "Isn't that sweet?" She was very proud of me then and pleased that I was interested in the church. When I graduated from high school and said that I wanted to go into the ministry, she quit smiling and told me I needed to think about a major in college that would lead to a successful career. I majored in religious studies with a minor in psychology, neither of which pleased my mother. After I graduated from college, I decided to go to seminary, and I finally told my parents of my plans.

My mother tried to make the best of it and said, "Perhaps you will meet a nice young man who is studying for the ministry."

My dad sat down with me and said, "What are you going to do with a seminary degree? Do you really believe that Southern Baptists are going to change their mind about women in ministry?"

I said, "Dad, I can only hope and pray that they will change their minds, and there have to be women prepared when they do. It is what I have been called to do."

My dad surprised me by saying, "Annie, I hope you are right, because I think you will make a heck of a minister."

As usual, my eyes filled with tears, and he burst out laughing and said, "You just got to get a grip on those tears."

Then he gave me a huge hug, and I felt closer to him than ever before. He seemed to see the real me, maybe for the first time ever.

When I had talked with my parents since coming to Covenant, they asked vague questions about my ministry.

I would tell them everything was just great, and that seemed to answer all their questions. I felt very attached to my parents, and they were wonderful parents, but they didn't seem to want to have meaningful conversations about my life, my beliefs, or my goals. For some reason, it seemed to make them uncomfortable when I wanted to talk with them about who I really was, my joys and my struggles, and how I saw the world and my role in it. Sometimes I wondered if they had those conversations with each other, and they have been married for almost forty years. We could spend hours talking about family members and what they were doing, about politics, and about movies or sports. I loved talking with them, but I would have liked to have had more in-depth conversations with my parents.

My brother and sister, Tom and Janeen, and their families didn't seem to care a whole lot about my chosen profession either. We had fun when we were together, and I loved being with them and my two nieces and three nephews.

My brother-in-law, Joey, a good Southern Baptist boy, actually sat down with me the last time we were all together and asked, "What is it like to go against expectations of the church?"

I said to him, "What I am doing doesn't seem like a huge deal to me. I am just doing what I have been called to do, and it's really a career for me. It's not like I am breaking any laws. But you know Mom and Dad are devout Southern Baptists and they tend to follow the teachings of the church on most spiritual matters. The only visit I had with my parents where they did not seem to mind about my calling was when I brought Mike home for a visit. I hadn't had a serious boyfriend since college. Mom was so relieved I had a boyfriend and that I was not gay, that she even told me she hoped I would be very happy as a minister."

Joey laughed and said, "I remember that. Not that your parents wouldn't have accepted you as a lesbian, but they were slightly relieved after that visit. Annie, just give them and everyone else some time. People have a way of coming around to new ideas in the church, but sometimes it takes longer than it should."

"You're right, Joey. But when you're in the middle of change, it is nice to have some people on your side."

"Tell you what, Annie. I'm there whether or not the rest of the family is, and I'll keep advocating for you and any other women ministers along the way."

"Thanks, Joey. You're a sweetie."

Sunday morning came, and I awoke at 6:00. My stomach was churning, and two cups of coffee did not help. What I did not want to happen was a discord between my love and commitment to my church, my "job" as my mom called it, and my love and commitment to my parents. I wanted my parents to see and accept me in my role as an adult professional, as a pastor. No matter what my job was, or for that matter, what any adult child's job was, it would be difficult for parents not to see us as children who still need to be told what to do and how to do it. I wished my parents, as well as others, could step back, turn off their parenting, and enjoy the results of all their years of hard work of rearing children. The good outcome might surprise them.

I peeked into the sanctuary about ten minutes before worship was to begin, and I saw my parents coming in the back door. My parents were both in their early sixties, but they were extremely youthful looking. With dark hair just beginning to gray, they were both fit and trim, and they walked and talked and dressed like forty year olds. They had moved from Mississippi about three years ago when my dad was hired as an assistant city manager in Columbia, SC.

I had mentioned to a few members that my parents were coming today, and they were graciously welcoming them. I had been working on myself, telling myself that I really was an adult, and that I was not here to please my parents, and that it did not matter if they thought I did a good job. But I kept regressing to that eleven-year-old in the school play who so anxiously wanted to make my parents proud. I prayed that I would just remember to address the needs of my congregation and to make this service a meaningful worship experience for everyone there.

When the service began, I introduced my parents as guests and welcomed them from the pulpit. Then I tried to forget they were there.

They shook almost as many hands as I did at the end of the service, and then we headed to civilization to find a nice restaurant. Dad led the way and after about thirty minutes, he saw a chain he recognized and liked, and he pulled in. I followed him. We took our seats, ordered our drinks, and then I became anxious again.

I did not want my parents to hurt my feelings or to discount what I was doing at Covenant Baptist Church. I thought perhaps it would be safer to talk about all the usual things going on in our family. Before I could get that conversation started, my father cleared his throat and looked at me and said, "Annie, your mother and I have something we want to say to you."

My stomach took a dive, and I could tell I was getting this pained look on my face, trying to brace myself for what was coming. He said, "Annie, you obviously do a very good job at Covenant. Your congregation seems to like you very much, and you handle yourself well in the pulpit."

I felt the "but" coming.

"Our only concern is where is this going? You're in an interim position for at the most a year. Then what? Do you think there's another Southern Baptist church out there that's going to call you as their pastor?"

"I don't know."

"Well, I can pretty much tell you that there are not many Covenants out there. We just don't want you to be disappointed when your stay here ends, and there is no other church to go to. Maybe you should start thinking about your future and where you can go from here. You really can't complain. You are one of a very small number of women who have had the opportunity to pastor a Southern Baptist church."

"So what you're saying, Dad, is that I, as a woman in ministry, should be grateful for any opportunity to serve even if it's for a short time?"

"Now Annie, there's no reason to get defensive. The reality is that you're doing something that most churches would not allow, and yes, I think you should be grateful for this chance. That's all I am saying."

"What about the rest of my life, Dad? Do I just keep looking back to this one year of service and be satisfied to never have the chance to serve as a pastor again? Is that what you want for me?"

"Of course not, Annie. We just don't want you to be hurt or disappointed if this is your only chance to be a pastor. You have to prepare for that."

"Actually, I don't, Dad. What I am doing now matters. For our denomination and for women. I have no doubt that God has called me to be a pastor, and if I really believe that, then what I am doing now is not a one-shot deal, but a chance to prepare for my next place of service. I'm going to stick with that plan until God tells me differently."

My parents shared a look of resignation, and with a sigh, my mother said, "What's good to eat here?"

Chapter 10

Monday morning found me sitting at my desk staring at a wall. The discussion with my parents had left me feeling abandoned. If they didn't have my back, then who would? I knew they were just worried about me and my future, but it would have felt good if they had overcome their concerns to encourage me.

Then I just shook my head and decided to start the week. There had been a few rumblings about the church's continuing support of Cliff and Sarah. I was visiting them as often as I could, and several ladies in the church were taking turns fixing meals about two times per week. Cliff was still getting his salary even though he was suspended until the issue was resolved, and some people had commented that perhaps there were others in the community who needed our help more than the Burnsides. Sarah and Cliff were having very little contact with anyone outside their immediate family, and I knew the love and support that was demonstrated by the church was extremely important to them, but I understood there were some members who had reservations about helping them financially by providing meals.

And to be honest, there were some members in addition to Erin and her family who just did not want to support Cliff. Child abuse is a tough issue for everyone to handle, and to keep showing love to an accused requires love beyond what we humans can give.

It was also time for the church's Fall Bazaar. I had little knowledge about how bazaars were run, so on Tuesday morning at 10:00, I headed for the church fellowship hall for a planning meeting. The committee was much larger than I expected with about fifteen women and one man present, so I caught on pretty quickly that this bazaar was a big deal.

Charlotte Wilburn was the person in charge, and she was an impressive sight to see. Charlotte was 5'9'', and she had the best posture I had ever seen. That, of course, made her seem even taller. She had a medium build, mostly hard and muscular but with the beginnings of a little softness around her middle. Her hair was salt and pepper, and with that, it was hard to tell how old she was. She had assignments printed out for specific people and handed them out with words of directions for each task. She was very thorough but also very efficient, and each person took their assignment willingly and with few questions.

Faye Emerson, a faithful member, asked, "Has it been decided how we would use the money earned at the bazaar?"

Charlotte looked at me briefly and then said, "Ideas have been mentioned informally, but a definite decision has not been made."

"I don't want to come across unloving or uncaring," Faye said, "but it seems that the Burnside family is receiving a lot of support from our church at this time, including help in the form of meals. I've heard it has been mentioned that they could use our further financial assistance, but it seems to me that there are more pressing needs in the church and our community right now."

"It sounds like you just want to abandon Cliff and Sarah, Faye," said Vivian Artz.

"Not at all. I just want us to look at all the options for our bazaar earnings."

"Well, it's hard for me to think of anything else as important as clearing Cliff's name. He's been a member of this church for a long time, and I think we ought to support him."

Faye asked, "Do you mean financially or emotionally because it seems to me that they still have a steady income coming in right now."

"I mean any way we can."

Pete Stoudemire, the only man present, said, "I'm not saying this myself, but a couple of people have said to me that they can't help but wonder if Cliff might be guilty of what he is charged with. You know, where there's smoke, there's fire. I think we have to consider how it will look if the church had helped to support someone found guilty of child sex abuse."

Joy Hearn said, "Pete, you can't really think Cliff is guilty, do you? You've known him a long time."

"I'm just saying what I've been hearing, and we need to be careful how this looks to the community."

Vivian responded, "What about how it looks to God? Maybe we ought to think about that, too."

"Now, Vivian don't get all stirred up. To be honest, I don't believe Cliff is guilty either, but we still have to use good sense about how the church relates to him."

Vivian just shook her head.

Joy said to Charlotte, "What other things are we looking at? Perhaps we can have enough funds for more than one project."

"One other big project is the church in Honduras that we have a partnership with. For a couple of years now, we have gathered clothing, tools, and furniture and shipped these things to this group. It's possible that we could use our earnings and buy other things that they need, particularly things for their church."

"There's also the local food bank," said Faye.

Charlotte said, "We don't have to decide today, but it's important to know what our options are, and I think we do have to look at all the possible consequences of which projects we choose. Pastor Annie, would you like to add anything?"

I stood up and addressed the group. "There are a lot of people being affected by Cliff's situation, and it has already caused so much pain for his family. I don't know what the end results might be, but I believe our best option is to pray diligently for guidance about how to relate to this man and his family. What I'm hearing from you is that we don't want to abandon them completely, and perhaps individual members can continue to provide meals occasionally for the family, but we want to be careful not to ignore other areas in which the money earned at the bazaar could best be used. Spreading the gospel through our ministry locally and internationally presents wonderful opportunities for our church members. We all know that there are other ways to be supportive of people than just financially. Perhaps when the time comes to decide on how to spend these earnings, we should look at all the ways we can serve others and evaluate which way is most effective for each group."

There were several committee members nodding their heads, and I took a deep breath, relieved that everyone's focus had returned to the bazaar.

Charlotte smiled at me and said, "We have been doing this the same way for nine years, and so far it has worked well. People know what needs to be done and how to do it efficiently. We have made a lot of money for mission projects and for improvements to the church. But you need to know that we are not rigid about this. If you or anyone else has a better idea for how to do things, we really do welcome your input."

Wow! I actually believed her. Even though this was how they "always did it," they really were open to new ideas.

I said to Charlotte and to the committee, "I don't believe in changing things unless there is a reason to do so. You have this so well organized that it seems perfect just the way it is. Is there anything you want me to do?"

Charlotte seemed to think about my question and finally said, "It would be lovely for you to be at the bazaar for at least part of the day. People from all around the community come to the bazaar, and I think they would like to meet you. Would that work for you?"

"I would be thrilled to be there," I said, and I meant it.

I had visited Charlotte in her home, but it seemed all we talked about was her deceased husband and her children.

I realized now that so much of my conversation with the older members of the church was about their families and not really about them. I did not know much about who she was as a person, and after this meeting, I wanted to know more. The last of the committee members headed out, and I said to Charlotte, "I don't believe I have ever seen a meeting run so well. Please tell me your secrets. Were you a CEO somewhere in your past?"

She laughed softly and said, "You might say that. I spent twenty years as a nurse in the army, and by the end of my time, I felt as if I could be in charge. It was a wonderful experience for me, and I learned a lot about leadership."

"This bazaar must be a piece of cake for you after your service."

She laughed again and said, "This year seems to be a little more controversial because of the choices about how we should spend the project funds. As you could tell from our brief discussion, this church is full of people with strong personalities and beliefs, and I have learned through the years to run a tight ship or we will not get a good end result. There was a lot of grumbling at first and almost an uprising one year, but our love for this church and our common goal of raising enough money to make a difference brought us together as a team, and it really has worked for the last few years. I can only hope we can focus on the bazaar for now and the decision about how to spend the funds later."

"I agree. This situation with Cliff created some pretty strong feelings, and it may take a long time to resolve them. I look forward to participating in the bazaar this year as well as observing the committee and its chair in action. Please let me know if you need me to do anything else, and I say that to you freely because I can tell you can handle this."

Chapter 11

I thought it was time to reach out to the community, not just to church members. I was not sure how I would be received. I thought back to Mr. Owens and his first comments to me. I was afraid they were going to be common expressions of how people felt, so I knew I had to be prepared for rejection. Mr. Owens and I had a working relationship now, and he had even complimented me on one of my sermons, but it had taken regular contact and several weeks to get to this point. I could not see that connection happening with other Baptist ministers in the community or even other residents

My first attempt at networking was with the local Baptist association, the local organization of Southern Baptist churches in an area. There is often a pastor or former pastor as the administrator and a small staff to provide support and training programs for the local churches. They, along with delegates from individual churches, do have some control over which churches are allowed to be a part of their membership. I arrived without an appointment and asked if I might speak with Brian Stanley, the administrator. The receptionist asked my name and when I told her, her eyebrows raised about one and one-half inches.

"Just a moment and I will see if he is in," she said and got up to walk to an office directly behind her office. I couldn't help but wonder how she would not know if her boss was in when his office was right next to hers.

She returned and said, "He does have a prior commitment in thirty minutes which is across the county, but he would like very much to meet you."

"Thank you," I said.

She gave me a big smile, and I didn't know if that meant she liked me, or if it was going to be fun to see me annihilated in her boss's office. I was hoping for the former.

Brian Stanley was sitting at a big desk in a very large office. He stood when I entered the room, walked from behind the desk, and extended his right hand in welcome to me. His smile seemed sincere to me, and I reached out to take his hand in greeting. Rev. Stanley was about six feet tall, dressed in a dark brown suit, a beige shirt and a nondescript tie. He was about thirty pounds overweight, which for some reason seemed to be an issue for a lot of pastors I know. Maybe congregations were just too eager to feed their pastors. Rev. Stanley had a beautiful head of white hair that made him look very distinguished.

"Please have a seat, Miss Adams. I have heard good things about you, and I am happy to finally meet you."

It was hard for me, but I let the "Miss Adams" go. I knew he would never have greeted a new pastor in the community without the title of "Reverend" or even "Brother," but we were charting new territory. He asked me to sit down, and I did.

"I don't have much time," he said. "I hope my secretary explained that I have to be in a meeting across the county in thirty minutes."

"She did."

"Then what can I do for you?"

"Mr. Stanley, I am the pastor of a Southern Baptist Church here in this county, and I have been here for almost two months now without acknowledgement from the association. I guess I would like to know if that is ever going to come."

"It's Rev. Stanley, Rev. Adams, and I wish I had better news for you. The Southern Baptist denomination recognizes the autonomy of the local church, however with that being said, if the local association wants to remain on good terms with the national organization, they tend to follow the guidelines offered by their denomination, and most Southern Baptist leaders do not believe it is Biblical for a woman to serve as a pastor of a church. The association as a group has discussed how to maintain a good relationship with Covenant, but I don't think our group has made any definite decisions. How is that for getting to the point?"

"You actually discussed doing that?"

"We did. Contrary to what you and lots of people think of us, we really are aware that the world is changing and has been for some time now. Other denominations in this community have female pastors, and they are respected colleagues of ours. We sometimes work with them in ecumenical efforts and services. But as you well know, the Southern Baptist denomination has stuck with the tenet of no female pastors, and since we want to remain a part of that group, we need to show respect for that belief. It is certainly not personal as we really don't know you very well. However, we are still not sure when or even if we will take a stand on Covenant's decision to hire you."

I just sat there and could not think of anything I wanted to say. I expected to be rejected, but this gentleman had done it in such a way that I could not be angry. He just presented the facts, and I knew them to be true.

Suddenly I just felt very tired and beaten down, and I guess it showed. The denomination that I had grown up in and had loved for so long really did not want me any more if I believed differently from the leadership. It felt almost like losing part of my family and part of my identity. Covenant called itself Southern Baptist, but how long could that continue if we did not follow their guidelines? Would we have ties to the national organization and a vote at the convention? Was I doing more harm than good in insisting that I knew my call was from God? Would members of my church be hurt by their having me as their minister?

I had lost my confidence, and I remained quiet.

Rev. Stanley looked at me for a full minute, and I could see in his face that he made a decision. I assumed he was going to tell me that for the sake of Covenant, I really should encourage them to find another pastor. He knew I was just hired for one year, and my guess was he thought I could lead them to make a better decision next time for the church's sake.

Then he said very gently, "Don't let anyone question your call from God. Not me or anyone else. This God we serve is bigger and better than we can even imagine, and He can and will use anyone who is willing to serve Him. Now, if you quote me on that, I will have to deny it because I am getting close to retirement and quite honestly, I still need a job. You are the future of Christianity, and that, my dear, is much bigger than any denomination."

I was shocked by his words, and as usual, I had tears in my eyes.

He laughed and said, "I've heard about those tears of yours from some of your church members, and I can tell they are not exaggerating. Rev. Adams, I really have to go but I wish you well."

When I left Rev. Stanley's office, I just went home. I was not sad or mad about our brief conversation, but I just felt kind of empty inside and needed some time to replenish my spirit. I appreciated what he said to me, but the conversation just reminded me of how outside the norm I was operating and how much energy that took.

Chapter 12

After an evening of no phone calls, mindless television, and a wonderful night's sleep, I woke up feeling as if I could conquer the world. I started by calling Sarah and Cliff and asking if I might stop by and see them. They said that would be fine, and I agreed to be there in one hour.

They greeted me at the door and Sarah looked pretty good. Cliff had lost some weight and had dark circles under his eyes. The three weeks since his arrest had taken a toll on him.

I asked if there had been any new developments, and Sarah said, "We have a close friend who works at the Sheriff's department, and she unofficially told us that the accuser had been brought in two times in the last week to speak with officers and with the department psychiatrist. We have no idea what that means, but at least it was movement in the case."

"Do you know when the next court date is?"

"Not really, but I think it is a ways off. We just spend a lot of time waiting to hear from Cliff's attorney. It's like our whole life has been put on hold. Also, we are a little afraid to even go outside to the store or to any event. Cliff is concerned his face has been in the local papers, and he doesn't want me or the kids harassed or embarrassed any more than has already happen."

"You are saying that you really can't make any plans for your family to go or do anything right now."

"Exactly. You don't realize how much time you put into planning and thinking about your future until you have to stop doing that completely. No one likes living in limbo, and now we are forced to. Unfortunately, our families live farther than thirty miles from here, and Cliff can't visit them because of the bail agreement."

Cliff finally spoke. "My parents are too embarrassed to come here to see me. They must think I did this awful thing. How can they think that?"

"Cliff, your parents don't think you are guilty of this," Sarah said. "They are just older, and they don't know what to do. Please Cliff, please quit dwelling on your parents."

Cliff put his head in his hands and just sat still. I felt so helpless. I had not realized how much of this situation Cliff was not handling well. I knew I should have some words of encouragement for him, but I was having a difficult time coming up with any.

Finally I said, "I can't even comprehend what you are going through, and even though I have only known you a short time, I do know that both of you have a tremendous amount of strength. It is going to take all of it to get through this. I have one practical suggestion that I have heard several people say helps them in a crisis. That is to start keeping a journal. People have told me that it is the best therapy they have found. They write down everything that is happening to them, and then they write down all the feelings they can't really say out loud. I've heard there are a lot of curse words in those journals, but you can feel free to use them because it is just for you to read. I don't know if that really helps, but it can't hurt anything. And as for the boys, how would you feel about them coming to the church Saturday and helping everyone do the fall cleaning and sprucing up the yard to get ready for the bazaar? I believe they would be welcomed and treated with love."

"You can help the boys, but there is no help for me. My life is over," said Cliff.

I exchanged a look with Sarah who reassured Cliff that his life was not over, that there was hope.

"Cliff," I said, "Look at me. You have a wife and two sons who love you very much, and they need you to keep fighting. This is a horrible situation, but you cannot give up. You are strong enough to get through this with God's help."

"I want to keep fighting, but it is so hard," Cliff said, and then he began to cry.

Sarah put her arms around him and comforted him. "It will be alright, honey. It has to be."

I watched her hold him and felt the despair in this home.

"Pastor Annie, it would be wonderful if the boys could help with the cleanup. They would enjoy seeing people at church."

"Okay, Sarah," I said. "I will pick them up about 9:00 and will bring them home when we finish or when they get tired of working."

"Thank you. It seems like such a simple activity, but it might be the first normal one they have done since this whole thing started."

"The other comfort I can always offer you is prayer. Will you pray with me now?"

They agreed, and I prayed for strength for each of them, for endurance, and most of all, for justice.

After leaving their house, I went by the community hospital where one of our members, Thomas Hearn, was having some tests. I thought I could at least speak with his wife even if I could not see him. As it turned out, I saw them both. He was in between tests and was sitting in the waiting room with his wife.

They are a sweet couple. They have been married sixty-two years. He is eighty-three, and she is eighty-one. Thomas is tall and slim with thinning brown hair and wire-rimmed glasses. He was a bookkeeper for forty years with a small auto repair business in Monroe, NC. Joy is of medium height and a little overweight, and she has a beautiful head of thick white hair that complements her striking blue eyes. Joy worked for thirty years as a school cafeteria worker at an elementary school in Monroe. The first time I visited them at their home, I found out that they had one son, Evan, who was killed in an automobile accident when he was in high school over forty years ago.

That night in their home, I had asked them what he was like.

They looked at me with shocked faces, and I thought. *Oh my God, I have done something awful by asking that.*

I started to apologize for asking, but Thomas said "No, no, please don't apologize. It's just that no one has asked us about him in so long. We would be thrilled to tell you about our son. We talk about him all the time, but other people seem to think we have forgotten all about him."

Joy spoke first, "It took us several years to get pregnant, so we were thrilled when Evan was born. He had dark curly hair and the bluest eyes you had ever seen. Just like me. He was a good baby and a good little boy. He was happy except when he got too tired, and then he could get right cranky. He stayed with Thomas' mother while we worked. That was a little unusual back then, but we needed two incomes. As he got older he was pleasant and well mannered. I expected him to get a little defiant when he was a teenager, but it never happened. Thomas always said he didn't have anything or anyone to defy 'cause we kind of spoiled him, but even if we did, he never acted spoiled."

Then Thomas spoke up and said, "He always loved music. He loved the children's choir, and he loved the Beatles and the Monkees and just about any other singing group you could name. He loved riding his bicycle and playing basketball. But what he was beginning to love more than anything was his guitar. He had taken lessons for several years, and all of a sudden, he was playing in groups that actually sounded good. His last group was called the Newbies, and they focused on songs written by the band members. That was hard, and sometimes they did not sound great, but they were creative and they were having fun."

Then Thomas added, "He was riding with a friend, a fellow band member, when the accident happened. They were not drinking or using drugs. They were just young. Our best guess was that his friend, Walt, and he were probably acting silly and singing songs, and Walt just did not see the stop sign at an intersection. They were both killed."

"I was so angry with God for a long time," Joy said. "How could he take my beautiful boy? People had the nerve to tell us it was God's will, and I was as angry with them as I was with God. I just will never accept that God wills young people to die and parents to experience such unendurable suffering. After several years, I finally came to peace with God. I believe He cried along with us that awful day. I think Evan died in a tragic accident that was caused by youthful exuberance and inexperience. It changed our lives forever, but after a while our anger at God decreased, and our faith in Him slowly returned. When I think about our lives now, I am so grateful that we did not completely lose our God as we did our son. That might have destroyed both of us."

"Thomas and Joy, I am both impressed and amazed that you two came through such a devastating loss without losing your love for each other or for God. I don't know if I could have done that."

"You would be surprised what you can do when you have to, Pastor Annie," said Thomas. "But let me be honest with you. Joy and I have both begun to yearn for that time when we will be reunited with Evan. Please don't panic or be shocked by what I am saying because we are not going to do anything to hasten our demise, but when it does happen, please know that we will be celebrating our reunion with him. It's been a long, long time, Annie, and we miss our boy and want to see him again."

"Your job, Pastor Annie," Joy said, "will be to remind the surviving spouse that through his or her grief, they, too, should be glad that their partner is with Evan again. It really will be a time for celebration."

Of course, after that visit, I cried all the way home, but after I had some time to think about it, I admired each of them so much for their strength and their honesty about how they felt. It is so easy for those of us who have not had such a tragedy in our lives to believe that the people who have will "get over" their loss and move on. With Thomas and Joy, they lived their lives, but they never quit missing their child or grieving his loss. It was only natural that as they approached the end of their lives, they got excited about seeing him again. I don't even know how I feel about seeing and knowing our loved ones in the afterlife, but I sure as heck can't say that it won't happen, so I could share their anticipation with them.

When I found both of them in the hospital waiting area, I greeted them with a hug and a smile. They looked a little tired, but they were reading the newspaper and patiently waiting for the next test. It was the last one Thomas had to have that day.

I asked if they were comfortable sharing what was going on with Thomas, and they said of course. Joy said, "Thomas has been having some pain in his upper abdomen, and the doctor wanted to do some tests. They thought it might be something to do with his gall bladder, but they needed the tests to verify that."

Thomas said "I have been raking leaves and cleaning up the yard. I think I just pulled a muscle or something, but Joy worries about me so I agreed to all these tests. They are a regular pain,

Pastor Annie, so I'm hoping I get an apple pie for my reward tonight."

"Thomas, you do not need more apple pie for a reward. What you need to do is slow down, so you won't have all these problems and then you won't need all these tests."

"Yes, dear," he said, with a big wink in my direction.

"I saw that, Thomas," said Joy, "but I will be keeping an eye on you from now on."

I said a short prayer with them thanking God for their many years together and for their son, and then I prayed for their continuing good health. When I finished, Thomas whispered to me, "I wish you had put in a good word about that pie."

Smiling, I left that hospital, and headed for a huge hospital in Charlotte. Another church member, Mai Anderson, had had knee replacement surgery three days ago, and I wanted to see her. She had met her husband Edward in Vietnam in 1966 when he was serving in the US Army there. He had been a clerk for a general, and in buying office products and other goods for the general, he had met Mai in a local business. They became friends. Then Edward learned he would be going home in two months because his mother was very ill. When they learned of that, Edward and Mai both became distraught and realized that they had fallen in love. They began the process of determining how he could take her home with him and discovered how difficult that would be. It took them four years to arrange for Mai to come to the States, but they never gave up and have been very happy together. They have two children, both of whom live in the Charlotte area.

I found Mai's room, and, of course, Edward was there. Mai is a petite woman with long, dark straight hair who looks younger than her age, while Edward is a tall lanky man whose face reflects the trials and tribulation of a former soldier. They were holding hands and giggling about something when I came in the room, and for a moment, I felt like an intruder. But when Mai saw me, she was so grateful that I had come to see about her. She said, "I am in some pain, but overall, I am okay."

Edward said, "The surgery went very well, and we are so glad it is over. Now she will start rehab, and from what I hear, that's the tough part. Mai is tough, though, and she'll work very hard."

"I am just glad you are doing well."

After determining that she was progressing appropriately, I said a prayer for her and then turned back around and headed for home.

I again was feeling overwhelmed by the lack of time to do all the things I wanted to do. These three visits had taken up a huge part of my day, but I just believed so strongly that was a vital part of my ministry. Now I had to go back to the office and go over the month's expenditures so I could be prepared for this evening's finance committee meeting. I had neglected to organize that morning gathering for those who wanted or needed quiet time to commune with God, and I was feeling guilty about that. I was again running low on energy and inner strength to do my job.

Chapter 13

After the finance committee meeting ended, I went home and found some time to just think. As happened too often when I paused for thought, my mind turned to Mike. Remembering our time together was all I had left, and I allowed myself to do just that. I still wondered how I could have misread his feelings for me. I had finally accepted the fact that he had loved me, but not in the way that I wanted to be loved or in the way that would make a marriage lasting and meaningful. I had begun to wonder if I would ever find that kind of love, and as much as I wanted that, I was trying to reach a point in my life that I could accept being alone if that was what happened. That was not easy to accept. After about fifteen minutes, I made myself quit focusing on that and move on to other areas of my life like what could I eat for dinner tonight.

While eating my dinner of cold cereal and milk, I began to think about the future of Covenant. In the time I had been there, I had attended numerous meetings about the daily activities of the church, and I would say that things were running pretty well. What we had not done as a group was talk about where we wanted and needed to go as a congregation and how we were going to accomplish that. The fall bazaar was in a week and a half, and it would be taking a lot of time and energy of the members, but I knew we had to all stop and take a look at our future. I already felt terribly invested in this congregation, and I wanted to see them survive and grow together. I also knew times were hard for mainline denominations, and we were going to have to evaluate who we were and who we wanted to be. I decided that I would recommend we set a date for our church-wide meeting on Sunday two weeks after the bazaar. I would prepare a short meditation, but the actual service would be primarily church members talking about what they wanted in a church and specifically what this church should be doing in the community. Meeting during worship was a pretty drastic step, but this church had made a pretty radical decision when they hired me, and I was hoping they wanted continued radical action.

The cleanup day on Saturday was a really good day for teamwork. I picked up Justin and Robbie, and they were excited to be headed for the church.

Robbie sat up front with me since he was the oldest, and after a couple of minutes, he turned to me and asked, "Pastor Annie, is my dad going to jail?"

I could not promise Robbie that would not happen, but what I could say was, "Everyone who knows your dad well believes this is all just a terrible mistake, and I think we just have to hang on to that idea and believe that our justice system will get it right. Robbie, it is scary, I know, but your dad needs you to believe in him like your mom does. It is one of those bad times that you just have to get through. I don't know if you ever pray, but that is something you can do that might give you some comfort. God will listen to your prayers."

Robbie did not say anything, and I felt sad that I could not completely eliminate his fears.

Justin and Robbie really seemed to have a good time just being around people who loved them. I stayed in the office most of the time because I had to finish my sermon for the next day. The boys worked very hard according to the cleaning crew, and right after lunch, they asked me to take them home. The place looked pretty good to me, so I was thrilled to have an excuse to leave.

A week later, we had the annual bazaar, and it was an amazing feat of organization. Charlotte had everyone in the right place and on time, and attendance was great. Approximately 250 people from all around the region attended the bazaar, and many of them purchased items. The vendors, both in and out of the church, seemed to be bringing in money, and I became an observer of what a small group of people could accomplish if they had a goal and a plan.

Edna found me to introduce me to her two adorable granddaughters, Emily and Ella. They were three-year-old twins, both with dark eyes and brown Shirley Temple curls. They smiled at me and giggled as they ducked their heads toward their grandma. She seemed to have her hands full with them, and I offered to help, but she said she was fine and that her son would be picking up the girls shortly.

I introduced myself to everyone I did not know, and several of them told me how lucky I was to be working in this particular church with this group of people. At first, I was kind of surprised, but one older gentleman asked me to sit with him, and when I did, he said, "I want you to know that this church has always taken a stand for what is right. Sometimes it has not taken a popular stand, but they have stuck to their guns throughout the years. I lived in this area in the sixties, and this church was the first to speak out clearly in support of civil rights, and they practiced what they preached by having joint services with the black Baptist church that used to meet down the road. I did not always agree with their ideas, and sometimes they made me angry, but in hindsight, their ability to see what was right and their courage to speak and act on that was pretty darn impressive. They were just always ahead of the rest of the county and sometimes the whole country. There were times when other Baptists in the county were pretty upset with Covenant, but if they complained about them, they looked bad so they had to keep quiet. You do know that some of them have complained about you being a pastor, right?"

"I had wondered about that, so thank you for telling me. I'm still pretty new and feeling my way as a pastor. It is always nice to know what I might be facing in the community and to have a little insight through history as well."

"You need to talk with Alexander Jones. He was a teenager in the black Baptist church that met with Covenant, and he is pretty outspoken about what went on during the Civil Rights Movement. He always comes to the bazaar, not to buy anything but to see old friends. He'll be here soon."

"I forgot to ask your name, sir."

"My name is Woody Henry, and I am a good Methodist. Been one for about seventy years, and it's served me pretty well."

"Thanks again for your insight."

I wandered around some more, and talked with members and vendors. Right before noon, when lunch was going to be sold, I saw a distinguished black gentleman come into the fellowship hall. I saw Mr. Owens and asked him if he knew the gentleman's name, and he told me it was Alexander Jones.

I walked over to him and introduced myself to him. I hoped he would not mind speaking with a representative of Covenant, the church who fifty-something years ago took a stand for civil rights.

He looked at me a long time, making me just a little uncomfortable, and then he said, "I can tell you are feeling very proud of your church, and perhaps you have heard enough of your history to know that this church made a huge impact on my life. I was an angry fifteen-year-old who had begun to hate all white people. I was suspicious of the church's motives when they first came to us, and said they wanted to worship with us. My dad was a deacon, and I kept warning him that they wanted something from us, and that they could not be trusted. But he knew our church had to accept the hand of friendship that was being offered even if it was not sincere, and he encouraged the pastor to do so. We did and it was a wonderful, loving and meaningful partnership. When I graduated from high school three years later, your church awarded me a scholarship so that I could attend a university in Charlotte. They renewed that scholarship for me until I graduated, and changed forever my opinion of white people and Christians. After I graduated from college, I attended a seminary in Salisbury, and I have served as a pastor for over thirty-five years. By the way, my church has always offered scholarships to our youth, and one of those per year is offered to a white student in a neighboring church. Your church has a wonderful history, but I hope what you are doing is leading them to make new history. The community continually asks the church, 'What have you done for me lately?'"

"I agree, Mr. Jones. I am very blessed to be at this church. I was the administrator of a food bank in Charlotte previously, and I was lucky enough to work with people who believed in my potential and shared those feelings with Covenant, but it is time for me to lead this church on its new mission. This church is known for being special, and I want to continue its pattern of fighting for justice and equality."

The bazaar ended at 2:00, and I could tell it had been a huge success. I was tired from all the "glad-handing" I had done, but I was also exhilarated about the conversations that had confirmed in my mind that this church needed to find its new mission. I could not wait to talk with the deacons about the Sunday morning meeting to plan our future.

Chapter 14

When I spoke with the deacons early Sunday morning and told them that I wanted to use most of a worship service for a discussion of our future, they seemed to think that was a great idea. I explained that whatever we planned for our future, we had to all be in it together and that often there were members who cared a lot but who could not or would not come out to a called meeting at night. There were only a couple of questions concerning any visitors we might have or how to handle the few children we would have during worship on the designated day. Since Cliff and Sarah were not coming to church right now and since Erin and her family had left the church because of our kindnesses to Cliff and Sarah, we really did not have any active members with children, but occasionally, a member brought grandchildren.

Alan Emerson, a deacon, and his wife, Faye, volunteered to take any children who were present to the fellowship hall and entertain them for the duration of the meeting. Jesse Akin, a member and chairman of the finance committee who always attended without his wife, said that if there were any visitors, he would first invite them to stay and hear the discussion, but if they did not want to do that, he would escort them to the fellowship hall, offer them coffee, and then sit and talk with them. That seemed to take care of any issues except for my concern if we announced this meeting too early no one would come that day.

Edna, who was chair of the deacons, looked at me questioningly, and said gently, "Oh ye of little faith, Annie. This congregation cares about its future, and our members will show up that day."

I felt properly reprimanded and just said, "That is wonderful."

My experience had been that even the best members of a congregation got excited about a day off from church, and any reason to stay home, such as a called meeting, was just the excuse they were looking for. I so hoped I was wrong.

The designated Sunday for our congregational meeting arrived, and I was a little anxious. I did not want any plans to be mine alone, and I wanted church members to speak up, talk with each other, and decide for themselves new ways we could serve. My greatest fear was that no one would speak, and they would look to me for all the answers. I knew that was not the right way to go, but I also hate silence in a group meeting, and I just did not know what would happen.

When 11:00 rolled around, I walked into the sanctuary and was pleasantly surprised. Actually, I was shocked. There were more members present for this meeting than we had been having at our worship services. We had our music, prayers, and offering as usual, and then I gave my devotion.

I began by saying, "Do you know someone who attended church as a child and maybe even as a teen but who no longer goes to church? I'm guessing that most of these people did not reject God, but somehow in their list of priorities of day-to-day living, church attendance fell lower and lower until it was no longer even on the list. Much of this probably started during young adulthood when these friends and/or relatives were either in college, were working new jobs, or were starting their families. Sunday became one of the few days they had to sleep late and lay around and not rush off somewhere. Saturday always seemed to have chores needing to be done, but Sunday was a day of rest and sleep, and they just got out of the habit of going to church. Years went by before they knew it, and pretty soon they had become the 'unchurched.' Often they were critical of organized religion, and eventually, they decided the church just was not relevant to them anymore, and they discarded any remaining idea that church was still a part of their lives. Some have rejected more than just the church, including the teachings of Christianity. As Christians and churchgoers, we have developed feelings of apathy and helplessness about being successful growing our churches. It just seems too overwhelming, and though we talk about reaching the unchurched, we really don't know how, and we really don't want to change anything about us or about how we reach out to people. This morning as we talk about our church's future, I think we need to look at three different areas of action."

I took a breath and a sip of water and looked slowly out over the congregation. A few heads nodded in agreement.

I went on to say, "First of all, we need to look at our product, a personal relationship with Jesus Christ and seeing Him as our pathway to God. As with any company, you can't sell something you don't believe in or something you haven't experienced. The person doing the 'selling' has to believe that the product will improve the buyer's quality of life. Furthermore, the 'seller' has to know how the buyer's life will improve and what steps have to be taken to make that happen. Second, we have to determine methods to let others know about our product. Most companies use advertising or word of mouth. Perhaps that would work for us, but we need to look at all ways to share our product information. Marketing Jesus Christ has been done the same way for a very long time, and perhaps we should look at new ways to do that."

My mouth was so dry I took another sip of water. This was a challenging devotion.

"Finally, we need to give a great deal of attention to our audience. It seems that churches often look for new members who are just like them. That is fine, but so many of that group consider themselves a member of a church even if they attend very infrequently. We certainly want to continue seeking those who have fallen away from the church, but perhaps we should begin to seek those that the church has pulled away from, those people who are not like us, those who don't look like us or talk like us and those who have different ways of living. Sometimes it seems that we beat on doors that hide people who reject us and the church while closing the church door to those who want to come in, but who don't fit the church mold. We need to offer guarantees and warranties, and we need to provide follow-up services. In other words, we don't just sell the product and walk away from the buyer. We need to be present to help with any issues, questions, or problems the buyer might have. We as a congregation need to be available to nurture new Christians in their spiritual growth as well as in other areas of their lives. As we gather to talk in a few moments, let's think about how we can implement these actions and make them a part of our faith as well as that of others."

Then I led the group in a prayer where I asked for God's guidance, his patience with us, our patience with each other, and for creative thoughts and ideas.

At this time, since there were no visitors or young children present, we began our meeting. Before anyone started talking, however, I asked that we gather in a circle with everyone facing each other. I did not like the idea of everyone having his or her back to each other in the pews, and as much as we had to rearrange ourselves on the seats, it was worth it to look at each other.

The deacons had written a letter explaining to the group what we were going to be discussing, and at this time, Edna began to chair the meeting. She asked if anyone had any opening comments, and a couple of hands went up.

Pete Stoudemire, my retired minister friend, cautioned the group not to sell out our important beliefs, that there were just some things we could never compromise on, even to bring others into God's grace or into our church fellowship. He turned to me and said, "Actually, I am a little offended by your calling Jesus Christ a 'product.' He is our Lord and Savior, the son of God, and we should always talk about Him with reverence and respect. I was a Baptist pastor for forty years, and I would say I never thought of Jesus as a product. I know the world is different now, but I honestly don't know how far I can go with all these new ideas."

"I appreciate your feelings about that, Pete, and I am sorry if my comments offended you or any other member here today. I agree with you about reverence and respect. It was actually hard for me to say some of those things because, like you, I was taught to honor God's name. I meant no disrespect. Sometimes I get so frightened about the future of the church here on earth that I feel like shaking things up. I was hoping my words might help us get started thinking and talking, but I will be more sensitive to your feelings about this in the future."

"Well, it didn't bother me a bit, Pastor Annie," said Thomas Hearn, "and, Pete, let me say something to you. You are a respected man of God. I visited your church in Charlotte, and I was able to spend time with you and your lovely wife, Belle. You reached out to everyone in your community, and Belle was one of the most accepting women I have ever known. I can say this to you because I have known you for fifty years. She would be leading the charge in putting these new ideas into practice, and she would want you to do the same. You serve as the caretaker of our tenets, and if we go too far in any direction, you speak up and tell us. I think we all know that if we don't change something about our message, it will not be received. I agree with Pete that there are some basic tenets of the church that must never change, but there are an awful lot of ways we've been doing things that haven't worked."

Edna spoke up and said, "I have a white board right here. Let's hear it guys. What can we never compromise on?"

Everyone became very quiet. Finally, Joy Hearn spoke up and said, "Edna, the phrasing of that question is a little difficult for me to swallow. Never is a very long time. I know there are the beliefs that make up the foundation of Christianity, and I certainly want to affirm them, but to say 'never compromise' is a bit intimidating to me."

"Jesus is the son of God. He died and rose again and is a living Savior," said Pete. "And because of that and God's grace, we may all choose to have a personal relationship with Him. I don't have a bit of trouble saying we can't compromise on that!"

"We are to love Him with all our heart, our soul, and our mind and our neighbor as ourselves," said Charlotte Wilburn.

There were a few seconds of silence, and I, along with the others present, was trying to figure out what would come next.

Jesse Akin, the local pharmacist, spoke up and said, "I am not sure how to say this, but I believe the Bible is the inspired word of God, but I don't think God dictated every word, and because of that, the Bible is not inerrant in my eyes. The message is infallible but not every word in the Bible is. I know that opens up a whole can of worms about what to believe, but I think if you look at the book overall, the message is pretty darn consistent and clear."

"Well, there's the virgin birth and the healing of the sick and there's the miracles and the amazing works. But as I am sitting here, I could stay quiet over these things, but I could never stay quiet over Jesus being the Son of God and his rising from the dead. Those are the things I could never compromise on or even bring up for discussion," said Mr. Owens.

"Well, I believe in the Trinity, and to me, that part is important, but I don't know if someone came to us and did not accept the idea of the Trinity if that would be enough for me to not let him or her be a part of us here," said Thomas. "But I do agree that believing Jesus is who He said and that He rose from the dead has just got to be a belief we must have in our church members."

There were several people who spoke up softly and said, "I agree with Thomas." This was followed by murmurings of "Me, too" and a few nodding heads. No one seemed upset with this line of discourse, and members continued to discuss what was important to them and on what they could not compromise.

Mai and Edward Anderson were sitting in the back because of Mai's wheelchair. She timidly raised her hand and waited for Edna to acknowledge her. Once Edna saw her, Mai spoke softly and said, "Forgive me if I don't completely understand what is going on, but it frightens me that we are saying some things in our faith don't matter to us while others do. I have not been a Christian my whole life, but I thought everything was important to my faith. I am confused about what we are doing."

Edna spoke up and said, "Thank you for speaking up, Mai. I think everything is important in my faith as well. What we are trying to do is to discuss what is most important to us so that if someone came to our church who did not believe everything we did, would there be any room for them in this congregation. For example, some people believe that every word in the Bible is literally true, while others believe that the Bible was written by humans who were inspired by God, and because of that, there is room for inconsistencies without the message being weakened. The question would then arise, 'Is there room in this church for people with these two different beliefs?' To me, the question is also 'If someone wants to worship with us who believes a little differently from some of us, will they be welcome?'"

I said to Mai, "I don't think we want to start giving up our beliefs or expecting any member to do that, but can we be open enough to allow those who believe a little differently from us or who live a different lifestyle from us to still worship God in this church? You were right to question us about that because I think we did sound like we were throwing beliefs out, and we don't want to do that."

Jesse Akin spoke up and said, "I don't want to do that either, but I don't want what I believe to keep others from learning about God and being a part of this church community. To me, that is the point. How do we hang on to what we believe and yet welcome those who are different from us?"

Edna nodded and said, "I think you just summarized the question beautifully, Jesse, and I appreciate your comments. We are talking about a mindset, not really about specific beliefs. Do we want to invite and include people to this church who are different from us? Will we invite those of another color or those who speak a different language? Will we invite those who are not residing in this country legally or those who have a different sexual orientation? Will we invite different types of families to worship with us? These are the really hard questions that we need to answer before we go on."

No one said anything, but I did not take the silence as dissent, but rather acknowledgement of the difficulty of the questions facing this and many other congregations.

The question came up again of how we would treat people of other faiths as well as other Christians who have very different ideas or lifestyles from a majority of our congregation. Interestingly enough, there were several members who spoke up and said, "If anyone wants to serve with our congregation, I think they should be welcome. I don't care what religion they belong to." Others commented that both Jews and Muslims or members of any other world religion would be welcome in our church. They could not accept membership, of course, without accepting our basic beliefs, but they could certainly be a part of our church community.

Vivian Artz spoke up and said, "Well, I may as well say what I am thinking. I would hope that our church would be open to those with a different sexual orientation. I was a young person here fifty years ago when the Civil Rights Movement was at its peak, and I was very proud of the way we stood up for equal rights. It is time to do that again. Several of us have been talking about this for some time, but I personally think it is time to do something rather than just talk."

Pete spoke up and said, 'Now, Vivian, that may be stirring things up too much. I believe we should welcome gays into the church, but I am not sure what you mean when you say 'equal rights.' I don't believe in gay marriage, and I can't go that direction."

"So, Pete, if you have a granddaughter or grandson who tells you he or she is gay, you will just say to them, 'That is fine, but because of that, you will not have the same rights as all other Americans, and I am just fine with that.'"

"That's getting a little personal, Vivian."

"For many people, even some in this church, Pete, it is personal, and that is exactly why we should take a stand."

"My stand would be against gay marriage, and that is not going to change," said Pete, his voice rising.

Vivian was visibly upset, and even though Edna usually let discussions play out, she did finally say, "This is a very controversial subject, and I think it is going to take a lot of prayer and a lot of discussion to reach any kind of resolution. What I am hearing is that even though we have some differences of opinion on how far to go with gay rights, we seem to be open to inviting people with varying sexual orientations to worship in this congregation. Am I correct on that?"

There were murmurings of assent and no apparent disagreement with what she said.

She spoke again and said, "We have a long way to go on these issues, but I am happy to see open and respectful discussion here."

I was amazed that this topic had even come up in a Baptist church, and I was thankful for the way it had been discussed, but I also knew this was a dangerous area for congregation unity, and we needed to be very careful with how it played out. I also knew that there were people who would have extremely different views about these issues who would not publicly speak about them, and somehow we would have to listen to what this group was not saying, also. I just sat quietly and waited for the rest of the discussion.

"Can we still call ourselves Southern Baptists if we don't make a bigger deal about all these beliefs and if we take a different stand on social issues?" Faye Emerson asked.

"I don't know," said Edna. "When I was younger, part of being Southern Baptist was a tenet called 'the priesthood of the believer,' and to me that meant I could sort out my beliefs with God on a personal level, that I could seek his guidance on issues, and that my thoughts might not be just like everybody else's. That seems to have changed now and there is more doctrine that I see as the church demanding members' compliance. I really don't like that, but I also know that being Southern Baptist is a part of my identity that I really don't want to lose."

"Well," said Joy Hearn, "we are already in the dog house for having Annie as our pastor, and it does not seem to me that they could put us there more than once. We might just remain there for a longer time."

Everyone laughed softly and just shook their heads.

Thomas spoke up and said, "We do have to accept that there could be consequences for any decisions we make that seem foreign to the beliefs of other Southern Baptists. But what I hear this morning is that this church would welcome participation by anyone who chooses to do that. Being a church member would require some agreement with our beliefs, but I personally don't have a problem with anyone of any faith or of no faith participating in the activities of this church. In fact, I would welcome it. As long as we are okay with that, I don't think we have to have our beliefs all decided and absolute today."

Vivian nodded and stated, "Now that is something I can agree with. If the church represents Jesus Christ to the world, we better make darn sure our doors are open to everyone and not just after they agree to be baptized, but from the first day they enter our building."

Again, there were other nodding heads. Edna took the idea of consensus even further when she asked if each person felt comfortable stating their agreement or disagreement with the idea of an open door, and if they did not or really were not sure how they felt, would they be comfortable just saying their opinion or just saying pass. Most members nodded their agreement, and out of the fifty-eight people present, forty-four affirmed their agreement with the previous conversation, ten abstained, and four people said they did not feel comfortable with all the statements made but did not want to make comments about them.

Edna thanked everyone for their attendance and said that we would meet again soon. She also mentioned that we had not discussed participation or membership of those of another race, or those residents who are undocumented, or those who speak a different language. Edna asked for everyone to keep thinking and praying about all of the ideas that were brought forward today and others that we still needed to discuss, and she urged everyone to come prepared the next time to express any concerns they might have. The next meeting was going to be on a Wednesday evening in two and one-half weeks. She encouraged people to talk with each other openly and in a pleasant manner and to listen to each other as well. She closed by saying that we all knew we could not all agree completely on a church philosophy, but that one thing we had always practiced was letting everyone be heard and their comments valued. With that, she said a prayer and sent us all home.

I don't know about the other church members, but I was mentally exhausted from trying to figure out beliefs that were such a part of my identity but were not regularly evaluated and verbalized. I thanked Edna for doing such a good job of chairing the meeting, and she noted the same reaction as I.

"We just believe this stuff," she said. "We don't usually rank it in importance. I don't want anyone to feel their deeply-held beliefs are being challenged, and yet I think we need some kind of definition of who we are as a church. Surprisingly, I got the impression that for each of us there are beliefs that are vital to our faith, but that we would accept different beliefs in others. I guess what I am hearing is 'Don't take my beliefs away but come and worship God with us in any way that you need.' It's very frightening to think like that, but it is also a freeing and enlightening stand for a Christian church to take. Maybe at the next meeting, we should make a point of noting that the goal of our church is to serve God in every way we can and to introduce others to a personal relationship with Him. If that is the case, it opens all kinds of doors on how to express our faith and how to let others in who are different from us but who want to express their faith as well."

"Edna, that was beautifully said. We need to write that down," I told her.

She laughed and said, "I will when I get home. I'm too tired right now."

This church was made up of an interesting and diverse group of people. They seemed so traditional in so many ways, but their thought processes were so open and they were not threatened by new and really somewhat radical ideas. I could not wait to see where we would end up as a community.

Chapter 15

The next week was busy as usual. I visited some of the church members who were not very outspoken at our Sunday morning meeting, but in most cases, they were supportive of those who spoke out loud.

Mrs. Maizie Jeanne Johnson, a ninety-two-year-old member served me a cup of tea and then sat down next to me on her couch and said, "I just want you to know that I believe every word in the Bible, that I believe the only way to heaven is through salvation with Jesus Christ, and that those who are not saved are going to hell. However, with that said, the world is different from how it was when I grew up, and our society has changed. My grandchildren and great-grandchildren are wonderful people, but none of them are active in any church. They have told me that the church is outdated and out of touch with today's world. I don't believe Jesus Christ is out of touch now nor will He ever be, and if we can develop a new Christian community that brings our families back to God and to faith in Him, I say 'Go for it.' If I can be flexible about this, then it should be an easy sell to everyone else."

I leaned over to her, took her hand, gave it a squeeze, and said, "Thank you for that lovely thought. I know all of this change is difficult for everyone, but people are stepping up and saying, 'Whatever it takes to get people back in touch with God, we are willing to try.' It seems to me that is why we are here."

There were two families, Fred and Edith Miller and their single adult daughter Belinda and Jake and Peggy Morton and their two college-aged children, Lucas and Ava, who told me they were not sure they could stay with the church if too many changes were made. I had made appointments with both couples to visit them at their homes and discuss their concerns. When I arrived at the Millers at the appointed time, I rang the doorbell and patiently waited. There was no response, and I rang the doorbell again. There was still no answer. I stood on the front porch for a few more minutes, and then I decided to just put my visitation notification on the door and leave. I hoped nothing was wrong, but actually, I was more afraid that this family had chosen not to have further discussion about the church's future plans. I tried not to jump to the most negative conclusions, but that was, unfortunately, my nature.

I drove to the Morton's house next. Jake had retired from being an assistant principal at a local high school, and Peggy had taught second grade for thirty years. They lived in what was called "town," which meant they were in the city limits of Bakerstown on a historic street with about a dozen beautiful old homes. The landscaping was perfect at each home, and the yards were beautifully maintained. The Morton house was a huge, two-story white stone house with a porch encompassing the entire front of the house. The shutters and the roof were a dark hunter green. A huge oak tree on the left side of the house looked as if it had been there for centuries. I parked my car on the street and quickly walked up the steps to the front door.

I knocked on the front door and was thrilled when it was opened promptly by Peggy.

"Come in, come in," she said. "We are so happy to have you in our home. Would you like something to drink? Coffee or iced tea?"

"Iced tea sounds wonderful. Thank you."

Jake came in from the back of the house and shook my hand warmly.

"Come have a seat in the den," he said, and led me to a large room in the back of the house. Things were moving so fast I didn't get a chance to see much of the house, and I had really been hoping to do that. It was such a beautiful house on the outside that I felt sure it would be gorgeous on the inside as well.

I took a seat on a large, comfortable leather sofa in the den, and, as I looked around the room, I saw a stuffed leather chair across the room and a beautiful wooden rocker next to it. Built-in bookcases on two sides of the room were full. There was a stack of newspapers beside the leather chair and a magazine rack that was overflowing next to the rocker. Houseplants were strategically placed around the room and several wooden tables were obviously antiques. A cream-colored afghan was thrown across the back of the leather chair. The room had a lived-in look, and I found it very comfortable and relaxing.

Peggy came back in with the tea and took a seat in the rocker. Jake had stood until Peggy came back in, and then he sat in the leather chair.

"First of all, Pastor Annie, welcome to our home."

"Thank you," I said. "I appreciate your taking a little time out of your day to talk with me. First of all, I want to hear about Ava and Lucas. They are getting close to the end of the semester, aren't they?"

Jake spoke up and said, "Yes, Lucas is in his senior year at Appalachian State, and he is majoring in history and political science. I'm a little worried about what he's going to do with that major 'cause he says he does not want to go to law school. He could teach, of course, but he would have to take some more courses to get certified. Ava is a freshman at Chapel Hill, and she just loves college. She's been going to the Baptist Student Union and has met some real nice kids there. She hasn't said anything about it lately, but we are so glad that she is involved with that group."

"Lucas has been dating a little girl from Hickory for about a year," said Peggy, "but I don't know if it is serious or not. We haven't met her parents so I don't know for sure what she is like, but I know Lucas would only date a good Christian girl. Ava seems to go out in groups so far and hasn't talked about any particular boy. She's young, though, and we really don't want her getting serious about anybody right now."

"Both of them were on the dean's list last semester, and we are as proud as punch of them," said Jake.

"I think you have every reason to be," I said. "I look forward to seeing them again over the holidays."

"We look forward to seeing them, too. Both of them have been so busy this semester we have hardly seen them," said Peggy.

There was a slight hesitation in the conversation at that time, and I figured I better get to the point of my visit.

"Jake and Peggy, when you left the congregational meeting last Sunday, you told me you were not sure you could stay in the church if all these changes were made, and I do want to hear what you have to say about that."

"We are happy to talk to you about that," said Jake. "You know, Annie, we have been members at Covenant for a very long time, and we're proud of what this church has accomplished and what it stands for. However, we have a little trouble with the direction that we feel the church going. Our family and its values are important to us. Our two kids have never been in any trouble at school or in the community. They are good kids and haven't really been exposed to a lot of values different from ours. We kept them in church all the way through high school and encouraged them to hold on to their beliefs and values. How can we now say that it is ok to be gay and to live a deviant lifestyle and that our church is supporting that idea? Help me with that, Annie."

I had to force myself not to react to the use of the word deviant. All I could think of was my friends in college and in seminary who were gay and who were the most honorable and dependable people I had ever known.

Then Jake said, "In the beginning of God's word, he created man and woman as mates, and I don't reckon I've read or heard anything in the Bible to contradict that. Annie, I just think people want to be inclusive and politically correct so they are ignoring what the Bible says about homosexuality. I just can't do that, and I'm hoping that we are not the only church members that feel that way."

I turned to Peggy and said, "How do you feel about that?"

She looked surprised that I would ask her opinion but then said, "I agree with Jake. It is not a lifestyle we can condone."

I paused to think for just a second and then said, "I understand where you are coming from. I have read the same Bible that you have. Let me try to explain why I don't end up at the same place you do. As you know, there are lots of rules and regulations in the Old Testament, most of which we ignore or we don't understand. We certainly can learn from the Old Testament, and it does have some wonderful messages for us, but there are just so many ancient laws that most people don't have any true comprehension of them. So we often go more to the New Testament for our direction. Homosexuality is mentioned a few times, but does not seem to be a major issue of the Christian lifestyle. Jesus does not mention it at all. What I try to do is to always interpret scripture in the light of the gospel that Jesus Christ lived and taught. When I do that, I cannot see the condemnation of homosexuality that others find in the Bible. To me, it seems that Jesus focused more on our relationships and how we treat and care for each other as a measure of our morality. Now, Peggy and Jake, please hear me say that I love the Bible, and I do honor it, and hear me say again that I'm not trying to change your mind or beliefs that you have been led to by your faith, but I am just trying to explain how I come out at a different place."

Jake and Peggy exchanged a glance and then Peggy said, "We appreciate your sharing with us, but we just can't agree with you on this issue. And our major concern is the message that our children would receive from these changes. What if one of them decided to become gay because the church said it was okay now. Why, that would just kill Jake and me and would destroy our family."

"I hear your concerns and fears, Peggy and Jake, but as you probably know, most people don't believe that homosexuality is a choice that people make, but it is a part of who they are. And I can't help but emphasize that it is only a part of who an individual is. They remain the same person they have always been after they let people know they're gay. I really do hear your concerns, and I appreciate your being so up front and honest with me. That means a lot to me. I so hope you can stay with the Covenant community. I don't think we all have to believe the same thing in order to worship together, but I respect your right to disagree."

There was an awkward silence at this point, and I smiled at them and said, "I have some other visits to make, so I better get going. Thank you again for having me in your home. Would you pray with me?"

"Of course we will," said Peggy.

I prayed for guidance and understanding and for tolerance among Christians. I think I was right on the line of offending Jake and Peggy, and I tried to be very careful about what I said. I had listened closely to every word they said and never tried to convince them that any particular way was the right way. I really did not know what to say to them because it seemed as if the majority of the church was willing to try some new ideas and possibly some new programs, and I supported the majority. But these people were wonderful Christians and faithful church members who loved this congregation, and I did not want them to feel alienated or hurt. I said to them as I left, "Let's just wait and see where this goes. We love you guys, and we value your opinions. I don't know where we will end up."

I returned to my office at the church to check for phone messages and was thrilled to hear from Edith Miller. She said, "Fred and I forgot completely that you were coming by today, and we decided to go spend the day with my sister in Concord. We never thought about it till we saw your card on the door, and we are so sorry. Hope to see you soon." I took their call as a positive sign.

I saw Edna in the grocery store, and she felt very good about the members' reaction to the discussion last Sunday. She said, "This is the most excitement this church has had in a long time. I was afraid it was dying a slow death, and now I believe with all this thought and discussion and new ideas, we have come back to life. And guess what? My youngest son, John, told me last night that he is thinking seriously of moving out of Charlotte and back to this community. He is the one whose wife died about a year and a half ago and he has the two little twin girls. I think he wants some help from me with the girls, and I am willing to do what I can. I am just excited that one of my children will live closer to me, and I am so excited that we might have a church that I can be proud to share with Johnny and his girls."

I was working at my desk at the church late one afternoon when the buzzer rang to tell me someone was at the outside door. I have a window I can look out through so that I can see who is there before they see me. Surprisingly, it was Rev. Stanley from the association office. I knew this was not going to be good, and I actually thought about not answering the door, but then I admonished myself for being so cowardly, and I went to open the door. I greeted him and asked him to come into my office. He was not smiling, and I dreaded what he had come to say. I offered him a cup of coffee which he accepted, and while I was getting that for him, I tried to compose myself for whatever bad news he was going to share with me.

When I sat back down with him, he looked at me and said, "You know that we as the leaders of the association had not made a definite decision in regard to Covenant calling you as pastor. They needed someone to come in and lead them back to being a vital congregation, and two people, two men, had already turned them down."

"I am aware of that."

"We just saw no reason to call you or Covenant out for going against what the denomination leadership believed. I actually just hoped that Covenant would survive and grow and that your leadership would be a good thing. I was personally comfortable with leaving the results to God. But now, all over the community, people are talking about Covenant and their willingness to change and be open to all people even if the new people don't always accept Baptist doctrine. I believe I heard that one comment made was that Covenant would allow anyone to worship with them even if their beliefs were totally different from those of the members. Is that true?"

"That's what I heard church members saying."

"Let me ask you. Would that include a Muslim or an openly gay couple? Are you just not going to have any standards at all anymore? What are you doing? We were not that upset about your being a woman, but how far do you expect us to go? Are you just someone who pushes the limits just to see how far you can go, or do you not have any sense at all?"

"Wow," I said, my voice rising, "You are really upset with me, and I guess I'm not sure why. Is it because you, in your mind, allowed me to serve as a pastor of a church, and that you believe I should be so grateful for that, that I would never want to be a part of any other controversial issue, that I would just sit back and quietly and meekly do my job and not make any more waves?"

There was silence for a moment. Then he said, "To be honest, I think there is some truth to what you are saying. I like you and began to think to myself, 'Who am I to tell her she can't be a pastor?' And I honestly thought any hoopla about your being female really would pass with time, and people would just gradually get used to you. I feel angry that now people are asking why you are pastor of a Baptist church and why we did not remove Covenant from our membership as soon as you came here. Other Baptists in the community are hearing about some of your ideas, and they are feeling a little outraged by what you have done."

I sat quietly for a few seconds and tried to figure out what to say. I was a little angry at Rev. Stanley that he had come to my church and started blasting away about some of our thoughts and activities. But I knew I needed to handle this in a Christian manner because whatever I did would be all over the community soon enough. The problem was I was not at all sure what the Christian way to handle this situation was.

Finally, I said to Rev. Stanley, "I am really sorry you are upset with me, but one thing you and this community have to understand is that I kept my mouth shut during most of our meeting, and although I support them one hundred per cent, these are the ideas and suggestions of Covenant church members. I did not come to Covenant to change everything radically, but I have been thrilled that the members recognize that if they do not want their church to wither on the vine, changes are going to have to come. Society doesn't even like churches anymore, especially Baptist ones, and if we don't become more inclusive, we will eventually die out. I will not stand by and let that happen. I tell you what. Why don't you come to our next meeting and tell us your ideas on saving organized religion in this world? I know our members would love to hear your ideas and those of your colleagues. Perhaps we will hear some things that we would want to adopt."

It was his time to sit quietly for a bit. Then he looked at me and said, "This is not going to go away, is it? Change is going to come, and I am not going to like some of it. In fact, I am not even going to understand all of it. If it is going to survive, my church is going to have to be different. I am sixty-three years old, and I don't want it to change. I want it to be the way it has always been. I have always believed that my church is Biblical, and that is why it must never change. But now, I am not even sure that is true. I'm not sure I can face what the future might bring."

"Believe it or not, I do understand what you are saying. As I look at scripture, I see that it was written at a time when the world was so different from now. But it is still relevant to the present. We just have to figure out new ways to get it out to the people of this day, and if we don't do this, scripture may be lost to future generations. I don't know about you, but I can't bear for that to happen."

"I just feel so old today and so out of touch. My grandchildren affectionately call me 'Grandpa Dinosaur,' and today it feels so true. What can I do to bring myself in touch with our modern world and how to share the gospel with it? Am I beyond hope when it comes to being a part of modern society?"

"Of course you are not," I said, "but I sure don't have all the answers. This is the first church I have heard of that is even asking the right questions. If you want, come to our next meeting. I think you would have a lot to contribute. I don't want you or anyone else to feel as if you have to change the tenets of your faith, but somehow that door to your beliefs has to widen to reach the world. It is just not happening now in most churches. I know people are terrified of the 'slippery slope' syndrome, but that fear of losing control of what you do and believe if you make even one change has stopped progress in the world for so many people. Believe that you can make changes and still have control over your own life."

"Thank you for saying that, Rev. Adams, but I feel unable to move beyond where I have been for the last forty years, and to be honest, a large part of me does not want to move. I think I am going to have to leave all of these new ideas and innovations to you and your congregation."

With that said, Rev. Stanley stood up and shook my hand warmly. "Thank you for understanding where I am. I wish you Godspeed in all that you do."

I unlocked the door for him, and as he walked away, my heart ached for him and other Christians who struggle with letting love become the primary focus of their faith as opposed to judgment.

Chapter 16

My brain was just fried, and I called Jane as soon as I got home and asked, "Can we meet for dinner tonight? I really need to laugh and have a little fun for a bit."

"I am so sorry. Normally, I am sitting at home wondering what to eat for dinner about now, but actually, Frankie is looking for his own place, and he wants me to help him decide on the best location. We are looking at two apartments tonight and one condo. I really have to do this with him."

"Of course you do, Jane. We do need to get together soon because this sounds like real change in him and in your relationship, and I want to hear all about it."

"Thanks for understanding. I hope everything is ok."

"I'm fine, but just a little stressed. I will just go for a run. Good luck tonight."

I know I made a resolution that I was going to live a healthier lifestyle, but I had not been very successful at making those changes. I had run a couple of miles two or three times since my decision, and I liked the idea of running this evening. I could have called Sheila to see if she was busy, but it was last minute, and I could not bear another rejection.

I threw on my running clothes and took off. My first thoughts were that I had to find some ways to handle this job better. Unfortunately, or maybe fortunately, I did not have any family close by, and my two closest friends were about forty-five minutes away. I was crazy about my church members, and I think most of them liked me okay, but I could not talk with them about my feelings or my stressors with the church. That would be inappropriate and unprofessional. I valued my relationship with God and my interaction with Him, but I needed more human interaction that was not based on my position as pastor. This was the first time as a pastor that I knew I needed an outlet other than friends and family and church members, and I decided then and there to seek out some type of support group.

As I walked back up to the church, I noticed Mr. Owens' car was there. I believed if I kept making the effort, he and I could have a better relationship so I went inside to say hello.

We had become friendly and greeted each other in a pleasant way each Sunday morning, but there had been no personal sharing.

I slipped into the education building and found Mr. Owens making copies in the office. He looked up and said, "Hello Rev. Adams. What brings you here?"

"I was just coming in from a run and saw your car and wanted to say hello."

He paused for a moment, and then said, "Thank you. That's nice of you."

There was a moment of silence, and just as I was about to say good night, Mr. Owens said, "Rev. Adams, I was baptized into this church, and it has been my church my entire life. Even when I went away to college, I came home most weekends so that I could go to church here. I love this church. It just seems like everything I have ever known is changing. When I grew up, ministers were men, and women worked behind the scenes in church. It was a team effort, but the pastor was the leader – of the church, of his family. Now everything is different in our society, and even though I thought the church would not be changing along with everything else, it is. Where does it stop? What can I hold on to that won't let me down?"

He stopped talking, and I could see his chin begin to tremble just a little, and I knew what effort it had taken for him to say all that.

"Mr. Owens," I said, "sometimes I feel the same way about the church. People, particularly young people, apparently don't see the church as relevant any more, and I grieve that so much for them. But also, I understand it. Even in my short twenty-eight years, the world has changed so much that around people younger than me, I feel a little out of touch and even a little old fashioned. As you know, the church is trying so hard to stay the same that the world is leaving it behind, literally. Believe me, if I had any answers, I would share them with you, but I don't. I struggle every day with these questions."

"What do we do then?" he asked.

"We do just what you and I are doing. We talk to each other, and even more importantly, we listen to each other and to the community."

"I haven't done that very well with you, but I think I'll try a little harder."

I grinned at him with relief on my face and said, "That would make me very happy."

I went home and was ready to jump in the shower when the phone rang. It was Belinda Miller, and she seemed very reluctant to talk. I waited for her to say what she wanted, and finally she said, "I just thought you ought to know there is a small group of church members talking to each other about where the church is going. They are not happy with the church's direction or with your leadership. Their goal is to take back Covenant and make it like it used to be."

I was and I wasn't surprised. I thanked Belinda for contacting me and assured her our conversation would be confidential. Then I sat down on the edge of my bed, and I prayed.

Was this going to result in a split in the church? That would be a disaster. Covenant is a small congregation, almost like a family. Members had known each other for years, even for generations. Family members could now be on separate sides of the issues. There would be anger and name-calling just like in a family dispute. This type of interaction in a church is part of what turns off those who are not involved in church. Society expects more from Christians, and so often, we don't live up to the expectations.

I wanted this church to be different and special, and I believed it was. I knew that I had to ask God to lead me to heal the breach that Covenant was experiencing. How could I do that? Churches everywhere had split, and so many pastors had tried so hard to keep that from happening. My prayer to God was for wisdom and courage and for hope because at this point, I felt very discouraged.

Chapter 17

Considering what I had just heard and been thinking about, I slept well that night and was actually still asleep when the phone rang. I struggled around to find my phone, and in doing so, was surprised that it was 8:05. I never sleep past 7:00. The run must have done me some good. Finally, I got the phone and answered it. I tried to sound as if I had been up for a while, but I know I was a little groggy. Sarah Burnside was on the phone, and she sounded both excited and terrified.

"Annie," she said, "We just got a phone call that Cliff needs to be in court this morning at 10:00."

"What? I thought your court date was a couple of months away."

I jumped out of bed, opened my closet door, and grabbed the first matching skirt and tee I could find.

"I know. That's what we thought. We're so scared."

"What does your attorney say?"

I walked over to a chair where my favorite blazer was hanging on the arm and grabbed it, too. Now I needed shoes.

"We can't get him on the phone. Annie, is there any way you can come with us? Just in case our attorney doesn't make it."

"Of course I can. Now take a breath, Sarah."

I headed to the kitchen for a cup of much-needed coffee.

"Okay, I'll try. But this just doesn't seem fair!"

"I understand, Sarah. Listen, do you want me to pick you guys up or just meet you at the courthouse?"

"I don't know. I don't know. I think I can drive so we will meet you there at 9:45. "

"That is fine. I will meet you in the front lobby of the courthouse. I will also say a prayer that all of us will be ready for whatever today brings. Be careful driving, Sarah. I know you are upset, but you can do this."

I rushed through my shower, wolfed down breakfast, got dressed, and had twenty minutes to spare. To be honest, I don't know if I have ever prayed so hard at one setting, but I decided that if it was ever needed, it might be today. "Dear God. Sarah and Cliff are very dear people, and they need you very much right now.

I want to be strong for them because, honestly, I don't think they can take much more. Please help me to do and say the right things to them. Please let the justice system work for them. If Cliff is innocent, and I do think he is, please let us all do and say the things that will show that to the courts. Give Cliff and Sarah and me strength and courage to face the day. Amen."

I took a deep breath and walked out to my car. I got to the courthouse about five minutes before I was to meet Sarah and Cliff, and, of course, they were already there. Sarah had been crying, but she was holding it together now. Cliff looked as if he were in a trance and hardly knew where he was. He really was not communicative at all. I gave them both a hug and said, "Ok, you guys have faced a lot in the last two months, and this is just one more thing to deal with. Take a huge breath right now, and reach way down deep inside to find more courage. You have not used your whole supply, and even if it is buried deeper, it is there. Don't tell me you can't do this because I know both of you, and you can and you will. Right now!"

They both looked at me and focused just a little bit better. I felt as if I were a life raft, and that I was the only thing that kept them both from going under.

"Put on your confident faces now and hold your heads up. We can get through this!"

They each raised their head just a little, but I knew they were extremely fragile, and it would take all of their efforts to get through this court session.

They called Cliff's name just as his attorney arrived, and without any time to talk, we all went inside the courtroom. When the judge looked his way, Cliff's attorney spoke up and said, "Your honor, I have not had the chance to talk with my client this morning, and I need a recess to do that."

The judge looked at him and said, "Sit down, Mr. Potts. I will explain everything to you and your client."

"But your honor…"

"I said sit down, Mr. Potts."

The judge began to speak. "We have had a grave injustice in this case. Yesterday evening late, it was brought to my attention that young Eddie Jamison was talking to his assigned therapist, and he admitted that he had lied about Mr. Burnside abusing him. He told his therapist that the abuser was someone else, and that it had been going on for two years. When Eddie told the abuser that he was going to tell someone what was happening, the abuser threatened both Eddie and his parents, and Eddie was terrified of him. Eddie was told to pick out his favorite teacher and tell the counselor at school that the abuser was him and when he did that, the abuse would stop. The abuser promised to stop the abuse if someone else could be blamed if it ever came out. Eddie felt as if he had no choice, and he wanted the abuse to stop, so he then accused Mr. Burnside. The court apologizes to you and your family, Mr. Burnside, for these charges and for the pain and suffering it has caused your family. Eddie also asked the court to tell you he was so sorry for what he said, and that you really are a wonderful teacher. At this time, is the prosecution ready to speak?"

"We are, your honor. We are recommending that all charges against Cliff Burnside be dropped and that this case be dismissed."

The judge said, "I am happy to concur. Mr. Burnside, you are free to go."

Then he adjourned court for a fifteen minute break.

I couldn't move, and I couldn't speak. Nor could Sarah or Cliff. We all just sat there and stared straight ahead. Finally, Mr. Potts turned to Cliff and said, "It's over, Cliff. This nightmare you have been living is over."

Sarah stood up beside me and walked behind where Cliff was sitting. Then she slowly put her arms around his neck and rested her head on top of his. He leaned back into her, and when he did, tears began to fall, from Cliff and from Sarah. I continued to sit quietly and stare ahead until Cliff was able to stand. He turned around and hugged Sarah. I heard him say to her, "Thank you for believing me and for standing by me. It means the world to me that you did that."

As they pulled apart, I reached for both of them and said, "Congratulations to both of you. I am so happy the truth came out. This is certainly an event to celebrate, but it's probably going to take a while for this to sink in. Just enjoy each moment as you take in what's happened."

We exchanged hugs as well, and then we gathered our things and headed for our cars. As we walked out of the courthouse together, none of us had much to say. This really was a life-changing event, and it would take time for the impact to fully hit each one of us.

Cliff and Sarah went on their way, but I held back and went over to the local newspaper office, the Bakerstown Post. I went in and told them I wanted to see the editor immediately. The receptionist explained he might not be in, and then I told her to give me his home address. She was a little taken aback, but she checked, and told me he would be available in ten minutes if I wanted to wait. I told her I definitely wanted to wait.

When the editor invited me into his office, I explained to him what I had just experienced in the courtroom. He said that was great news, but asked what it had to do with him. I responded to him, "Just what you said. This was great news, and it needs to make the headlines in the local paper. Tomorrow. This family's life has been turned upside down for over two months, and Cliff's reputation is damaged beyond complete repair, but this newspaper which so faithfully reported all of these charges will have as its headline tomorrow, 'All Charges Dropped in Local Child Abuse Case.'"

"Now see here, Miss…"

"It's Rev. Adams, sir, and I know I am coming on strong to you, but if you had seen the pain of this man's family in the last two months, you would be eager to help start their healing process. I know you are a Christian and a member of First Baptist Church here in town, and I really do expect you to practice your faith here and now. Please help give this man and his family their lives back."

He looked at me for a while, and then he said, "Tomorrow seems like a slow news day so far, so I guess this story can be on the front page. It won't be at the top of the page, but it will be on the front page, and we will get all of the information in the article."

At that point, I knew I was close to losing it, and so I thanked him profusely and then I quickly left and ran to my car. I knew the road ahead for Cliff and Sarah would still not be easy, but I was so happy they could be free of this burden. I also acknowledged to myself that this would mean one less conflict with which Covenant would have to struggle.

When I got to my car, all I could do was just sit there. The emotional toll of my chosen career was more than I had expected, and exercise and a healthy diet were not going to take care of my stress level. When I got back to the church, I called the local ministerial association and asked if they had any pastoral support groups that met on a regular basis. They responded that they had a prayer breakfast once a month, and that I would be welcome to attend. In fact, they were looking forward to my becoming a part of their group. I responded that I would love to come to the prayer breakfast and asked if they might email me with the date of the next meeting. Then I had to continue my search for what I needed, a group where I could talk about my concerns as a pastor as well as those of my congregation. I hoped there wasn't something wrong with me because I felt this need. Perhaps if I were married or had immediate family or close friends living nearby, I might not have a need for such a group, but I experienced these intense emotional times with members of my congregation, and then I had to go home and try to process it all alone. As a pastor, I felt like I had relationships with church members, but I must stay in my professional role with them. It was different from friendship.

Later that evening, I contacted a pastor friend in Charlotte, and he immediately knew what I needed. In fact, he invited me to go with him to the next meeting. I hoped it would be helpful for me as I continued to learn about this path God had chosen for me.

Chapter 18

Vivian Artz, one of our most active and outspoken members, called to tell me she needed knee replacement surgery, and she was concerned about who would teach her children's Sunday school class for the next three or four Sundays. Sometimes a couple of children were present, and sometimes there were none. Sarah and Cliff's boys, Justin and Robbie, had not been coming for the last two months, but I was hoping they would feel comfortable coming back to church.

I knew it was crazy, but I told Vivian that I would take care of her class while she was out. How hard could it be to prepare a few Bible stories and activities for a small group of children?

The first Sunday after Vivian's surgery, there were no children present for Sunday school, and to be honest, I was disappointed. Then came the next Sunday, and Justin and Robbie were there. I was so excited to see them back in church, and I asked if their Mom and Dad were coming that day. Justin said, "Mom brought us but she said to tell you if we saw you that they were not quite ready to return. I hope that's okay."

"Of course it is, Justin. I am just excited to see you and Robbie."

Also attending that day were Alan and Faye Emerson's two grandchildren, Brayden, aged 6, and Julia, 8. The Emersons' son was divorced, but he and his ex-wife were friendly and civil, and the grandchildren visited their grandparents regularly.

The room where the children met for Sunday school was small, but it was painted in bright, cheery colors, one color for each wall. The room held two small tables and eight smaller than normal chairs and a bookcase with coloring books, Bible story books, bags of crayons and washable markers. Across the room, a bulletin board covered with yellow background paper displayed pictures of church children taken during the last ten or fifteen years. Each child's picture was set on a stem as if he or she were a flower, and it made for a beautiful garden. On the third wall, a white board hung with several dry markers placed on the edge of the board.

I was afraid the children might not feel comfortable as Brayden and Julia were visitors to the church, and Justin and Robbie had not been there for about two months, but when I entered the room, they were all four chasing each other and tripping over chairs and giggling because the room was so small.

I told them they needed to take a seat. Ignoring their pained expressions, I smiled and said, "Let's start with a prayer. Does anyone have anything they want me to pray for?"

There was pretty much dead silence, and just before I said, "Please bow your head," Robbie looked around very tentatively and said, "I think I want to thank God for helping my Dad. He has been very sad for a long time, and now things are better."

I said. "I will be happy to thank God for that."

Then Brayden said, "Could you pray that my mom and dad would love each other again and that my dad will move back to our house?"

I hesitated a moment and said, "Yes, I will pray for that. Anything else?"

Julia said, "My friend Morgan has a bad cold, and I want you to pray that she gets better. Also, my dog is getting older, and he is having trouble getting around. I want him to get better, too, so we don't have to leave him at the vet's hospital."

"Of course. Anything else?"

No one else said anything, and I very carefully said a prayer asking for all the things the children had mentioned and thanking God for helping Robbie's dad. I also asked God to help us have a good lesson today.

The children looked up expectantly after the prayer, and I said, "Today we are going to talk about what it means to pray."

This was not what was written in the lesson for children that day, but I knew that I had to say something to address the idea of prayer and how it worked. My heart was hurting for Brayden as he seemed to be struggling with his parents' divorce.

"Show me how people pray," I said. "Get in the position and put your hands and feet and head where you think they have to be to pray."

They looked at me as if I were a little crazy, but then one by one they got in position. Robbie stood up and bowed his head.

Julia got on her knees and bowed her head as well. Brayden decided he would stand up, look upward, and hold his hands out to his sides, palms up. Justin kept sitting in his chair, and said, "I don't want to."

"That's fine, Justin, because by doing that you have made a great point. There is no 'right' position for prayer. You can be standing or sitting or even lying down. You can be riding your bike or driving a car. You can look up or down or just straight ahead. God does not care about what you are doing or how you are standing or sitting when you talk with him."

"How can you talk to God? You can't see Him or anything," asked Julia.

I agreed with her and told her that was one of the most confusing parts about having a relationship with God. How could you talk to somebody you could not see or hear if He talked back? And did He ever talk back to you? I had a quick flashback to the hurtful things Mike had said to me about my relationship with God, but I cleared my head of those thoughts right away.

I asked the children what they had been told about prayer in the past.

Brayden said, "We always thank God for our food before we eat, but I don't know why because He doesn't give it to us. My mom buys it at the grocery store."

Justin said, "My mom and dad always come in at night and ask me if I have said my prayers, and I always say 'yes' even though sometimes I don't. Does God get mad at us if we don't pray?"

"That's a very good question, Justin, but first, let's start with Brayden's question. Brayden, your mom is not the only person to pray before a meal even thought she buys and cooks the food herself. Why do any of you think people pray to God before meals?"

Robbie said, "Maybe they don't want their food to be poisoned, and they think praying will prevent that?"

Everybody giggled at that and looked to see if I was mad at Robbie for that answer.

I continued to look very serious and said, "I guess our mothers could be trying to poison us, especially with broccoli."

More laughter followed, and I could sense the children relaxing. They were having a little fun in Sunday school, and it seemed like a good thing to them.

"Brayden, let me try to give you a serious answer to your question. Even though you're right about your mom buying the groceries at the store, our prayers before we eat help remind us of God's many gifts to us, including the ability to think and learn so we can work to pay for our food. Most of us have enough to eat, a place to live, people who love us, clothes to wear, and places to learn, and sometimes we need to be reminded to appreciate all these 'blessings' and to thank God for His allowing us to have them. Saying grace before meals reminds us of how God loves us and cares for us. Even if we say grace as a habit, we still take that moment to appreciate God's love."

I paused for just a few seconds, and then I said, "Now, let's talk about these prayers at night or the times we don't pray."

Justin said, "I think prayers at night help keep monsters and boogey men away from us while we sleep."

Of course more laughter followed, and I told them, "I certainly hope so because I have always been a scaredy-cat at night."

Julia looked at me with awe and said, "Me, too, Pastor Annie, and I am too embarrassed to tell my parents. I wish I could have a night light."

"I wanted the same thing as a little girl, but my parents thought it was silly. Have you asked your parents for a night light?"

"No," Julia said, "I've been too embarrassed, but since I know you wanted one, maybe I will ask."

"Good luck, Julia. I hope that works out for you. Now back to our question. I don't think God gets mad at us when we don't pray, but I think we miss out on something really good when we don't talk to God. And when we tell a fib to our parents about praying, we not only miss out on talking to God, we miss out on being trustworthy to our parents. I want to ask you a question that might help us to think about why praying is important. Do you know what a conversation is?"

"Sure," said Julia, "It is when you and another person talk about something."

"Do you like having conversations with other people?"

"I do," said Robbie, "but only when they really listen to me and act like they care what I am saying. Sometimes grown-ups just nod their heads and say 'Uh huh, that's nice.' That's when I am pretty sure they are not really listening to me."

"You may be right about that sometimes, Robbie, but I don't think that will happen with God. That is what prayer is to me. It is a conversation with God, and because He is not here with us in a human form, we have to learn to talk with Him and then listen in silence to see if we can figure out what He might be telling us. Sometimes it seems like we don't hear from God, and then it gets discouraging. Then we have to keep trying until we feel as if He has heard us and maybe even given us an answer. Sometimes that answer comes from something another person says, from a scripture in the Bible we might read, or sometimes from our own minds when we figure out what is right for us to do. Even though it might feel like that answer came from within ourselves, sometimes God can put ideas in our heads that help us make decisions. The first few times this happens to you, you don't always know God is helping you, but sometimes you think back to a problem you had, and how you figured out what to do, and then you realize that you didn't come up with the answer all by yourself. It kind of takes a while to start believing that God really does communicate with you but once you can see that, it is really cool. Now, I have another question for you. Does God always answer your prayer like you want Him to?"

Brayden got a scared look on his face, but he did not say anything. Each of the children sat there quietly and didn't seem to know what to say.

Finally, Brayden spoke and said, "Why wouldn't God give us what we want?"

"That's a good question, Brayden," I said. "I have wanted to know the answer to that for a long time. What do you all think?"

Robbie looked very serious and then he said, "If it was that easy, we would just treat God like Santa Claus, and we would always want more of everything for ourselves. Maybe God knows if we could always get what we want, we would only think about ourselves and not be very nice to other people."

"But what if we always ask for good things?" said Brayden. "Why won't he say yes to what we ask for?"

"Well, guys, that is the part I don't have the answers for, and this is when people get mad at God. They ask for something that is good and that makes sense, and then don't get the answer they want. Sometimes people start saying, 'What's the point of talking with God then?' The only thing I can tell you from my own experience is that over time, maybe even from now until you are grown up, there will be times when God answers your prayers with what you want, but there will be other times when He doesn't. But having the conversations with God is one of the best parts of being a Christian, even when you don't like the answers you get. Don't give up on your prayers or on His answers, but just know they may not all be the answers you want."

We sat for just a few seconds and thought quietly. I was struggling with my feelings of inadequacy when it came to teaching these beautiful children about prayer when I couldn't even find time to pray as often I should. Finally I said, "You guys have been great. Y'all have made me really think today. I have a sheet with a prayer word search on it, and I have a little treat for those who finish the search. Now you can all start."

They all started to work quietly, and fortunately the word search was easy enough that each of them could finish it. They got their treat, and then I said, "I guess we should pray again before we leave. Is that ok?"

Julia said, "Can I pray?"

"Of course you can," I said.

"Hey, God. I still don't understand everything about prayer, but I am going to try to start talking to you and see what happens. Pastor Annie says it is a good thing, and I hope it is. Amen."

Chapter 19

Fortunately for me, there were no children in Sunday school the next Sunday, and the week after, Faye and Alan Emerson volunteered to cover the class, and I agreed. Never before had I appreciated children's Sunday school teachers so much.

Also, during that week, I got an email from my friend in Charlotte who had invited me to the support group for pastors that he had been attending. The next meeting was the following Monday night, and he suggested I come into Charlotte, have dinner with him and his wife, and then we could go to the meeting. I agreed to that as well.

On the Monday night of the meeting, I almost changed my mind. I did not want to get involved in some heavy therapy group, and I was not sure what I was getting into. Chad, my friend, texted me at 5:00 that day and said, "No backing out. It will be fine."

How could he know I was so close to canceling on him?

I arrived at his home about 6:00, and his wife, Laura, answered the door and invited me in. She apologized profusely, and said "Pizza is on the way. I had two parent conferences after school today, and I just got home. Chad is picking up the pizza for us."

"Laura, please don't worry about that. I am not very hungry and I hate to impose on you and Chad."

We moved into the kitchen and she sat down at the table with me and said, "Unfortunately, this is a typical night for both of us. With preparing lesson plans and grading papers, I come home from school and start working almost immediately at home. I always think I am going to prepare dinner, but it seems like most of the time, Chad and I both just grab something to eat on the way home. His schedule, as you probably know, is worse than mine. We almost always have to make appointments to have a few hours a week to talk, to make love, or to even watch a television show together. But you know what? We make those appointments, and we keep them. That is what is keeping us both sane and keeping our marriage alive. I am also so grateful for this support group you are going to with Chad. I don't have the time to talk with him and reflect with him on all the needs and concerns of his congregation, and this group gives him just a little time and support to do that. From the little I have heard from Chad, I think you will find it very helpful."

"I hope so, Laura, because to be honest, I feel a little needy to be going to a meeting like this. You would think a pastor of all people would have the strength to help others without it wearing her down, but that is not true for me."

"Annie, the only difference between you and Chad and all the other pastors that you know who are not actively involved in finding a support system, is that you are being honest about needing some help. The best thing about getting that help is that it will make you a better pastor and a happier human being. That is definitely worth an hour or two out of your monthly schedule!"

Just then the garage door opened, and a car pulled in. A door slammed, and then the back door to the house flew open.

"Sorry I'm late. Hey, Annie. Hi, honey."

Chad gave Laura a kiss and me a hug, and then he said, "Annie, it's good to see you. It has just been a hectic day, and I am sorry we are rushed with dinner. I wanted to have more time to sit and talk leisurely. But let's enjoy our thirty minutes of pizza, and then we will head out for the meeting."

We sat for just a few minutes, but we took time to ask about our families. Chad and I had known each other since high school, and even though we had gone to separate colleges, we always caught up with each other at least once a year.

Chad and I arrived at our meeting at 7:30. There were only eight people there, including Chad and me. Ministers are often hesitant to present their needs before those of others, and the small group allows them the time to share. There were two other women in the group, and that made it a little more comfortable for me. We introduced ourselves by first name only. No one seemed to care where you were a pastor, but only that you faced the same issues as others in the group. To be honest, I felt a little like I was at an AA meeting, but I decided to try to have an open mind.

The apparent leader of the group was a man named Daniel. I couldn't help but notice that he was extremely handsome with long, curly blond hair, deep blue eyes, and a cleft in his chin. He also did not have a ring on his left hand.

We all took a seat, and Daniel looked around at each of us and said, "I'm glad you are here. I'd like everyone to take a deep breath and relax. This time is all about you."

I believed him, and it made me feel as if I were important to Daniel and to this group. Then Daniel began with a prayer for us, the group members. It was as if he had a direct line to God, and I felt the comfort of intercessory prayer.

Then Daniel explained how the group worked. "The first two ministers to speak tonight will be Frank and Lucy. After they share, there will still be some time for discussion."

Frank, a middle-aged man, said, "Lucy, you start."

A woman not much older than me, Lucy tried to start speaking but she was having trouble staying composed.

"It's been a really hard month for me, and it's kind of amazing that I get to be the one to talk tonight. I… uh, I seem to have lost sight of God recently, and I feel like I am floundering. In my congregation, there is a young family with two children, a girl aged two and a boy four. Two weeks ago, the boy, Jude, was diagnosed with leukemia, and all I have seen is a family nearly destroyed by this diagnosis. They keep asking 'Why?' and I don't have an answer for them. I keep asking 'Why?' and I don't have an answer for myself. I need to feel God's hand on me and this family, and I can't seem to make that happen."

"What do you feel about this boy's illness?" asked Daniel.

"I feel very distressed, of course, and very sad. I also feel frightened for this family and what they have to face."

"What do you feel toward God?"

Lucy looked a little confused and she said, "I think I just told you how I feel."

'Yes, Lucy, you did tell us how you feel about the boy and his family, but I don't think you told us how you feel toward God."

"I don't know what you mean, Daniel."

"Ok, that's fine, Lucy. What is the boy's prognosis?"

"The family just got that word a couple of days ago, and I believe it is pretty good. But this family is special. They are a loving, caring family, and they love God and our church. And this poor child has been through agony already with all the needles and the heavy doses of medicine. I just can't understand why this has to happen to any family. Where is God in this?"

Lucy's voice had gotten a little louder, and then she made a great effort not to lose control.

I looked at Lucy, and I had to speak. "Lucy, sometimes I have a hard time, too, finding God anywhere. All I look for is just a brief connection to remind me that God is near, but sometimes it just doesn't happen, and I don't know how to make it happen."

Chad spoke up and said, "I would be surprised if we didn't all feel that way occasionally, but I don't have the answers to how to make that work either."

Frank said, "I don't want to come across simplistic, but that is when I have to fall back on my previous experiences with God. It's like I keep reliving them in order to remember that God is in my life even though when I reach out for him, I don't feel his presence. I guess that is a part of faith."

Lucy spoke very adamantly, "Faith is a wonderful thing, but that is not helping Jude and his family in this time of crisis. They need God now, not in their memories."

Her voice was so intense that it was followed by a somewhat awkward silence. She looked around and began to cry.

"I'm sorry, Frank, and everybody else, too. I'm not mad at you."

"Who are you mad at, Lucy?" asked Daniel.

She looked back at Daniel and was silent for a full minute. The she cried out, "How can God allow this to happen? I am so angry with Him that I can't pray, I can't hear His voice, and I'm having a really hard time preparing a sermon for Sunday. It just all seems so pointless. If God is not in charge of the world, then why bother trying to relate to him?"

Adam, another young pastor, said, "And if you can't understand what God is doing, how on earth can you lead a congregation to keep loving Him and following Him as their Lord?"

"Exactly. I feel like a failure because I can't explain to this family why God let this happen to their son."

Daniel spoke and said, "Lucy, I am so sorry this happened in your church, and I am sorry you feel like a failure. I'm also sorry you are hurting over this young boy's illness. It sounds like God has not been there for you through this."

"He hasn't,' she practically screamed. "Where is He and why won't He help me understand this? Where is He for this family?"

She started to cry again. I wanted to put my arms around her, but I didn't know if that was okay or not. After a couple of minutes, I couldn't stop myself, and I walked over to Lucy, got on my knees in front of her, and held my arms out to her. She reached out to me and continued to cry as we shared a hug.

After a few minutes, she sat up and said, "I so desperately want to feel God's love because if I don't, how can I tell his parents that His love is there for them. When I reach out for Him, there is nothing there."

She looked at me and said, "You are the first person who has hugged me, and I appreciate that so much. I just needed to feel someone's touch."

I stood up and went back to my seat.

Daniel said, "Lucy, I heard you say that because you can't feel God's love right now, you feel like a failure with these parents."

"Yes, what kind of a minister am I that I can't offer them God's love and comfort?"

"You are the human kind of minister," Chad said to Lucy. "The kind who struggles with the illness of a four-year-old boy. Maybe it's okay to let this family know you are angry with God, also, and that you are questioning His love. That might help them feel okay about their anger and their feelings of loss of God's love."

"I don't feel like I can do that. I feel like I have to be a rock of faith for them, and I just can't do that now."

"Let's stop talking for a few minutes and ask God to let us feel his presence in this room. Maybe if we can experience Him here, it will be easier for Lucy to experience Him in her church with this family," said Daniel.

There was a very emotionally-charged silence. Lucy was still crying softly, and then she quietly came over to where I was sitting and asked if she could sit by me. Chad switched seats, and Lucy sat down next to me. I held out my hand and took hers as we continued to sit in silence.

After a short time, she said, "One thing I have needed is human contact and support. Perhaps that is where I will find God again."

Daniel spoke to Lucy, "It sounds like you have isolated yourself from others in trying to be the rock for your church and this family, and perhaps you are right. Perhaps one of the best ways to experience God is to feel love from other humans."

"How should we handle our own issues with God with our church family?" Frank asked.

There was a moment of silence and then Adam said, "I think we can be honest about our struggles with our relationship with God up to a point, but with our congregations, I think we have to affirm our faith is still strong even if sometimes it is not. Here in this group, we can express our doubts about God and our relationship to Him, but our church members look to us for strength and faith when they are in despair. Lucy, I hope that your words here will give you the strength to go back to your church and help them feel God's presence again."

"Thank you, Chad. And thank you, Annie, for having the courage to hug me and to help me believe I can feel love, maybe even God's love again. Please pray for me during these next few weeks."

We took a short break. I was overwhelmed by Lucy's feelings, but I also realized that I could identify with her needs, and that someday, I might feel just as she does. This group might be something I could really use.

When we returned to the group, Frank began to speak and said, "I do think all the illness and death we have to deal with is hard, and Lucy, you will be in my daily prayers, but I have just as hard a time with the living. I am still having a really hard time learning how to get through a day and how to get everything done. At the end of the day, I am so exhausted that I have a hard time having any kind of life. My wife is very understanding, but I am beginning to sense us drifting apart, and that terrifies me. Our kids are old enough, they don't need us to take care of them so much, and my wife is trying to find herself. I just don't want her to find herself apart from me."

"You're saying your marriage could be in trouble?" asked Daniel.

"I don't know for sure. I just know I'm tired of putting my wife last, and I think she is tired of it, too. Yet I don't know how to save enough time and energy for her."

"Let's stop and discuss that for a bit," said Daniel. "It seems that the most common concern of all the ministers that participate in any group that I lead is time management and having a life. I don't think that issue is limited to ministers, but perhaps we experience more guilt about it. What are some of the ways you handle this problem?"

"If we could handle it, no offense, we probably wouldn't be here tonight," said Adam.

Everyone grinned at the leader of the group who just shrugged and said, "I actually know that. Yet here you are. What's up with that?"

Chad answered, "I think part of our problem is we think we should be able to take care of everyone else and then our families, too. When our faith means so much to us, how could we draw a line on how we can serve our congregations?"

"I agree," said Frank. "But as I get older, I just can't do that anymore. I'm tired of taking care of everyone else. Does that mean I have to leave the ministry?"

There was silence, and that scared me. Didn't anyone have any answers for Frank?

Lori, the other female pastor in the group said, "If that's true, Frank, then we'll all have to leave the ministry, and I don't think that's what God wants for us."

There were a few chuckles all around the group, and then Daniel said, "Let me ask. How do you handle the issues of time management and guilt?"

There was an uncomfortable silence. Then Chad said, "Well, I tell myself that I deserve some time with my wife and for myself. Sometimes I will watch a football or basketball game and not worry about anything or anybody else during that time. I enjoy that a lot, but then I might feel guilty for being so selfish."

"Anyone else?"

Tanner, the only other group member who had not spoken, said, "I occasionally go to a movie with my wife, but when I do I always worry that one of my parishioners will see me and wonder why I am not available to them."

"Wow," said Daniel. "I didn't realize I had a group of saviors of the world. I should really be honored to have each of you here in this group, and there really should be people serving you and meeting your every need so that you can continue your great work. Get real, people. You are not the only answer to the world's problems and the solution to all of your church members' pain and sorrows. Get over yourselves. Perhaps that is the first step in solving the problem of time management. Listen to what you are saying. You are telling me people cannot get along without you. Whose needs are being met by your thinking that? What you do is meaningful and important, but you will not last in your job if you don't realize that you are only one person, one very human person who has his or her own needs that must be met. Somewhere in your career, you must learn enough discipline to draw some lines between your parishioners and yourself and your family. You will be a much better servant to others if you do that."

There was total silence in the group. I, for one, was thinking that Daniel's message was so simple, and why hadn't I thought all of that on my own? The burdens of the ministry are primarily mental and emotional, and in order to keep functioning, we had to keep ourselves in a healthy mental and emotional place. We had to do whatever it took to do that. For me, I needed to actually do all those physically healthy things I had thought of, and I also realized that I probably needed a group like this one. In fact, I might even need an individual mentor with whom I really could share names and details of church members. I had come tonight thinking I would find out that I really did not need any support, and instead discovered I needed as much as anyone could.

Other group members began to mumble some agreement with Daniel, but I think he hit a lot of us in our ego, and for some, it was hard to accept.

He looked at me then and said, "You are new to our group tonight. How does all of this sound to you? Your name is Annie, right?"

"That's right. It was helpful for you to point out how we all seem to have these 'savior' complexes. I had not thought about that before, but I think it is important that we recognize what we can do and what we cannot do. It is hard for me to admit that I can't help all of my parishioners with all of their problems, but it kind of makes my sense of responsibility a little bit lighter, and that is a good thing."

Daniel looked at me with his intense blue eyes and said, "It's good to hear that something I said to you tonight has actually been helpful. You will have to come back next month just so you can help me feel good about myself."

Everyone laughed at Daniel's comment, and it reaffirmed how needy so many of us were.

Then Daniel went back to Frank and asked, "Are there changes you can make in how you serve your church that would help your marriage?"

"I think there are, but it is so hard to do after being in the same church for nine years. I'm afraid I have set precedents that might need to be changed."

I said, "Frank, tell me how you are going to communicate with your wife that changes are going to be made?"

I saw Daniel's eyebrows go up, but I didn't care. Frank needed to think about what I said.

Frank looked at me, somewhat confused, but with a determined look in his eyes.

"I'm not very good at that kind of talk with my wife, but Annie, I am going to go home tonight and tell her what you said and ask her to help me figure it out. She is a very smart woman, and I just want her to know I want things to change."

I gave him a huge smile and said, "Good for you, Frank."

Everyone talked a little more about how to set limits on what we could do and on the responsibilities that we would take on, and by the end of the group, I felt as if I could identify completely with the group members.

As we were wrapping up, Daniel said, "There were some difficult things to hear tonight, but we are talking about your survival as a pastor and as a person, and I feel very strongly about helping you do that. Think about what was said, and come back next month with some more of your ideas."

Chad and I headed for his house where I had left my car.

"Daniel did not mince any words, did he?" I said, not really knowing how receptive Chad had been to the comments.

"No, he certainly did not. As I think about it, it is so true for me. I really believe my church members need me desperately, and my job is to be there for them all the time. That is crazy, and I'm going to try to make some changes."

"Me, too. By the way, I assume Daniel is a pastor also. He did not say much about himself. I saw he didn't have a wedding ring so I assume he is handling all this as a single guy as well."

"Dan is a priest. He provided support groups for other priests and when we heard how effective he was, my ministerial group asked him to do one for us."

A priest. *Just my luck.*

Chapter 20

I woke up the next morning feeling a little more in control of my life. Balancing the need to be productive in a career and taking care of my own personal and physical needs seemed to be the challenge of the day. In fact, it might be a major challenge of adulthood.

Turning my mind back to my parishioners, I realized that I had not heard from Thomas and Joy Hearn about Thomas's test results. It was 8:30 in the morning, and I thought it would be fine to call them.

Thomas answered the phone and said, "Good morning, Pastor Annie. Good to hear from you. We have been meaning to call, but we have been a little overwhelmed with some information we received from the doctor. We have had to make some decisions, and we don't agree about the next steps to take. The 'Mrs.' has been a little out of sorts with me, but I think we are on the same page now. It is kind of complicated so why don't you come over for dinner tonight, and we can talk more leisurely."

"Should you check with Joy and make sure that's ok, Thomas?"

"I don't think that will be necessary. Who do you think does most of the cooking in this house anyway?"

"I guess I never really thought about it. Are you telling me that you are the cook in your house?"

"I am telling you that. It is not completely true, but that is my opinion at this moment."

"Thomas, are you going to get both of us in trouble?"

"Not at all. Trust me on this. Just show up this evening about 6:00 and we will have food to share."

"That sounds great. I will see you both then."

Thomas is funny to talk with. He is kind and generous, but he pretty much says what he wants without holding back. Joy often just rolls her eyes at him, but they seem to have a connection with each other that protects them from the world and the hurt one can experience from it. When I am around them, I feel I am seeing love at its very best. I was really looking forward to sharing a meal with them.

It was early in the week which is when I try to visit church members. No one was in the hospital at this time, but I knew Vivian Artz and Mai Anderson were now at home recuperating further from knee surgery and rehab, and I wanted to see both of them.

I made quick calls to both women, and they were at home and glad to have some company.

I went to Vivian's house first because she lived closer to the church than Mai. She had told me on the phone that the back door would be unlocked and that I should come in and go to the den. I followed these instructions carefully, and ended up just where Vivian wanted me to be. Vivian was sitting in an overstuffed, faded tan chair with a low fake leather ottoman directly in front of her. Her right leg, the one on which she had the surgery, was lying straight out on the ottoman. Her face showed slight strain, and I wondered if she was in a great deal of pain.

Before I could ask, she told me, "I know I kind of look out of it, but I am doing very well. There is a little pain, but the medication is taking care of that. The only time it doesn't take care of the pain is when the physical therapist comes by and makes me do my therapy. That is tough, but I am getting around pretty well, and I am planning to be at church on Sunday. I can't stand not being able to get around better so I am working very hard to become even more mobile."

Vivian's daughter, Heather, was visiting with her. I introduced myself to her as both she and Vivian invited me to sit down. Heather was going to get her mother a cup of tea and asked me, "Would you like some tea or coffee?"

"I would love some coffee. Two teaspoons of sugar if you have it."

"No problem," Heather said.

Vivian and I chatted a few minutes about her doctor and the surgery. She asked me how her children's Sunday school class was going, and I told her it was fine when there were children there, but that had only happened a couple of times. I decided not to go into the story of how and why I changed the lesson that one time. It was probably better that she not know.

Heather returned with our coffee and tea, and after thanking her, I asked her where she lived. She said, "I live about six miles from here on the way toward Charlotte, off of Highway 74."

"Oh, I didn't know you were local."

"Yes, I am. I see my mom regularly, but a lot of times she comes to visit us at our home, or we eat at a restaurant closer to Charlotte. It's just easier."

"Do you have a family?"

"I do. My partner and I have adopted two children, a boy seven and a girl ten, and we have two cats and a dog."

I smiled at her and said, "That sounds like a full house."

She smiled back at me and said, "It is, but we love it."

"You know I have to ask, right?"

"What do you mean?"

"Do you have a church for your family to attend?"

She looked at me for a few seconds, and then she said, "Not at the present time. There are several gay-friendly churches in Charlotte, but we don't want to have to drive that far just to go to church. No one in any local church has ever invited us to come."

"I am inviting you and your family to join us any time you want. We would love to have you."

"Thank you for the invitation. I really do appreciate it. Mom has been telling me we would be welcome, but we have been made very uncomfortable several times in the past when we have attended other churches, and we are a little afraid, for us and our children. We seem to make some people very uncomfortable, and even though the people have been pleasant, they don't seem to know what to do with us."

"Trust me on this, we will find a place for you, and we will probably put you to work. I am not very good at evangelizing, but think about coming to visit us."

"I will."

"Is this where I get to say, 'I told you so?'" Vivian asked.

"Yes, mother, I knew that was coming."

We laughed and talked for a few more minutes, and then I said, "I should be going. I want to get to Mai's house before lunch time. Can we pray together?"

"Of course," Heather said.

I asked God to continue to bless Vivian in her recovery and Heather and her family in their search for acceptance and a church home.

It was beginning to seem that everywhere I went and every conversation I had involved issues that were more complex than I had expected. Being a pastor invited people to present themselves in their purest form, hoping that in some way talking to God's representative allowed them to communicate with God. It was, as they say, a blessing and a curse. I enjoyed hearing about the lives of people, but sometimes knowing about the burdens or concerns they had weighed heavy on my heart. I hoped Mai was having a great day!

Mai was indeed having a great day. She greeted me at the door and welcomed me in. Edward was in the kitchen, and she called for him to come into the living room. When he did he brought steaming cups of coffee and thick slices of cinnamon nut bread, right out of the oven.

"You timed your arrival perfectly," he said. "I just got this bread out of the oven and got it sliced. Please join us in a morning snack."

The aroma of baked cinnamon bread was incredibly enticing. "I will be happy to have some of your bread, Edward. Did you bake it yourself?"

"I did, Pastor Annie. It is one of my many specialties."

"Edward Anderson, you had better stop lying to our pastor or you are going to be in big trouble. Pastor Annie, I made this bread and all Edward did was take it out of the oven when the timer went off. I have tried to teach him not to tell these big lies, but he can't seem to learn. What can I do?"

I laughed. "I'm not sure. Just keep setting his audiences straight and perhaps he will get the message one day."

She just shook her head and gave her husband a look of tender adoration. He looked like a little boy who had been caught with his hand in the cookie jar, but who knew the woman he loved would not really care.

We had a nice chat about Mai's excellent recovery, and I also learned a little more about Mai's extended family members who still lived in Vietnam. She had three sisters and two brothers with numerous nieces and nephews, and the primary reason that she had the knee surgery was because she planned to go see them soon and wanted to be able to get around on her trip.

"Are you going with her, Edward?"

Edward and Mai shared a quick look followed by a slight pause in the conversation.

Then Edward said, "No I am never going back to Vietnam. I am happy for Mai to visit her family, and I would love for her family to come here, but, for me, it holds too many painful memories of guys I knew who did not come home whole or at all. I don't want to stir up those memories. I think Mai understands how I feel."

There was a bit of an awkward silence, and then I said to Edward, "Thank you for your service, and I am sorry that you do have these painful memories."

I looked at Mai and said, "I hear that Vietnam is a beautiful country, and I hope your trip will help you remember the country of your youth. Are you okay with Edward's feelings about your home country?"

"I think I understand them, and although it makes me a little sad that he will not meet all my family, I am okay with his decision. The war was a terrible thing for my country, too, and for my family. Both my parents were killed in the war. We do not know which side killed them, but that was true for lots of people then. I was the oldest girl, and it was my responsibility to take care of my younger brothers and sisters until my brothers got older. The oldest of my brothers enlisted in the army when he was sixteen, and he was killed in action just two months later. That is why I was so lucky to get a job in a business. It was a safe place to work, and I made just enough money to buy food for my family. And of course, that is where I met Edward."

"You were very blessed to find such a good job that helped you support your family."

"Yes, I was. My family depended on me. It is unbelievable to me that it has been eight years since I have seen my brothers and sisters. I still think of them so often and remember all of our experiences as children. It is strange that I have a good life here with Edward, but in my head, I have a life of memories that I go to all the time. I have been back to Vietnam two other times, but the last time I was there for just two weeks. This time I will be staying for three weeks. When I am there, that becomes my life, and my memory life is the one I have here with Edward. I am blessed to have Edward who is happy for me to visit my family. Will you check on him while I am away and make sure he is eating right?"

"Let me know when you will be gone, and either I or a fellow church member will contact him at least once a week during that time."

I had a prayer with them before I left asking for safe travel for Mai and comfort for each other while they were apart. As soon as I got in my car, I took out my phone and put in a reminder for me to check on Edward when Mai was gone.

When I left the Andersons' house, I actually felt at loose ends. There was nothing I had to do right now, and I felt a freedom I had not felt since I had been pastor at Covenant. I checked on my phone, found the closest movie theater and took off for an afternoon adventure. I had a big box of popcorn and a huge coke. It was a great escape.

Chapter 21

After my movie, I went home, had a short nap, vacuumed, cleaned my bathroom and kitchen, and put in a load of laundry. I was looking forward to this time with Thomas and Joy Hearn, although I was a little concerned about what they might have heard from the doctors. This was the first time I had been invited to any member's house for dinner. Sunday lunch was a popular time to invite the pastor, and I had shared that time with a couple of families in the church, but this evening during the week felt very special.

Thomas opened the front door to their home before I even reached the porch. They lived in a ranch style brick home with a double carport. Their yard was neat and tidy and full of trees and shrubs and flower gardens, but since it was the fall season, the only evidence of any color were several maple trees whose leaves were a vivid red.

Joy was getting a casserole out of the oven. She was wearing an apron made of yellow-flowered cotton, and before she shook my hand, she raised the apron to wipe the sweat from her brow and then to dry her hands.

"Welcome to our home, Annie. It's good to see you."

'Thank you, Joy. It is good to be here. Something smells wonderful."

"Joy is the best cook in the church," Thomas said. "Ask anybody. They will tell you."

We had a wonderful dinner of a delicious chicken and rice casserole with cheese and crunchy stuff on top, home-canned green beans from their summer garden, cornbread and salad. Then for dessert, we had a cherry cobbler with vanilla ice cream. I had not had a meal like that in a long time, and I told Joy how much I appreciated her hard work. I helped her clear the table even though she protested my assistance, and then Thomas suggested we go sit in their den and talk.

Thomas and Joy sat on the couch right next to each other and held hands. Both were very calm, although Joy seemed to be a little anxious.

Finally, Thomas said, "The results from all the tests that I had were not what we expected. I have stage four pancreatic cancer, and I have less than a year to live, probably quite a bit less. I could have more time if I chose to be treated, but I have decided not to take any chemotherapy or radiation treatments."

I was stunned by what Thomas said. I wanted to say something, but I was struggling. Finally, I said, "Thomas and Joy, I'm so sorry. Are you confident about your decision?"

"I am at peace with this decision, but Joy is still struggling with it. Intellectually, she knows this is the right decision, but it is very difficult emotionally."

While Thomas spoke, I noticed Joy's struggle with her tears. Her eyes would fill with tears, but then she would blink them away so that they did not escape from her eyes. It seemed to be taking a heroic effort on her part to keep from breaking down completely.

I wanted to run over and hug both Thomas and Joy, but I made myself sit very still and wait.

Joy spoke up then and said, "I know this decision is the best one for Thomas. Neither of us wants to spend the last few months we have together on this earth with him throwing up and feeling miserable, but it is so much more difficult than I ever expected to sit back and do nothing but wait for the inevitable. We told you a while back that we both long to be reunited with Evan, and I still want that, but the reality of our life here on earth is all I can think about right now, and I don't want to live without Thomas here with me."

I again questioned my ability and my maturity to handle this situation. These two people who I really cared about were baring their feelings of fear, loss, and grief as openly as anyone I had ever heard, and I needed to make a response to them without being trite and without my feelings being involved. This wasn't about me.

I responded to Thomas first and said, "Thomas, I am sorry there is not an option for treatment that you would try. I respect your decision because I know you would not have made it lightly or without carefully considering all of the options. I hope you also know that should you change your mind about treatment, I would support you in that decision as well. Can you help me understand what you have been going through since you heard your diagnosis?"

"Well it seemed to take them forever to get back to us so, of course, I was thinking there wasn't anything to be worried about. Then the doctor's office called and told us to come in on a Tuesday morning, just about two weeks ago. When we sat down in his office, he came out and told us the news. I remember he then left the room and gave us a few minutes to digest what he had just told us. Neither of us said anything 'cause we didn't know what to say. I reckon we still don't."

"How have your friends and family responded to this information?"

"You are the first person we have told. We needed the two weeks to get our heads around what was happening. The only productive thing we did was to update our wills, but we didn't tell our attorney why we were doing that. I am beginning to find peace a little bit at a time. At first, I just could not believe it was true, but then I said to myself, 'Thomas you are eighty-three years old, you have lived a great life, had a great love, and maybe it is just time.' I tried to tell myself that there did not have to be a reason for this happening to me, that it just happened. Like when Evan died. I never did think there was this great plan where he had to die at seventeen, but it just happened, and it was something I had to accept and live with. That took me a long time to do, but I am moving a little faster with myself. I say that I am not afraid of dying, but the reality is that it is an unknown to me, and it is frightening. But what I have realized is that there are not other options, and if I want to live the rest of my life in joy and peace, I have to come to grips with all this. My biggest worry is Joy and how she will handle everything. We are awfully close, and I am afraid she's going to fall apart and not be able to go on."

"Thomas Hearn, thank you so much for your faith in me. I am just a frail little old lady who will never make it on my own. Is that what you are saying?"

Thomas looked surprised and looked at Joy as if he couldn't believe what she was saying.

"Oh Joy, of course I didn't mean that. You are a wonderful woman, but you must admit that I take care of all our business dealings and paying the bills. That's something you never wanted to be involved in."

"Why would I when I had you to do it? I am smarter than you give me credit for. Just tell me a few things, and I will be fine to take care of the house and our business. Don't you spend a minute worrying about that!"

Thomas just continued to look at Joy. I could not tell if he was feeling a little relieved that Joy was coming across so strong, or if he still wanted to think of her as the "little woman" that he had always taken care of. I don't think Thomas could tell either.

"Both of you are showing a lot of courage, and I am very proud of both of you, but just in case either one or both of you get a little nervous or afraid, please know that I will be here for you. Thomas, when you are ready, we can talk about your fears, both for yourself and for Joy."

Then I turned to Joy and said, "I am also very sorry for what you are going through right now. I know you are asking yourself, 'What is going to happen and what can we expect?' I hope you have a physician who will answer those questions for you. Sometimes having the facts is better than not knowing exactly what the future holds."

We were all quiet for just a moment, lost in our own thoughts, and then I asked them, "What can I do to help?"

"Well now that you mentioned it," said Thomas, "we were wondering if you could get the word out about my illness to church members. You know we don't have a lot of extended family, and the church has filled that void for us. We want everyone to know, but it is very difficult to go over this time and time again. If everyone knows, then we talk about it differently and then move on to other topics. I know you can't announce it from the pulpit, but you know there are other ways to dispense information. Would you be able to do that for us?"

"Of course I can, Thomas. I can share this with smaller groups like the deacons and the Sunday school classes. The word will spread quickly, I'm sure."

"Thank you, Annie. I don't think we will be in church this coming Sunday, so that gives us a little time for people to share the information. I have two first cousins living in Gastonia, and we are going to go see them on Sunday to tell them about the situation. It will be an all-day visit with them. I want to spend time with them while I still feel good. We were all pretty close growing up."

"Of course, Thomas, I will call you on Monday to see how your visit with the cousins went."

I knew I should offer to pray with them, but I wasn't sure I could. Thomas, ever the gentleman, looked at me and said, "Why don't I say a little prayer for us tonight before you leave?"

Chapter 22

I wanted to complete two tasks before any more time passed - setting up a prayer time for church members and finding an individual mentor. The conversation with Thomas and Joy had been very difficult emotionally and confirmed that I needed someone to talk with about what was going on at Covenant. I decided to make these two concerns a priority.

The Sunday after my visit with Thomas and Joy, I did what I told them I would do. I shared the information about Thomas's illness with church members. When I walked into the church office, Edna and Mr. Owens were already there. After a quick greeting, I gave them the news.

"Oh my," said Edna, as she sat down in an office chair. "I've known them for such a long time. This is such a shock."

Mr. Owens just looked at me and said, "How sad."

Then he asked, "Are you okay repeating this over and over?"

I shook my head as tears flooded my eyes. "Not really, but I am willing to do this for them."

At Mr. Owens suggestion we agreed that he would tell the two adult Sunday school classes, and Edna would talk with the deacons. I agreed to speak with some of the members as they left the church at the end of the service.

I could've hugged Mr. Owens.

People were shocked and upset as Thomas was a beloved member. Several members came up to me between Sunday school and worship and asked what they could do for Thomas and Joy.

I suggested, "Besides telling them of our love for them and spending time with them, why don't we start this prayer group in Thomas's honor? He would never want us to limit our prayers to him or Joy or even to focus on them, but if we started the prayer group to honor him and Joy, I think he would like that. What do you think?"

Charlotte Wilburn said, "I think that is a good start, but I want us to be careful that we really become a source of comfort and strength for Thomas and Joy. We always have such good intentions when people are sick or grieving or needy in any way, but so often in the chaos of our individual lives, we lose track of who needs us the most."

Vivian spoke up and said, "I agree. People, including me, always have such good intentions about helping others and being a source of strength for them, but usually I get so involved in my own life, that time passes, and I find I haven't done anything that I planned to do for other people. We could get a list of volunteers, and to keep them organized, I could develop a spread sheet which I could keep current. What do you all think about that idea?"

"I love it, particularly since you are willing to do the organizational part of it," said Charlotte. "You know we may have more than one person sick at a time, so we have to have someone who lets Vivian know who is sick or in the hospital or who is just going through a bad time. Annie, I think that might have to be you. Is that okay?"

"Yes, that will be fine. Sometimes I get distracted by issues in the church and problems in church families, so I will have to ask you to be willing to kick my butt occasionally to make sure I remember to get this information to Vivian. Everybody up for that?"

Pete Stoudemire stood up, laughed, and said, "I see that as my calling these days, so I will certainly support you on that idea."

I laughed. "Pete, your support is always appreciated."

Faye Emerson said, "Annie, I will take care of a sign-up sheet. I'll even encourage members to sign it as they leave worship this morning. If no one cares, I would like to call this committee the Helping Hands committee."

"What a great idea! Thank you, Faye. That is a huge help. Now we better all head in to worship."

After worship, Faye brought me the list, and there were nineteen names on it.

On Monday morning, I made several phone calls to check on the status of some of the members I had not seen in several weeks and found three additional names to add to Vivian's list of those needing attention. This included the name of Edward Anderson as Mai was leaving to visit her family in another week. I also sent her the names of the nineteen members who had agreed to help care for the congregation. My last call of the morning was to

Thomas and Joy who reported that other than being a little tired, they were okay and had had a wonderful visit with his cousins.

I would continue doing what I had been doing, but it was a tremendous relief to know that my church members would get more care than I could give them by myself.

That same morning, I gathered all my courage and called Rev. Stanley at the association office. I wanted to ask him if he knew of any other pastor who would serve as a mentor or advisor to me. I left this message with his secretary as he was not in, but to be honest, I was not sure I would get a response from him. It was, however, a place to start.

Chapter 23

I spent the next morning outlining my sermon for Sunday and also trying to put together an agenda for the next congregational meeting which was scheduled for the next week. I was really struggling with my role as pastor in leading the church versus letting the church members make all the decisions about the future of the church. It was really hard trying to figure out how many of the ideas I had running around in my head were my own creation and which ones might be the result of God's revelation.

Yes, I really needed the help of an experienced mentor, and I was grateful Brian Stanley had returned my call that morning. We'd scheduled time that afternoon, and I arrived about five minutes early. The office manager, Evelyn, greeted me warmly. That felt good. Now if only Rev. Stanley would greet me as warmly as she did.

The door opened to Rev. Stanley's office, and he smiled at me and said, "Come on in, Rev. Adams. It is good to see you."

So far, so good, I thought.

"How are things going?" Rev. Stanley asked.

"Pretty good overall. One of our members has just learned he has terminal cancer, and that was difficult for everyone to hear. We are still struggling with how to change our outreach agenda. And, of course, there is never enough time to do all the things I want to do, but I just keep plugging away."

"Are you taking care of yourself?"

I gave him a half smile. "Kinda, sorta, I guess. Sometimes I feel pretty alone, and being strong for church members takes a toll on me emotionally. I don't really have anyone I can share my concerns with on a regular basis, but I did attend a pastor support group in Charlotte a couple of weeks ago, and I plan to go to that again soon."

"That sounds like a good idea. Are you going to the one led by the priest? I can't remember his name."

"Yes, that's the one.

"I hope that works well for you. And I am assuming that you are still interested in finding a personal mentor as well?

"I am. I absolutely love what I am doing, and I am trying to maintain a social and personal life apart from the church, but that has been difficult. I've learned that as a pastor, you open up your heart to all of the joys and all of the pain of your congregation and their families."

"And as you do that, they become your joys and pain as well."

"That is so true. I guess it sounds pretty heartless and not very Christian, but I've already found that the burdens that my congregation faces are pretty overwhelming if I let them become my burdens as well. I know I won't last in this career if I don't do a better job of taking care of myself, both emotionally and physically."

"Rev. Adams, you have learned a very important lesson about being a pastor, and to be honest, you have learned it a lot sooner than I did. It took me several years to get to where you are now."

"Well I might be there intellectually, but I am not sure I am able to practice this lesson in real life. I still get pulled in emotionally almost every time a member has a problem or a concern. By the way, please call me Annie. We have shared so much, both good and bad, that I feel like we are friends."

"Thank you, Annie. I feel the same way, and please call me Brian. Annie, I want to propose that I be this mentor that you are looking for. Don't say anything yet. Let me explain why I think this is a good idea. Even though we are at different places in regard to a lot of beliefs of the church, the pastor's role is something I do know about. I have accepted that you are serving as a pastor of a church, and I know a lot about what you will be facing in that role. Now, I don't want your answer right away. I won't be offended if you say no as I know we are different in many ways, and if you would like, I will continue to look for someone else to serve as your mentor. As my role as Association Pastor, I have done this before, and actually, it is one of my responsibilities so there would be no charge for my services. You take some time and think about this idea, and then you give me a call."

I sat quietly for about thirty seconds, and then I looked at Brian and said, "I don't need any more time to think about this. I would be honored if you would be my mentor. I did not think about your doing this because I know you don't support my role as pastor, but if you can move beyond my being a woman and see me in this role, I would be ever so grateful. I already feel better today after our brief conversation, and I will look forward to more meetings with you."

"Thank you, Annie. To start out, I think we should meet once a week for a while, and then we can probably cut back to less often. I know scheduling an hour session per week will be difficult with your schedule, but it is very important that we keep these appointments. Does that sound okay?"

"That sounds wonderful."

Evelyn scheduled three weeks of appointments for me, and I left there feeling as if the burdens I had been carrying were already lighter. This was not what I expected from this meeting with Brian, but I was very happy with this outcome.

Chapter 24

The next congregational meeting was for Wednesday night, and I spent many hours thinking about how to approach this meeting. I also thought about what, if anything, I could do about the group that was opposed to changes in the church.

We had a very strong group of leaders in Covenant, and I wanted to determine how to take everyone's ideas and concepts and put them into effect in the church, but I also knew that just like any other group, there was diversity of ideas. The problem with diverse ideas in a church was that sometimes these ideas and beliefs were a central part of who people were, and to suggest that they compromise in these areas was heresy to many of them.

I wanted this church to be different. I wanted people to be able to hold on to their most important beliefs while helping to build a church congregation that might not represent all those beliefs. I wanted the end result to be a place where all people felt welcome and where individuals could get to know God in a personal relationship. I wanted a church where love and service, not doctrine, were the prevailing themes. Baptist theology and doctrine would be taught, but acceptance of that would not be a prerequisite to church participation. We would not be following the Southern Baptist ideas on social issues.

These were the things that I wanted in the church, but I also knew that the first person who had to be willing to compromise was me. If this church wanted to be traditionally Baptist, I would lead them in the best way I could. If members did not want to be inclusive, then I would have to accept that.

The night of the meeting arrived. The Women's Missionary Union had made cookies, a lot of cookies, for this meeting. They also had two forty-two cup coffee makers going which filled the fellowship hall with a wonderful aroma, and they had hot water for tea and hot chocolate. I personally thought it was a bit much, but the president of the group, Anita Fleming, a quiet and dignified woman who had retired from the high school cafeteria as manager, came over to me and said, "Pastor Annie, let's have conversation with coffee and cookies before, during, and after our discussion. People will always talk more with each other when it is perceived as a social group rather than official business, and we want honest discussions, don't we?"

"Of course we do," I said. "That is really a good idea."

I did not know Anita well at all, but I thought then and there I should definitely change that. I immediately went over to Edna and whispered Anita's idea to her. She agreed that would be helpful.

Edna, as Chairperson of the deacons, called the meeting to order. She opened with a prayer for tolerance, for wisdom, and for guidance. Then she welcomed everyone and explained how the meeting would work, including the fact that everyone would be encouraged to share their opinions and their ideas with the group. Then she summarized our last meeting and distributed a document about the beliefs we had agreed could not be compromised or devalued. She waited for everyone to have the list and to have a minute or so to look over it. Then she asked if anyone had any questions about the list.

Wayne Fleming, Anita's husband, asked, "Is this like every belief that we as a church are going to have?"

"That's a very good question, Wayne. Let me see if I can answer it. My understanding of these beliefs is that they are the most important to us as Christians, and that we would not be comfortable compromising on them. It would not mean that we would reject people from participating in our church community who had different beliefs, but that these basic tenets are the core of who we are, and we are going to hang on to them no matter what. Anybody have comments about these beliefs?"

Pete Stoudemire spoke up and said, "Wayne, I had some problems with the idea that we would welcome people who don't agree with everything we believe, but the more I thought about it, the more I liked it. We have a wonderful product to market, that of Jesus Christ as a personal savior, but if we don't have the opportunity and the audience to market Him to, then how will other people learn about Him. For years, it seems we have gone to foreign countries and to other communities to tell them about Jesus, but it may be time to bring people to us, and in order to do that, we have to let them in. Wayne, don't be too shocked by my use of the terms product and marketing. Pastor Annie used them at our first meeting and I about had a stroke over it, but after a day or two of thinking about it, it kind of made sense. Hope I didn't offend anybody with those words."

Charlotte Wilburn spoke up and said, "I don't have a problem with the terms you used, but I would have a problem if the only reason we welcomed people different from us was to be able to convert them to Christianity. I am not opposed to that being an end result if it happens because the community sees us as showing God's love and acceptance to everyone, but I don't want this church to turn into a witnessing machine just for the sake of increasing our numbers."

"I agree with Charlotte," said Faye Emerson. "What I would like to see is a church which welcomes all to participate and to fellowship with us without having to draw lines about who would be welcome and who would not."

Vivian Artz spoke up and said, "I would like my daughter and her partner and their children to be welcomed into this church without being judged for their lifestyle. I don't know if they are Christians or not, but they are a beautiful family."

There was a moment of silence. Then a small voice from the back said, 'I would like my son who is being released from prison next month to be welcome here and not be judged."

I could not see who said that, but I was hoping someone was keeping notes.

Libby Smith, one of the oldest church members, said, "My granddaughter has two children, and she is not married. I would like for her to come to church, and she will only do that if she can believe that she won't be condemned or stared at or talked about. She has actually said that to me and I would like to be able to tell her that she would be welcome here."

Mr. Owens spoke up and said, "I have two nieces living in this community who are both living with their boyfriends. Even though I know this happens all the time now, I have not invited them to come to church here since they were little girls because I was embarrassed that they might introduce their boyfriends and say they are living with them. I want to have a different attitude about them myself and when I do, I want to be able to invite them to church and know that no one else will be judging them either."

No one said anything for a while, but then a child's voice was heard. Very softly, Robbie Burnside spoke up and said, "I want my daddy to feel like he is totally accepted here again. He did not do anything wrong, but he was accused, and it feels like to my family that some people here might not want him to come back, that they might be judging him. This church is important to me and my brother, but we won't come here without our parents."

Now there was total silence. And then way in the back, a small woman stood up and started applauding what Robbie had said. I tried to see who it was, but then people in front of her and all around her started clapping as well. Pretty soon, everyone in the room was standing and applauding.

Edna had tears in her eyes, but she was able to get everyone's attention and announced that we would take a cookie break for about ten minutes.

Edna and I made a point of wandering through the small groups of people talking and enjoying their cookies, and both of us felt that from what we were able to pick up that most people had positive feelings about the things that had been said in the meeting so far. Only two couples, who were actually talking with each other, were overheard to question whether or not it was wise to invite homosexuals and ex-cons into the church. I made a point of remembering who they were, the Millers and the Mortons, and even though I had tried to visit the Millers once and had actually visited the Morton home once, I knew I needed to go back again.

While walking around, I was shocked to see Erin and Danny O'Reilly. After Cliff Burnside's arrest, they had declared they were never going to come to this church again. I did not have time to stop and talk with them, but I smiled and waved at them, and I was thrilled to see them at this meeting.

Edna gathered everyone together again, and then she said, "Please tell me if I am wrong, but I am hearing that most of you want to have an attitude of acceptance in this church, an attitude that because this is God's house, everyone will be welcome here. We have mentioned some people whose lifestyles a lot of Christians have problems with, some who many Christians feel must change their lifestyles before they can be children of God. I am not hearing that from this congregation. Am I correct?"

There were nodding heads and voices murmuring in agreement.

Then Edna said, "I think many of us are excited about these attitudes in our church, but I must tell you I have a lot of concerns. How can we change the attitudes we have had for years about some of these groups we are talking about? How can we keep that initial reaction that we have had for years from being visible to new people coming into our church? Will we be afraid of a person who has been to prison, and if we are, won't he know that as soon as he meets us? Are we so conditioned by society to disapprove of gay couples that our attitudes will show as soon as we see two women come into the church together with their children? And what about Cliff? Most all of you know him, but how many of you have reached out to him since all the charges were dropped? Maybe we want to show love for all these people, but just maybe we don't know how to do that. I think our next challenge is to figure out how to practice the acceptance that we talk about."

"Edna, I think you are right about this," said Pete Stoudemire. "My heart and my head tell me that if Jesus were a member of this church, he would open his arms to everyone, and I want our church to be like that. But you are right about our gut reactions to certain things, and before we open our doors to everyone, we need to make sure our actions will reflect our new attitudes. What do we do?"

"May I say a few things?" I asked.

"Oh please do," said Edna.

"Yes indeed," said Pete.

"My parents grew up in Mississippi, and so did I, as some of you know, and even though I love my home state, it was not a hotbed for racial equality. By the time I was born, feelings and attitudes had changed. I went to a school that was fully integrated, and students were very comfortable with that. My parents, on the other hand, went to school during the sixties when everything was just changing. My mom has shared with me that she was so frightened of the black students who went to her junior high because she had never had any personal contact with black people before that time. Her parents had lived in a very rural area and had black families all around them, but there had not been much social contact. One day, my mom went to the bathroom at school, and while she was in there, she could hear someone crying in one of the stalls. Being a compassionate young lady, she spoke to the girl through the door and asked if she could help. The young lady in the stall said 'No one can help. My mother has cancer and she might die.' My Mom's response was that she went to church and that she would pray for the girl's mother. Just then the stall door was pulled open and this lovely young black girl flew out the door and gave my Mom a huge hug. Then she took off down the hall to her class. My mom said she just stood there and all kinds of thoughts ran through her mind, but her primary thought was 'She is just like me.' She told me it might have been her greatest revelation of all time. The point of all this is maybe we have to get to know people who are different from us in order to see how they are like us. Perhaps our first step might be determining a way to meet and get to know people who are different from us."

"Good point, Annie. I know we only have about fifty people here tonight, but I think the best use of our time that's left might be to break into small groups and make specific suggestions about where to go from here. Does that sound okay to everybody?"

"Tell me specifically what you want us to talk about, Edna. I am not clear about that," asked Faye Emerson.

"Sure. Talk about two things. One is 'Who do you want to encourage to come to our church?' The second would be 'How can we reach out to groups we want to attract to our church, particularly if those groups are different from us in some way?' We will take about twenty-five minutes to think about this."

People gathered with their closest friends and created six different groups. I observed the interaction in the groups and saw friendly, caring, and comfortable conversation. There was obviously serious conversation going on, but there was also teasing and laughter among the groups. I watched all of this very closely and as I did, I began to worry about how new people would affect the culture and the growth of the church. Was all of this a mistake? Would changes in who we invited to worship with us destroy the church and its members? What were we thinking that people could accept those so different from themselves? I felt overwhelmed by the risks we were taking. Are changes worth the possibility of ruining a good thing?

Edna walked over to me and said, “Everything is going great, don’t you think?”

“Yes, it is,” I agreed, and I hoped and prayed that was the truth.

Spirits were high as everyone left to go home. Everyone seemed excited about their ideas, and I couldn’t wait to read what the groups had written down. I just kept worrying that maybe we did not know how difficult change was going to be or what some members would do to resist these changes.

Chapter 25

With all of the chaotic but expected concerns of individual church members, I was barely keeping my head above water, but there was another issue that had been worrying me. We were trying to figure out ways to get more people to come to our church, and, if by some miracle that actually happened, I wanted to make sure we had a worship service that would meet visitor's needs as well as those of the church members.

Mr. Owns did a wonderful job with the music for worship, and he and I met occasionally to discuss things, but I thought we might need a more formal meeting and planning time. I asked him if he would be okay with that and with asking another person to join us at this meeting, and he agreed. He suggested Edna Allen be on the committee with us, and I thought that was an excellent idea, which seemed to please Mr. Owens.

We set up our first meeting for the following week.

Mr. Owens, Edna, and I sat in the small church library for our meeting. I started by saying that I thought it important that we look at our present worship services and evaluate how effective they were, with our present membership and with any new members that we might gather along the way. I expressed my feeling that we had a good worship service most Sundays, and I praised Mr. Owns, telling him that I thought the music choices and planning were exceptional. My question was could we make any or part of the worship service any better? I was terrified to ask this question, but I asked them to be honest and make suggestions as to how I could improve my sermons and make them more meaningful.

After I said these things, everyone was silent for a short spell, and of course, my anxiety level shot sky high. I just knew they were going to tell me my sermons were awful.

Finally, Mr. Owens spoke up and said, "Thank you for your positive comments about the music. I do believe that music is vital for effective and meaningful worship, and I try my best to bring that every Sunday. I know that a lot of churches are doing less traditional worship services and singing more praise choruses, and I am not crazy about that idea. However, if you guys think that would enhance our worship service, I guess I am willing to compromise on that a little."

"I have to be honest," Edna said, "I like our traditional worship service. And Annie, you do a wonderful job with your sermons. Something new now and then could be good, but to give up traditional hymns and prayers is not something I really want to do. I know that is my age speaking, and I do want you both to know that if we need to, I can live with some changes. I must go on record saying, however, that I do not feel a need to provide entertainment in worship. The message of Christianity should be enough to entice people into our doors without rock and roll and dancing and clapping of hands. Perhaps we are not presenting the true message of faith in as attractive and meaningful way as we could, and that is worth looking at for change."

"I don't think I know what you mean," I said to Edna.

"When I was a child, the main message of Christianity that I was exposed to was to be saved so I would go to heaven and not to hell. That was pretty cut and dried, and it was easy to understand. Then the message moved toward the kingdom of heaven being on earth and the idea that having Christ in our hearts would make our lives here on earth more meaningful and full of purpose in the here and now. Along with that came some ideas of more service to our fellow man, and therefore we started soup kitchens, home building for the poor, care for the homeless, fund raisers for those in need, and special activities for youth and children. But it seems to me that most of our service projects we do for the church are done outside the church, and I am not sure we have figured out how to bring the community into the church sanctuary. It is wonderful that we took the church to the community, but now maybe we have to bring the community into the church. To be honest, I think that scares us more than anything. If we bring homeless people into our church, we ask ourselves, 'Will they be dangerous? Will they fit in? Will they mess up our services? What will they wear? How could we become friends with them?' If we invite undocumented residents who don't speak English into our churches, we ask, 'How will they understand what is going on? Don't most of them want to be Catholic? How could we become friends with them?' If we invite members of the Lesbian-Gay-Bisexual-Transgender community into our churches, we ask, 'Won't our children want to copy their lifestyles? Aren't they all sinners? Won't they want us to think that they are loved by God? How could we become friends with them?' I think our worship services are usually just fine, and the only changes that will really enhance them are those we invite to join us."

"Okay, just hold on a minute," said Mr. Owens. "This is just too much for me to take in. Are you all saying that it does not really matter what the message is as long as we are sharing it with all kinds of people?"

"No, of course not," said Edna, "but I can understand why you are thinking that. As usual, my mouth is running faster than my brain. Of course it matters what the message is, and I think we can agree on what that message should say, but the problem seems to come when our focus is only on sharing that message with people who are just like us. Christians aren't the only ones who like to hang out with like-minded people, but our purpose and our message is so much bigger than that. I think all I am saying is that we really need to figure out a way to bring those groups of people who are not like us into our church."

"I agree with you, Edna. And it seems to me that we need to change a mindset concerning who belongs in our church and who might not fit in."

"I understand what you guys mean," said Mr. Owens, "but I have to say that thinking about these groups you named being members here at Covenant scares me to death. All those questions you were suggesting as problems are very real concerns of mine and would be for a lot of other church members. We can't risk losing our current members just to bring in people who may not become a part of us or who might leave us very quickly. That is certainly not good 'business sense,' is it?"

Edna looked very perplexed. "I guess it's not, is it? How can we get people comfortable with the idea of having a really diverse membership? We talk about that a lot, but the reality is that none of us know how to make that work, do we?"

We sat there quietly, feeling defeated and recognizing that we did not have any answers for the same questions that churches all over the country were asking. Where were our new members coming from? How did we recruit new members? How did we make our church and its message relevant to our current culture?

Finally I said, "If we try to solve every problem in our church in this meeting, we will get nowhere. I agree that we as a church must look outside of ourselves in order to grow, but for us right now, I still think we need to focus on making worship as meaningful as possible for everyone who joins us, both members and visitors."

I had come into this church thinking I would make a huge difference in this community, and that I would be able to lead them in a way that would bring in new people and keep the old. I thought that because I was young and energetic and open to new ideas, we would put the out-of-date ideas about church behind us, and that everyone would welcome the new way of doing things. The center of that plan seemed to be about me. Just like all my young and upcoming professional friends, I wanted to be a success in my field, and I believed I could make that happen all by myself. I forgot about God. I felt truly humbled, which was a new feeling for me and not a very comfortable one. I had prayed a lot and studied scripture, but I am not sure I ever really thought about asking God where He wanted the church to go.

I knew I had to say something to Mr. Owens and to Edna, and so I said, "I agree that we don't seem to have a lot of answers tonight about specific things to do or new ways to have worship, but I appreciate the fact that it seems you are open to trying new worship ideas even if they are not our favorites. Perhaps, Mr. Owens, we might insert one praise song during worship or maybe at the beginning of the service. Would that be something you could live with?"

"Of course I could, and if you'll give me a few days to think about it, I'll come up with a plan that will be comfortable for all of us."

"Thank you so much."

"I was also thinking that we might try a brief fellowship time during the service just to give everyone a chance to say hello to each other. How does that sound?"

"I actually like that idea, Annie, because so often I don't have time to speak to everyone. What about you, William?"

"I think that's okay. We are planning lots of changes for this congregation, so maybe it is a good idea to go slowly with worship changes."

"Well, I sure think that is enough for now. As with everything, as our membership changes, we will have to continue to evaluate our services."

"Rev. Adams, you look a little stressed. You okay?"

"I guess I am a little stressed," I said, "but I'll be okay. Would you lead us in our closing prayer?"

"Sure," he said, and he prayed earnestly for God's guidance and leadership and for our acceptance of how God wanted the church to grow, even if it wasn't what each of us wanted. I felt as if he had looked inside my soul and prayed the prayer that I had needed but had not been able to find.

Edna picked up her purse and said she had to get home. She had mentioned that her son and two granddaughters were moving home with her the next day, and she wanted to be sure everything was ready for them. We wished her well and said, "Goodnight."

I planned to go home as well, but Mr. Owens asked me to hold up a minute. He said, "I certainly do not want to offend you, but I have this bottle of Cognac in my desk that at times when I am tired and feel overwhelmed, I drink a little of it. Would you like to join me?"

Without even questioning why or how, I said, "I sure would."

We went into his office where I sat in his guest chair across the desk from him. It was a dark brown leather wingback chair into which I could sink forever, and then he pulled out two small glasses and poured a small amount of Cognac in each of them. He handed me one and said, "Don't drink it all at once. It is to be sipped and savored."

"Thank you. I will do that."

He raised his glass to me and said, "To the future. To change and to staying the same."

I drank a small sip of the Cognac, and as it entered my system, I immediately felt a warm glow and a relaxing of my muscles throughout my body. I closed my eyes and sat still as I felt my body lose the tension in my neck and back.

Wow! That was some powerful drug.

I looked over at Mr. Owens, and he had a silly grin on his face. Then I did something I rarely do. I giggled. When Mr. Owens heard me, he laughed out loud, and then I giggled even more.

"You know, Annie, I think we needed this," he said, as he continued to smile. "By the way, while we are talking and relaxing, I need a favor. Please call me William. I know I'm old enough to be your father, but I am not, so I would rather be a friend."

"I would like that a lot, William."

Chapter 26

I spent the rest of the week trying to catch up on visitations. I saw Thomas and Joy, and they seemed to be more at peace with Thomas' illness. They were very excited about a trip to the beach they were planning.

Thomas told me, "We have not been to the beach since Evan died. We had our honeymoon at Oak Island, and after Evan was born, we tried to go back every year. Evan loved it there. After he died neither of us could face going there again, but now we are ready to go back, and both of us are very excited about it. I think we will stay just a couple of days, and so we should be home for church next Sunday."

"That sounds wonderful, Thomas. I hope you guys have a great vacation."

I went by the Andersons house to tell Mai good-bye and to tell Edward I would be checking on him as would some of the church members. I told him to call me if he needed anything.

Vivian Artz had been at church since her surgery, but I just wanted to stop by and say hello. She was looking a little tired and told me she had been doing too much and was trying to take it easy for a while. I encouraged her to do that. I also told her how proud I was of her for speaking up for her daughter and her family. She just smiled and said, "I probably should have been doing more all along, but at least I did it when I really needed to."

There were two other names on my list of members to be visited. Both had expressed a need at the congregational meeting. One was Libby Smith who had spoken about her unmarried granddaughter with the two children and the other was Mary Leblanc, a Katrina transplant from New Orleans who mentioned her son's release from prison.

Mary lived in a small trailer park just off Highway 218. Her home was a small mobile home that was rusted all around the lower half of the outside walls. Two broken windows had plastic over them, and the front concrete steps were turned almost crossways in front of the door whose screen had been torn in half. Parked outside the trailer was a twenty-year-old Honda Accord. Just to the right of the dirt path leading to her front door was a small flower garden. The only color in the garden at this time of year were the purple and yellow pansies, but it was easy to tell the garden had been cared for. There were no weeds, and it looked as if the perennials had been carefully trimmed in preparation for the spring. I knocked on her front door, stepping very carefully on the steps. Mary opened the door with a smile and invited me in. The linoleum floors were torn in several places, but they were immaculate. The couch was covered with a clean sheet, and the rest of the furniture in the living room was two folding chairs. She had a nineteen-inch television on a small table in one corner of the room. There was no cable box nor a satellite dish.

I took my seat on the couch, and Mary brought out a tray with two cups of coffee and a small plate of four vanilla wafers. She asked if I needed sugar or cream, and not seeing either of those, I told her black was fine.

She sat down on one of the folding chairs and said, "I am so happy to have you in my home. I have lived here for seven years, but I have not had much company. My son Damien was twelve when we moved here. It was right after Katrina. He was not happy about the move because he had friends and his father's family in New Orleans. He did go to school and graduated a little over a year ago. But then he could not find a job, and he got angry about that. I have worked as a waitress off and on since we moved here, and that kept us afloat. Eventually, Damien decided to sell drugs for one of his friends, and of course he got caught. He was given community service at first, but before he could even complete his hours, the police had him again, and this time he had to serve eighteen months. He will be released soon, and I want him get back on the right track. I've only been coming to Covenant for several months, but I really like what I am hearing there."

"I am glad about that, and I am happy that Damien will be released soon. Will he be coming back to your home?"

"That is the plan. I hope Damien wants to make changes in his life. I don't want to lose my son. He did tell me he will have to stay one month at a halfway house, and while he is there, he thinks they will help him find a job. I have just started working again cleaning tables and washing dishes at a small diner in

Bakerstown. I am hoping if I can keep working, and Damien can find a job, we will be a lot better off."

"I hope so, too. One thing I know is that both of you will be welcome at Covenant. Maybe when Damien gets home, you can bring him by to meet me. I hope we will keep seeing you there, too."

Even as I welcomed new people to Covenant, I could only hope and pray they would be accepted.

We chatted a little more about what happened to her in Katrina. Mary told me, "Damien and I did not leave our home when we were told to because we were so afraid looters would come and take our possessions that we had worked so hard for. We got trapped on the roof of our house. The water came up quickly, and pretty soon we couldn't have left even if we decided to. By the time the waters were so high in our neighborhood, most of the wind had died down, and we sat on our roof for twelve hours. I have never prayed so hard in my life, mainly that Damien would be safe. I felt that I had made a terrible mistake by not leaving when they told me to, and I did not want Damien to pay for that with his life. Finally, a helicopter flew over, and then after a short distance, he turned around and circled above us. A man and a belt for us was let down from the helicopter, and eventually, we were lifted up to safety. The Red Cross helped us for about two weeks, and then we were relocated to Houston and finally to North Carolina."

"I cannot imagine that kind of terror. You were very blessed to survive that."

Mary acknowledged that she knew that was true. She talks about once a month with her sister who stayed in Houston, but Mary admitted she was lonely and looking for people to get to know. She had been a faithful member of a Baptist church in New Orleans, but since she had been in North Carolina, she had not attended church regularly.

"I want to make some changes in my life, and I am hoping I can begin those changes at Covenant."

"I hope so, too. Can we pray before I have to leave?"

"Of course. Would it be okay if I pray?"

"That would be fine," I said.

Mary prayed, "Thank you, Heavenly Father, for this beautiful day and for Rev. Adams coming to visit. Please bless Damien today, keep him safe, and let him know that I am thinking about him all the time. We are trying to get our lives back where You want them to be, and we need a whole lot of help from You. Help us to make the right decisions for our future. I love You, Amen."

"That was a beautiful prayer, Mary. Thank you for that."

"I will be there on Sunday unless I have to work. I'm trying to get Sundays off because of church and because that is when I can visit Damien, but right now, I have to take what I can get. I will see you soon, though."

After a fast-food cheeseburger lunch and a quick stop at a local drugstore to pick up hand cream and bath soap, I headed for Mrs. Smith's house. I had visited her once when I first came to Covenant, but I did not know her well.

Mrs. Smith's house was quite different from Mary's. It was a two-story red brick home on a large piece of land covered in trees that had been there for decades. There were pecan trees, and oak trees and a few maples thrown in. Most had lost their leaves, but the oak trees had some bronze leaves, and the maples still showed a little bit of red color. There was a long gravel-covered driveway to the house. A porch extended across the front of the house, and on that porch were wooden rocking chairs placed sporadically along with a couple of outdoor tables. Mrs. Smith still had her ferns hanging across the front of the porch, and they looked beautifully healthy. I noticed that particularly because I have tried to grow these ferns, and it never seemed to work for me. Lucille's home was not new, but it had been lovingly cared for.

When I was walking up the steps, I heard the front door open, and when I looked up, there was Mrs. Smith in a pair of baggy blue jeans and a faded flannel shirt.

She called out to me, "Come in, come in, and please excuse my appearance. I have been working in my yard, and I kept thinking I should clean up and get ready for your visit, but I just kept finding more things to do."

Mrs. Smith's accent was as Southern as it gets, and the charm just oozed out of her. I said to her, "Please don't worry about that. I am jealous that you have time to work in your yard, and in my eyes, you are dressed just right for a fall day in the yard."

She laughed and said, "Why thank you very much. I just hope there is no perspiration odor on me from all my hard work. Please come in and have a seat in the parlor."

With that, I could not help but think. *The parlor? My goodness, I have entered a time machine and gone back to the Antebellum South.*

The parlor was a warm and welcoming room. One wall was covered in built-in bookcases full of books, many that looked as if they were very old as well as plenty of current books. Family photos lined another wall. Some were recent, as I recognized Mrs. Smith and her three children, but many of them had to have been of her parents and grandparents. A long sofa with brown and white stripes covered another side of the room, and there were overstuffed chairs throughout.

I sat on the sofa and immediately thought I could stay here forever. The one thing I knew I could not do was fall asleep on this sofa so I made myself sit up very straight. Mrs. Smith sat down in one of the chairs and picked up a bell which she rang gently. Within ten seconds, a middle-aged woman brought a tray holding a silver tea service, two fine china cups, and a plate of homemade oatmeal chocolate chip cookies.

The woman put the tray on the table closest to Mrs. Smith and then asked her "Will there be anything else, Mrs. Smith?"

"No thank you, Frances. Everything looks lovely."

Fortunately, Frances was white, or I really might have thought I had gone back to Antebellum days.

Mrs. Smith poured a cup of tea and put a cookie on a small plate. She asked if I wanted sugar or lemon in my tea, and I told her sugar would be fine. She brought me the tea and the cookie, and then she served herself.

While she was doing that I said, "I want to thank you for your comments at the meeting the other night. I know that took a lot of courage for you to speak up. I hope you have only received positive responses to your concerns."

"I have. I know I am an old fogey when it comes to this, but I just wish Elizabeth had waited to have her children until she is married. I don't condemn her and haven't done anything drastic like take her out of my will, but I know how difficult it is to rear children, and I hate to think of her struggling on her own. She has ended the relationship with the father of the children for some very good reasons, but now she is responsible for these two babies all by herself. She is still in school, and she is a junior at UNCC, but that makes it even tougher for her."

"You must be proud of her for trying to continue her education."

"Oh I am. Elizabeth is a very hard worker. Her mother and father, my son and daughter-in-law, have almost completely abandoned her, and I am angry with them. One does not abandon one's children, no matter what they do. I have been trying to help her out a little, but chasing these two children, ages one and three, is more than I can handle. I have also tried to give her a little money, but she is very proud and has to be completely destitute before she will accept any."

"It sounds like you have been a tremendous support to her."

"Well, I have certainly tried. I have even asked her to come to church with me, and she just looks at me and says, 'Sure, Grandmother, I will fit right into that Baptist church. They are known for their compassion for sinners.' It breaks my heart that she feels that way, but, to be honest, I am afraid she might be right. Until the other night, I did not push her coming with me because I thought people might make unkind comments or even talk about her after church, and I did not want that to happen. I love this child dearly, and I only want what is best for her."

"I believe that you do, Mrs. Smith, and I hope the church can help you give her that. If she is interested in bringing the children to church, I think she would be accepted. What's happened to church members is that they are more aware of how they respond to visitors, and they are thinking about how to show acceptance of those who might be a little different from them. You know that doesn't mean that everyone will love and accept every visitor to the church, but I think the culture of the congregation is slowly changing in a positive way."

"I believe that, too, Rev. Adams, but I guess I am not ready to bring Elizabeth in as a guinea pig to see if church members are more accepting. I think I might wait and see how that works with someone else. I don't want to turn Elizabeth away from church completely."

"I understand your caution, but hopefully, we will be inviting some different groups to visit the church rather soon, and it won't be too long before Elizabeth can try us out as well. I personally would look forward to having some young children in the church."

"They are beautiful children and very well behaved. I am very proud of how Elizabeth is rearing them. I do believe the time is close when I will feel confident enough to bring her to church, and I look forward to that time."

"I do as well, Mrs. Smith."

She told me a little about the rest of her family and then talked about her husband who had been dead for ten years. She said that Frances had worked for her since before her husband's death, and that even though she was her employee, she thought of Frances as a sister.

"We actually do most of the work together, but when I have company, she insists on being the 'maid' and playing that role. She says I have to keep up my image in the community."

I smiled at her and told her I was glad she had Frances' companionship, and then I said a prayer, told her goodbye and left the plantation.

Chapter 27

The following Sunday was a really good day at church. There was an excitement in the sanctuary that had not been there before. People were greeting each other and actually looked very happy to be there. I noticed Cliff and Sarah Burnside coming in the back of the church, and they were greeted warmly by almost everyone they passed. Two of the people who shook their hands were Erin and Danny O'Reilly. All of those people who spoke about their personal situations at the congregational meeting were present, and church members were going out of their way to welcome them.

I took advantage of all the excitement in the air and announced that we would be having our first "Thomas and Joy Hearn" prayer and meditation gathering on Tuesday morning of the following week. I explained that we would meet at 7:00 that morning for quiet time to reflect and pray.

My sermon was entitled "Finding Courage Within," and I used the scripture found in the book of Acts describing the courage of Stephen. Stephen had been brought in to be questioned by the religious authorities regarding his preaching and performing of great wonders in the name of Jesus. He had been accused of blasphemy, and when questioned by the high priest, he simply poured out his heart about the early history of the Hebrews and the faith of the leaders, and then he verbally attacked those who had killed the one he called the Righteous One or Jesus. Stephen knew that what he did and said was going to make the authorities angry, and yet he showed no fear of them. The authorities did become very angry with his words, and they stoned Stephen to death, and as he died, he prayed that God would not hold this sin against those who were attacking him.

I spoke to the congregation and said, "I want each of us to look inside our hearts to see if we have the courage to take a stand and make some possibly unpopular decisions in this community. Now don't get me wrong. I don't think any of us are going to lose our lives over being an inclusive body of people, but you and I both know that if we invite gay families into our church and if we invite those of a different color or religion and those who are undocumented or have been imprisoned, we are going to raise the ire of some of our fellow Christians. They may catch you in the grocery store or at the Pizza Palace or at a fast food restaurant, but they will find you, and they will criticize you and this church. Some people will be hateful and mean, while others will just be distant, but you will pay a price for being a part of a radical group with new ideas. It will be difficult both for us and for our families. It will take courage, and my prayer is that if this is the path our church wants to take, each of us will look inside our hearts and find the amount of courage that we need."

I shared two other stories of courage in the Bible, and then I prayed for our congregation and for each of the members of our church.

After the service, I shook everyone's hand, and when I faced Harry Williams, I knew he was not happy with me. Harry and his wife Earlene had been very active in the church when their children were younger, but in the last few years, they had come to church less frequently. Interestingly enough, they sent their tithe every Sunday, and we as a church really did appreciate that. Harry had not approved of the church calling a woman as pastor, but he stuck it out because he had been a long-time member of the church. Now with everyone talking about making even more extreme changes, I knew he was on the edge of walking away from this church. I asked him if I could come and visit with him on Monday afternoon at 1:30. He was quite frank with me, and said to me, "I don't think it will do any good if you are trying to get me to accept these new ideas in the church, but I will be happy to talk with you. Earlene will be at home then, too, so it will be a good time for you to come."

"Thank you, Harry. I will see you then."

Monday afternoon came way too soon, and I arrived at the Williams' home promptly at 1:30. I was quite anxious about this visit as I did not want to alienate Harry and Earlene, but I knew Covenant was making some moves that could be upsetting to some of our members.

Earlene greeted me warmly at the door. I had not visited with the Williams before because we had some scheduling problems at first, and then to be honest, I got busy and forgot I had not been in their home.

We walked down a short hallway into a large oak-paneled den. Two large, comfortable looking recliners faced an entertainment center. On the side of the room across from where we stood was a comfortable looking red and black plaid sofa with an end table lamp combination on one end and a brass colored floor lamp on the other. To the right of the couch was a desk with a laptop computer centered on it.

Harry was sitting in one of the recliners, and when he saw me, he started to get up.

I said, "Harry, keep your seat. You look so comfortable."

He responded, "I might just do that 'cause I am worn out. I have been raking leaves and burning them all morning, and that is a big job. If you really don't care, I will just stay sittin' here."

"You are fine. I have raked a few leaves in my time, and I agree with you that it is hard work."

Earlene hurried off to bring me a glass of tea, and I looked at Harry and said, "I appreciate your willingness to talk with me about the church. I know we see things differently, and I guess all we can do is talk and see if we can find any common ground."

"I don't mean to be pessimistic, Annie, but I don't see any place we can meet. The Bible says very clearly that homosexuality is wrong, just like it says women should not be pastors of a church, and I don't see any way around that. I don't hate gay people, but if they are going to be in our church, they need to change their ways. To invite them in with their boyfriend or girlfriend is about as sinful as being homosexual. I just don't understand the other members of this church who seem to think it is okay to do that. It seems like they want to do anything to get new members, but I think God might have his limits. This church is important to me, but to be honest, I can't stay a part of something I don't believe in."

Ignoring the dig about women pastors, I said, "Harry, I do hear what you are saying. As young as I am, as a child, I remember hearing some of those ideas in church and at my school. It was only after I went to college and made some friends who were gay that I started looking at those teachings a little more closely. As your pastor, I am not here to talk you out of your beliefs. I would never do that. Those beliefs are a part of who you are, and it is your God-given right to believe as you want. To be honest, I am not even sure why I am here. Maybe I just want to let you know why I believe as I do.

"Annie, I don't care if you tell me what you believe. I just don't want you to expect me to change. And to be perfectly above-board, you need to know that some of us in this church may go elsewhere if these ideas continue."

"I have heard that, Harry, and it breaks my heart. This church has fought a lot of battles together for many years, and I would hope we could continue to do that, even if we don't agree on everything."

Earlene had slipped in with my tea, and I took a long drink of the sugary concoction. It was like nectar in my mouth.

I turned to Earlene and said, "What do you think of all this?"

She smiled at me and said, "To be honest, I haven't given it a whole lot of thought. I have never known a gay person personally, and it just hasn't been an issue for me. I have always believed like Harry says, that the Bible says homosexuality is wrong, but I am probably a little more open than he is to hear if you have something different to say."

Harry looked at Earlene as if she had just questioned the resurrection, but he did not say a word.

"Well, to be honest, I have studied this issue quite a bit because it is difficult for me to understand a God who would condemn a man or a woman for being born a homosexual. And I do believe that happens. I have never known a gay man or woman who said that they had chosen to be gay. I am not saying that that would never happen, but I just have not known it to be the case. Let me tell you where I am with the few mentions of homosexuality in the Bible. First of all, these statements are never given a high priority in the scriptures. In the New Testament, it is mentioned in I Corinthians and I Timothy. There is a list of behaviors that would prevent people from inheriting the Kingdom of God. However, when some study the Greek words, many interpret these verses to be condemning of homosexual prostitution and not homosexuality. That would be no different from a condemnation of heterosexual prostitution. In Romans, there is a mention of the men leaving the 'natural' feelings toward women and going toward men. One interpretation of that is that Paul is talking about doing what is natural to oneself, not in the sense of what is right or wrong, but simply following one's identity as a heterosexual. This passage would have nothing to do with someone who is by nature homosexual. Guys, I don't want to get too complicated here, but these are some of the interpretations that have helped me believe that God loves and accepts gay people just like he does everyone else.

Earlene said, "That is really quite interesting. I certainly have never heard those ideas from any other pastor."

Harry frowned at her and said, "There are probably good reasons for that."

I refused to take offense and went on with my explanation, "The Old Testament is full of rules and laws of ancient tribes wandering in the wilderness, and it is hard to even imagine following a small portion of them. I have always wondered why it is that the idea of sexual misconduct is so much more important to people than all the other rules that we break on a daily basis. I want you to hear me very carefully now. I have told you all this so that you know where I am coming from as a pastor. I really am not trying to convince you that my way of thinking is the right way. I just want you to know I have some justification for what I believe."

There was silence, and I immediately worried that I had gone too far with everything I had said. I didn't know what to say, so I tried to stay silent. The Williams were good people, and I did not want to alienate them.

Finally, Harry spoke to me and said, "Annie, I believe you are sincere in your study of the Bible and in what you believe, but I still think you are wrong. We can take verses out of context and interpret them all different ways, but I still believe that God condemns homosexuality. I don't think I can worship with gay people, but I don't feel angry with you. I just don't agree with you, and to be honest, I don't want you to do anything to hurt Covenant."

I wanted to cry, but I didn't. There are so many issues that separate Christians from each other, issues that we make bigger than our faith, and I had absolutely no idea how to change that.

I said to Harry, "Thank you for listening to me. I want you and Earlene to worship with us at Covenant, but there is absolutely no way I can see Jesus not opening His arms to anyone and everyone who wants to be in His house of worship."

Earlene surprised me by speaking up and saying, "Pastor Annie, both of us needed to hear what the other had to say. So much of the problem between groups of people in this community as well as in the whole country is that they don't spend any time listening to each other. They just want to hear themselves talk. I thank you for what you said, and I will think about it and pray about it. So will you, won't you Harry?"

Harry tried to hide the surprise in his face as he looked at Earlene. Then he said, "I might do that."

I looked at both of them and said, "I will do that, too."

Then I asked Harry if he would say a prayer before I left, and he did, asking that each of us would be open to God's leadership and direction in this matter and all others.

When I walked to my car, I felt very discouraged because I did not think I had made any impact on Harry and Earlene, and I was afraid they were going to leave Covenant for another church or try to get enough votes to prevent any changes at Covenant, but I had to acknowledge that at least we had a very civil conversation about a very controversial topic.

Chapter 28

Tuesday morning I wanted to do a few things to set the tone for our first prayer session so I headed over to the church earlier than usual. It was still not completely daylight, but I only turned on a minimum of lights in the sanctuary. Then I set up a CD player with religious music to play softly in the background. It was a mixture of music styles, with some being rather formal or classical, some choir groups, and others country music groups. I sat in a chair on the floor facing the congregation and tried to relax as 7:00 quickly approached.

The first to enter the sanctuary was Vivian Artz. She smiled at me as she entered quietly, walked in slowly using her cane, and took a seat on the second row of the church. Closely behind her came Sarah Burnside and then Mary Leblanc. It was very quiet for a few minutes, and those present seemed to be trying to be quiet and meditative. I find that very difficult to do, and I don't think I am alone with that problem. About ten minutes after seven, just as I was about to say a few words, Earlene Williams walked in and sat down about five rows from the back.

I raised my head and said softly to the group, "We are here to take some time out of our day to commune with God. You may be in pain, either physically or emotionally, and this is your time to ask God for his help. Perhaps your family is in trouble and you need to pray for them. Maybe you are just feeling lonely and want to be assured that God is alive and that he cares about you. Whatever your reason, please take advantage of the peace in this place and talk to your Heavenly Father."

I kept an eye on my watch, although I did take advantage of the quiet and had a wonderful conversation with God. At 7:30, I spoke to the group again and asked if they had any prayer requests that they wanted to share with the group. There was a comfortable silence, and then Sarah Burnside said, "I am just so very grateful to God that my family's life seems to be returning to normal. To be honest, I was never sure that was going to happen. But now, we go to the grocery store or out to eat, and people speak to us and wave to us from across the parking lot. At school, the boys' teachers report to me that they seem to be laughing and playing again just like they used to. They also say their grades are returning to normal as well. Cliff has not returned to teaching, and I am not sure he ever will, but he, too, is beginning to laugh a little again and is occasionally playing with our sons. He is concerned about his professional future, but even that seems less important after what he has been through. We feel welcome in this church again, and that has been an enormous blessing to us. Thank you all very much."

We sat comfortably in silence again for about ten more minutes, and then I told them I would say a prayer to close our session. I prayed for each person there and their families, I thanked God for being in each of our lives, I prayed for our church and all of the decisions we had to make, I prayed for guidance, and I prayed for peace for church members. I expressed thanksgiving to God for these members who were present and for each person who was associated with Covenant. I asked that we would continue to love each other even though we might have differences in beliefs. I ended with thanking God for his love for each of us and asked that we would continue to experience that love every day so that we could share it with others. Then I closed the prayer and sat quietly for just a moment more.

I looked up and saw Sarah and Mary wiping away tears. But they were smiling as well. We seemed to need to gather closely for just a moment, so we walked to the center aisle about five rows back, shared a few hugs, and then we went our separate ways. I had a need to discuss how this first prayer group went, and to ask for input, but I controlled my insecurities and just said goodbye to everyone. My ever present need for affirmation had to be put on hold.

Chapter 29

I had not seen my parents for several weeks, so when I realized I had Friday off, I called and told them I would like to come home Thursday night and spend the day with them. My dad said he would try to get off at noon on Friday so we could have more time together. I felt as if I had also been neglecting my best friends so I called Jane and Sheila to catch up on their lives. Jane was very apologetic about not calling in a while, but then she shared that she had helped Frankie move into a townhouse, and they had bought a puppy together. Frankie was the primary caretaker, but they did share ownership.

"Have you made plans that you are not sharing with me, Jane?'

"No, really, we have not made definite decisions yet. Frankie has been amazingly attentive lately, but no commitment has been made. I feel really good about our relationship, but I do not want to rush anything. I really am happy when I am with him. He told me last weekend that he could not imagine life without me, and I told him I felt the same way about him, but I don't want to push him in any way so I am truly just enjoying the moment. I am so happy."

"That is wonderful, Jane. I am so happy for you guys."

"How is everything with you and Covenant?"

"Actually, things are going rather well. I am feeling more comfortable each day in my role as pastor. I am going to see my parents this week, but maybe we can get together for lunch soon. We are only about forty-five minutes away from each other. Let's really do this."

"I agree," said Jane. "I will text you in a couple of weeks."

I left a message for Sheila, and she called me back about 9:00. Sheila was not nearly as outgoing as Jane or I, but she was very special because of her ability to listen and to carefully reflect on what people said to her. I always knew that Sheila really heard what I said and that she paid attention to my concerns and questions, both expressed and unexpressed. The youth that she served spent hours with her discussing and planning meaningful projects. They also talked with her about their own lives, their families, and their futures. Sheila loved her work but she often questioned if she was enough of a "fun" person to be a minister to youth. Jane and I had both encouraged her that she was truly in the right place of service. Young people had lots of friends and family to have fun with, but to find someone who would really listen and care about what happened to them was a rarity.

Sheila and I spent a short time catching up on our jobs and our churches. Sheila served in a large Baptist church in Charlotte and was responsible for about fifty youth and their activities. She had told me that she had wonderful parental support as well as that of other church members, and that she did stay busy all the time, especially in the summer. The previous summer, she took thirty-six teenagers on a mission trip to Jamaica. It was apparently a huge success and a wonderful learning experience for the youth, but Sheila said it was as stressful as it gets.

I asked her if she had recovered completely from the trip over the summer, and she laughed and said, "I think I have recovered, but to be honest I think I might wait a while before I plan something like that again. I just felt so responsible for every young person involved, and it was terrifying to think of what could happen."

"Well I am glad you are feeling better. Is the responsibility getting so huge that you might decide to do fewer activities with the youth?"

"To be honest, it is getting so overwhelming that I might think of changing jobs."

"Sheila, I thought you loved what you did, and you are in such a great church. What's getting you down?"

"I don't always know, but sometimes when I am planning a party for after a football game or a trip to the skating rink, I wonder what it all means. Is that really the ministry I need to be doing? Sometimes I feel like a cruise ship activities director whose main purpose is to assure that all participants have fun, and I think I want more than that. There is definitely a need for someone to plan activities for youth in the church, but I just don't know if that's enough for me anymore."

I was totally surprised at Sheila's concerns, but I was sympathetic to her. If you were called to any type of ministry, there was always, as there was in any job, a lot of extraneous work to do. No one did only the serious and meaningful work of any job. There was always going to be paperwork and reports and busy work that had to be done.

I said, "I am sorry. Are you taking care of yourself both physically and mentally? Do you take time off and get away from the work at least once a week? Do you have a mentor to talk to?"

Sheila burst out laughing, and in fact, she laughed until she cried.

I asked her, "What's so funny?"

She said through her laughter, "Talk about the pot calling the kettle black!"

I giggled and said, "We make a great pair, don't we? But seriously, Sheila, I must tell you that I attended one meeting so far of a minister's support group, and I had a session with my new mentor. It did not take me long to learn that I needed that kind of support. I recommend these programs to anyone in the ministry."

"You're serious, aren't you? That was quite a change for you."

"It was a big change for me, but one that I really needed. Let me know if you continue to have concerns about your own ministry, and we can talk more about it."

"I'll do that, Annie. I'm glad you called."

The following Thursday afternoon, I drove to my parent's home in Columbia and retreated into the world of my childhood and youth. My brother Tom and his wife, Debbie, and their three kids came over for a late family dinner, and it was total chaos, as usual. We ate too much and brought up every funny family memory there was. Then all of us played two games of Scat, a great little card game for all ages. I lost thirty cents and regained the sense of having a life. It was money well spent.

My sister Janeen and her husband Joey could not come that night as they had a PTA meeting, but Janeen was coming over the next day for lunch.

Best of all, my parents did not question me about my future plans.

I always leave my number and where I will be with Edna when I go out of town, but I did not hear a word from her, and it was a wonderful time.

Chapter 30

In the midst of all the discussions and ideas and controversy that we as a congregation were dealing with, the business of the church had to go on.

Covenant usually had between six and ten deacons who were responsible for overseeing the actions of the church leading to service, spiritual growth, and financial stability. Presently, there were eight because that was all they could get to serve, but two of them had served for three years, and it was time for them to go off the deacon board. Church members had been asked to nominate any man or woman of good standing in the church as a deacon. Usually, according to Edna, the deacon chairperson, there were quite a few nominations, but by the time people took their names off the list, the number had decreased to one or two.

The names of those nominated had been printed in the bulletin, and those people were asked to let me or Edna know if they were willing to serve. Out of nine nominations, six had called early in the week to tell us they would not be able to serve at this time. I could only hope and pray that no one else on the list called.

I was working in the church office trying to bring order out of chaos and planning my week when the doorbell rang. When I looked out the window to see who was there, I saw Jesse Akin.

I opened the door and greeted Jesse with a smile. He said, "Good morning, Pastor Annie. I was wondering if I could have a few minutes of your time."

"Of course you can, Jesse. I am always happy to see you."

We walked into my office, and I offered Jesse a cup of coffee. He declined and then took a seat across from me.

"How have you been, Jesse?"

"I am fine, but I think I am going to have to ask you to take my name off the deacon nomination list."

Normally, I just thank the person who tells me this, and I do not try to make them feel guilty about their decision. For some reason with Jesse, I wanted to talk with him about it.

"Can you tell me why you would think that, Jesse?"

Jesse looked embarrassed and uncomfortable. Before I could tell Jesse that he did not owe me an explanation, he started to speak.

"Pastor Annie, about twenty years ago, I was nominated for deacon for the first time, and to be honest, I was tickled to death. Lorraine and I had been married for about a year, and we had been coming to church here since we got married. The week before the vote was scheduled for the whole church, I got a visit from the pastor. You see, both Lorraine and I had been divorced, and he felt like I was not qualified to be a deacon because of that. That hit me hard, Pastor Annie. I have been a Christian since I was eleven years old, and I really love the Lord. So does Lorraine. We tithe, we pray together every night and we read and study the Bible, and we were faithful members of the church. Rev. Hughes was in his seventies then and was an interim pastor, but I did not feel like I could go against his wishes, so I took my name off the list then and every time I have been nominated since then. I know people must think I am not willing to serve, but I just did not want to make any trouble. I don't think any of the deacons who are serving now are divorced, so I reckon I better follow the rules."

I felt a surge of anger and frustration go through me when I heard Jesse's story. How could a judgmental call from twenty years ago have kept this lovely man from serving God as a deacon in this church? If someone has the desire and ability to serve God, why must other Christians put up barriers?

"Tell me something, Jesse, if you don't mind. How did Lorraine feel about what Rev. Hughes said?"

"Well, that is the hardest thing about this situation. Lorraine just sat down and said, 'How can I worship in a church that doesn't think you are good enough to serve as a deacon?' and she has not been back to this church since then. She always watches a church service on the TV, but she won't come with me. Lorraine has a stubborn streak, Pastor Annie, and she is set in her ways."

"I don't much blame her, Jesse. When you love someone and know what kind of person he is, it is hard to forgive someone who hurts him so badly."

"Thank you for understanding about that. To be truthful, Pastor, I came in to talk to you in person because I was thinking that with all the new ideas and changes in our church, maybe there was some new thinking about deacons and divorce. That's probably just some wishful thinking on my part, but I guess I keep hoping that will happen."

"Jesse, I know there have been definite changes in how people feel about deacons or ministers who are divorced and actually toward divorce in general, but I don't know if Covenant has a policy about that or not. Seems to me, if mistakes kept us from serving God and the church, there wouldn't be anybody left to be a deacon or a minister."

"You got that right, Pastor."

"Jesse, let me talk with some of the other leaders of the church and get back to you on this question. For now, if you are willing to serve, you keep your name on the deacon nomination list."

Here I go again. I really don't look for controversy, but it just seems to find me. I would be shocked if this was still an issue in this church, but then I won't know for sure until I ask.

The next scheduled deacon's meeting was the following Thursday evening. I always attend deacon's meeting, but usually I let the deacons take care of their business, and I just observe or sometimes I answer questions. I always do a report to the deacons on my activities for the month and while doing that, I usually get a new list of people who need me to visit them or someone close to them.

This time I wanted to talk with the deacons about Jesse's question. Six of the eight current deacons were present. Those present included Edna Allen, who was, of course, the chairperson, Charlotte Wilburn, Alan Emerson, Thomas Hearn, Edward Anderson, and Fred Miller.

Edna called the meeting to order and gave the opening prayer. She asked if there were any questions or corrections about last month's minutes, and when there were none, the group voted to approve the minutes as written. The deacons had been charged with gathering the written suggestions from the last congregational meeting, and Edna had compiled a list of every suggestion that had been made, eliminating any duplications. She had distributed that list to every deacon and to me and asked that we read the list and evaluate the suggestions that were made before the meeting today. I had spent two evenings reading the list and trying to determine what might be good for the church and what would not be. There were twenty-two suggested activities or projects on this list, and they each had possibilities. For me, however, there were six projects that stood out above the others that I believed could be successful for our church. I was going to wait to see how the deacons felt about the list as they were the ones who would have to approve any projects.

Edward spoke first when Edna asked for opinions of the items on the list. He said "This was a difficult task, but with Mai gone, I had plenty of time to think about it. I felt like I was back in school doing homework."

There were a few murmurs of agreement here and a little nervous laughter.

Then he continued, "Right off the bat, I eliminated the ten activities that were just for children. They are all good, but I felt like we were looking for a new way to attract families. Then I actually eliminated eight of the remaining twelve because they did not sound like activities that would unite members with visitors. For example, the dinners-for-eight program is a great idea for churches, but it seems to me it would be difficult for new people to get to know the church if they were just meeting a small group of members. I liked the idea of having a church-wide picnic at a park and have special entertainment and prizes for people."

"I kind of agree with what you said, Edward," said Alan. "The church-wide picnic was high on my list, too. I also liked the idea of a 'getting to know you' potluck after church where visitors would be paired up with church members at lunch and would really spend some time getting to know each other. We church members would have to know we couldn't sit with the same old friends or family that we usually sit with, and we might need a little training or advice about how to get conversations going with strangers."

Charlotte spoke up and said, "I guess great minds do think alike 'cause I am with you guys. Whatever we do needs to be church-wide and geared toward the whole family, not just the kids and not just the adults."

No one else said anything for a few minutes. Edna spoke up and said, "Anyone else have any thoughts on this?"

Thomas said, "I am still not hearing anything that is going to pull people out of their beds on Sunday morning. These ideas are good, but what makes them stand out from all the other ideas that were presented? I am still convinced people long for the communion that one can share with other Christians, but getting them to do anything about that is the challenge. We have got to find that one appeal that might reach the hearts of people in our community, and we have to have the courage to use that appeal, whatever it is."

"Why aren't we just cutting to the chase here," Alan said. "If we care about this church, we have to make some big changes to keep it alive. It seems like we have all been walking on eggshells even though we have been talking about this for almost a year, way before Annie came to us. We want to be an inclusive church, and that means we make a point of inviting couples and families that have not been widely recruited to a small rural Baptist congregation. We invite people who would not normally walk through our doors because they would not feel welcome. Not only do we need to invite these families to our church, we also need to change our hearts so that we can sincerely and truthfully welcome these groups into our congregation. I just keep thinking, if Jesus was a member here, which side would he be on, the one that said you have to be a certain kind of person or have a certain kind of lifestyle to be welcome in God's house or the one who would say 'Come on in whoever you are, and I will love and accept you.' I don't know about all of you, but if every aspect of my life was examined closely, I might not be welcome in this church either. It is not our job to judge others, but to present the gospel of Jesus Christ to everyone, and there is a lot more important stuff in the gospel about how we should love each other than there is about condemning each other. Now there, I have said my piece. You can take it or leave it."

Alan was flushed and visibly upset. I thought for a moment that he might cry.

Again, there was that moment of silence.

Then Fred spoke up and said, "Alan, I never really thought about these groups as people I should love because I am a Christian, but instead I saw them as people I should not love because I am a Christian. How could I have been so blind? I told Annie a while back that if the church made all these changes and invited all kinds of people to come worship with us, that my family and I would probably have to leave the church. I apologize for that, to Annie and to the Lord. What you just said touched my heart, and I am ready to get on board with these ideas. I am going to need some help figuring out how to accept and love everyone who walks in our front door, but at least I am willing to try. I still have my concerns and I particularly feel uncomfortable with gay people, and I think Edith and Belinda do, too, but I will try to talk them into accepting these changes as well. Don't expect too much from us, but we won't be running out on you."

Edna looked at both Alan and at Fred and said, "I couldn't be prouder to call both of you my friends. Thank you for your comments. Does anybody else have anything to say?"

"I think they have said it all," said Charlotte, "and I am in full agreement with them."

"Me, too," said Thomas, "and all I can add is that let's get started because I want to be here to see this happen."

Edna looked at me and asked if I had anything I wanted to say.

"Of course I do," I said. "I am very proud of each of you for these thoughts and ideas that you have presented tonight. Several months ago, you called me to this church to lead you in making changes in this congregation and broadening your vision, but I will say to you tonight, you are the ones who are leading this congregation in a new direction, and I am proud to be your pastor. I believe you are following God's leadership and that you are laying an innovative path for the church of tomorrow."

Edna, ever the persistent chairperson, said, "Now that we have the direction we want to go, we will have to decide how to get there. I hate to ask this, but could we meet next week again after thinking about concrete ways to get people invited to our church. All of us may have some personal contacts with people we want to invite, but I think we are going to have to go bigger than that to make this work. Is another meeting ok with everyone?"

Everyone agreed, and I was asked to close the meeting with prayer. "Let us pray. Father God, we thank You for every good gift that You have given us, and we pray that we will be able to share the most wonderful gift of all, a relationship with You through Jesus Christ, with any and every person who walks through our door. I pray that You will help us to cleanse our minds of old stereotypes, old prejudices, and old fears that we have held for so long. Help us to be your representative of love here on earth so that anyone who comes the way of this church will be able to see You through our treatment of them and our acceptance of them as your children. Forgive us for all the times we put people in categories and reject them because of our biases. Give us Your mindset of love and acceptance. With a grateful heart I pray, Amen."

We said our goodnights, and I headed for home. I felt at peace about what the deacons had decided, and then I realized I had not asked them about the divorced deacon question. That would have to wait until next week. I was meeting with Rev. Stanley tomorrow, and I knew he was going to have to hear all about this meeting whether he liked it or not.

Chapter 31

My meeting with Rev. Stanley was what I would first call uneventful. However, as I thought back over it later in the day, I realized that I had told him my concerns about the church and the changes I saw coming to it. I was scared that no one was really speaking his or her mind about some of these issues and that as soon as we announced some of these new ideas to the present church members, everyone would leave the church. I was afraid everyone would say we, but what I really meant was I, had ruined the church.

I was also afraid for Thomas, and by Thomas, I meant for myself. Would I know what to do to help Thomas be at peace with his own death, and did I know the right things to say and do to help Joy get through this time?

This time with Rev. Stanley was all about me, and I realized I needed the time desperately. Could I lead this church to growth and service? Could I perform a funeral if I had to? Could I serve a grieving congregation when I would be devastated myself by the loss of a man like Thomas? Was I getting too close to the church members, and should I maintain a wall of professionalism with them? How could I keep my distance emotionally when I cared about so many of the church members?

I think my questions for Rev. Stanley might have been a little overwhelming for him, but he really helped me answer several of them. His words of understanding and experience helped me to feel more confident in my role as pastor. The greatest gift he gave me, however, was an opportunity to talk for a whole hour about what I was doing and feeling. I felt as if I had a clean slate after my meeting with him, and I felt so much more ready to face a new week with new problems.

The following Sunday, I arrived at the church about ten minutes before Sunday school was to start. We never had too many people at Sunday school, but this morning it looked as if there were a few more cars than usual in front of the church. Pete

Stoudemire was the teacher for the adult class, and members had told me that he was a really good teacher. They said he always gave a brief history about whatever book of the Bible they were studying, then he would give a brief summary of the lesson, and then he asked discussion questions about the lesson. Edna's description of Pete's questions were that "they always got people thinking and pretty soon a full-fledged conversation was going on, so much so that the class would be over before you knew it."

There was also a discussion class which usually involved the younger adults of the congregation.

I had just opened my office door when I looked up and saw John Allen, Edna's son, coming in the door with his two little girls. He was quite handsome with thick brown curly hair and dark eyes. He was about six feet tall, and very trim. This morning he had on faded jeans and a Carolina hoodie. I had met him once before when he visited the church with his mom, and all I remember about him is how dead his eyes had looked. He had seemed numb with grief.

This time when my eyes met his, I was happy to see that life had returned to them. I turned to him and said, "Good morning, John. Welcome."

He said, "Thank you, Rev. Adams. I am glad to be here. The girls want to go to Sunday school, and my mom told me she thought they would go in a class with Vivian Artz. Is she right about that?"

Most of Vivian's children were in school already, but she had always told me if younger children showed up for Sunday school, she would be happy to take them. The twin girls, Emily and Ella, were three so they were indeed younger, but I knew Vivian meant what she said.

"Yes, that's right. Let me show you where they meet."

John was struggling to hold on to both girls and a bag he was carrying for them, so I asked Ella and Emily if they would take my hands and let me show them to their class. I suggested John could bring the bag to the class. Each girl eagerly grabbed one of my hands, and we walked toward the children's classroom swinging our arms.

The O'Reilly children, Bobby and Erin were the only ones there today so far. They were excited to see the twins and wanted to help take care of them. I looked at Vivian and said, "Are you going to be okay?"

"Of course I will," she said, "the more the merrier. The older children are my helpers this week."

John handed the bag to Vivian and whispered a few words to her about the girls. She smiled at him and reassured him they would be fine.

John and I headed back toward the office, and I asked him if they had completed the move to Edna's house.

He nodded and said, "Yes we have, and I have hired a part-time nanny to help with the girls. I welcomed the help I could get from my mom, but I don't want to wear her out. She has her own life, and I want her to continue with that. It is just so nice to have her around the girls, and they are crazy about her."

"She is crazy about them, too, and I know she is glad to have you at home. How are you doing, John?"

"Actually, I am feeling more human every day. It has almost been two years since Lucinda died, and I am beginning to believe I will survive. I wondered about that for a long time, but I knew I had to keep going for the sake of the girls. Thank you for asking."

"If I can help in any way, please let me know."

"I will, Rev. Adams."

"Please call me Annie. If we are going to be seeing you here more often, we need to be less formal."

"All right, Annie it is, but don't expect to see me here too much. I am not on the best of terms with God right now, and I don't know if I ever will be again. But I do want the girls to be brought up in church, and from what I hear, this church is going in a very exciting direction. I would be proud to have my girls grow up in this congregation."

"Thank you, John. That's good to hear."

I watched him walk to his car and realized that he had moved forward in his grieving process, but that it would be a part of him for the rest of his life.

Thinking I could now return to my office to read over my sermon, I opened the door only to hear a voice behind me saying, "Pastor Annie, could I talk to you a minute?"

I turned around to see Robbie Burnside standing right outside my door.

"Of course, you can, Robbie. Come on in and have a seat. Did you guys just get here because I was just over at the children's class?"

"Yes, we did. We were running a little late. I told Miss Vivian that I needed to talk to you, and she said it would be fine."

"What's up, Robbie? What can I help you with?"

Robbie is a blue-eyed blond who wears glasses with dark frames that make him look very intellectual. I have heard that he is very bright and an excellent student. He is presently in the fourth grade and is a little smaller than his classmates because he has a late September birthday.

He looked a little nervous, and I was not sure what I could do to help him relax. I decided to just smile at him and wait to hear what he had to say.

"Pastor Annie, I have been listening to your sermons, and I have been thinking about this a lot, and I want to be baptized and become a church member. I feel like I kind of have a relationship with Jesus already, and I just want to let the world know that I have accepted Him as my savior."

I thought I was prepared for this moment as a pastor, but the absolute joy that I felt when Robbie told me what he wanted took my breath away. I wanted to stop and savor this moment.

"I am very happy to hear that, Robbie. Have you asked Jesus to come into your heart?"

"I have. I did that back when my Dad was having all that trouble. I was so worried about him that I had to ask God to help us, and He did. I understand all those things you preach about, how none of us are perfect and we all sin, and that is why God sent Jesus to live on earth and become one of us, but one who did not sin. And I know that Jesus died for all our sins, and all we have to do is acknowledge that and ask Jesus to come into our heart. I really do want to be a Christian, Pastor Annie."

"I believe you already are one, Robbie, and all you have to do now is let people know that and be baptized. Then you will also become a member of the church."

"That is what I want."

"Have you told your parents yet, Robbie?"

"No, I haven't. I wanted to talk with you first to make sure I was doing everything right. Will you help me tell them?"

"Yes, of course. When can we do that?"

"Maybe we can do that right after Sunday school. I was hoping that I could walk down the aisle today and let everybody know that I was joining the church."

I looked at my watch and knew that time was short, but I knew we could figure out a way to make this work.

"Stay right here, Robbie. I will go get your parents right now. I know this will make them very happy."

"Pastor Annie, don't scare them when you go get them. After what happened to my Dad, they get very nervous when something unusual happens."

"I understand, Robbie. I will be very careful with what I say to them."

I walked quickly over to the young adult class and knocked on the door. I walked in and apologized for interrupting them. Then I said to Cliff and Sarah, "Robbie has some very good news for you guys, and we were wondering if you could come over to my office to hear it?"

They looked a little surprised, but said of course they could.

We walked over to my office quietly and went in.

Sarah immediately said, "What is it, Robbie? Annie says you have some good news for us."

"I just wanted to tell you, Mom and Dad, that I am going to join the church today and let everyone know that I am a Christian. Is that okay?"

Cliff put his head down and began to cry. Sarah just reached over to give Robbie a big hug. Then Cliff lifted his head, and looked at Robbie and said, "That is better than okay, son. We are very happy for you and very proud of you. You know that your mom and I are both Christians, and this is what we want for you as well. You have made us both very happy."

Robbie stood up and went over and hugged his dad. It was a beautiful moment.

"Okay, Robbie. After the sermon when we sing the last song, that is when you can come down and talk to me again. I will be waiting for you. After church is over, we might all take a minute and talk about when Robbie can be baptized."

"That will be fine," said Sarah. "Thank you so much, Annie, for everything you have done for us, both today and in the past."

"You are more than welcome. Now all of you scoot so I can get ready for worship."

Chapter 32

I didn't set an alarm for Monday morning and had a wonderful night's sleep. When I woke up and looked at my clock, it was 8:45. That's probably the latest I had slept in a couple of years, and I felt great. My exercise routine had fallen by the wayside again, so I decided that as soon as I felt more awake, I would take a run. I didn't have any appointments for the day, and I felt completely free.

I stumbled to the kitchen, turned on my laptop and made a cup of coffee with my Keurig. Life was good.

I toasted an English muffin, spread peanut butter on it, and sliced a banana on top. While I ate breakfast and drank two cups of coffee, I read the Charlotte paper online. As usual, there was lots of "bad" news in the paper, but I was not going to let it get me down.

When I finished with breakfast and the paper, I put on my running shoes and some shorts and a sweatshirt. The temperature outside was fifty-two degrees, and the sky was clear blue. It was a perfect day for running, and I took off and ran three miles without having to stop and without too much gasping for air. I was still about a half mile from home when I couldn't run anymore, so I walked rather leisurely back to my house.

After showering and getting dressed for the day, I decided to go shopping. I had not bought anything new in several months, and it was time for some new clothes. I decided to go to Carolina East Mall where there were several stores in which I loved to shop and buy clothes. There was also a great deli there where I loved to eat.

Arriving at the mall just a little before noon, I decided I should eat first to keep up my energy level. I had a delicious Southwest Cobb salad and a giant glass of sweet tea. A couple of young guys in suits checked me out as I left the restaurant, and I just gave each of them a huge smile. I spent three hours shopping, got no phone calls, bought three new outfits, and felt completely renewed as a woman and a human being.

As I drove back home, I had several revelations. First of all, I loved my job, my church and the congregation. I loved the life I was living right now. I also realized that taking care of myself occasionally renewed my spirit, both emotionally and physically, and that I would be a better pastor if I would do that more often. I had spent the first few months of this job desperately trying to prove myself to the church members, to the community, to my parents, and probably to God, and it was time to slow down a little and accept the fact that I believed this was where I was supposed to be, and that with that faith, I didn't have to continue to try so hard to be perfect. I accepted the fact that God could take a person like me, someone with all my failings and frailties, and actually do some good in the church and with his people.

Life was indeed good.

Thanksgiving was right around the corner, and I had no clue what, if anything, the church usually did to celebrate that day. Since the deacons were meeting in a couple of days, I just waited until that meeting to ask my questions.

Before we started our deacon meeting, I told the group that I had a few questions that I needed an answer to. First of all, I needed to ask if there were any rules about a deacon being divorced. The same six deacons who were at last week's meeting were present again with the addition of Cliff Burnside. When I asked this question, each one of them looked at me as if I were from another planet.

Fred Miller spoke up and said, "You guys know I am one of the more conservative members of this church, and I don't have a problem with a deacon being divorced. Now of course that is as long as he or she is respected as a Christian man or woman by the church members and a faithful member of the church. And, to be honest, I might have a problem with someone who has gotten divorced several times, not because it becomes a bigger sin, but because it might indicate a problem with that person's judgment."

Edna asked why that question had occurred to me, and I told her about my visit from Jesse Akin and his concerns. She just shook her head. "I can't believe poor Jesse accepted what that interim minister said all those years ago. We would love to have Jesse as a deacon, but we just thought he didn't want to serve."

"Hopefully, we can correct that mistake. I think he would really like to be a deacon, and maybe we can win Lorraine's forgiveness in the process," I said.

Then I raised my second question. "What does the church do to celebrate Thanksgiving, if anything?"

Again, the group looked at me rather strangely.

Charlotte looked at the others and said, "Correct me if I am wrong, but I don't think we usually have any kind of special service for Thanksgiving. I don't know why." The others nodded to indicate Charlotte was right, and I just thanked them for the information.

Edna called the meeting to order and said a prayer. Then she said, "Folks, it is time to make a damn decision. Please pardon my language, but it is time we decide how we want to move forward in making this church an inclusive church. Like we said before, this has been up for discussion since before Annie came here, and so far, all we have done is talk. Has anybody thought and prayed enough about this to come up with a plan?"

Edward spoke up kind of tentatively, and said, "I have an idea, but I just don't know how well it might work."

"Your plan might be all we have, so let's hear it," said Edna.

"I was thinking we might have a big family day celebration, and we would celebrate all different kinds of families, those with two moms or two dads, those with one parent of one color and one of another, one parent who speaks English and the other one who doesn't, one where one parent is a Christian and the other one is another religion, and on and on. You get my drift, don't you? Somebody else had this idea earlier, but I like it for this celebration. We'll feed everybody, of course, and each church member would like adopt a family on that day and sit with them for lunch and really get to know them. And one more thing. We would have to advertise this event in the Charlotte paper, which is going to cost a fortune. And we probably need a bunch of signs to put up all over, too. That's my idea."

Everybody just sat completely still staring at Edward.

"Somebody say something. Don't just sit there," Edward said.

"I love it," said Charlotte. "It is so simple and yet so perfect."

Fred said, "I think it's ok. Kind of low key, not making a huge production of it. I'm in favor of not stirring up too much trouble."

"I wouldn't count on not making trouble, Fred, but at least this way is a positive statement, and the focus is on families," said Alan.

Edna looked at me. "Pastor?"

"I think it is a wonderful way to honor and include all different kinds of families. Edward, I'm so happy that you came up with this plan. It's fantastic," I responded.

"Thank goodness we finally have a plan. I like it, too. A lot, in fact," said Edna. "The next step is to report this to the church and get their approval, and after that we have to figure out how we are going to make this work and when we can do this. Edward, let me just ask you. Do you have some opinion about when we ought to do this?"

Edward grinned and said, "Well, since you asked."

We all burst out laughing at the pure delight on his face.

Then he said, "Let me finish now. I know this is coming up awfully fast, but it seems to me that the time of year that focuses on family the most is Christmas, and so I was thinking we should put this together in the next month or so, like maybe two Sundays before Christmas."

This time we all looked at him like he was crazy.

"I know, I know, you all are thinking we just can't possibly do that. But just think about it. We are going to have a worship service and a lunch after that. That's our specialty, preachin' and eatin'. Most of the work is going to be between now and then, and I think we can do it. Mai won't be back for another couple of weeks, so I got all kinds of time to do stuff, and I will be happy to do it. Let's make a list right now of what we would need to do besides prepare for worship and lunch, and then we can decide if it is possible. Okay?"

It was impossible not to get caught up in Edward's excitement, and maybe he was right. If we waited until after Christmas, then we had to worry about the weather being bad on our chosen day, but then if we waited for spring, the excitement about this project might be wearing thin.

I spoke up and said, "Edward, I am willing to work right along beside you in the next four or five weeks. I agree with you. I think we can do it."

Edna looked around and said, "What about the rest of you? Are you in?"

Thomas said, "I will do what I can, but I just don't know what will happen with my health in the next few weeks. I think Joy will certainly be willing to help as well."

Fred and Alan looked at each other, nodded and then Alan said, "We're in, also."

"Me too," said Charlotte, "but I guess I better go out this weekend and get my Christmas shopping done."

Chapter 33

The next morning in the light of day and at my desk in my office, I looked at Edward's list and said to myself, "What were we thinking?"

I really went into a panic wondering how on earth we could get this event scheduled and prepared in just five weeks. That's how long we were going to have to put this all together. I had to prepare the best sermon of my life, but on top of that I knew I would have a lot of responsibility for this program. That was okay because I was the only paid staff, but it still felt a little overwhelming.

The doorbell rang, which was a surprise since it was 9:00 in the morning. I looked out the window and saw John Allen standing there.

"Good morning, John. You're up and around early."

"I am on my way into my Charlotte office, but I just wanted to stop in and tell you how pleased I am to hear about this program the church is planning. Mom came home and told me about it last night. I know the whole church has to approve this idea but if they do, I would like to volunteer to help in any way I can. Also, I have a check to give you right now for this program. If for some reason it doesn't get approved by the church as a whole, then use this money for some other good program in the church."

He handed me a check for $200.00, and I said, "Thank you very much, John. Your positive comments are very much appreciated. This is an amazing group of people I'm getting to work with. They are not all alike, but somehow they have all reached a point where they see ministry in a similar way, and as you know, their way is pretty darn radical. It is a very exciting time to be a member of Covenant Baptist Church."

"It always has been, Annie. I think this church attracts Christians who believe that Christianity is and always has been a radical movement."

"I agree with you on that, John, but I am worried about the community's reaction to this program. I just don't want any church members to get hurt or hassled by their friends or family outside of the church."

"Annie, just remember that these people are tough. When they were supporting the Civil Rights Movement nearly fifty years ago, some of the members received threatening phone calls, and a few had graffiti spray painted on their houses. None of them backed down then, and none of them will now. This is more than a 'program' of the church. It is a part of a much larger movement across this country to fight for the rights of gays, undocumented residents, and families that don't fit into the fifties mindset that is so rampant across our nation. Whatever happens, these people in this church are doing what they believe is right and what they want to do. You don't have to feel so responsible for them."

I didn't know what to say, and when I looked at John, I saw sincere concern for me in his eyes.

"Thank you, John. I'll try to remember that."

"Good for you, Annie. You have a great day today. I better head out for work now. Let me know if something comes up I can help with."

I locked the door and headed back to my office. Even though I knew we had to wait for the approval of a majority of church members, I decided to study the list of things to do we had created at the deacon meeting to see where I needed to start. We had broken the activities down into several headings. Probably the first area was the one we needed to address most quickly, and that was under a general heading of publicity. Following closely behind that was sensitivity training for all church members, program development, security for the designated Sunday, and lunch coordination.

Publicity was the obvious place to start, and I started a list of activities that I personally might have to be involved in. It seemed to me that writing a press release in which I presented the program, including its goals and objectives, time and date, intended audience, location of the church, and why the church was doing this particular program would be the place to start. This could be something that we would submit to the Charlotte paper and to local newspapers in surrounding counties. This could also be sent to local television channels, and maybe they would mention it on one of their local shows. I guess we could also send it to local radio channels and ask them to do a public service announcement.

That would take care of traditional publicity sources, but I knew we had to include social media. The church had a Facebook page, and I could handle that, but I had never tweeted anything in my life, and that was another resource we might need to investigate. Maybe a church member with twitter skills might step up and offer assistance.

The office phone rang, and I picked it up promptly. There had been some complaints from church members that no one ever answered the phone at church. There was a lot of truth to that because I spent very little time sitting at my desk. I had made my cell phone number available to all church members, but some of them still wanted to use the office phone.

"Good morning, this is Covenant Baptist Church."

'Is this the pastor Annie Adams?"

"Yes it is. Can I help you?"

"Yes ma'am. This is State Trooper Eddie Jackson. I am investigating an accident on Highway 74, and I have been unable to find any family members of the driver or his passenger. I went to the home of the victims, and neighbors told me that they were very fond of their pastor, and that is where I got your name."

"Who was involved in the accident?"

"Well, ma'am, I would rather talk with you face to face, and so I am headed on to your church. Will you be there for another half hour?"

"Yes, of course. I'll be here. Can you tell me how badly these people are hurt?"

"Ma'am, I will be there in about twenty minutes."

Oh my God. Who on earth could he be talking about? He didn't even say when the accident took place. My heart was pounding, and I decided I needed to calm down and regroup before he got here. If people were in the hospital, I was going to have to be ready to help them and their families. I almost couldn't think about the alternative, that someone had been killed. That would require even more strength for the family. I put aside my paper work, walked into the sanctuary, sat down on the front pew, and prayed.

It seemed like no time at all till I heard the doorbell ring. I walked to the window, looked out and saw a state trooper standing there. I opened the door quickly and said, "Please come in."

"Thank you, ma'am. I am Trooper Jackson."

"I am Rev. Annie Adams. Let's sit in my office."

He followed me down the short hallway, and we each took a seat.

"Please tell me what's going on," I said.

"This morning at 6:45 a.m. on Highway 74 west, a silver sedan ran off one side of the road, the driver over-corrected, and the car crossed the road and hit a bridge abutment. We are not completely done with our investigation, but it appears that it was a single car accident. The driver and the passenger in the sedan were both killed instantly. Their driver's licenses identified them as Thomas and Joy Hearn."

"Oh no," I cried, and then I covered my face with my hands. "No, no, no, it can't be. That's not fair, it's just not fair. Oh, God, no."

"I'm very sorry, ma'am. Are you ok? Do I need to call someone for you?"

"No, you don't have to do that. I'm supposed to be the person you call for help."

Trooper Jackson said to me, "Ma'am, it seems to me that you are pretty upset, and I am more than happy to stay with you until a friend or family member can come. I've got to find someone to make a formal identification of the bodies, but I don't want to leave you alone. I was hoping that you would know some family members I could contact about identifying the driver and his passenger just to confirm their identities."

"I'm afraid I don't, but I will try to find the names of their closest kin, and I will call you. Do you have a card?"

"Yes ma'am. I have one right here."

"Thank you, Trooper Jackson. I will get back to you as soon as I can."

"Thank you, Ma'am. I appreciate your help. Are you sure you don't want me to wait with you until someone else can come be with you?"

"I appreciate your concern, but this church where I serve is the family of these two victims, and we will gather together to get through this. Again, your kindness is greatly appreciated."

I walked him to the door, and when he left, I locked the door, and went to my desk and fell apart completely. I cried for Thomas and Joy and for Evan and for how much they wanted to be together again, and then I cried for everyone who has experienced a shocking and tragic death of a loved one. I cried for the pain of separation that death brings, and I cried for everyone who is missing the physical presence of someone here on earth. I tried to regroup a little so that I could make some phone calls, but I couldn't pull myself together. Finally, I called my parents and asked them to come. When I told them what had happened, my mother and father told me they would be here as quickly as they could.

After I knew they were coming, I got it together enough to make some phone calls. I started with Edna because I knew she could advise me about who else to call. She told me she would get the phone tree started for when a tragedy happens in the church. She suggested that since Thomas and Joy had no close family that we might have to plan the funeral, and she told me she would be happy to help with that. She suggested we go to their house and look around a little so that we could find phone numbers of Thomas' cousins and possibly that of his attorney. As uncomfortable as that made me, I knew she was probably right, and I told her I would meet her at their house in thirty minutes. She said that she knew where they hid a key in the back yard.

Before I left for Thomas and Joy's house, I went to the bathroom and held a cold, wet paper towel to my face. I felt awful that I couldn't get it together, and I didn't want church members to see how weak I was. The tears just kept coming, and I didn't know how to make them stop. Finally, my brain thought of asking God for strength, and as I did, I began to have a sense of peace and of courage that somehow I would get through this process and that the church would as well. I was ashamed it was all about me, but the shock of their deaths had been totally overwhelming for me.

I was selfishly thinking about the fact that I had thought Thomas was so brave to refuse treatment in order to enjoy the time that he had left, and that I really wanted to tell him that, but I thought I would have more time. I had also wanted to tell him that we would look out for Joy, and that I would stay in touch with her even if I wasn't at Covenant after this year. But I didn't tell him that either, and now there wasn't a need for that. I really had wanted to tell him goodbye and how much he meant to me in this short time I had known him, but again, I had been waiting a little longer to do that.

I had lost three of my grandparents to death, and somehow as bad as that was, this seemed so much worse. I think it was because I felt some responsibility for Thomas and Joy. I was their pastor, their shepherd, and I was supposed to help take care of them. I had failed, and they were gone. These feelings didn't even make sense to me, but I couldn't help how I felt.

Ten minutes had passed since I talked with Edna, and I knew I had to get going to the Hearn house. I took a deep breath, washed my face one more time, put on a little powder, and walked to my car.

Edna and I shared a long hug when we met at the house. She had obviously been crying, too, but we were both trying to think about what needed to be done. She found the key to the house, and we entered the back door. The silence was a little overwhelming as we walked through the kitchen into the living room.

Edna took charge and said to me, "I will go into their bedrooms and look for metal boxes or files that might give us information. Why don't you look in this room and also the small den next to the kitchen? Just call out if you find something significant."

I couldn't believe I was walking around Thomas and Joy's house without them there. The room looked just like it did when I had dinner with them a few weeks ago. The morning newspaper was lying on the floor next to Thomas's chair. I smiled when I remembered that Joy fussed at him that night that he had not picked up the newspaper before I came. He told her, "I have a system. Each morning I take yesterday's paper and put it in recycling before I sit down to read the one from today. It doesn't hurt anything if the paper is on the floor for one day."

I had to keep reminding myself that they were not going to walk in and ask me what I was doing. I looked in the drawers of the china hutch and the end tables and found nothing. In the small den, there was a desk that held their computer, and it also had several drawers in it. Their land line phone was on this desk, and I found a local phone book, a Charlotte phone book, and finally a little address book with their personal numbers in it. I called out to Edna and said, "I think I have found something."

She walked into the den, and I showed her the address book. I suggested she look through it because I thought she might recognize more names than I would. She sat in their desk chair and began to peruse the little book. I turned back to the desk drawers and looked for file folders that might have information about wills, their attorney's name or life insurance. In the bottom drawer, I found what I was looking for. There were two folders lying flat at the bottom of the drawer. One said "In case of my death" and had Thomas' name on it, and the other said "In case of my death" and had Joy's name on it.

When I saw those folders, I had to stop and breathe. Reading what they had written was going to make their death real, and I was trying to delay that as long as possible.

Edna spoke up and said, "I have found two names and addresses in Gastonia, and I believe these are Thomas' cousins. Would you want to speak with them first? Maybe you can break it to them more easily than I can."

"Of course I will, Edna. Let me have their names and numbers."

She handed me the address book and pointed out the two names of people who lived in Gastonia. One had a last name of Hearn, so I was pretty sure we had the right people. I picked up the phone from on the desk and dialed that number.

A man answered the phone and said, "Thomas, you old dog, how was your trip to the beach? Was it a second honeymoon?"

"Hello, I'm assuming this is Oliver Hearn," I asked.

"Yes it is, and who is this and why are you calling from Thomas' house?"

"My name is Annie Adams, and I am Thomas and Joy's pastor. I have some bad news, and that is that Thomas and Joy were both killed in an automobile accident this morning. I am so sorry for your loss."

I spoke very slowly and clearly because people often don't hear you the first time you give them bad news, and even if they do, they cannot process the information very quickly.

"What did you say? Thomas and Joy? Both gone in an accident?"

"I'm afraid so. The state trooper came to the church just a couple of hours ago and gave me the information. The chairman of our deacons and I came to the house and found your number. They need someone to go to Charlotte and confirm their identities. We thought as family members you might want to do that."

"Oh no, we can't do that. We will try to come to the services, but I am not even sure about that. My wife has had a stroke and is in a wheelchair. I really don't leave her alone without a neighbor coming in to sit with her. My sister lives in Gastonia as well, but her health is not good either. My son and his wife live in Charlotte, but they have not seen Thomas and Joy for over ten years, and I don't know how they would feel about identifying their bodies. I am so sorry. Is there anyone in the church who could do that for us?"

There was no way I was going to ask a church member who had known and loved Thomas and Joy for so long to do that, and so I immediately spoke up and said, "Yes, I can do that for you. I will contact you when that task has been accomplished."

Right after that conversation, I called Trooper Jackson to find out where to go to confirm identities, and I told him I would be the one to do that.

I was incredibly embarrassed that I felt as if I needed my parents to get through this ordeal, and I certainly didn't want anyone to know that. However, after Edna and I had gathered Thomas and Joy's folders on their deaths and had looked through them and found information about their life insurance and their wills, I was physically and emotionally drained. Knowing that I had to still identify their bodies was a burden I did not feel I was up to, but it had to be done. I called my dad to tell him what I still needed to do, and he told me to sit tight, that they would be at my house in another twenty-five minutes. He asked if I could wait for him, and I said "How could I not wait for you?'

I went to my house to wait their arrival and took the time to lie down and relax for ten minutes. When that time was up, I took a quick shower, and slipped on a multipurpose black skirt and sweater over a white silk blouse. Just as I finished dressing, my parents arrived, and I was so glad to see them. How could I ever be unhappy or annoyed with them again?

I tearfully apologized for calling on them for help, but as soon as my dad parked the car, he took four giant steps and wrapped his arms around me. I needed him at that moment more than I had in a long time. My mom reached around him to hug me as well, and suddenly I didn't care if people knew I needed them.

We walked into my house and my dad said, "I am going to go with you to the morgue to identify the bodies, and your mother is going to fix dinner while we are gone."

"Please tell me there is a grocery store in this town, honey."

"Yes there is, Mom, and it is two miles down this road to the right. It's a nice store, and they should have anything you need."

"Okay, good. You guys can take off, and I will take care of everything here."

I stopped for a minute and looked at both of them. "I can't tell you how much I appreciate your coming to help me through this. I thought I was ready to handle most anything in the ministry, but this has really overwhelmed me and shaken my faith in myself. I am worried about getting through the funeral, and I know I will have to do that for the sake of the congregation. Your being here for me tonight is going to give me the strength to get through the rest of this. Thank you."

"Sweetheart, you may be a grown woman, but we are still your parents and always will be," said my mom. "Now get on to Charlotte, and get that task done. I'll be waiting for you."

My dad stayed with me every minute of the identification process, and it was not as bad as I feared it would be because of him.

Chapter 34

My parents left early the next morning to return home. They had asked me if I wanted them to stay for a few days or to come back for the funeral, but when I woke up that morning, I had decided that this was my responsibility, and that I could handle it. I was ever so grateful for their help in the beginning of this crisis, and I believed that their presence helped allow me to prepare for the coming days.

I waited until 8:00 to call Edna, and when I did, she answered promptly. She had taken home the insurance papers we had found in the den, and she assured me that there was more than enough life insurance for every expense. She also found in the insurance papers a notebook in which Thomas and Joy had written what they wanted at their funerals.

"What do you mean?" I asked.

"Well I have seen these before. You can get them at funeral homes anytime. It is a little book with several questions about funeral preferences, and it gives the person a chance to make his or her requests known without freaking out their family. There is just one book, but answers have been written out by both Thomas and Joy."

"Does it say when they wrote out these answers?"

"I don't think so," Edna answered. "I wasn't really looking for a date, but I'm not seeing one as I look through here. They have each selected songs they would like sung and scriptures they would like read. Their most interesting request is that they want people attending the funeral to have a chance to speak, and they would like them to share a story about Thomas or Joy at the funeral service. Thomas said he would prefer funny stories, but that he would take any kind he could get."

"That sounds like Thomas. Can we do that at a funeral?"

"I think we can do anything we want, particularly if it is what the deceased wants. Remember there is no close family for us to ask."

"Just what we need as a church. An unusual funeral service that is outside the norm. Do you think we will get much flack about that?"

"Annie, this is one time I don't care. Thomas and Joy wanted this to be their funeral service, and by God, we are going to do it that way."

I felt her reprimand sharply and was a little embarrassed about my concern.

"I agree," I said. "Shall we meet at the funeral home in a little while?"

"I have already talked with the owner of the funeral home nearest us, Mr. Edgar Heard. He asked me to bring the booklet and wondered if we could be there about 10:00 to make plans. Would that work for you?"

"Yes, that would be fine, Edna. I will see you then."

I hung up the phone and just sat at my kitchen table finishing my third cup of coffee. I wondered how it had been for Thomas and Joy. Were they in a lot of pain? Were they conscious? Were they able to talk to each other? What was it like when they passed from this life to the next? Was Evan there to greet them and did they recognize him? Do we all just become spirits and no one recognizes anyone? The state trooper said they were killed instantly, but what does that mean? Their faces had a few scratches on them, but nothing that looked fatal. Did they have any idea at all that they were dying or did it really happen so fast that they didn't have time to even think about it?

And is there any life after death?

I always had kind of a morbid fascination with death and the afterlife, mainly because I did not have any way of really knowing what it was like. I believed people who had near death experiences who said they saw a light or that they had seen loved ones who had passed away before them. I really did. But there was always a part of me that thought, "Maybe we see what we want to see." I wanted there to be an afterlife where I would see my grandparents again and recognize them, but how could that happen?

I had to literally shake my head to get all of these doubts out of my mind. I believed completely the recordings of Jesus being seen among his disciples after his resurrection, and if that could happen, then there is some basis for believing in the afterlife and in the bodily resurrection. I could not completely understand all of that, but I did not have to. My faith, based on my study of scripture and primarily on my life experience of a personal relationship with Jesus Christ, was enough to begin to quell all these doubts.

I got up from the table, showered, dressed, and headed over to the church office. Before I went to the funeral home, I wanted to check for messages. I had a feeling there were going to be a lot of them.

Chapter 35

The funeral services were scheduled for Saturday afternoon. The deacons decided not to fix a meal because there were going to be so few family members at the funeral.

Thomas'cousins, Oliver and his sister were coming with Oliver's son. Joy had some cousins as well, but they lived in Virginia, and they could not come that distance. She had a brother who was deceased, and he had two daughters. One lived in DC and the other in central Ohio. They seemed genuinely upset about Joy's death, but neither felt they could make it to the funeral. One was eight-and-one-half months pregnant, and the other was a single parent to two boys who had soccer tournaments out of town that weekend.

The church members had been and were continuing to be Thomas and Joy's family. We used the phone tree again to give out the information about the funeral and about what Thomas and Joy had wanted. We asked church members to think about sharing a story as requested. We also put the obituaries in the Charlotte newspaper and the local newspaper, the Bakerstown Post.

With the request made by Thomas and Joy, I did not feel a funeral sermon or meditation was necessary. Mr. Owens, Edna, and I put together the funeral service using the songs and the scripture that Thomas and Joy had requested. We left plenty of time for the congregation and other friends of Thomas and Joy to share their stories, and we had some stories of our own in case no one else was willing to talk.

I had prepared myself as best I could for this service. I had experienced so much shock and pain when I first heard about the accident that I felt as if the worst was over. Now was the time to celebrate the lives of Joy and Thomas.

It was a dark and rainy Saturday morning. Somehow that seemed appropriate for the occasion, but it made travel and getting in and out of the church more of a challenge. The service was to begin at 1:00, and by 12:45, the church was full. I asked several men of the church if they would get some of the folding chairs from the Sunday school building, and they did. They filled up as well. We had put in a new camera in the sanctuary that would transmit services to the fellowship hall, but we had never used it. A church member had donated it saying that someday we might need it for our services or for our children to observe and be a part of worship.

It actually worked. Those gathered in the fellowship hall could hear the entire service. Pete Stoudemire stayed back there as close to twenty people were directed to that area. It was decided that those people would just come into the sanctuary if they wanted to say something about Thomas and Joy.

We began the service with prayer and the singing of "Amazing Grace," Joy's first song selection. Then I read the scripture selections, and we sang "Abide With Me." Then I explained about the booklet describing what Thomas and Joy wanted at their funerals.

I said, "Thomas and Joy wanted a celebration of their lives, and the way they chose for that to happen was to ask people to share stories about them or about experiences that people had had with them. We are respecting their wishes, and I will start. After my sharing, please feel free to stand or go to the front of the sanctuary and share your stories. I had only known Thomas and Joy for five months, but I already loved them. They were loving and gracious friends and church members. My fondest memory of them is the night they introduced me to their son Evan. Evan died in 1974 in a car accident, but that night when they talked about him, I felt as if I had met their son. Their love for him was as strong that night as it was in 1974. They also shared with me that as they got older, they looked forward to seeing Evan again when they passed away. They told me not to worry, that they were not going to rush things along, but that there was some comfort in thinking about seeing their child again. Today, I believe Joy and Thomas are holding their blue-eyed son in their arms again, and along with my grief, I can feel happiness for them because of that."

I sat down and bit my bottom lip to keep from crying. I wasn't sure how I got through my brief story about Thomas and Joy, but I knew I could not lose it now either. Stories started and kept coming. Several of them were stories about Thomas' humor, and the entire church laughed heartily upon hearing some of his antics and his funny stories. Stories of Joy were more tender and kind, which certainly reflected her personality. It really was a celebration of their lives, and for the first time, I understood that phrase when it came to funerals. After about thirty minutes, the stories seemed to stop coming, and I stood up, asked one more time if anyone else had anything to say, and when there was no response to that, we sang "Shall We Gather at the River." Then I closed the service with prayer.

After the service, most of the congregation walked together to the church cemetery and quietly said our final goodbyes to Thomas and Joy.

Chapter 36

When everything was finally over, I went into my office at the church and sat at my desk. I was experiencing a terrible letdown, almost a numbness that made me feel incapacitated. I wondered if I would still be sitting here tomorrow morning when everyone showed up for church services.

There was a tap on the door and William Owens was there with his bottle of cognac and two glasses. I couldn't help it. I just started crying.

He just looked at me and said, "I thought it might be cognac time again."

I grinned at him through my tears and said, "We have to quit meeting like this."

He sat down across the desk from me, poured each of us about a half inch of cognac, handed me my glass, and said, "To Thomas and Joy and to family reunions."

We tapped our glasses gently and let the cognac ease into our systems.

I looked at William and thought to myself, *I met this man almost five months ago, and all I know about him is that he is a music director for my church.*

"William, tell me about yourself and your family."

He looked surprised at my question, then very pleased as he answered, "What do you want to know?"

"Anything you want to share."

"I don't really know where to start," he said. "I was born and raised in Bakerstown. I have three sisters and one brother, all of whom are still living, two in Charlotte, one in Salisbury, and one sister and me still in Bakerstown. My mother was a warm and loving parent who made us toys when we couldn't afford to buy them. She taught me to read before I went to school and taught me to love music. She played the piano for the church, and when she knew I was interested in learning to play, she and I would sneak off to the church on Sunday morning before anyone else got there and she would give me lessons. If I had a spare minute during the week, I would sneak into the church and practice. Back then, the doors were not locked at the church, and I could get in any time I could get away from my chores or my schoolwork."

"So your love of music as well as your talent came from your mother? Did your father appreciate music as well?"

"My father was a strict and rigid taskmaster. He was an unskilled laborer for a local construction company, and his job was hard and not very rewarding. He believed that hard work is what made the man, and he wanted my brother and me to be 'men.' If we didn't do something the way he wanted us to, he would whip us with a belt and make us redo whatever it was he was displeased with. That usually happened at least two times a week for me. The piano was my escape, but I knew my father could never know about it, and my mother and I had an unspoken agreement about that."

"Your mother must have been a very strong woman."

"Indeed she was. She was my rock. She died when I was fifteen and my brother was seventeen, and my sisters were all younger than me. We were all devastated. My brother left home and joined the army one week after she died, but I stuck it out until I graduated from high school. Then I joined the army as well and spent a year and two months in the jungles of Vietnam. I did my duty well and was promoted twice while in the army. My lieutenant really wanted me to re-up, but to be honest with you, Annie, there wasn't a chance in hell I was going to do that. I had to kill some people during battles, and I have never forgiven myself for that."

I was completely shocked at what William had told me.

"William, I had no idea you were a veteran, much less that you served in Vietnam. You should be proud of your service for our country."

"I am proud that I served my country, Annie, and I did what I had to do for my safety and that of the men around me, but I still can't accept the fact that I took the lives of other human beings. I guess I should have been one of those 'conscientious objectors' that I heard about, but I didn't know exactly what that meant, and I didn't know what it would feel like to kill someone. By the time I found out, it was too late to change my status, and I just had to do my duty. I don't regret my time in the army, but I don't like to think about it either."

While I sat there quietly, William poured each of us another half inch of cognac, and to be honest, I was happy to have it.

William went on with his story, "When I got out of the army, I came home and went to college. I never lived with my father again, but he was getting old, and I tried to help him whenever I could. It still was not a pleasant experience. He was critical of everything I or my siblings tried to do. But I was a man when I came home from Vietnam, and he only tried to hit me one time after that. I knocked him down and told him not to ever try that again with me or with any of my siblings. He backed down from me, and I realized then that he was just a bully with us kids, and that as soon as we stood up to him, he would leave us alone. He passed away in 1980."

"I'm sorry, William, for the bad relationship with your father and for the pain you suffered in the war. You certainly have become a wonderful, kind, and productive man. For that you should be very proud."

"Thank you, Annie, for those kind words. I taught music for thirty years in high school, and I think I made an impact on some of those students. I have served this church for a long time and I am very proud of that as well. My life has been good."

"I know I shouldn't ask this, but have you ever thought about getting married. You are such a great guy. I can't help but wonder why you never married."

William smiled somewhat sadly. "That's a story for another day."

I said okay, and we both got up to leave to go home. I just had to walk, but I was concerned about William driving. He said he was going to practice about an hour for services tomorrow and by then, he thought he would be okay. He said he had also brought a sandwich and some snacks and he would eat that in the middle of his practice time. He said he would call his sister who lived close by if he needed to.

I locked my door and walked into the hallway with him. He turned and looked at me a minute, and then he stepped forward and gave me a big hug. I hugged him back, telling him how grateful I was that we had become friends.

He laughed, "I'm pretty sure we are more than friends. We are drinking buddies."

I laughed and headed home. I was desperate for a nap. Never having been much of a drinker, anytime I had alcohol of any type, I always got sleepy. I made it to my bed and had just laid down for this wonderful nap when the phone rang.

No, I thought, *what now*?

I answered the phone, and it was Edna.

"You don't need to be alone tonight, so you are coming to my house for dinner," she said.

"Edna, thank you, but that is not necessary. I will be fine."

"Yes, you will be because you will have a great meal and fellowship at my house. I am sending Johnny over to pick you up at 6:00 sharp. Be ready 'cause he is not the patient sort."

Then she hung up. I was left holding the phone and trying to figure out how I was going to review my sermon and take my nap before it was time to get ready. The nap won out, but I did set an alarm so I would not sleep too long.

I took a shower when I woke up and felt totally refreshed. I started looking around for what I was going to wear. I opened my closet door and just stared. I had nothing to wear. I didn't want to wear jeans. That just seemed too casual. But I sure as heck didn't want to wear a dress or skirt. That didn't feel right either. No t-shirts. No blouse that was too dressy or too proper either. *Oh my God. What is wrong with me? I haven't worried this much about what to wear since I did my trial sermon here at Covenant.*

I sat on the end of my bed and realized my fretting had something to do with the fact that John was coming to pick me up. *Annie, don't go there. The work we are doing at Covenant is too important to get caught up in fantasies or what ifs. And you know how you are. You can get obsessed with a fantasy in a heartbeat. That does not need to happen right now.*

I took a deep breath, grabbed a pair of slacks and a cotton blouse, touched up my hair and went to the living room to wait for John.

Edna gave me a long, loving hug as soon as I walked in her door. We were all hurting about losing Thomas and Joy, and although we did not talk about them every minute of dinner, our minds continually reverted to our loss. We laughed about some of the stories that were told at the funeral, and there were a few tears shed as well. It turned out to be just what I needed to let go of the knot that had been in my stomach since the state trooper had told me about the wreck. I knew I would continue to feel sad about Thomas and Joy, but this gathering helped to relieve the tension I had been carrying for the last few days.

Chapter 37

A lot of tears were shed during worship the next day, but somehow we all got through it. The only unusual announcement was that Robbie Burnside would be baptized the following Sunday. That brought some smiles to several members' faces, and I realized that this baptism would help the church move on. It was a new life coming into membership in the church, and it was a symbol of the future.

When I was shaking hands after the service, I saw Jesse Akin and realized that I had totally forgotten about calling him about his election as a deacon. I called him aside and told him what the deacons had said.

"You mean I can freely serve as a deacon, and people really want me to do that?"

"That is exactly what the other deacons said, Jesse. I am sorry that you have felt hurt by comments made by an interim who probably did not have the authority to say what he said. Knowing you as a man who respects the wishes of the church pastor, I understand why you never questioned his comments, but I am so glad you did this time. We need a person like you to serve as a deacon, and I am hoping your name can remain on the list of nominations."

"I would be proud to serve this church as a deacon, and I just can't imagine what Lorraine is going to say."

"Jesse, I think she will be very proud of you, but more than that, I hope she is proud of this church."

The next morning, after a shortened run, I dressed and walked over to the church. It was a cool, crisp morning, and I put on the jacket I had grabbed as I left home. I knew there was a baptistry up behind the pulpit, but there had always been a curtain in front of it, and I had never even looked at it. I wasn't even sure which door to go through to get in the right place. I opened one door, and it was a storage closet that held mainly cleaning tools and supplies. I felt a little embarrassed that I had not known where the mops and vacuum cleaner were kept. The church paid a local woman to come in once a week and clean the sanctuary and the education building, and she did such a good job that I had never needed these supplies. I needed to remember to thank her for doing such a good job.

The next door opened into a narrow hallway which had two doors. I opened each of them, and the small rooms they led to were identical. These were the dressing rooms for both the pastor and the person being baptized, each with a small bench on one side of the room, and a cheaply-made, full-length mirror on the opposite wall. Hanging on a hook in each room were two white cotton choir robes for both the pastor and the person being baptized to wear into the water.

I stepped back into the short hallway and followed it to an opening that ended with steps leading down to the concrete baptismal pool. It was empty, of course, and I had no idea how it got filled with water. I walked down the four steps into the pool and looked around for a pipe or faucet which would fill the pool area, but I couldn't see anything.

There's nothing as bad not knowing how to do something like fill the baptismal pool to make a person feel stupid. I looked but the walls of the pool area were all solid and sealed, with no way to allow water in. Finally, I decided I would have to show my ignorance and ask someone how to fill the baptismal pool.

Since Pete Stoudemire was a retired minister, I decided to call him first to see if he knew how to fill the pool. He didn't laugh at me, which I appreciated, but he did say it was very simple. He told me, "At each end of the baptismal pool, in the middle of the walls, there are two plugs which open up to let water flow in. The plugs are painted the same color as the baptistry, and so to find them, you just run your hands over the wall until you feel the plugs. They come out easily, and the faucets which turn on the water are found just outside the pool in the small room on the left. To keep the water somewhat warm, you should not fill the pool until just before the worship service, and someone has to be responsible for turning the water on and off. The faucets are old and sometimes they can be hard to turn."

I told Pete, "Thank you so much for the information. I appreciate it."

To myself, I thought that this process sounded like a disaster waiting to happen. Old faucets. Holes in the wall. Maybe we should just go down to the lake down the road where water would be guaranteed.

I knew Charlotte was coming by in about half an hour to talk about the process for visiting the sick or delivering food where needed. I figured I had time before she came to try to fill the baptismal pool just to make sure everything worked.

First, I went back down the steps into the pool area to find the easily-removable plugs. It took me ten minutes of rubbing my hands on the ends of the pool over and over again to finally feel the plugs that were, of course, the same color as the entire pool area. After I finally found the plugs, I tried to pull them out and that just was not going to happen. I could feel the sides of the plugs but I could not get my fingers under the edges.

I sat down on the steps that led down to the pool and thought about how to solve this problem. I had a small box of tools at my house so I ran over there to get that, hoping that I would know what to do with the tools. I brought the entire box back with me and the first tool I tried was called a nail puller. At one end of this tool, there was a flat prong that could fit under something and pry it open. I slid it as far under one of the plugs as I could and pushed as hard as I could. Amazingly, it pulled the plug right out. I stood up and yelled "Yes" as loudly as I could. Now for the next plug.

Fifteen minutes later, "Yes" was not the word I was yelling out loud.

Finally, I sat back and told myself to take a break. I was so mad. Why does everything have to be harder than it's supposed to be? This task seemed so simple when I started it.

"Annie, are you in here?"

"Shoot!" Charlotte was here already. "Yes, I'm up here in the baptistry."

She worked her way up to where I was, and she found me sitting in the bottom of the baptismal pool with several tools lying beside me.

"Surgery, I presume?" she said with a smile.

I grinned up at her and said, "Yes, and I think I have killed the patient."

"What's going on, Annie?" She joined me on the floor.

"I've been working on this plug for twenty minutes, and I can't get it out, and the other one came out real easy, and we can't very well baptize anybody if we can't get the water in here, and …"

"Hold on, Annie. Tell me what I can do to help."

"Would you see if you can get this plug out of the wall?"

"Yes, hand me the tool that you think will work the best."

I gave her the nail puller and told her how easily it had worked on the other plug. She took it and scooted over closer to the second plug. Slowly and carefully she tried to slide the prong under one side of the plug. I sat and watched her quietly, and after about five minutes, she got the prong all the way under the plug and forced it out.

I just looked at her and said, "Thank you, Charlotte."

"You are welcome, Annie. Now what else do we need to do to make sure everything works right on Sunday?"

"I want to fill the pool area here to make sure the pipes are clear and the faucets can be turned on and off. The faucets are just in the hallway at the top of the stairs."

"Ok, let's do it."

We got up and walked up the stairs. Charlotte was moving slowly and seemed a little stiff. I felt so bad that she had gotten on the floor with me, but I didn't want to say anything to her. We found the faucets and tried to turn them on. At first nothing happened, and I thought I might have to curse a lot, but then Charlotte said, "Bring your tool box up here, and let's see what you have."

The box had been a gift from my dad, and it was mainly tools he didn't need or had duplicates of. Charlotte looked through the box and pulled out a funny-looking tool that reminded me of the dentist's office. She explained to me, "These are vise grips, and I think they might work on this old faucet."

She took the tool and attached it to the faucet and pushed down as hard as she could. Sure enough the faucet turned, and once she got it started, it could be turned by hand. I heard the water start running into the baptismal pool, and then she repeated the action with the other faucet. She explained to me that one faucet was cold water and the other hot, so we had to adjust them to make sure the water was the right temperature. I was just so glad the water was running that adjusting the temperature seemed like a minor task.

We just kept sitting at the top of the stairs talking quietly as the water ran.

She said to me, "Are you ok, Annie?"

"I am now, Charlotte. This sort of task makes me feel so inept, and I just don't like that feeling. I have never been good at projects around the house or now the church, and I just hate it when I feel that I can't take care of myself or my responsibilities completely. I don't like asking for help."

"I am the same way, Annie. I took care of myself for so long that when I married Walter, it took me a long time to let him do things for me and to help me do things. After being married to him for several years and having him see me at my most incompetent, I finally realized that I didn't have to prove anything to him or to anyone else about my abilities. There were some things I couldn't do well that he could do better or help me with or that we might have to pay someone else to do, but then there were things that I could do better than him or anyone else, and I begin to value those abilities in myself. I quit expecting myself to be totally self-sufficient and allowed myself to need other people. Even though Walter is gone now, I still allow myself the luxury of asking for help when I need to."

I thought about what she said and wished I could be there. I was in this position where I had such a need to prove myself that it was difficult to see myself admitting my failures or my weaknesses, but perhaps I would become stronger if I could do that. It was definitely something to think about.

I said to her, "Thank you for explaining that to me. I will give those ideas some thought."

The baptismal pool filled up nicely, and the water was nice and warm. We were able to turn the faucets off pretty easily, but then I had a slight panic. I had no idea how to drain the pool. I looked at Charlotte, and suddenly, I began to laugh.

She looked back at me and said, "Do you want to share the joke?'

Once I could talk again, I told her the problem and she started laughing, too.

"This is a good time to practice asking for help," she said to me with a grin, and I agreed.

I called Pete again, and he said, "Oh it's easy to drain the pool. Look to the left of the faucets, and there is a lever that can be pulled in two directions. One way is to open the drain in the bottom of the pool, and the other is to close it. It should be easy to operate."

I said, "I'm sure it will be. Thanks, Pete." And it was.

Charlotte and I walked over to the office, and she told me that people had been faithfully doing what they signed up for on the Helping Hands committee, and that the people they were visiting and taking food to were thrilled with the attention they were getting from the church. I had been busy with so many other things the last couple of weeks that I was relieved that members were being cared for so well. She also gave me a written report of the bazaar earnings and how the committee had voted to use them, and asked me to review it and let her know if it met with my approval.

After Charlotte left, I decided to ask someone else to be responsible for filling the baptismal pool on Sunday. The first person to come to mind was Danny O'Reilly. He was young and strong. My only hesitation was that nasty business when Cliff was arrested, but I had seen the two families together at church, and hopefully, they were friends again or at least friendly. When I called Danny to explain the situation and to ask him if he would take this responsibility, he said he would if I would show him how everything worked. I told him that would be no problem. He agreed to come in on Thursday morning for his instructions.

Almost half of my Monday had gone into solving this problem, but that is so typical of this career for which I had been chosen. You just never know what struggles you will have to face.

Chapter 38

That night I got home about 8:30 after a Christian Education meeting at the church. I was tired but more than that, I could not stop thinking about Thomas and Joy. They had been together for so long that neither of them could imagine life without the other. Thomas was so worried about leaving Joy in so much despair and loneliness. He had also told me that he was a little afraid of the pain of cancer lasting for an extended period of time. He actually said to me, "There is no reason to suffer like that."

Ever since the officer had told me about the accident, I had a question in my head that would not go away. Could Thomas have caused the accident that killed them, hoping to assure that he and Joy would die quickly and together? I couldn't believe I was thinking like this, but this thought just would not leave my head. I had not said a word about this to anyone, and I never would, but I was trying to figure out a way I could get some answers.

As I was sitting at my kitchen table that night, it occurred to me that I could go and talk to the officer who had investigated the accident. Maybe he would give me a copy of the accident report. As I sat there by myself, I wasn't sure I wanted to find out anything else about the wreck, but knowing how I am, I didn't think these questions would go away until I had answers. Later as I drifted off to sleep, I couldn't stop thinking about the depths of despair that Thomas must have been feeling and wondering if he had taken extreme measures to assuage that pain.

I woke up in slightly better spirits but still determined to find answers. My first step was to call the local State Troopers office to see what I had to do to get a copy of the accident report. It was going to be more complicated than I thought because I found out I would have to contact the Department of Motor Vehicles in Raleigh to get that report. I was more than willing to do that, but I thought perhaps I should start with the local office which was not too far away in Monroe.

First things first, however, I hurried over to the church for our morning meditation and prayer time. I felt a powerful need for this quiet time this morning, and from the turn out of ten members, I knew I wasn't the only one. Of all of those attending, I continued to be most surprised by Earlene Williams. It seemed that she was trying very hard to stay connected to Covenant Church, and I was thrilled to see that. There was also something else going on with her but I could not figure out what it was. I would just have to wait to see if she would share it with me.

Taking some action helped me feel better, so I dressed quickly in my serious professional clothes, and I headed out to Monroe. When I arrived, I sat in the parking lot for a few minutes trying to think of how I was going to frame my concerns so that I could get answers without the trooper asking me too many questions. I did not want to stir up a bigger investigation than was needed.

I finally decided that the truth was the best way to go. I wasn't doing anything wrong, and I didn't really know why I was feeling anxious about asking some questions. I just needed to take a deep breath and relax.

I walked into the Highway Patrol Offices and was greeted by a gracious and well-mannered trooper. He asked me how he could help me, and I tried to think of the best way to answer his question.

"I was wondering if I could talk with Trooper Eddie Jackson about an accident that happened in Union County on Highway 74 west. It happened last Thursday morning."

I had found out from some notes in Thomas' calendar that he had a doctor's appointment in Charlotte at 8:30 the morning of the accident, and that is how I could remember they were headed west.

"Are you a family member?"

"No, not exactly. I am Rev. Annie Adams, the pastor of the two victims. They do not have any children or siblings living. Our church was their family, and I just had a few questions for Trooper Jackson. I met him when he came to notify me of the accident."

"I see. Trooper Jackson is off today and won't be back on duty until Thursday evening."

My face must have reflected how disappointed I was, because the trooper immediately said, "First Sergeant Greg Barrow would probably know about the accident because he would have the written report from Trooper Jackson, and he is in today.

Would you want me to check and see if he would be available to talk with you?"

"Oh yes, thank you so much."

The trooper directed me to a small waiting area and told me he would let me know if First Sergeant Barrow was available.

I sat down in the hard chair and took a deep breath. Part of me wanted to run out the front door and forget all of my questions about this accident. Why was I doing this to myself? And if I found out there was some truth in my concerns, would it have to become public knowledge? Did I really want to go there? Did I really want this information shared with everyone who loved Thomas and Joy?

"Ma'am?"

I almost jumped out of the chair when the trooper spoke.

"Yes?" I said, trying not to look as nervous as I felt.

"First Sergeant Barrow can see you now."

I followed him down a hallway past six or eight offices into a somewhat larger office near the back of the building.

The man sitting at the desk in the small office was much younger than I expected, and he seemed to completely fill up the room. His hair was cut very short but you could tell it was a very dark brown. When he looked up and saw me, he stood immediately, and came around the desk to shake my hand. His hand was warm and strong, and I had to resist the urge to lean forward and put my head on his chest. There was a powerful sense about him that he could take care of whatever problem you brought his way. When he first looked at me, there was a brief flicker of surprise on his face, but he immediately controlled that and became First Sergeant Barrow. His eyes were brown, but they were light and almost had a golden color to them. They were quite mesmerizing, and I had to force myself to look away from him.

"Please come in, Rev. Adams, and have a seat."

"Thank you, First Sergeant Barrow."

"Trooper Smith has told me that you would like more information about a fatal accident that we investigated last week. He tells me that you are not family, but that you are the victims' pastor. Is that correct?"

"Yes, it is. Thomas and Joy Hearn, the uh…, the uh…victims were members of my church.

I was struggling to stay in control but talking about them was still very difficult for me.

First Sergeant Barrow looked closely at me and said, "You obviously cared about this couple."

"Yes. I have some questions about the accident that I would like to have answered for my own knowledge, but I don't want to stir up any trouble for you guys or for anyone else."

"I'm not sure what you mean."

"I would just like to know a little more about how the accident happened. I was told it seemed to involve only the one car, but that was still not definite when Trooper Jackson came to notify me of the accident. Has the investigation been completed? Have there been any unusual findings from the accident? Did everything happen the way I was told originally?"

First Sergeant Barrow sat up even straighter in his chair. Then he looked at me almost gently and said, "Why don't you tell me what's going on and what you are worried about? Then I think I can better answer your questions."

I looked back at him and got lost in his eyes again. This was crazy. This man had a very powerful presence, and I was having trouble not telling him all my concerns. But if I did, he might start a new investigation, and then everyone would know what I was thinking.

"Well, for example, are you sure that there were no other cars involved?"

He seemed a little disappointed with my question, but answered it thoroughly by stating, "There were two other cars nearby that morning, and both of them verified that no other car was involved in the accident. It happened quickly but from both their recollections, it seemed to be a textbook example of a driver over-correcting after running off the side of the road."

"Do you know what made him run off the side of the road?"

I held my breath as I waited for his answer. He said, "No, I don't think we know for sure. Do you?"

I looked back at him again, and I said, "No, I don't but I just want to eliminate one possibility."

"What possibility would that be?"

I felt almost as cornered as a criminal who was being interrogated. The First Sergeant was being kind and gentle, but he would not stop asking his questions.

"If I tell you something, can it just stay between us?"

His look of compassion changed to one of incredulity, and he said, "What do you think?"

I realized that I had begun chewing on my left thumb nail, and I quickly stopped that.

Finally, I spoke up and said, "Thomas Hearn had stage four pancreatic cancer and only had a few months to live. He was concerned about the pain that he might experience for an extended period of time, but even more so he was frantic about leaving Joy, his wife, behind and worried about how she would handle the loss as well as taking care of herself. They had been married for sixty-two years, with no children or siblings living, and I think Thomas was having trouble leaving Joy alone. I just want to be sure that he did nothing to cause the accident. I'm sorry I didn't just come out and ask you that in the first place, but I don't want anyone else to know that I am having these concerns."

There was silence after my outpouring, and I had trouble looking at the First Sergeant. I wish he would just tell me that I could just call him by his name so I didn't have to keep thinking the "First Sergeant."

"Thank you, Rev. Adams, for telling me what your real concern is. I know that must have been difficult for you, and I appreciate the effort. Let me share some information with you. In the coroner's initial report, there was a mention of Thomas' cancer, and any time that becomes known to us, we always look a little deeper into the accident. We, too, are aware that some older couples might make decisions that would cause them to pass away at the same time, and we did look very carefully at all of the factors that seemed to cause the accident. We looked very thoroughly for any indication that this accident was caused by a purposeful act, and there was absolutely no evidence of that. Does that address your major concern?"

I looked down and began to cry. First Sergeant Barrow got up and walked around his desk and handed me a tissue. He didn't tell me to stop crying or to get it together, but he just sat there quietly on the edge of his desk. After a short time, I managed to stop crying, blew my nose and wiped most of my tears off my face. I knew my mascara was probably running down my cheeks, but there was nothing I could do to fix that now.

"I'm sorry," I said to him, "I know a crying female is the last thing you want in your office, but I was just so relieved to hear what you said. I was really afraid that I had failed Thomas and Joy as a pastor and had not recognized their level of despair. They were wonderful people, and I loved them, and I couldn't bear to think of them making such a courageous and yet tragic decision."

"I understand your fears," First Sergeant Barrow said, "but don't worry a bit about being a crying female in my office. I have three younger sisters who have cried in this office, in my bedroom growing up, in my car, and practically every place I have ever spent time. Besides, I think you had some legitimate fears and questions, and I hope I was able to take care of most of them."

"You did, and thank you very much."

"Now, I have a couple of questions that you might need to answer for me. What's a nice girl like you doing in the ministry?"

I smiled at him and said, "I ask myself that same question about five times a week. I was called to the ministry, and I was blessed to have a church want me to be their minister."

"Where is your church?'

"It is Covenant Baptist Church near Bakerstown."

"Baptist? It's not Southern Baptist, is it?"

"I'm afraid so."

"You can't be that. They don't allow women pastors, do they?"

"Covenant is a very special place, and by the way, God allows it."

"I'm sorry. I didn't mean anything by my comment. I don't have a problem with a woman being a minister. However, I grew up Southern Baptist, and I'm pretty sure my pastor talked about what women could and could not do in the church. I always wondered when that denomination was going to move into the current century, so I guess they have."

"Actually, I would not assume that. My congregation is kind of a renegade group, and they called me to be their minister even though the denomination does not believe it is Biblical."

"Renegade, huh? Is it a bunch of young people?"

"Not exactly. It's a pretty gray church, but they just have new ideas."

"Cool."

"I think so. Look, I am sorry I have taken up so much of your time. Thank you again for listening to my concerns and for answering my questions. You have helped me a lot."

"You are very welcome. Hey listen, I might stop by Covenant one day next week just to make sure you are okay. Would that be alright?"

"That would be great, but I am not always at the church. I am often out visiting in someone's home or at the hospital. Here is my cell phone number, and you can check with me before you come by."

"That sounds great. I'll see you soon."

Chapter 39

As I drove home feeling more at peace about Thomas and Joy's accident, I asked myself the question, "What just happened?"

It seemed to me that a compassionate, gentle, gorgeous man just told me he was interested in seeing me again. I wanted to be very careful and not jump to any conclusions. I was so anxious about our discussion concerning the accident that I never even looked for a wedding ring. I can't believe I missed that opportunity. I knew it was possible that part of First Sergeant Barrow's professional responsibilities included a follow-up visit, but it did seem like a little more than that.

However, I could not dwell on any of that as I had way too much to do in the next few weeks.

When I got back to the church, I went to the office and checked messages. Some days I would kill for clerical help. I had to return twelve messages, most of which were responses to simple questions that anyone could answer. When this happened, and I felt frustrated, I always said to myself, "I am where I am supposed to be and where I want to be so I need to get over it." It usually worked after a while.

Then my frustration turned to panic. It was almost a week ago that the deacons met and decided to have this special family day two weeks before Christmas. After Thomas and Joy's accident, everything was put on hold, and now it was time for action. We put off the church-wide vote for approval of the plan until next week out of respect for the church's time of sorrow, but there were things we needed to start on so that we would be ready after the vote. I also remembered that the Worship Committee made up of Edna, William and I was supposed to keep working on improving worship.

Before Trooper Jackson had called me that horrible day last week, I had been thinking about an article to submit to several local newspapers, one of the few tasks I could work on before the church voted on this special day. No one would know that I was writing it ahead of time.

I pulled out my laptop and began to write. Not only did I put who, when, how and where, I also tried to write about the why, and that was the complicated part. I sat staring at the screen for a long time trying to find just the right words to describe why this church was planning this event, but nothing was coming to mind. Even though I believed this church felt led by God to develop this plan, it seemed like such an arrogant cop-out for why. How could I describe my feelings for the people we were trying to include in our congregation? How could I describe my belief that if Jesus were here on earth today, His church would look like the one we wanted to create? That might not make other Baptists and other Christians happy, and our intent was not to offend others. I didn't think we were even really trying to change the world, but if we professed to be Christians, how could we not seek justice and equality for all people? And if we succeeded at that, then the world would change whether we wanted it to or not.

I wrote quickly, but I knew that after the church voted, I would need to go back and look at the article again and maybe have it read by a couple of other people to make sure that it was positive, accurate, and not too inflammatory.

The deacons had planned to meet again tomorrow night, and I couldn't believe I was saying this, but with Thomas gone, I needed to make sure all the other deacons were going to be present.

Cliff Burnside had been at the last deacon's meeting, but when I looked at the list, I realized that he had not said anything during the meeting. Cliff was still somewhat fragile after everything he had been through, but for him not to say anything at all probably indicated a concern. I called him and asked if I could come by for a visit.

He said "That will be great. I am here by myself most of each day, and I would love the company."

I felt as if I had been punched in the stomach. How could I have ignored Cliff for the last few weeks? The charges had been dropped against him, and his nightmare was over, but the isolation and the after-effects of his trauma were obviously still a big part of his life. I just assumed he would be okay now, and I was wrong. Thank goodness this other question had come up, and I had a reason to visit with him.

I had a policy of not visiting men by themselves unless I had someone with me, and I called Edna to see if she was available. She was keeping her two granddaughters that day since they had colds, and she could not join me. Then I thought of Vivian Artz, and I called her and explained the situation, and she told me she would be happy to go with me. She even said she would come by the church and pick me up at 10:45. I had told Cliff that I would come by about11:00

Vivian was right on time, and we arrived at Cliff's house about five minutes early. He greeted us at the door with a big smile. Fortunately, he seemed very comfortable with Vivian being with me and said, "It is great to see you, too, Vivian. I heard about your surgery, and I'm glad to see you getting around."

Vivian surprised me and leaned over and gave Cliff a kiss on the cheek as she said, "I am happy to see you, too."

Cliff looked at me and said, "You seem surprised at our closeness, Annie. You probably don't know that I dated Vivian's daughter Heather for a couple of years in high school. They were my second family, and I loved them. Still do actually."

Wow. I certainly did not know that, and as I usually do when this situation arises, I get frustrated over how much history there is to learn about church members. How long would I have to be here to catch up on all the members and their interactions?

"That is wonderful, Cliff. I'm glad you guys are close."

Cliff invited us to sit in their den. The other times I had been in their house there was such a sense of crisis that I had never really looked around. The focus had been squarely on survival for the family. I took a moment now to look around and was pleasantly surprised at how cute their house was. It was almost like a dollhouse. There were lots of windows in the den and in their living room, and each window was decorated with colorful curtains. The living room had white cotton curtains that stopped just below the window sill, pulled back with a multicolored band. The furniture in the living room was very simple, made of wood bases and overstuffed cushions of varying colors. The den was a little more traditional, with bright red curtains and white tie bands. The furniture was darker in color, and there was one leather chair.

Brightly-colored paintings on the walls kept the room bright and cheery.

I sat down on the couch next to Vivian, and Cliff sat on the leather chair. I apologized for the lack of notice of our visit, but Cliff just laughed and said, "Our house usually looks pretty good because I do a lot of cleaning to help pass the time, and we always have sweet tea available. I'm pretty hooked on it."

I knew the feeling.

"Are the boys doing well?" I asked.

"They seem to be, and we have seen a definite improvement in their grades at school. Sarah is back to working full-time since I am not working right now. I am drawing my salary for the rest of this school year, and then after that, I don't know what I will do."

Vivian spoke up, "Will you return to teaching?"

"Probably not," he said. "I think I would always be on guard with my behavior towards students and also a little fearful about how I would relate to them. I just would be terrified about someone else making false accusations against me. I feel a little frozen about my interactions with children."

"I am sorry to hear that, Cliff," I said. "But I can understand how you must feel. I will keep you in my prayers that you will find the right way for you to go from here."

"Thank you, Annie. I do appreciate that."

"The reason I wanted to talk with you is that I realized this morning that at the last deacon's meeting, you did not say anything at all, and I am concerned that you may have some issues with what the deacons want to do. I would never want you not to speak out about your thoughts and feelings about any project we are planning."

Cliff hesitated just a few seconds and then spoke. "I know this is going to sound strange, but I believe I am still recovering from the trauma I went through, and I often feel like I am on the outside of everything that's going on and that I am looking in on it but am not a part of it. I still feel like I don't have the right to speak my opinion about anything. No one has said anything, but I feel that way on my own. I think what the deacons are planning is wonderful, and I support it one hundred per cent, but I don't feel a part of it. I really don't know how to break through the shell that I feel is around me and reconnect with the world. Please don't take this personally because it is all coming from me.

"What about your family, Cliff? Are you having the same problems staying connected with them?"

Again, he hesitated, but then he said, "It is better with them, but it is not back to normal. Sarah has been talking with me about it, but I just can't seem to make everything right. I guess it will just take more time."

All of a sudden, my concerns shifted from what Cliff might think about the deacons' project to Cliff's state of mind, which made me feel like I was way out of my realm of experience

"Have you thought about talking about your concerns with a counselor? I don't know much about what you are feeling, but I am wondering if it could be a situation like PTSD."

"That's crazy, Annie. What I went through in the last few months was nothing compared to what soldiers go through on the battlefield."

"I know that, Cliff. But what you are experiencing is affecting your quality of life as well as that of your family. I admit freely I don't know much about reactions to trauma, but I was just wondering if talking to someone about it might be helpful to you. Maybe it would just speed up your full recovery."

"Annie, I know you are just trying to be helpful, and I appreciate that, but I think you are way out of your league to discuss my mental health. I am not the kind of person who gets mad at someone who is sincerely trying to help me, but I will just tell you nicely to butt out."

I was shocked into silence. That comment was not what I expected from Cliff. However, I had to think about what he said and when I did, I said, "I hear you, Cliff, and I apologize if I have offended you. I just wanted to make sure today that you were not opposed to what is going on."

"Rest assured, Annie and Vivian, I do support where the church is going, and I will do my best to be helpful in planning this event. Does that make you feel better, Annie?"

"Yes, of course, Cliff."

Actually, I was terribly embarrassed to have offended Cliff, particularly in front of Vivian. I did not know where to go from here in the conversation.

Vivian bailed me out by saying she had a prior commitment and needed to leave.

When I got in Vivian's car, I just sat back with my head on the back of the seat. She got in quietly and started the car. As we pulled out onto the road, I said to Vivian, "I am so sorry to have put you in the middle of that.

Vivian spoke softly, "Annie, I don't think you were wrong in what you were saying but maybe Cliff is not in a place to hear it. I will share with you that when my husband came home from fifteen months in Vietnam, he was not the same man as he had been. Some of the things Cliff was saying sounded just like my Marvin, particularly the part about being on the outside looking in on everyone around him. I think all you can do now is to keep in contact with Cliff and his family and be there for them if a need arises."

"I just feel so bad that I would presume to judge Cliff or to analyze him. Who am I to do that? Sometimes I can barely keep my own shit together. Oh, I'm sorry, Vivian for my language."

"Ok, Annie, you need to take a breath. You are getting all worked up because you are not perfect and have upset one of your members. I know you feel badly about what happened with Cliff, but I believe we all have to accept our frailties, both you and him. I'm going to make my analysis of you if I may. You are still very insecure and scared of failing in your role as pastor, and you are putting way too much pressure on yourself. You are actually doing a wonderful job as our pastor, and people have grown very fond of you. Celebrate that, and when things don't go just right, forgive yourself and move on."

"Vivian, thank you for being honest with me and for still supporting me. My insecurities have gone wild, but I will try to recover from that and move on to more positive thoughts."

Vivian let me out at the church, and I immediately went into the sanctuary. I needed some quiet time to think and pray about all that had been said in the last few hours. I needed to regroup so that I could be strong again and face all the challenges of my ministry. I spent time during the rest of the afternoon working on my sermon for Sunday. I decided I was going to preach about the need to accept ourselves as we were, the good and the bad. To be honest, I thought it would be therapeutic for me and helpful to others.

Chapter 40

I kept worrying about what Belinda Miller had told me about another group discussing the changes that Covenant was considering. It frightened me that some people might leave this church or even gather enough votes to change the direction of the church. If either of these things happened, I could not predict what would happen to the church or to me. But there was little I could do about it. I did not believe that I should say anything to the deacons at this time because to be honest, I did not know who to trust. And I did not want to stir up trouble where perhaps only rumors existed.

I decided all I could do for now was to try to keep communication open among church members. I also knew that I would continue to actively meet with those families who were uncomfortable with the direction Covenant was going. I wanted our disagreements to be discussed face to face.

On Wednesday evening, I met with the deacons again, and this time we hit the ground running. Edward was almost as organized as Charlotte Wilburn, and together they worked to write down what needed to be done and who needed to do it. Cliff was there as were all of the other deacons, and he seemed a little more involved with what was going on this time. We all assumed that the vote to have the family day would pass in the congregation, and we were planning for what needed to be done starting next Monday.

Charlotte began by saying, "Fred and I are going to be in charge of the lunch and the adoption of visitors by church members. We really believe that having one person or one family to relate to will make the guests feel more welcome and more connected to the church. And also, we will find someone to be in the nursery."

Edward said to Charlotte and Fred, "Thank you for agreeing to do all that. I really believe you will be able to get church members to volunteer to help you."

He looked at Edna and me and said, "I understand you two are interested in focusing on publicity. I would like to help you with that as well. I think getting the word out about this event will be vital to its success."

Edna said, "I am happy to help with publicity, but I don't have a clue about where to start. Do either of you have any experience in this area?"

Edward looked at me first and I shook my head no. He then shared with us, "When I was a lot younger I actually worked in public relations. While I was in the army in Vietnam, I actually had to put out a newsletter for the troops, and I learned a little about writing and advertising events. When I came home, I worked for a while in the advertising department of a big department store, and it gave me a little bit of experience in publicity. Other than that, we will be making it up as we go along."

I nodded. "Come to think about it, when I was Director of the food bank, I did have to work a little on publicity and advertising for our programs. Maybe we can help each other figure out what we need to do."

Alan had some connections with the local police and sheriff's office, and he thought he could get a couple of officers to work that day just to be sure nothing unpleasant happened. Cliff was a little vague about what he would do, but he seemed willing to think about how we would proceed with follow-up after the service. When the sensitivity training was mentioned, everyone looked at me, and I told the group that I thought I could put together something that could be helpful. I had no clue what I would do about that, but I would reach out to other church groups or maybe some of my counselor friends and hopefully I could come up with something.

We were all eager to get to Sunday so that we would know that we had the full support of the church with this plan. Once that was done, we were going to ask for volunteers to help with each of the committees.

It was as if we all believed this could happen and that it would be successful. I might have been the strongest doubter there, but I did not let on for one minute that I wondered if we could pull this off and if anyone would come to our family day. Faith was a very strange thing. It helped you to believe that fears and prejudices observed in people for years could be changed. I was trying very hard to believe that could happen.

Even though we couldn't act yet on publicity, I worked several hours the next day making a plan. I listed every group or company that I could think of who might want to hear about this special day. I got a list of all the newspapers in a twenty-five mile radius along with the mailing addresses and email addresses of their editors. I got phone numbers and email addresses for every television and radio station in Charlotte. I was sure we would think of other ways to get out information about this event when we met as a group again.

I also started writing an extra sermon to have ready just in case there was a crisis between now and the Family Event day, and I happened to get in a bind. I also started thinking about the sermon I would give on that date. Whether or not anyone showed up who was not a member of the church, I wanted to have a powerful sermon about love, acceptance, and what the church of Jesus Christ should look like. I actually spent the entire day in my church office, thinking, writing, praying, and of course, answering the phone.

Chapter 41

We had postponed the baptism of Robbie Burnside last week because of the trauma of losing Thomas and Joy. I was so glad that such a joyful event would happen this Sunday. I was hoping the celebration of Robbie's baptism would help the church begin to heal and to somehow regain its perspective about life and death. I don't know if anyone else needed that, but I know that I did.

Danny O'Reilly had been officially trained to fill the baptismal pool, and when I went in to check on it about fifteen minutes before the start of the worship service, I found the pool perfectly filled with extremely hot water. I looked up at Danny with panic on my face and said, "It's hot, Danny."

He said, "I know, Annie. Trust me. When you get in there in about twenty minutes, it should be perfect. I called the preacher at First Baptist in Bakerstown and another church in Monroe to ask for their advice, and they both gave me the same information. It takes about twenty minutes for the water to become pleasantly warm in a baptismal pool, even at this time of year. It will be fine when you and Robbie get in it. In fact, it may even be a little chilly, but I figured you'd rather have it that way than it being too hot."

"Thank you, Danny. I have to confess to being a little nervous about this service. I want it to be perfect for Robbie, and since this is my first time to baptize anyone, I can't help but worry about every little detail."

The service would start without Robbie and me being in the church. We would both be in the small rooms next to the baptistry. I would go down into the water first and say a few words. Then Robbie would walk down his steps, take my hand and come all the way down into the water. The water was to be between three and four feet deep, which would be about chest level for me. There was a heavy metal stool if we needed it for Robbie to stand on. He was about four feet tall, but I did not want him to be scared of the water.

I heard William begin to play the prelude, and I stood at the top of the steps waiting patiently. Then I heard Pete Stoudemire open the service with prayer and then explain that we were celebrating a baptism this morning. There was silence for a few seconds, and then I heard the organ start playing again softly. That was my cue. I walked down into the water, and just as Danny had predicted, it enveloped me with warmth. A microphone had been placed just outside the baptismal pool, and we hoped it would pick up my voice clearly for the congregation.

I welcomed everyone to the service. Then I said, "Today we are welcoming into our church membership Robbie Burnside. Robbie came into my office two weeks ago and told me that he had accepted Jesus as his Lord and Savior and that he wanted to be baptized and become a member of the church. In our church, baptism is a symbol of the burial of the old self and the birth of the new person in Christ. We copy the baptism of Jesus Christ as described in the New Testament of how he went down into the water to be baptized by John the Baptist. We believe baptism to be a symbolic act of obedience into a new birth. Now I will baptize Robbie Burnside into a new life of obedience to Jesus Christ."

I turned to my left where Robbie stood at the top of the steps. His dark eyes seemed as big as saucers, and he looked scared but determined. I nodded to him and as he started down the steps, I reached out my hand to him. He grabbed it and held on tightly. He got down to the bottom step and tried to find the stool with his right foot. He missed it the first time, and when he stood on the bottom of the pool, the water was at his chin. I reached over and pulled him up, and then he took one more step and found the stool. He grinned at me, and I smiled back at him, both of us exhaling as we did that. He was standing in front of me on the stool where I could put my left hand beneath his back, and after I did that, I raised my right hand above his head and said, "On your confession of Jesus Christ as Lord and Savior, I baptize you, Robbie Burnside, in the name of the Father, the Son, and the Holy Spirit. Amen."

Then I put a dry towel over Robbie's face and with him leading the way by leaning backwards, I immersed him in the baptismal pool. The warmth of the water and the emotion of the moment was an amazing combination, and I felt a joy in my faith that permeated my soul and my mind. Robbie came out of the water with a big grin on his face, and I smiled at him again just as he turned and started up the steps. His father was standing at the top of the steps to help him get dressed for the rest of the service, and there were tears running down his face. I walked up the steps to my dressing room and quickly began to dress for the service as well.

The rest of the service was wonderful, and I felt as if I was floating on air. Right after the sermon, the church moved into a business session. The first order of business was to approve new deacons for the coming year. Jesse Akin, Danny O'Reilly, and Anita Fleming had all agreed to serve, and all were approved unanimously by the congregation. Then the question of the family day was put to the congregation. Every family in the church had received a written report from the deacons, so church members knew what they were voting on. The motion to carry out the family day was made by Edward Anderson, and the motion was seconded by Charlotte Wilburn. Edna called for a vote by the show of hands, and then she said, "All in favor of this motion please raise your right hand."

There were hands up everywhere, and even though I did not know I was holding my breath, apparently I was, and I let that breath out very slowly when I saw the number of hands go up. Then Edna said, "All opposed to this motion, please indicate this by raised hands."

I looked out into the audience as a few hands came up very slowly. "No" votes were made by Harry and Earlene Williams and Jake and Peggy Morton which were expected, but also by Wayne and Anita Fleming which was a surprise to me.

My heart broke for their pain and for the division between these long time church members and the majority of the other members. I could only pray that long term friendships would not be destroyed by this differing of ideas, and I asked God to let me know if there was any way of reconciliation without capitulation of the majority's goals and objectives.

Chapter 42

On Monday morning I was sitting in my office at the church totally overwhelmed by the four weeks of preparation needed for our Family Appreciation Day. The doorbell rang, and I was grateful to be able to escape from staring at my computer screen. I peeked through the hole to see who was there, and oh my, it was First Sergeant Greg Barrow. I opened the door, peeked out, and looked at him and said, "Hi."

He grinned at me and said, "Don't look so shocked. I told you I was going to come by and see how you were doing. I got the feeling these people in the accident were really important to you, and I want to make sure you are doing alright."

I smiled back at him and said, "That is very kind of you, and yes, they were important to me. Would you like to come in and sit down for a little bit?"

"I would. And I brought you coffee."

I looked down at his hands, and he had two big cups of coffee in them. He handed me one of them, and I took it gratefully.

"Here's a couple of sugars if you need them."

"Oh yes, I definitely need them. Thank you."

Back in my office, I sat at my desk, and he took the office chair across the desk from me. I poured the sugars in my coffee and swirled it around.

"I also brought you a copy of the accident report. I kind of asked them to rush it to me so I could get it to you quickly."

"It doesn't describe their injuries or anything, does it?"

"No, it's just a statement of the results of the investigation of how the accident happened. At the end of the report, there is a simple comment stating that both passengers in the car were deceased, but that is all it says."

"I appreciate you getting it and bringing it to me. I am pretty much at peace about the accident, but looking at the report will help me finalize all my concerns."

"You're welcome, Annie. That is, may I call you Annie?"

"Please do."

"And I'm Greg."

"Thank goodness. Even in your office that day, I kept thinking your title was way too complicated. Greg sounds much easier."

I think we had chit-chatted about all we could now, and I was starting to feel a little awkward.

He looked at me and said, "Annie, please tell me how you came to be a pastor in a Southern Baptist church. I have to say that I have wondered about that since our conversation. I would wager that you have explained that many times, but if you could give me a brief version of how you got here, I would greatly appreciate it."

I hesitated for just a minute because I felt a small sense of disapproval from him, but then I told myself not to get paranoid. I shared my story about wanting to be a pastor since childhood, my graduation from seminary, and Covenant's call.

Then I said, "So far it has been a powerful experience, both good and bad."

"Did anyone ever talk with you about pastors of churches being men only?"

"Of course they did, for my whole life and even now. Just like they told women and African Americans they could not vote for a very long time and that they should not be seeking a formal education, that they were not capable. Just like they told women they could not serve on the battlefield or become President. It is a bunch of hooey, and if you think those ideas make sense, then our friendship will be short lived."

"Whoa, Annie. I'm on your side. I was just curious about how much flack you've had to take through the years. Obviously, it has been quite a bit. I have to tell you that my father has been a Baptist minister in Charlotte for thirty-five years, and I am afraid he would be appalled at your being a church pastor. But I am not him. I guess I still consider myself Baptist, but I just can't hold with a lot of their positions. I think a while back they talked about women being submissive to their husbands, and that one appealed to me a lot, but I really couldn't imagine the reality of that."

I rolled my eyes at him over that, and he laughed.

Then he said, "Annie, I would like to continue this conversation with you if we could. Would you go to dinner with me one night this week?"

If I remember correctly what it feels like, I think he just asked me on a date. I just sat for a few seconds and tried to remember what that was like.

Greg looked a little flustered and said, "I'm sorry. I should have asked you first if you are seeing somebody. I didn't mean to put you in an awkward situation."

"Oh you didn't, Greg. I am not seeing anyone. I was just trying to think about my schedule, but of course, I can't remember everything, so let me check my calendar."

I pulled out my phone and saw meetings on Tuesday and Wednesday evening and a Women's Missionary Union party on Thursday night. I was supposed to go to my parents' house on Friday evening for my nephew's birthday party, and I had planned to spend the night. I usually spent Saturday night preparing for Sunday, and that got me into the next week that was Thanksgiving week. I explained my schedule to him, and he looked a little pained.

"Are you blowing me off or is this your real schedule?'

"Oh, I'm afraid this is my real schedule. I'm sorry about this week."

"I hate to even ask, but what about Sunday night? Do you guys have Sunday evening services?"

"Not regularly. Let me check." I looked again at my calendar, noting that both Monday and Tuesday night of next week had commitments, but Sunday night seemed free.

"Wow, that actually works for me. I would love to have dinner with you next Sunday night. Let me get your number in case of some emergency, but if you don't hear from me, I will expect to see you then."

"I will pick you up about 6:00 if that's ok, and we'll drive somewhere toward Charlotte to eat. Is that ok?"

"That is great. I will see you then. By the way, I do live in the parsonage which is just to the right of the church."

"Good to know."

After I walked him to the door, I went back to my desk and sat there staring for a few minutes. That whole interaction with Greg felt like an out of body experience. I knew it was real, but I couldn't feel anything about it. I just felt too pressured with what I needed to do.

I felt torn between enjoying being a woman who had a date to prepare for and a professional who had overwhelming responsibilities in the next few weeks. At that point, I chose to focus on my pastoral duties.

It was frightening to finally be at a place where we needed to start taking action. All the talk and planning about this event had felt safe, but now getting this information and this message to the community was going to make this church and its members vulnerable, and I felt frozen in time, afraid to "push the buttons" that would start this process. Tears filled my eyes because I was afraid these actions were going to mess up the best thing I had ever had in my life, and because I was scared and not courageous like others who had fought for equal rights in the past. What the hell was the matter with me? I wasn't like these other people who had changed history, even some of our present church members. I felt way out of my league. What if I did something so wrong that I messed everything up? That would hurt so many people. What if this process destroyed this church? Maybe I should have let somebody else take on this church and this project, somebody much stronger and more capable then me.

I reached for my Bible and tried to think of a scripture that might address my fears. I couldn't help but think of Moses who tried to repeatedly explain to God why he was not the right one to lead the children of Israel out of Egypt. In Exodus 3 and 4, Moses points out everything that could go wrong with him being the one to lead God's people, and for each of Moses' concerns, God had an answer. God eventually became angry with Moses' fears, and Moses manned up.

Needless to say, I didn't consider myself on the same level as Moses. But in trying to conquer my fears, it was always good to know that those so much greater than I weren't volunteering to be on the front lines either.

I stopped thinking for a moment and quietly prayed for direction and for courage. I prayed for God's touch and for his presence in my life. I always knew that if he were by my side, I could do anything, and I needed that now more than ever.

After a bit, my pity party was over, and it was time to get busy.

First, I emailed the article I had written to the Charlotte paper, to the Bakerstown Post, and to the local paper in Monroe. I had considered other local newspapers, but I thought I might wait and see the responses from these first three. I also contacted all of the television stations in Charlotte. I was asking for public service announcements, but I also told the station managers that I or a representative of the church would love to be interviewed by a reporter or by one of the local talk show hosts. That last idea was not mine. I couldn't imagine being interviewed on television. I would be petrified. However, I would do what I had to do to make this work. It was too important. I also posted the information about our family day on the church's Facebook page.

I had put together a list of the ideas that should be on a flyer that we were going to have printed and then distributed all over our area and the Charlotte area. Edward and Edna and I needed to get together and approve the final ideas for the flyer, and then Edward was to get it printed and distributed to church members who were willing to put some of them in a public place. Maybe I was fooling myself, but I thought we had a handle on publicity.

Edna was doing one other thing. She was contacting all agencies and groups that had shown themselves to be open to undocumented residents, the LGBT community, minority groups, and single parent families and asking them to send out this information in their newsletters or to announce the information in their meetings. This must be the easy part of publicity because it was going far too well.

Chapter 43

The biggest concern I had about planning this whole event was the "sensitivity training." The worst reaction that might happen at this event to honor all families would be for someone to cringe or pull away slightly or perhaps even to react with a negative facial expression. Our congregation needed to be conditioned to seeing new participants in common behaviors such as a biracial couple or a family with two moms.

When I worked in Charlotte, I had two lesbian friends, Linda and Allison, who were the kindest and most caring women I had ever known. We went out to dinner about once a month, but I found myself reacting on a small level to their public displays of affection. I knew intellectually that that was not only okay, but expected behavior between two people who love each other, but I often looked around to see if anyone saw them. I am not proud of that reaction, but I also know that it is a behavior that comes about because of what our culture has taught us to expect and what we are used to.

One night I asked them to take me somewhere that might help me become more accustomed to displays of affection between them, and we ended up in downtown Charlotte at a lesbian bar. I was a little uncomfortable at first, but eventually, after explaining that I was straight, I had a few dances and some good conversation with several women. They were mainly professionals who lived in the Charlotte area who were looking to meet someone special or to just have a good time in a place where they could be themselves.

Going to a gay bar for sensitivity training was not going to happen for the members of my church. But what I found happening to me as I talked with these women and observed them dancing and having a good time together was that it mattered less and less that they were lesbians and more and more that they were just people. At least for me, exposure to those who are different from me helped me be more comfortable with them. Even watching television shows where gay couples were a part of families helped me feel more comfortable with homosexual relationships in real life. I realized that lots of people would say that we should get those shows off the air because they were corrupting us, but I saw them as helping me to love my neighbor as myself.

I called everyone I could think of to see if there were already programs set up to desensitize groups to different types of families. I left a message with a large North Carolina Baptist group asking them to call me back if they knew of someone who could talk about diversity in the church. I contacted Chad in Charlotte to see if he knew anyone who could lead such a group, and he referred me to the good looking priest, Father Daniel. I contacted him and although he found the idea of sensitivity training fascinating, he did not know of anyone who could deliver such training. He also said he was sorry I had missed the last meeting, and he hoped to see me at the next one.

No one seemed to have any answers for me.

I even talked with Rev. Stanley about this at our weekly meeting, but all he could do was look at me and say, "Please don't ask me these questions. You know what my answer will be, and I want our relationship to stay positive and productive." I knew he was right and that I was pushing the limits just a little with him. I backed off immediately.

Out of desperation, I called John Allen. He was a professional in Charlotte and had lots of contacts in large corporations and businesses. I thought maybe he had heard of some type of group that could do training like we needed.

When I was able to talk with John, I explained what I was hoping to do and what I was looking for. He listened very carefully, and then he said gently, "Annie, what you are doing is admirable, but I am afraid you are ahead of your time. My mom has mentioned to me that she participated in groups years ago that were to help participants identify stereotypes and prejudices toward African-Americans, and it was very eye-opening and very helpful, but I don't know of anything like that for the new kinds of families of today. I've got a couple of friends who are social workers and psychologists, and I will check with them, but I'm not hopeful. I will let you know if I find someone who can help you."

"Thanks so much, John. I appreciate your help."

"You know, Annie, you may be trying too hard here."

"What do you mean?"

"Bringing in an unknown 'professional' may not be what the congregation needs. Maybe they just need a few people telling their story to make it up close and personal to them. You might consider a panel of a couple of gay people or their families, an undocumented resident if he or she is willing to speak out, a single parent, or a biracial couple. They could prepare a few words and then answer questions from the group. Maybe a more low key presentation would be better received by the church."

I sat quietly for about half a minute until John said, "Annie, are you there?"

"Yes, John, of course. I'm sorry. I was just processing what you said, and I think you might be right. I'm so nervous about this whole event. I want this to be a positive experience for the church and not something that could turn out to be destructive. Thank you for your comments. I'm sorry I bothered you."

"Annie, you are never a bother to me. Please call me any time you think I can be of help. I'm honored that you think I might have some good input for you. Let me know what you work out."

I sat for a moment longer and thought about John. I was beginning to see how wise he was. He was not showy or outspoken, and sometimes I thought he seemed a little shy socially, but in a one-to-one conversation, he was attentive, empathetic, and willing to make observations. His comments always seemed so relevant. I needed to use him as a resource more often.

For now, I needed to get out of this office. My visits to church members had slacked off, and I needed to catch up on those. I made several quick calls, made contact with four members, and took off for these visits.

Lucille Smith was first on my list. She looked great, although she told me she was a little worn out. She had kept her two great-grandchildren two days in a row, and even though she had Frances to help, she was tired. I told her a little about what the church was planning, and she got very quiet. I was afraid this was going to be too new for her to accept, and I wondered if she would reject the plans of the church.

But when she spoke, all she said was, "This is not like it was in my day, but the reality is it is not my day any longer. I wish the church well in what it is doing. Please keep me informed so that I may share this with Elizabeth."

Mary Leblanc was next. Mary had been to church a few Sundays, but she seemed to be having a hard time fitting in. I wanted to ask her how she felt about the church and see if there was anything I could do to make her feel more a part of the church.

I had explained to all the members I called that my visits would be sincere but limited in time. Mary greeted me at the door before I had a chance to knock, and she welcomed me into her trailer. She looked as if she had been crying, and I was immediately concerned.

"What's happened, Mary?"

"Oh, it's wonderful news. Damien has been released to the halfway house. He got out a month early because of his good behavior. I just feel like he will be so much safer there than in prison. And I can visit him twice a week at the house. I just can't wait to see him there. Visiting Damien in prison was one of the worst experiences of my life. I put up a good front for him, but it was hard, and when I left him, I would cry all the way home. I am so relieved his ordeal is almost over."

"Will the halfway house help him find a job?"

"They already have. Damien is a smart boy, and while he was in prison, they had him working with the maintenance crew. His job is working in maintenance for all the county buildings and for public housing in the city. He'll be like an apprentice for a couple of years, and if he does well, he will be promoted after that time. He will actually have health and dental insurance. I am so proud of him. They will also pay for half of his tuition at the community college if he chooses to take some classes. Damien wants to do that. He has always wanted to be an engineer, and I know that sounds impossible, but I believe he can do it."

"Mary, all of this sounds wonderful, and I am so happy for you and Damien. I am looking forward to meeting him. May I ask you about something else, Mary?"

"Of course, Annie. What is it?"

"I've noticed you haven't been at church the last two Sundays, and I was wondering if everything is okay with you and the church. I want you to feel comfortable there."

"Most of the time I do, Annie, but it's hard. People are friendly and always talk to me and ask me how I am doing, but it just seems so superficial, and I don't know how to move it forward. I still feel kind of like an outsider there, and when I'm tired, I just don't make the effort. I don't feel like I contribute anything there. I give a little bit of money but it just feels like the church will be fine without me, and I like to be needed."

"I understand that, Mary. When you were back in Louisiana, what did you do in your church there that made you feel needed?"

"Oh my, lots of things. They told me I made the best coffee in the church, so I got there early every week and had a big pot of coffee ready before Sunday school. When it was cold, I would also make hot chocolate for the kids. I also sang in the choir every Sunday. I sing alto, and I felt like an important part of that group, too. Time played a part, too. I was a member there for six years, and Damien was baptized there. It was our church, and I want to feel that way again."

"Mary, I want you to feel that way again, too. You are such a wonderful woman to talk with, and I want the rest of the church to know that. You have a lot to offer the church, and we've got to figure out a way to get that to happen. Will you give me time to think about it and see what I can come up with?"

"Of course I will, Annie. If I'm not working, I'll make a point of being there this coming Sunday."

"That'll be great, Mary. I am sorry I don't have more time today, but let's pray before I leave."

After the prayer, I headed to my car and made a note in my phone to think of ways Mary could serve the church.

My next stop was Edward Anderson. I was glad I had contact with Edward through the deacons, because I had not checked with him since Mai had been gone. The Helping Hands committee had taken him a couple of meals a week until he told them he did not need any more food, but that he did like the company. After that, some of the committee members took turns stopping over to visit him twice a week, and a couple of them even had him over to their house for meals. I think I was hoping to make up the time I had not seen him by visiting him today.

The first words out of my mouth when he opened his door were, "Edward, I am so sorry that I have not seen you more over the last couple of weeks. I feel like I have let you and Mai down."

"Darn it, Annie, I wanted to tell you right away not to feel bad 'cause you hadn't been by here since Mai left because I know what all you have been doing, and I have been fine, but you beat me to the punch. Several church members have come by, and people have been nice enough to invite me over for supper a couple of times. Really, I have been just fine."

I got tears in my eyes and said, "I know you are fine, Edward, but I still feel like I should have done more for you. I am sorry about that."

"No need for being sorry, Annie. Really. I've been excited about our plans, too, and thinking about them has also kept me busy. Is there something I should be doing? I got some ideas for the flyers, and I thought you might want to look at them."

"I would like that a lot."

In keeping with my policy of not visiting men alone in their homes, and since it was an unusually warm November day, I asked Edward if we could sit on the screened porch at the front of the house. He agreed, and I looked at what he had designed so far. His design was very good. There were drawings in crayons of different kinds of families, and at the top of the flyer was the comment, "Let's all be one big family at Covenant Baptist Church." Then in one corner there was the time, place, and date. "Everyone is Welcome" was written in the other corner.

"I really like it, Edward. Let's run it by Edna and the rest of the deacons to make sure they are okay with it as well, and then we can get some printed. How many do you think we will need?"

"If we are going to put them on this side of Charlotte and the surrounding counties near us, we might need about 300. That might be overkill so let's think about it for a while before we do anything definite. It will take a few days to get them printed so we also have to allow for that."

"Edward, I think you have thought this through pretty well, and we can talk about it some more at our next meeting. Right now I have to head out. You take care of yourself. Mai will be home soon, and I don't want her to find you sick."

My next stop was the home of Jesse and Lorraine Akin. Jesse said he was off work for the day, and they would love for me to stop by. I was worried about how this visit would come across to the Akins, particularly Lorraine. I was worried she would think I expected her to come back to church just because Jesse had been approved to be a deacon, and that was not really what I wanted her to think. I just wanted her to know she was welcome, and really, that she always had been.

The Akins had a beautiful brick home on a large lot right on the outskirts of Bakerstown. It was a two-story house with beautiful landscaping across the front of the house. The lawn was obviously professionally designed and maintained. When I arrived at their front door, Jesse opened it wide and invited me in. Standing just to the left of him was a lovely African-American woman with just the beginnings of gray in her hair. Her milk chocolate-colored skin and dark expressive eyes did not give away her age, and she carried herself with the vigor of a woman quite a bit younger than Jesse. Then I looked at Jesse again and realized he was younger than I thought he was. His hair was white, but his face had few lines or crevices.

"Welcome to our home, Annie. This is my wife, Lorraine. Honey, this is Pastor Annie that I have been telling you about."

"Welcome, Pastor Annie," said Lorraine.

"Thank you very much. I'm sorry I haven't visited you before. I guess we had a couple of scheduling conflicts early on, and then I neglected to get back to see you. I apologize for that."

"From what I hear, you have been a little busy, Annie, so please, no need to apologize. Come on in to the den. Would you like some iced tea? Coffee?"

"I have been talking a lot today, and iced tea sounds wonderful. Thank you very much."

We moved into a room that could have been in any decorating magazine in the country. The colors were black and white, which seemed so appropriate. Occasionally, there was a red pillow or vase throughout the room, and the paintings on the wall were mostly of very vivid colors. The sofa was a decadent black leather that looked as soft as a baby's skin. A white bearskin rug and a smoky glass table were in front of the sofa. White linen-like chairs looked as if they had never been sat on. Yet the room felt lived in. An open book lay face down on the coffee table, and two empty cups sat on the table between the chairs. A massive stone fireplace had ashes in it from several days burning. It was a beautiful room, but certainly one that was comfortable and used.

I sat in one of the white chairs, and it was as comfortable as it was beautiful. Lorraine had excused herself to get our drinks, and Jesse took a seat on the couch.

It was almost 4:00 on a day that had been very busy and productive for me, and I was suddenly aware of being very tired.

Jesse took one look at my face and said, "Long day?"

"Very," I responded. "But a good day."

I became very aware of how energy depleted I felt, but I knew I wanted to have a special time with Jesse and Lorraine, and I tried to think myself into an adrenaline surge. Maybe the iced tea would help.

I said to Jesse, "You told me you and Lorraine had been married about twenty years, right? How did you two meet?"

"We actually met in Pharmacy school at UNC," said Jesse, "although I have to point out that I graduated, and she did not."

"I heard that, Jesse Akin," Lorraine called out from the kitchen.

I didn't know what to say about that, so I just sat there expectantly.

Then Jesse said, "Instead, she made more money in acting and in commercials than she ever would have made as a pharmacist, and she continues to receive royalties to this day. She did not become a star, much to her dismay, but she has had recurring roles in television shows that had predominately black casts. She always had very small roles, but she had a lot of them, and she was paid well. She loved what she did and has certainly made enough money to support herself. Her parents were very unhappy when she dropped out of pharmacy school, but now at seventy-three, her father is proud as a peacock."

"Are you telling Annie stories about me, Jesse?" said Lorraine as she walked back into the room.

"I'm afraid so, sweetie, but only good ones."

Lorraine handed me a glass of tea and served a plate of snacks, including grapes, homemade cheese straws, and sliced cheese and crackers. Since I had skipped lunch, I was thrilled to see this food, and I had to force myself not to gobble it all down.

While I munched on the snacks, Lorraine said to me, "Thank you, Annie, for finding out that Jesse could serve as a deacon at Covenant. It was a very big deal to me, not just because he was allegedly excluded because of our divorces, but because I could not help but wonder if it was because I was black. I tried not to be paranoid about that, but the interim minister who told him he could not serve had met me, and I recognized his disapproval of our marriage in his first glance at me. The members of the church seemed welcoming, but none of them came to our defense. As I look back now, perhaps they were unaware of our situation, or perhaps they were just too busy with their own lives. It was almost twenty years ago, and many of the members were still rearing their children. I had not really cared to be a part of Covenant before now, but with what is going on, I think I might want to be now. Do you think that would be okay?'

"Lorraine, I think it would be more than okay. I think it would be outstanding. I am incredibly sorry for what this church did to hurt you and Jesse. I think we all have to bear the guilt of the actions that were taken to exclude you and many others from participating fully in this Christian congregation. Times are different now, but we can never make up for the hurt caused by fear and discrimination. I just want us to stop hurting other groups now because of the same fear and prejudices. I hope you and Jesse will help us as we move forward toward being an inclusive church."

"It will be an honor to do that, Annie," Jesse said, and I believed him.

Chapter 44

I was not quite ready to let go of the idea of having a professional be a part of our diversity/sensitivity training, so the next morning, I contacted a large Baptist church in Charlotte to see if they had someone on staff who might come in as a consultant. I had to leave a message, but no one returned my call. I also called a state government number and got their switchboard. The person who answered the phone seemed not to understand what I was asking, and then transferred me to a number that rang between twenty and thirty times with no answer and no way to leave a message.

I sat for a long time thinking about who else might know of a professional person who was knowledgeable about diversity training. Maybe that was all in the past now. Just like Edna, my dad had attended a meeting on diversity in the workplace when he was younger, and one day when we were in the car together, he told me about it.

He said, "The leader asked lots of questions about how we would react to young people with certain style clothes, hairstyles, and skin color, and he was so descriptive that the audience got very uncomfortable. Then the leader acted out certain behaviors which actually made us laugh, but his point about our reactions was right on target, and I have never forgotten that."

When I went back to school after our discussion, I looked around at the students who were different from me, and I realized that I was prejudging them like crazy. That might have been the beginning of the radical me because I reached out to students who were Goths, rednecks, preps, special ed students, alleged gang members, and non-English speaking students. It was amazing. Some of these students who I really had not related to before became some of my best friends in high school and enriched my life tremendously.

I was beginning to realize that if we wanted to help the congregation become more comfortable with our focus groups, we were going to have to do it ourselves. And the reality was that I was going to have to put something together. I did not believe there was a program already set up that we could just bring in and use. At least I had tried. I saw no reason to reinvent the wheel unless it was absolutely necessary, but in this case, it was.

I decided to start with the people that I knew. I called Heather Artz. There was no answer so I left a message with her to call me back at her convenience. I called Lucille Smith and asked her if I could call her granddaughter Elizabeth, and she, after a brief hesitation, told me yes. She asked me not to hurt or embarrass Elizabeth, and I assured her that would not happen. I could only pray I was right about that.

I called Elizabeth and asked if I might stop by her home this afternoon. She was still on campus between classes and told me that would be fine.

Then I called Mary Leblanc and asked if I might contact Damien. She said that would be fine, but I would have to go through his probation officer. She gave me his name and number and wished we luck. She also thanked me for including Damien in this program, and she told me he would represent himself very well. Again, I could only hope that would be true.

The obvious biracial couple to get involved was Jesse and Lorraine Akin, but I felt really uncomfortable about that because I had just met Lorraine. I did not want her to think I met her just so I could involve her in this program although I hadn't even realized she was African American when I went to visit. I had to think about that for a while.

I went home for lunch, and right after that, I headed for Elizabeth Smith's house. She lived in a rundown apartment complex in downtown Monroe. Old lawn chairs and toys had been left in the yard in front of the complex. The yard was just dirt in most places with a scattering of grass here and there with no trees or shrubs. As I walked up the outdoor stairs to the second floor, I couldn't help but notice that there was a desperate need for paint all around the building. I found Elizabeth's apartment and knocked on the door. I heard a baby crying and another small child yelling about being hungry. Elizabeth opened the door with a frazzled look on her face. She almost looked like a child herself. She had on a faded pair of jeans and a threadbare sweater over a white cotton blouse. Her blond hair was pulled back into a pony tail with a Minnie Mouse band.

"I'm Rev. Annie Adams from Covenant Baptist. Is this a bad time?"

Holding one small, screaming child with the other pulling on her sweater, she just looked at me like I was an idiot, and I felt like one.

"Let me rephrase that," I said. "What can I do to help?"

"I'm sorry for this disaster. I just got in and the kids missed lunch at day care so they are starving, and I can't put Jeremy down 'cause he'll scream even louder if I do that. Lacy won't let go of me either so I am really at a standstill."

"Ok, tell me what to fix for lunch, and I can probably handle that way better than two crying children. You go sit with them while I fix lunch."

"Really?'

"Yes, really, but I do need some direction."

"For Lacy, I was going to fix a peanut butter and jelly sandwich with a cut up apple which has to be peeled for her. For Jeremy, I was going to heat up some leftovers from last night. It is spaghetti and meatballs, and after I heat it up, I run it through my food chopper so that he can eat it more easily."

"I'm on it."

I went to the kitchen and found the bread, peanut butter, and jelly for Lacy. I put those on the counter and looked in the fridge for the leftovers and an apple. I found all that, and there was quite a bit of the spaghetti left, so I took out a small portion for Jeremy and a larger portion for Elizabeth. Both of those went in the microwave. I got a glass of milk for Lacy and a sippy cup of juice for Jeremy, and then I peeled the apple and cut it up. Then I made the sandwich, chopped Jeremy's spaghetti, found some plates, and put it all out on the kitchen table. The last step was to pour two glasses of tea, one for Elizabeth and one for me.

Elizabeth came in to see if she could help, but it was all done. I told her just to sit down with her kids and have some lunch. I told her I would feed Jeremy while she ate if that was okay. She just stared at me, but she did sit with her children and they all started to eat. Jeremy wasn't too sure about me, but I had food on a spoon, and he got over his shyness pretty quickly. It was actually a pleasant lunch, and feeding Jeremy brought back memories of my nieces and nephews when they were younger and stirred up some other feelings in me that I just did not have time to think about.

Suddenly Elizabeth said, "Oh my God, I didn't think to ask you if you had eaten. I'm so sorry."

"No problem, Elizabeth, I ate at home before I left."

"Good. Thank you for all this. You certainly know your way around a kitchen."

"If you knew me better you would know what a joke that is, but I can do peanut butter and jelly and leftovers. Is there anything else I can do to help?"

"You're not like most ministers, are you?"

"That's probably a huge understatement, Elizabeth, but in some ways I am just a Baptist minister. That's really all I want to be."

"At least you know what you want to be. I'm still trying to figure that out."

"We'll talk about it sometime if you would like."

"Let me put these two babies down for their naps, and then we can talk about this program Grandmother told me about."

"Alright, I will clean up the kitchen."

"Wow, could you just move in?"

I laughed. "You just don't know what you'd be getting into, Elizabeth."

Elizabeth disappeared into one of the bedrooms with both children, and after a few cries of protest, there was silence, and Elizabeth reappeared in the kitchen. She had taken off the pink sweater and let down and brushed her hair. It was thick and silky smooth.

"Thank you so much for helping me with lunch. Most days I am a little better organized, but this morning was just one of those days."

"You are more than welcome. I enjoyed it. I imagine being a single parent to two small children can be a little overwhelming at times."

"I guess it is occasionally, but my children are the most important part of my life right now, and I want to make sure they have everything they need."

"Do you ever feel like you are missing out on things that other people your age are doing?"

"Of course I do, but I just don't care. As my parents often tell me, I created this life for myself, and I just have to deal with it. What they don't know is that I love my life, and what I am missing out on doesn't interest me a whole lot. I hope someday to fall in love again and to be able to go out and have fun, but for now my fun is with my kids. Let's go sit in the living room where we can talk some more."

I took a seat on the couch, and Elizabeth curled up into an overstuffed chair. Both were worn but clean and comfortable.

"Tell me about this program your church is planning, Rev. Adams."

"First of all, please call me Annie. Second, this program is an effort to honor different kinds of families. We hope to have single-parent families such as yours, families with two moms or two dads, biracial families, families who don't speak English or who might be undocumented along with more traditional families. It's a day to recognize that God loves and values all different types of people and families, and that no one type of family is more valuable to Him. Our members feel that most churches only reach out to people just like themselves, and we want to open our doors to everyone."

"Wow, that doesn't sound like any church I've ever been in, but it sounds very exciting. Was it your idea?"

"Not really. When I came to Covenant, the congregation was already trying to figure out a way to reach out to different kinds of people, and through our discussions, this was the idea they liked best."

"Grandmother really wants me to go to your church that day, and I think I would like to do that. Will there be child care for my kids or will I keep them in worship?"

"Child care will be provided, but if you are not comfortable with that, you may certainly keep your children with you."

"Good to know."

"There is something else that I wanted to talk with you about."

I explained to her our concerns about having negative reactions if we didn't prepare as a congregation and our idea for a panel discussion to help the members prepare.

"I was wondering if you would serve on the panel to represent single parents."

"When would this be?"

"We would like to get together on the Monday after Thanksgiving. I think we can make a difference with this panel discussion. What do you think?"

"I don't know how much I can offer, but I would be happy to be a part of the panel."

"That's great, Elizabeth. I think your grandmother will be very proud of you."

"Me, too," Elizabeth said, "and Annie, when I say you're not like other ministers, that's a compliment."

I grinned at her and said, "I appreciate that."

When I got back to the church, there were nine new messages. I started listening to them right away, because if I didn't, I would put them off forever, and that is not a good thing.

Four of the calls were questions about the times of committee meetings this week, and I was able to return them quickly. Two were calls asking if our early morning prayer group was still meeting, and I responded to those callers affirmatively. One call was from Heather who said I should call her this evening. One was from Mary LeBlanc who told me Damien was excited about being on our panel, and all I had to do was clear it with his probation officer.

The final call was a lovely surprise. It was from Lorraine Akin who told me she had heard about this panel we were trying to put together and how much she and Jesse would like to be on that panel. I called her immediately and told her how thrilled I was that they were willing to do that, and I told her that I or another member of the church would get back to her with details.

This was actually coming together and I felt more hopeful about it every time someone else agreed to be on the panel.

Chapter 45

The week was quickly getting away from me. I had committee meetings at night, I needed to buy a birthday present for my nephew who was turning thirteen, and I had a date on Sunday night to think about and prepare for. First, however, I had to call Damien LeBlanc's parole officer.

Harold Feamster answered the phone with a gruff, "Hello, what 'ja' want?"

I explained to him what I wanted and told him the date of the panel presentation and the date of the family event.

There was total silence when I finished my explanation of what I wanted, and I held my breath.

Then Mr. Feamster said, "Here it is. I found Damien's file, and it looks like he is okay to go out as long as he has a sponsor with him. You got somebody who can pick him up, be responsible for him, and bring him home after it's over?"

I only hesitated for a few seconds, and then I told him, "Yes, I do."

If I had to do it myself, Damien was going to be a part of this program. I could not let Mary down.

"Okay, that's fine. If he behaves himself, let me know. I'll make a note of that in his file."

"I sure will," I told him. "Thank you so much, Mr. Feamster."

"Yeah, anytime."

Yes! The only other panel member I was waiting on was Heather Artz. I had talked with her last night and explained what we wanted. She seemed interested and actually said that her partner, Dawn, was better at public speaking than she was, but that Dawn was out of town, and she would have to call me later today. She also told me she wanted to talk with her mom and make sure that she was okay with such a public outing of her family situation. I was rather surprised at that comment since Vivian seemed so open about Heather's status, but maybe she was completely open only when she knew the person with whom she was sharing would be accepting of Heather's situation.

It occurred to me that parents don't go around announcing their son or daughter's sexual orientation if they are heterosexual, so why would parents of gay and lesbian children do that. It is part of who they are but does not require public disclosure or discussion.

Edna and I had talked on the phone about the gathering on Sunday. The worship service would go as normal except we would only sing one song and instead of a sermon, I was going to present a meditation. Then we were going to ask the congregation to share their questions and concerns with us about the family day event. We wanted to be well prepared for the Sunday of the event, while at the same time making it just a regular day of worship. The deacons had worked very hard at their assigned duties, and I believed we were prepared for that day. Each of them had involved other members by giving them assignments, and these assignments had been well received by church members.

I needed to get to a mall, and after lunch when all seemed quiet, I headed for Carolina East Mall again for a couple of hours. I bought a gift for my nephew's birthday, and while I was at the mall, I bought a new sweater to wear Sunday night.

Late Friday afternoon found me driving to my parents' home in Columbia for the family's birthday party for my nephew, Derek. As much as these family birthday parties were not very exciting, I was happy for the distraction. I needed to get away from the pressures of my job, even for just a little while.

The overnight visit was great. Derek was a little more sullen with us on this visit, and I can only attribute that to his age. Later Friday night after the family party, my brother Tom was going to take Derek and seven of his friends bowling at midnight, so Derek knew he had to put up with the family fun in order to get to his late night event.

When I could get Derek alone, he was a sweet kid who loved to talk about sports and movies, but for some reason, he did not like the whole family thing. I was okay with that, but his dad and mom pushed him hard to be on his best behavior when he was with all of us, and there was always a little tension in the air.

Chapter 46

Attendance was high on Sunday morning. Even if members were a little worried about the family day, they wanted to know what was going to happen. Edna Allen was to chair the discussion meeting, and as usual, she seemed well prepared. After our abbreviated service, Edna asked the members to gather near the front of the sanctuary while keeping everyone as visible as possible. She stood at the front of the church and began by explaining how the event would work. The plan was for the twenty-one members who had agreed to be greeters to gather in the narthex thirty minutes before the start of worship, about 10:30. As visitors arrived, greeters would step forward to welcome them, to introduce themselves, and to get the visitors' names. Those greeters would then escort the visitors and their families to a seat in the church. Warm and welcoming conversation would be a plus for the greeters to initiate, but if that didn't happen, just a welcoming smile would be fine. The greeters would say their names to the visitors again and would say something like, "Please let us know if we can help you with anything. We will check with you after the service to help you find a table for lunch."

Edna explained that The Family Day Event Sunday would be a regular day of worship for everyone there, but we were hoping that it would also be a welcoming day if we did have any visitors. "If" was the operative word used here because we had no idea if anyone would respond to our invitation to come and worship with us. I personally felt sure that Lorraine Akin would come that day as would Elizabeth Smith and her children. Heather Artz and her family and hopefully Damien and Mary LeBlanc would be there as well. Ten visitors in one day would be an amazing feat for the church, but I know the deacons and I were hoping for more.

Erin O'Reilly raised her hand and asked, "What if we have more visitors than we have greeters?" Everyone burst out laughing and Erin looked embarrassed.

Edna said, "If that happens, we will cope with it, Erin. I wish we were all thinking like you instead of being afraid that no one would come."

Faye Emerson said, "I hate to even say this, but I have never met a gay person. I'm worried about saying the wrong thing to a gay couple or to their children. How do I know what to say?"

Suddenly, Jake Morton stood up in the back of the church and said, "I can tell you what to say to these people. They are sinners and are going to hell if they don't change their behaviors. I am here to tell you that this church is wrong to be inviting all these people to worship. What has happened to all of you? Don't you read the Bible anymore? Do you not care about the morals of our children? I've been a member of Covenant for a long time, and this is the first time I have been ashamed of this church. Please, please some of you take a stand with me, and let's turn this church back around to God's way. Stand up with me now against what this church is doing."

There was absolute silence in the sanctuary.

I think everyone was waiting to see if anyone would stand with Jake. I was watching Harry and Earlene Williams, and just when it looked like Harry was going to stand up, Earlene put her hand on his forearm. He looked at her, and she mouthed the word, "Please."

When no one stood with Jake, he turned around in disgust and left the church.

Everyone was shocked at Jake's outburst, and no one seemed to know what to do. No one moved or said a word.

Finally, I stood and said, "I am at just as much a loss as to how to respond to what just happened here as you must be. All I know to do is pray. Please pray with me. Dear God, please be with Jake right now as he must feel so alone and so abandoned by this church. We love him. Show us how to tell him that we care about him. What you have asked us to do is hard, and it's causing hurt feelings and anger. Yet we believe this is what you want us to do. Please help us to continue our work in the most loving way we can so that others who don't agree with us do not feel hurt or separated from this congregation. We thank you for the opportunities you have given us. Give us courage and strength to do your will. Amen."

I realized that Jake had been the main person who was unhappy with the direction of this church. Perhaps there had been others who had encouraged him along the way, but they had either given up hope or decided not to protest what we were doing.

Then I said to the congregation, "I am so sorry that this kind of hurt and anger has come to Covenant. Does anyone have anything they want to say?"

Pete Stoudemire stood up slowly and said, "This animosity from within is very difficult for any church, but as a former pastor, I will tell you that we cannot let this stop our momentum. We are on the right path, and as difficult as it may seem, we must not stop. There are too many people counting on us to let one person stop us. I'm saying we must continue our meeting and carry on with our plans. Does anyone object to that? If you do, speak now."

For the second time that day, there was total silence in the room.

Edna said, "I agree with Pete. Let's move on."

Faye's question was still floating around in the air, but we were all having trouble moving beyond what happened with Jake.

Finally, I responded to her question.

"Gay families are just like other families in that they want to be welcomed to a new place in a kind and sincere manner. They would like you to recognize their children if they have any, and most of all they want their family to be treated with respect and courtesy. Faye, one of your gifts is being kind and courteous to those around you, and if you treat our guests like you treat other church members, you will be fine. All of this goes for other family groups as well whether they are non-English speaking, homeless, biracial, or single parents. We just need to treat everyone with kindness and respect, the same way we should always treat anyone who visits our church."

Pete Stoudemire spoke up again, trying to get everyone's mind back on preparing for the event, and said, "I have to be honest, Edna. I really am okay with all of these groups coming to worship here because I am convinced Jesus Christ would welcome them, but if these gay couples kiss or hold hands, I'm just not sure how I might react. What if my face says something that my mouth don't wanna say?"

There were quite a few nodding heads after his question, and as strange as it sounds, I felt a surge of pride in this group of people. We were moving beyond Jake's outburst, and as difficult as this whole situation was for many of them, they knew in their hearts this is the way Jesus would do it. I think they just had trouble believing they could be as good as Jesus.

Edna spoke in her quiet but eloquent way. "Pete, I really do understand what you're saying. I have been blessed with some gay friends through the years, and I might be a little more comfortable than you in relating to them, but this is all new for our church. We have been so selective for so long as to who would be welcome in our churches that opening the doors to people who are different from us terrifies all of us. What will this do to our church? Will some people leave? Will we be condemned by the community we live in? Will this event be a total failure, and then everyone will think we were wrong to try it? You are not alone in your fears. But I don't think I can stand not doing this any longer. I am sometimes ashamed of how Christians and churches have treated people in our society because they are not just like them. How can we claim to follow Jesus Christ and not go after anyone and everyone to be a part of our community? As a nation, we are always worrying about the declining numbers in church membership, but what we really mean is, 'Where are all of those white, middle class Christians who used to go to church?' This is our chance to grow this church and to become an inclusive community, and we would be crazy not to take it."

No one else said anything else for a minute, and then quietly from the back a voice started soft and then got louder singing, "Amazing Grace, how sweet the sound. That saved a wretch like me.' Other voices joined in, and before the end of the first verse, it was a loud chorus among quite a few tears. I thought to myself. *We didn't cover everything that needed to be covered, and we had a crisis in the middle of our meeting, but I think we are all on the same page now, and that is what matters.*

Edna closed the meeting by reminding everyone that we would continue our training and dialogue with a panel discussion a week from Monday at 6:30 p.m. in the fellowship hall. She told us there would be coffee and tea and dessert, so everyone should just get up from the dinner table that night and come on over. She thanked everyone for being there today and encouraged anyone with further concerns or questions to call me at the church office. Then she closed the meeting with prayer.

I sat there quietly for a moment because I had just experienced one of those mountaintop experiences Christians get so excited about, and that was after experiencing an individual's moment of despair. The contrast had been pretty severe. Soon, though, church members came by, thanking Edna, and then asking me about some of the details of the family day. I answered all of the questions I could, and then started writing down the ones I didn't have answers for. Those would be referred to someone else, but I would make sure the person with the question got his answer.

I was the last to leave the church, and it was with such gratitude that I had been given the opportunity to be a part of Covenant Baptist Church. My life would never be the same after serving this church.

As I walked home, however, my thoughts turned to tonight. It had been a while since I had been on a date, and I hoped I could remember how to do that.

Chapter 47

I kept looking in the mirror at my front and then my back. I had boobs but not a great butt. I was wearing a straight, black skirt with a long sleeve, bright blue blouse. I wore matching blue earrings and a dainty gold chain around my neck. I had on my three inch heels, not stilettos, but high enough to emphasize my slim, muscular calves. My hair and make-up were the best they could be, so overall, I looked okay. I was a little nervous because it was a first date, but this wasn't my first rodeo, and I felt pretty confident about the evening.

My doorbell rang, and I took a deep breath and went to open the door. Greg stood there looking pretty darn good. He had a bouquet of lovely flowers which he handed me. I invited him in, excused myself to get a vase from the kitchen, and then I placed the flowers in the vase and put them on my coffee table. Then I took a longer look at Greg. He was wearing great looking jeans with a button up white shirt and a dark blue blazer. He smelled like he had just gotten out of the shower where he had used the best scented soap ever. He looked like he had just shaved, and his skin looked so soft I wanted to reach out and touch it.

Suddenly he said, "Do I pass?"

"Pass what?"I said.

"Your inspection."

I realized I had been staring at him so I grinned and said, "You'll do."

He laughed and said, "So will you. Shall we go then?"

"Sure. Let me get my jacket."

We walked out into a chilly evening and got in his car. He made a further good impression because he drove a hybrid Honda Civic. Apparently, he did not need to drive a macho car to be confident in his manhood. Perhaps the fact he was a state trooper was enough.

On the forty-minute drive to the Charlotte restaurant he had picked out, we talked about Covenant's family day and some of his work situations from the previous week. We then agreed that we both had stressful jobs and decided to talk about other things.

He said, "Tell me about your family."

I told him how my parents had moved to Columbia, SC recently, and that they were much closer to me and to my brother and my sister. I told him I had grown up in Mississippi, and he was very surprised.

"I don't expect too many radical women to come out of Mississippi."

"It shouldn't surprise you. Southern women are about the strongest in the country, and Mississippi is one proud Southern state. It gets a bad rep sometimes, but it was a great place to grow up."

"Good to know. What do your brother and sister do for a living?"

"My brother is an attorney and my sister is a stay-at-home mom. Her husband is a firefighter in Columbia. They have two kids, and my brother and his wife have three."

"Takes the pressure off to produce grandchildren, doesn't it?"

"Yes, it does. You know that because the pressure is on you?"

"No, there's no pressure on me. I have a son already."

"Oh, I didn't know that."

"Yes, I have been divorced for about a year, and I am the proud father of a two-and-a-half-year-old son named Anthony. My ex-wife and I share custody, but she has primary physical custody of him for now."

"How long were you married?"

"Four and a half years. And if the next question is 'What happened,' I'm afraid it was mainly my fault. I loved being a trooper, but I loved moving up in the ranks even more, and I did what I had to do to make that happen. I worked all the time and when I wasn't working, I obsessed about work. My ex, Mandy, was a teacher, and after teaching all day and grading tons of papers, she wanted to go home and have a family life. I guess I wasn't ready to help make that happen, and one night when I got home late from work, she told me that she had met someone else that she was beginning to care about, and even though she cared about me as Anthony's father, she wanted out of our marriage. I made all kinds of accusations about her having an affair, but she resolutely stuck to her story that she had not cheated on me physically, but was falling in love with someone else. She wanted out of our marriage to pursue this other relationship."

"How did you handle all this?'

"Not well. I threatened to divorce her on the grounds of adultery, and I threatened to get custody of Anthony because she was an unfit mother, but being the person she is, she let me rave about this and make threats for several weeks. She even let me cry and beg for forgiveness, but eventually she told me this divorce was going to happen and then we were both going to continue being Anthony's parents. I found after some time that I did not so much grieve our relationship but the end of my fantasy life as super husband and father. After some of the anger left me, I became depressed because I figured I had screwed up what should be the most important relationship in my life. I determined then and there that I could still be a good father, and that has been my main focus since the divorce was final."

"I'm sorry for everything you had to go through, but I am happy you have decided to be a good father to Anthony. Do you get to see him very often?"

"Since he is still pretty young, I see him for an overnight visit every week-end, and then I stop by his daycare and have lunch with him any time. I try to do that at least once a week. We negotiate about holidays, and we both celebrate his birthday together at this point. I don't know how long that will last. Mandy is getting married in a couple of months to the guy she had met while we were married. He's a good guy and seems to be good with Anthony."

"This whole thing sounds so civil. That speaks well for you and Mandy."

"Mainly Mandy. But I finally got a hold on my temper and my ego, and I've done better than I expected. Anthony is definitely the most important person in my life now, and I want him to know both his parents love him and like each other. Now, that's enough about me. Catch me up on your love history."

"There is not much to tell. I dated a couple of guys in college. One of them wanted to be serious, but I wasn't ready for that. I started dating a guy seriously about a year and a half ago, we had talked about a future together, but when I got called to Covenant, he dumped me."

"What? Just because you became a pastor?

I told him about Mike and our break-up, and then we moved on to other topics. We discovered that we were both college sports fans, basketball being our favorite, with football a close second. He, of course, cheered for the wrong team. He was a Duke fan, and I cheered for Carolina. We both liked Carolina Panthers football and even talked about going to a game.

We talked about our families where we grew up and found a lot of similarities. I guess since we were both raised Southern Baptist, it was understandable that our families might be similar. The difference now was that I still was close to my family and saw them fairly frequently, while Greg said that after his divorce, his parents had become somewhat distant with him. They liked to see Anthony a lot, and they tolerated Greg in order to do that, but he could feel disapproval from his parents, particularly his dad.

He told me, "It makes me incredibly sad that my dad's love seems conditional on my living a certain way and believing just like him. He never did like it when any of his children made mistakes, and he always let us know how disappointed he was in our behavior. I always felt that I had to live a certain way for my father to really love me, and divorce just did not fit into his realm of acceptable behavior, particularly not for his children. My mom is much more accepting and loving toward her children, but she never shows that in front of my father, which somehow makes her worse than him. As I told you at the office, I have three younger sisters, and they have been great. I see them quite a bit, and all of us see our parents because we know we need to, not because we particularly want to."

I said to him, "You know what, I hear about a lot of parents like that. They expect very high standards of behavior from their children, both when they are young and when they are grown, and if that is not there, they withdraw their love. I don't understand that. I am realizing more and more that the greatest gift my parents ever gave me was and is unconditional love. Sometimes they don't like my choices, but their love is a constant for me."

"You are very lucky. I just hope I can be that kind of parent for Anthony."

We had a lovely dinner at a Spanish restaurant. I had a dish with pork tenderloin served with black beans, plantains, and rice. It was delicious. Greg had a steak and potatoes. Granted it was cooked in a new and exciting way, but I couldn't help but tease him about his entrée choice.

I felt very comfortable with Greg. I had not known about his divorce or about his son, but to be honest, I didn't care about that. I figured at my age, it might be difficult to find a man to date who had not been married before.

After dinner we headed home, and all my high school insecurities came roaring back. Would he kiss me goodnight? Would he want more than that? How did I feel about him? Was he just a friend or was there romance brewing? We talked nonstop, but inside all of these questions were churning. This was why I hated dating!

Greg pulled in the driveway next to my house. There are two motion lights around the house, one in the front and one in the back, and the one in the front lit up the car and everything around it.

He came around and opened my door, and when I stood up next to the car, he was standing very close to me. I looked up at him, and then he said, "I'm going to give you a quick kiss, and then I will walk you to your door, see that you get in safely, and then I will leave. Ok?"

Rather breathlessly, I said, "Ok."

As I was backed against the car, he leaned down and gave me a firm but gentle kiss. It lasted less than five seconds, but it certainly got my heart racing. He pulled back from me, blew out a breath, and said, "Okay then." He then did just what he said he would.

After I locked my front door behind me as he walked away, I leaned against the door and said, "That was a very nice ending to a very nice evening."

Chapter 48

Monday was the beginning of Thanksgiving week, and I had a ton of things to do before I went to my parents' house on Wednesday. I was slowly moving toward a state of panic as I realized that because Thanksgiving was so late this year, we only had a week before the Family Day Sunday. Publicity had been going strong for about a week, but I had not heard any feedback. I was beginning to worry that no one was paying any attention. I found out later that day that that was definitely not true.

First came the call from the Charlotte newspaper. The reporter wanted to know when she could come and interview me about the family day event. The article I had submitted to them had been in Saturday's paper, and the reporter who called me said they had received over thirty calls asking questions about this event.

When I asked her if that was a lot, she said, "When it became known that a popular television series would be doing some filming in Charlotte, we received thirty-two calls asking for details and commenting about that. When the state legislature passed a bill that seemed to restrict voting rights, twenty-five calls were received about that. So as you can tell, over thirty calls about anything is a very big deal. It's almost as many as we get if we change the comics. So when will you be available for an interview? Would tomorrow morning work for you?"

I hesitated only a moment. "Tomorrow will be fine. Ten o'clock here at the church?"

"Sounds good. Thank you. I just want to tell you that what you are doing sounds like a really good thing, but I will have to be objective and ask the hard questions."

"I am aware of that, and I look forward to talking with you."

I told myself this was a good thing and not to panic. I didn't want to become a controversial figure or make the church known for a radical stand, but I think it was too late to worry about that.

The rest of the morning, I was working on my sermon for this coming Sunday. Then I would be free to work on the one for the family day. Just before lunch, I received another call from a woman who hosted a local TV talk show in Charlotte. She had read the article on Saturday as well, and she wanted me to be on her show.

"Could you join us this Wednesday? The show is an hour and your part would be about fifteen minutes."

The host's name was Cindy Perkins, and the few times I had seen her show, she was pleasant and gracious. I again knew this was something I had to do whether or not I felt comfortable doing it.

"Ms. Perkins," I said, "I would be happy to come and talk with you about this event. However, I do want to make it very clear that I am not willing to debate this event with anyone, whether it is you or another guest. What I am saying is that I do not want to get into a situation where you bring in someone who is opposed to what we are doing to debate the merits of this event. We are not doing this to alienate other Baptists or other Christians. Am I clear about that?"

'Of course, Rev. Adams. I would not put you in that situation."

"Okay, then, I would be happy to join you on Wednesday morning. What time and where do I come?"

"If you will give me your email address, I will have my assistant get all of that information to you. Thank you, Rev. Adams. I will see you on Wednesday."

I went back to writing my sermon, but with everything going on it was a little hard to concentrate.

I also allowed myself five minutes to think about my date with Greg the night before. It really had been fun. I felt almost like it had happen to someone else. I had been so consumed with the church that I forgot what it was like to be a woman that a man finds attractive. It brought good feelings to me, and I was going to enjoy them when I had time.

Thinking about the newspaper and television interviews did not bring good feelings. I wasn't really scared to talk to the media as I had to do that several times when I worked for the food bank in Charlotte, but this was different. This was controversial, and I knew the media liked it when people get fired up about their reports. That was not my goal. I wanted to use the media for free publicity, not for agitating the Christian community.

I spent the rest of the day trying to finish one sermon and thinking about the second. I also made some notes for myself about how to address the questions from the media about this event. I went home about 7:00 ready to crash for the evening and had just put on sweatpants and a t-shirt when I got a call from Sarah Burnside. She had taken Cliff to the emergency room because he could not stop crying. He had cried for about eight hours and had been sitting on the floor of their bedroom all day. She had a friend to stay with the children, but she was at the hospital by herself. I told her I would be there as soon as I could. When I arrived at the hospital and saw her, she hugged me and started to cry herself.

"Don't worry, Annie, I'm not going to cry for hours. I just needed to do this for a little while," Sarah told me.

At that point, we both started giggling nervously and then more tears came, this time from both of us.

"It's okay, Sarah. You can cry as much as you need to. Tell me what happened."

"Oh, Annie, he has not been himself for weeks. He puts up a good front around other people, but at home he just sits and stares. He has been crying a lot but today was the worst. He just could not seem to stop. He kept saying, 'I'm sorry, Sarah. Our lives are ruined as long as I'm still here. Without me, you can go on.' I was terrified, Annie, so I finally called a teacher friend of Cliff's who stood by him throughout this whole ordeal, and he came over and literally picked Cliff up and took him to his car and then here to the emergency room. He stayed with me for an hour, but then he had to go home. I don't know much yet, but I hope to have some answers soon."

"Have you eaten anything? Or do you need something to drink?"

"I can't eat right now. I'm too upset."

"Okay, that's fine, but I could use some coffee and crackers, so I'm going to get you some, too. I will be right back."

We sat together for about an hour and a half. I tried to give her a pack of the crackers but she said she really could not eat. We prayed together and cried some more.

Finally, a doctor asked Sarah to take a seat in a room off the waiting area. Sarah asked me to come with her. She introduced me to the doctor, and we all sat down.

"Mrs. Burnside, I believe your husband needs to be hospitalized mainly because I think he is a danger to himself right now. He seems to think he has ruined both your lives and those of your children, but he won't tell me what he did. Do you know what he is talking about?"

"Yes, I know, but he didn't do anything."

Sarah put her head down and started to cry softly.

The doctor looked at me, and I told him the whole horrible story.

He was appalled by what had happened to Cliff and told Sarah how very sorry he was for Cliff and for her. "I believe your husband can get help and overcome this trauma, and I would be happy to admit him here, but since he is a veteran, I am wondering if you would like me to get him transferred to the VA hospital in Salisbury. I believe Cliff has symptoms similar to PTSD, and even though they are not related to service in the military, I believe the VA staff can help him. It won't be as convenient for you to visit him, but he may have to be hospitalized a couple of weeks, and I think your charges would be less.

"Does Cliff know that he needs to stay in the hospital?"

"Yes and he seems relieved to know he will be hospitalized. That's a good sign. Somewhere deep inside him, he wants to get help and get his life back. I think he has a good prognosis, but it may take some time."

"I just want my husband back. I don't care how long it takes or how inconvenient it is to visit him. I want him to have the best care we can get, and I am okay with the VA hospital. I have a sister who lives in Salisbury so I can stay with her sometimes if I am there for a day or two."

"Okay then," said the doctor. "I will get everything arranged, and he will probably be transported there tomorrow. Do you want to see him tonight?"

"Oh yes, can I?"

After the doctor walked away, I hugged Sarah and asked her if she wanted me to go back in the room with her to see Cliff. She told me that she would be fine, that Cliff was still the man she loved and that they would work their way through this dark tunnel. We sat together for another hour, and then an aide came to get Sarah to take her to Cliff, and I told her I would see her soon and to call me if anything new came up.

After she left, even though it was getting late, I sat in the waiting room and ate the other pack of crackers that I had bought. I thought about the human spirit and wondered how much any one person could take. I questioned God about why all of this had happened to Cliff and Sarah, through no fault of their own. I was angry about the unfairness of life and raised the age-old question of why bad things happen to good people. After a while, and without any answers to my questions, I drove home and went to bed.

Chapter 49

I was awakened at 6:00 by a piercing alarm clock so I could prepare for the early-morning prayer group. Why did I set this up for so early, and why did it always come after a night when I had been out later than usual? I staggered to the kitchen, got coffee, retreated to the bedroom, showered and got dressed.

The one bright spot of the morning was that I had a text from Greg wishing me a great day and telling me how much he enjoyed being with me on Sunday. He wished me a happy Thanksgiving and said he was looking forward to seeing me after the holiday. That got my adrenaline flowing more than the caffeine from the coffee.

I made it to the church with five minutes to spare, opened doors, turned on lights and heat. I knew it was going to be chilly in the sanctuary, and I felt guilty about that, but I was moving a little slowly this morning. We had brought some afghans and throws that we left on the pews up front for anyone who got cold in church, and we would definitely need them this morning. The same small group of people had been faithfully coming to these prayer sessions, and I do believe it was meaningful to them, and it usually was for me. This morning I just wanted to get through it.

All of the regulars were there this morning except Sarah. Vivian Artz, Mary Leblanc, and Earlene Williams all gathered together at the front of the sanctuary. Pete Stoudemire and Faye and Alan Emerson were also there this morning. We each grabbed a throw to snuggle under and talked softly for a few minutes. I was just about to say that we should have silent prayer time when I heard footsteps coming in the side door. We all looked up and saw Peggy Morton coming in the door. She seemed distraught, and I immediately asked her if everyone was okay.

She looked at me and started crying. And then she said, "I just need lots of prayer so I came here today."

Vivian got up and said "Come sit by me, Peggy. I'll get you a blanket. We were just about to pray silently for a bit, and then we will pray out loud a little later. You can share as much or as little as you want to about what is worrying you this week."

Peggy sat down by Vivian, and we had about ten minutes of silent prayer. We could all hear Peggy crying softly, and so I decided we should move on pretty quickly to our time of sharing concerns.

When I asked about weekly concerns, no one said anything for a few minutes. Vivian asked for prayer for a cousin who was to have hip replacement surgery on Wednesday in Charlotte. Mary asked for continued prayers for Damien as he continued in his job and his present living arrangements. I decided not to say anything about Cliff because I had forgotten to ask Sarah if that was okay. After a couple of moments of silence, Peggy asked if what we said in this group would be kept private. That had not come up before, and I looked at the group and said, "What do you think?"

Earlene said, "If someone asks us to keep something private, then I definitely think we should do that. Is everyone okay with that?"

"Yes, of course," said Mary. "We have all told private things in here, and I don't think any of us have shared information with anyone outside the group."

"I agree," said Vivian. "This group has turned into a safe haven for each of us."

At this point, Peggy just fell apart. I assumed this was in response to Jake's outburst at our congregational meeting, but I waited to hear. Peggy and Jake held such strong beliefs against homosexuality, particularly because they wanted to protect their children from exposure to the tolerance of gay people that they had not been coming to church very often except, of course, for Jake's appearance on Sunday.

Finally Peggy spoke. "Our son Lucas has been dating a lovely girl from Hickory. We have met her a couple of times and found her to be so sweet and well mannered. Jake described her as a 'keeper.' This past weekend Lucas came home on Saturday night, and he told us that he and Lisa were engaged, and that they planned to marry next year. We were thrilled, and told Lucas that we were so happy for them, and that we really wanted to set up a time to meet Lisa's parents."

Peggy paused and took a breath.

"Lucas got a very serious look on his face and said, 'I think I better prepare you for that.'" And then he told us, 'Both of Lisa's parents are men. She has two dads. Her parents are a gay couple. They are wonderful parents and really nice guys. I don't want you to say or do anything to hurt Lisa's feelings about this so that's why I am telling you ahead of time.'"

No one said a word.

Peggy continued, "I thought Jake was going to have a stroke. His face got red, and he just kept saying, 'Damn it all to hell.' I didn't know what to do. Lucas decided to drive back to school that night, and before he left, he told us that he loved us very much, but that he was going to make a life with Lisa, and he hoped we would be able to adjust to that. Adjust to having two men be parents to our son's wife and even to our son? That is just asking too much. Jake told me it would be a cold day in hell before his son married the daughter of two queers, and I know if he talks like that around Lucas, we will lose our son. I'm desperate for help. Please help us."

The silence continued. At least now we better understood Jake's enraged comments on Sunday.

I realized that Peggy and Jake's view of reality had been shattered, and somehow, they had to find a way to reconstruct it.

I said to Peggy, "I am so sorry that you and Jake have had such a shock. I admire Lucas for telling you the truth, but I know that must have been incredibly painful for both of you."

"We are not like other people, Pastor Annie," said Peggy. "We can't just change our beliefs because they are not convenient for us or because we are in the minority. We believe homosexuality is sinful so how can we condone or approve of our son marrying into a family put together by sin? Jake says if he marries that girl, we will disown him. Lucas will not be welcome in our home any more. I can't stand that either. What do I do?"

I just looked at Peggy with great sadness, but I couldn't seem to come up with any words to offer comfort or advice. How could a situation like this or any other sever the parent/child connection? How do people abandon their children? Is that God's will for our families?

Vivian spoke up and said to Peggy, "I hope you and Jake will think long and hard before you lose your son. I understand that this must be a terrible shock for you, but please don't say or do things you can't take back. When I first found out Heather was gay, I wanted to run from her. I didn't want to accept it. It was not my dream for my daughter. Eventually, I realized her life was not meant to be my dream but hers, and I began to try to figure out how I could work though my own feelings and attitudes and accept my daughter as she was. For you, it may get easier because it's not your child you have to learn to accept again, but it will be a relative of his and his wife's."

Earlene spoke up as well and said, "Peggy, Harry feels the same way that you and Jake feel, that homosexuality is a sin. I thought I believed like he did but I have been listening to some of the conversations in the church, and I have been coming to this prayer group for several weeks now, and I just can't bring myself to feel hatred or even dislike for gay people any more. I believe most gay people are born that way, and if that is true, how can we or God condemn them? That just does not make sense to me. I have actually begun to be excited about the family day coming up, and I am eager to see where God leads us. I know it must be different when it's in your family, but please ask for God's guidance before you alienate your son and his fiancé. This is your child you are talking about, Peggy."

"Believe me, I know that, but it is also the core beliefs of my faith that are at risk as well. Don't assume I can just walk away from what I have been taught and have believed my whole life."

Tension was developing in this conversation, and I thought it best that we end our discussion with prayer for resolution, love, faith, and endurance which I did to the best of my ability.

We all thanked Peggy for coming today and for sharing with us, and we told her we would continue praying for her family. We also invited her to come back any Tuesday, but there was a part of me that doubted she would return.

We said goodbye to each other, and then I walked over to my office. The reporter was coming at 10:00, so I focused quickly and worked very hard to finish the sermon for this Sunday. I was able to do that by 9:30, but instead of starting on the family day sermon, I decided to freshen up my make-up, comb my hair, and pray. I was scared about how this interview would go, and I needed to feel God's presence in my spirit and my mind.

At 10:05, the doorbell rang, and after glancing quickly through the window, I opened the door to a young woman and a man with a huge camera. I introduced myself to both of them, and they told me they were Dora White and Donald Peterson. We walked to my office, but then Donald asked if he could walk around the church and take some pictures. I told him he could but asked if he would mind showing me the pictures he made before he left. He said that was routine, and he would be glad to.

Dora and I got comfortable. I offered her a cup of coffee or tea, but she declined. She seemed very professional, and I got the feeling she wanted to get down to business. I asked how I could help her.

"First of all, I've been told by my Southern Baptist colleagues and friends that it is very unusual for a woman to be pastor of a Southern Baptist church. How did you get this position?"

I immediately did not like her tone. I thought about answering "I slept my way to the top," but thought better of it.

I explained that I had been trained for the ministry at a seminary, and that I had waited several years for a call to a church. I was recommended to this church by a board member of the food bank in Charlotte where I was director, and then I gave a sermon, and they voted to hire me.

Then she said, "Tell me about the direction you are leading this church."

I didn't like this question either, but I answered as I always do. "This congregation has voted to go in a certain direction of inclusiveness, and as pastor, I am doing my part in helping them reach their goals. There have been several people who have asked me if I have come in and changed this church and its goals, and I will tell you that is not true. This church was very active and innovative during the Civil Rights Movement, and the members' goals and actions have not changed much since that time. Many of those members from the sixties and seventies are still here, and although they have continued their ministries on a smaller scale while raising their children, they now think it is time to expand the church's involvement with groups such as the LGBT community, undocumented residents, non-English speakers, biracial couples, single parents and whoever else feels as if the church has not welcomed them into their building in the past. That really is all we are trying to do, and we do believe, based on His life and His teachings, that this is what Jesus Christ would do if He had a physical presence here on earth today."

"Wow, although I have heard similar comments from some pastors in Charlotte, I have not heard these thoughts from rural Southern Baptist churches. How did you come to these ideas yourself if you grew up in a Southern Baptist church?"

"I haven't thought about that before, but I believe I took the teachings of Jesus and of my church and applied it to everyone. When I was growing up, we were always praising missionaries who went overseas or into our inner cities, and it just occurred to me that there were lots of other groups here at home that we were not ministering to. I asked myself why and realized that it was due to our prejudices and fears, particularly of our churches being invaded by people who were not like us. For many people, churches are our primary social group, and though we are willing to share the gospel with those far away who are different from us, we seem to be afraid to invite the black couple down the street or the gay couple across town to come and worship with us because it will change our group. All of us are afraid of that, but this church is brave enough to step out and take some risks."

"Where did you grow up?"

I looked at her and said "What?"

This time she laughed and said, "People in Charlotte are going to wonder where you grew up and assume you are a Yankee. Is that true?"

I grinned back at her and said, "Not hardly. I grew up in a small town in Mississippi."

"I love it." she said. "Now give me the scoop about this day you are planning so I can give you some free coverage."

"I'll be glad to."

And I did.

Now all I had to do was worry about how she would write the information I had shared with her. After about twenty minutes, Donald came back into my office and asked how we were doing. Dora told him we were finished, so I guess we were. He had taken some beautiful shots both inside and outside the church, and I complimented him on his work. He thanked me graciously and said he also needed a picture of me in the church. We went inside the sanctuary, and he had me stand beside the table in front of the pulpit and then at the pulpit as if I were preaching. He and Dora thanked me for my time and told me the article should be in Saturday's Times. I thanked them for coming out to the church and told them that they would both be welcome to worship with us any time.

Chapter 50

I worked on my sermon for the family day most of the afternoon. About four I went home and took a short nap. For dinner I ate a bowl of cereal, and then I headed back to the church for the deacon's meeting.

We gathered for our meeting at 6:30, and it was great to hear what everyone had been doing. Sometimes when you have volunteers doing most of the work for a project, things are left undone, but not with this group, especially since our group was smaller due to Thomas' passing and Cliff's illness.

We began with a prayer for continued courage and guidance. Charlotte and Fred were so excited about what they had been doing that they asked to speak first.

Charlotte spoke first. "We have fifteen families who have agreed to make at least a couple of dishes for lunch. That will truly be pot luck, but it usually works out okay. Additional food is to be brought in by professionals just in case we need it. That is costing quite a bit, but Jesse and Lorraine have agreed to pay for the catered food."

"And beyond that, Jesse and Lorraine have also suggested we pay the caterers to serve lunch so that all of the church members can be talking with our guests and not worrying about serving food or drinks," said Fred.

Then Charlotte spoke again and said, "Another wonderful thing has happened. Fred has found two women who work in a local day care who will come in and be in charge of the nursery for a minimal fee. One of them, Angie, has a gay brother, and the other is a Hispanic woman named Elena who shared that she had several cousins who were undocumented. Fred had also told the women that their family members would be welcome to worship with us any time, but especially on the day of our event. These women wanted to be of service for this event. If there are more children than we expected who need child care, Erin and Danny O'Reilly have agreed to help as well."

Charlotte took a big breath. Both she and Fred were as excited as two seven-year-olds on Christmas morning.

Fred had talked with Mr. Owens about music for worship, and apparently, William had a great plan for that. Fred explained, "William is going to play his guitar and sing 'His Eye Is on the Sparrow' for the special music. And he has picked out some of the most familiar hymns known to man for the congregation to sing."

"William has a solo voice?" I asked.

"Oh my, have you not heard him sing by himself?" asked Charlotte. "He has a beautiful voice, and he plays the guitar almost as well as he does the organ. It will be wonderful."

Fred told us that Edna was going to greet everyone at the beginning of the service and talk about our church and this event. Then we would worship just like always.

"That all sounds wonderful," said Edna to Charlotte and Fred. "You guys have done a great job. Thank you!"

Alan Emerson was next to report and he said, "I have hired two sheriff's deputies to be at the church the morning of the event from about 8:00 until 2:00 just in case outsiders decided to harass churchgoers. We know people might protest out on the road, but we don't want them on our property. Hopefully, all the deputies will really have to do is help with parking, but I'm afraid we have to be ready for the worst."

At that, we all got very quiet and just sat very still for about thirty seconds.

But Charlotte could not be contained, and she then explained, "I have one more thing to say, and then I will hush. All of the people who volunteered to be greeters for our visitors will be attending the panel discussion next Monday night. They want to be as prepared as possible for their job."

"Great," said Edna, and Charlotte grinned from ear to ear.

Edward and Edna had taken all of the flyers we had printed and distributed them throughout the community and into the eastern side of Charlotte as well.

Then I spoke up and said, "I had an interview this morning with a reporter from the Charlotte Times, and it went very well. Tomorrow morning I am going to be interviewed on the Cindy Perkins show."

"Faye and I watch that show as often as we can. Cindy seems like a really nice person, and she does a good job with the interviews. We'll be sure to watch."

"Me, too," said Edward and Fred at the same time.

I smiled and thought, *Oh goody.*

Then I said, "The panel discussion is pretty much all set up, even though I am still looking for a representative of an undocumented family or possibly a homeless family. I feel as if the people on the panel will be very helpful to us as a church, and I want to be very careful about who else we might invite to participate. Each of the panel members is going to say a few words, and then they will take as many questions as we have time for. There is one other thing I need to share with you, and that is Sarah has asked for our prayers because Cliff is having some health problems. Because of that, we might have to figure out some other follow up plan for our visitors."

No one seemed surprised about Cliff so I assumed word had spread about his issues, and then Fred spoke up and said, "We will be sure to get all the guests to complete a visitor's card, and then we can decide later how to follow up with them."

We all sat there quietly for a minute and looked at each other.

Edna said, "This is really going to happen, isn't it?"

"Yes, I'm afraid so," Charlotte said, and we all laughed.

I had to speak to this group. I told them, "Working with each of you has been a pleasure for me. I don't think I have ever worked with a group that believed so strongly in what they were planning, and it shows. Whatever happens on this family day, each of you can be very proud of what we have put together. Edward, you started this and you got us going on it quickly. Thank you for that. And thank each of you for all your hard work."

"Amen to that," said Edna. "Now let's close this meeting with a prayer and get home."

After Edna's closing prayer, everyone headed out, and I just sat for a few minutes. I was in a panic. Part of me thought we would not have any response to our event, while another part of me was afraid we might have such a large turnout that we couldn't handle everyone. The not knowing was driving me crazy, and I really needed to find some peace about it. Again, I turned to prayer.

While I was sitting there, Edna stuck her head back into my office and said to me, "Have you eaten lately?"

"I had crackers for supper last night and a bowl of cereal just a little while ago. I am fine."

"You go home and don't leave there. I will be bringing you some dinner."

I tried to tell Edna that was unnecessary, but she gave me a look that said, "Don't speak" and I didn't. I packed up what I needed to take home to review for the talk show tomorrow, locked the church, and headed home.

In about twenty minutes my doorbell rang, and I pulled open my door to let Edna in. It wasn't Edna standing there. It was John.

I looked at him and said, "How did you get stuck with this duty?"

"I didn't get stuck. I volunteered," he said. "My mom was pretty tired, and I needed to get out of the house for a little while."

"Please come in. We can go into the kitchen. Would you like something to drink?"

"I don't suppose you have a beer, do you?"

"Sam Adams ok?"

"Only my favorite. You sit down and eat your dinner. I'll get the beer. You really told my mom you had cereal for dinner and crackers last night. That horrified her, and thank goodness, we had lots of leftovers from dinner tonight."

I took the container and opened it. The smell was incredible. It was a huge serving of chicken pot pie. The chicken and the vegetables were in a creamy white sauce, and the crust was a golden brown. There was also a container of salad with an oil and vinegar dressing. I couldn't help myself. I was so excited to have this food that I dug right in.

John watched me for a minute, and when I looked up I said, "I'm sorry. I haven't even thanked you for bringing this to me. I was so hungry I couldn't wait."

"I noticed. Even I know you need to eat to keep up your energy. I assume there is a lot going on this week and next to get ready for the big family day event."

"Oh, my gosh, it's just overwhelming. Tomorrow I am going to be on a Charlotte talk show, and I am a nervous wreck about that. I have been interviewed by a news reporter before, but not for fifteen minutes and not about something like this. I really don't want to say anything to alienate other Baptists and Christians, but I want to express what we are doing and why we are doing it."

"Annie, you are not being very realistic. What you guys are doing is going to make some people furious, and they are going to rant against you. You seem to think if you explain it carefully enough, everyone will understand what you are doing and support it. That is not going to happen."

I put my fork down and just looked at him. He was right, but I didn't want to believe him.

"It will be okay. Some people will support you, and others will not. That's just how it is with controversial issues."

"John, I am not very brave. I'm not like your mother or some of the other people in this church that supported civil rights so many years ago. I'm afraid of causing trouble and controversy."

"Do you believe in what the church is doing?"

"Of course I do."

"Then take a deep breath and get ready for a bumpy ride. You have a lot of support around you, and when people are yelling at you on that Sunday or telling you that you are going to hell for what you are doing, you just keep believing. Annie, let me know if it gets rough. You are in a leadership position, and I know you don't want to look weak, so if it gets bad, call me and as the song says, 'I'll come runnin.'"

"Thank you, John. I may take you up on that."

I kept eating, and John just sat quietly and watched me eat. The silence between us was very comfortable.

"Annie," he said, and then hesitated. "I like you, and that scares me to death."

I looked up at him and said, "Why does it scare you, John?"

He took a deep breath and eventually said as his eyes filled up with tears, "I'm afraid if I like talking to another woman, then I am headed toward losing my memories of Lucinda, and I can't bear that."

I wasn't sure what to say to him, but finally I said, "It must be so frightening to feel like you really might lose some of those memories and might allow someone new to be in your thoughts."

"It is. Now don't get me wrong. I know she's gone and is not coming back, but holding onto my memories and not letting anyone get in the way of them has been very comforting to me. That doesn't mean that I don't want to find someone else to love one of these days, but actually allowing that to become a reality takes more courage than I have right now. That's why it scares me that I like you."

I finished eating my dinner and sat there for a moment. Then I said to John, "I like you, too, and it doesn't scare me to death, but it makes me nervous because you never know what's going to happen when you like someone. There's the pull to find out how much you might like the person and the opposite pull to avoid any emotional attachment that could lead to pain. To be honest, I don't have a lot of energy for that right now either, but I'll always take a new friend. Perhaps we could just leave it at that for now."

John nodded his head and said, "That I think I could handle. I like the idea of being friends."

"Good. That's settled for now."

"Okay. I think I better head home so you can get some rest, and I can beat myself up for crying in front of my new friend."

"I don't think beating yourself up is necessary. Are you okay to drive?"

"After just one beer? I think so."

"One can never be too careful. Let me fix you a cup of coffee for you to take with you. I'll feel better."

"That's fine. I'll drink it."

He gathered the dishes that he needed to take back home while I fixed the coffee. I handed him a styrofoam cup full of hot steaming coffee, and then he leaned over and kissed me on the cheek.

"Thanks for the talk," he said. "Goodnight."

"Thanks for dinner," I said.

I closed the door and locked it. Then I headed for bed. I truly did not have the strength to even think about what all just happened.

Chapter 51

When my alarm went off the next morning, I allowed myself just a moment to think. *Two really great guys seem to be interested in me right now. Wow. That's a first. But just like that famous saying, "I'll think about that tomorrow." There is just no time or energy to deal with it right now.*

Then I got out of bed and dressed in the same outfit I wore for my trial sermon. In that dress, I felt professional and confident, and I needed that for the television show this morning.

I arrived at the television studio about fifteen minutes before 10:00, and to be honest, I had a smile on my face. I felt great, and I felt prepared for this interview. An assistant named Rylee came and took me to a room where I could freshen up and wait for the right time for the interview. A comfortable couch, and water and snacks were available as well as several current magazines spread out on the coffee table. I felt like a celebrity.

Rylee said another woman named Sofea would come by to see if I wanted any help with my hair or make-up, and I thanked her for that. Then I sat down and went over my notes.

About 10:05, Sofea came by and asked if I would like a touch up, and I said, "Sure." She applied a little powder which she said would help keep my face from being shiny in the lights and a new color of lipstick for me.

Then she said, "Rylee will be coming back to get you in about five minutes."

I think I kind of went into a zone and didn't actually think about being interviewed on television. Rylee came back in, took me to the edge of the set, and then told me when it was time to walk toward the host.

Cindy Perkins and I shook hands and she directed me to have a seat across from her. She started quickly by asking, "Tell us about the Family Appreciation Day event that your church is planning for December."

I gave her the now-familiar details, and she said, "What your church is doing sounds very admirable, but to be honest, isn't it a little different from how most churches honor families?"

"I guess I don't really know how most churches honor families, but our congregation feels that the church in a general sense has neglected many people in our communities because they are not just like their members. It may be other churches don't feel as called as we do to open our doors to everyone and welcome them in. I'm not saying that is good or bad, but it is just how it is."

Cindy was looking at me rather strangely, almost apologetically, and I began to have a bad feeling about what was coming up.

"Rev. Adams, in order to hear both sides of this issue, we have invited Rev. Franklin Burns, pastor of the Kings Glory Baptist Church to come in and express his views on inviting the gay community into our churches. Rev. Burns, please come in and have a seat with us."

I looked at Cindy with an obviously upset expression, and she mouthed the word "Sorry" to me.

Rev. Burns came in and shook my hand and Cindy's hand. He had brought his Bible with him, and it was a worn and obviously used book about the size of Webster's dictionary.

Cindy turned to Rev. Burns and said, "Rev. Adams and her church are having a big event called Family Appreciation Day where they are going to honor all types of families from gay couples to biracial couples and undocumented families. What do you think about this program?"

"This goes against the teachings of the Baptist Church, and I'm afraid Covenant Baptist might be seen as a radical group defying the teachings of the Bible," said Rev. Burns.

My smile went away.

"Rev. Burns," I said, "I like your choice of the word radical, because certainly any true follower of Jesus Christ would have to live a radical lifestyle. We are not trying to defy anyone or any church's teachings. We are just doing what we feel led by God to do."

"I don't believe God is leading you to honor this abominable lifestyle, and instead of welcoming them into your church, you need to be condemning them to hell if they don't change their ways. Furthermore, in the Old Testament, let me read scripture to you that explains…"

"Excuse me, Rev. Burns. I came on this show to share with the community what we are doing at Covenant and not to debate the merits of our programs. I know you must be a godly man, but you seem to be somewhat judgmental, and I am not interested in having a debate with you. This is not a healthy conversation, and I am terminating it. I was told by Miss Perkins that I would not be ambushed during this interview, and I am holding her to her word. Thank you, Miss Perkins for giving me a chance to talk about our event."

Before I walked off the set, I turned directly to the camera and said, "Anyone who wants to come and be a part of a radical group of followers of Jesus Christ is welcome to join us for worship at 11:00 any Sunday. On December 8th we will be honoring all types of family units. All are welcome."

Then I turned and walked off the set. Cindy Perkins said, "Rev. Adams, please don't walk away in the middle of our interview," but I just kept walking. Just as I got to the edge of the set, I heard her say, "Go to commercial right now."

When I got to my car, I was shaking all over. I couldn't believe I had walked out on the interview, but I was not going to listen to this crap. What Rev. Burns was saying was hurtful to many people and not representative of our church. He had his own agenda and was not really interested in what we were doing.

My cell phone started ringing, and I was afraid to see who it was. Before I pulled out of the parking lot, I looked at it, and it was John. I was grateful he was calling but I couldn't talk with anyone right now. I turned my phone to silent and started the long drive home.

All I could think of were all the people counting on me to get out the word about this family day, and how I had screwed everything up. I didn't want to go back to the church. I wanted to just keep driving till I was out of the station's viewing area where nobody would know what had happened. I had told John last night that I wasn't very brave, and I meant it. I did not want to face my church members. I really do hate disappointing people. I felt sick to my stomach. Maybe I could just go to the church and hide. Maybe nobody watched the show, and no one will know what happened. Those thoughts made me feel better. This show is on during the middle of the day when people are busy. They are not sitting in front of the television. Obviously, John was watching, but that's just because I told him about it last night. Maybe there really was hope that no one saw the show.

For the rest of the forty-five minute drive to the church, I thought about what I could say to excuse my actions, but I was having a hard time coming up with anything. I should have stayed and talked calmly with Cindy Perkins and Rev. Burns and not let them get to me. I just couldn't stand what he was saying when all we were supposed to talk about was the program we were planning, not their beliefs.

When I got to the church, I couldn't believe what I saw. Oh, no. Someone must have died. Ten or twelve cars were parked in the lot. I parked my car up close to the church, and when I got out of the car, someone started applauding. More people got out of their cars, and the applause got louder. As I began to realize that this was for me, I was in shock. I had felt like I failed this church, and they were telling me that was not true. They actually seemed proud of me, and in turn, I could not have been prouder of a group of people who continued to stand up for what they believed was right and just and fair. Their courage would be what kept me going and what would make this family day a very special event. I started getting hugs from everyone, and lots of comments about how I did the right thing by leaving.

When Edna hugged me, she said "You probably got more publicity for this event by walking out than you ever would have by staying and having a boring conversation. Good job!"

Somebody opened the church and then someone else made coffee, and suddenly we were having our own type of revival. People were mad and excited and energized, and everyone was talking about how glad they were we were having this event, and they were coming up with ideas for the next big event we would plan.

I finally realized everything was going to be alright, and maybe this event was going to be a really good thing for this church.

This was the Wednesday before Thanksgiving, and after everyone left the church, I went home, packed a bag and headed for my parents' house in Columbia. Traffic was horrible, but I didn't care. I loved my family, and I really was excited about spending this special time with them.

And especially, I couldn't wait to spend some time in a place where I was not in charge and where the only controversial topics included whether or not to put marshmallows or pecans on the sweet potato casserole or whether to use whole cranberries or the jellied cranberry sauce.

Chapter 52

Saturday morning after brunch with the family, I packed up and headed back to my real world.

The time away had relaxed me, but as I got closer to home, I begin to feel the tension. I prayed for peace and for courage.

What John had said to me about people being upset and angry about our stand on families made a lot of sense to me, and as much as I did not like that, I wanted to be able to face that hostility with grace. I had a slight natural tendency to mouth off to people who were unreasonable or judgmental, but I knew I had to overcome this reaction. I needed to rise above the fray and be firm but not reactive. I wanted to be one of those people who could say "God bless you" to someone who was screaming at me that I was going to hell or that I was a terrible sinner.

I knew it would not be easy, but for the message of our church to be heard, I really believed that was what all of us needed to do.

About 9:00 on Sunday morning, I was walking over to the church office when I noticed six or eight people out on the road near the driveway leading to the church. They were gathered there with signs which I could not read from where I was, but I knew they were going to be negative.

I stopped in my tracks and tried to figure out what to do. Should I walk out and greet them? Should I call the sheriff's office to prevent any possible trouble? Should I ignore them?

As I thought about my options, I realized that they were standing on public property, and that as long as they did not interfere with members coming to worship the best thing to do was ignore them. They were the ones seeking attention, not our congregation.

I made a point of standing outside to greet members. People started arriving about 9:45, and of course, all they could talk about was the crowd near the driveway entrance. Apparently, the signs said the usual stuff. "Homosexuals are going to hell," and "God hates queers," and "If you love fags YOU are going to Hell, too."

The venom in these words was difficult to accept as coming from Christians, but that was definitely the source. A couple of the demonstrators had signs that said, "Come worship with us at the Open Arms Baptist Church."

The irony of that name was not lost on me, but again our goal was not to argue with these demonstrators, but just to practice our faith as we believed.

Sunday school and worship went on as planned, and after a little time in the sanctuary, members seemed to relax and focus on worshipping God. I thought it was good practice for us to be able to go on with our service even with the distractions of the demonstrators.

We reminded the congregation that the panel discussion that would help us prepare for next Sunday was to be held Monday night, and we encouraged everyone to come. There was excitement in the air again, but it was muted just a little as people began to realize that there was indeed going to be a price to pay for our efforts.

Jesse, Pete, and Danny walked out to the road as worshippers began to leave for home. They stood by to make sure there was no trouble from the demonstrators. Other than demonstrators repeatedly yelling "You are all going to hell," there were no other problems.

This was difficult. Next Sunday was going to be even worse, and I couldn't help but wonder if what we were doing was worth it. I had been so excited about our event, but now I felt immobilized and couldn't seem to think about what else needed to be done. I was standing on the front steps of the church when Jesse came back from the road. He looked at me and said, "Pretty rough, huh?"

I nodded my head and said, "Yeah."

He hesitated a moment and said, "I can't tell you how many times people made hateful remarks to me and Lorraine, or perhaps they just looked at us with disgust. It happened a lot when we first got married, and then as local people got to know both of us, and times began to change, it seldom happened around here. When we went on vacation or went into Charlotte, there were still the ugly looks and sometimes the snide comments. You never get used to it, but you learn to value the friends and acquaintances that love and accept you and your relationship, and you try very hard to not let the ugly looks and the hateful words destroy the special love that you have. We have been able to do this because what we have matters. What we are doing as a church matters, and we have to find a way to continue on this path even if the words hurt us and those we are trying to include. Believe me, as much as I would like to protect our guests from the hatefulness next Sunday, it won't be the first time they have heard it."

"Thank you, Jesse, I needed to hear that. The reality of hate-filled speech is not as easy to accept as I thought it would be, and your words have helped me so much. I am so sorry that you and Lorraine have heard these words simply because you fell in love and got married. Maybe what we're doing will make a difference someday."

"I believe it will, Annie, and that's why we're doing it. I gotta go now, but I will see you tomorrow night."

I was focused again, and there was one other person that I wanted to invite to be on our panel. One of the women who were going to help serve in the nursery, Elena, had told Fred that she had some undocumented cousins. Expecting undocumented residents to come participate in a public forum was unrealistic because of the legal ramifications, but perhaps Elena could come and be a spokesperson for her cousins. I called Fred and got Elena's number, and then I left her a message telling her what I wanted her to do. Hopefully, she would call me back.

I went home and felt extremely restless and anxious. It was as if there was nothing left to do but wait for the event. I knew that was not true, but I just couldn't decide what I should be doing today.

My phone rang, and it was Greg.

"Is Sunday afternoon a good date time? I am bored and restless and need to go to a movie. Are you interested in going with me?"

I hesitated for just a moment and then said, "I think that might be just what I need. How 'bout I meet you at the theater? We are talking about the one on 74 just outside of Monroe, right?"

"Yes, I guess that might work. I am interested in seeing anything funny. Is that okay?"

"That sounds great. I just need to escape all my crazy thoughts for a little while. What time should we meet?"

"There are a couple of options both starting a little after 5:00. Why don't we meet at 5:00? Then we can have dinner afterwards."

"That sounds wonderful. I will see you a little before 5 in front of the theater."

The movie was entertaining, and afterwards we went to a local Italian restaurant for dinner. We laughed about the movie and then caught up on our week's events. When he heard about the demonstrators out in front of the church, he said, "Do you want me to come next Sunday or send a couple of guys by to evaluate the situation?"

"I really don't know. I don't want to make a bigger deal of it than it's already going to be. We have two off-duty policemen hired to keep an eye on things, and surely that will be enough. Would they call for help if they needed it?"

"Yeah, I think so. Even if they are working off duty, if a crowd gets out of control, they can certainly ask for assistance. You can call me Sunday morning if you need anything, and I will come."

"Thanks, Greg. That does make me feel better."

It was pretty cold after dinner, so our goodbyes were short. It did involve another very pleasant kiss that lasted a little longer than five seconds, but as nice as it was, I was glad I was taking myself home. I really didn't have room in my life right now for anything more complicated.

By the time I got home, I was tired enough and relaxed so that I knew I could sleep. I did check my messages on my phone, and Elena had called me and said she would be happy to come and talk about her cousins, what they were like and what they wanted for their lives. I returned her call and confirmed time and location. I told her I did not know how it would go or how many people would be there, but that we would give it our best shot. She agreed that it was worth the effort.

Chapter 53

I woke up Monday morning with a burning anxiety in my stomach, so I decided a run would be a good thing. It did feel great and helped keep my mind off the panel that evening. I had to concentrate on breathing, and that became my highest priority.

Twenty-two phone messages were waiting for me when I arrived at the church after my run. Several were questions about the panel discussion tonight ranging from what time it started to whether or not they should bring a dessert. Faye Emerson was handling the food so I called her.

"I think we have plenty, Annie, but maybe I'll call them and let them bring something just to help them feel more a part of things," Faye said. "People can take leftovers home if they have to. By the way, as you suggested, I did ask Mary LeBlanc to make the coffee for tonight, and she was pretty excited about it. Hopefully, she will feel more a part of us."

I returned the calls asking about time and location of tonight's program. All of the ones I called were church members or families of the panel participants so I felt pretty safe about that. We had not publicized this event except in the church.

Five hate-filled messages told me that I was going to hell for what the church was doing, and that God would punish us for our actions. I hated that it was happening, but I felt tougher than I had felt a few weeks ago, and those actions made me more determined than ever to celebrate Christian diversity.

I called Sarah to check on Cliff, and she sounded pretty upbeat. "Annie, I can see real changes in Cliff. For one thing, he has gotten a little angry about what happened to him, and instead of taking in all the blame himself, he is beginning to recognize that he did nothing wrong, and that the 'fault' if we want to call it that, lies with Eddie Jamison's uncle Sam. I think he needs to be angry for a while, and then I hope he can move toward forgiveness. That is what will be best for Cliff."

"Very well said, Sarah. I think you are probably right."

It was lunchtime, and so I ran home and made a turkey and cheese sandwich. I knew I was going to need both strength and courage for my afternoon's plans.

I was going to drop in on the three church families who had voted not to go forward with the family day event. I was not sure that was the right thing to do, but I just could not leave them hanging outside the work of the church. I wanted them to know they were still welcome to worship with us, and if they did not, it would be because they chose not to, not because we did not want them.

First I stopped by Harry and Earlene Williams where I was welcomed warmly. They asked me to come in and sit down, no questions asked, and I got right to the point of my visit.

"Harry I know you are not in support of what the church is doing next weekend, and I just want you to know that I respect your right to have your own opinion and to stand by it. But I also want you to know that you are welcome to continue worshipping with us whenever you might want and whenever you feel comfortable. My hope is even though you may not support this particular event that you will still feel a part of Covenant Baptist Church. We still see you as a valued member of our congregation, and we always will."

Neither Harry nor Earlene responded to my comments, and we sat there in an uncomfortable silence.

Then Harry said, "Pastor Annie, Earlene and I have talked about this situation more than we've ever talked about anything in our lives, and we don't really agree on it. However, our relationship is the most important thing we have, and our church is right up near the top in importance, too. Because of that, we will continue to talk and to pray about the issues the church is facing. I can't make you any promises, but some of the things you and other church members have said to us make a lot of sense to me. But thinking about all these things, praying about them, and letting them work through our minds is going to take some time, and I don't think I feel sure about our future with Covenant. However, we thank you for letting us know the door is still open to us, and for right now, Covenant is still our church."

"That is all anyone could ask, and I thank you for your honesty. Please let me know if there is anything I can help you with on this journey."

Earlene said, "We will, Annie, and we really do appreciate your stopping by and talking with us."

"Harry, would you say a prayer for us?"

"I will, Annie. "Almighty God, I praise Your name and thank You for all Your love and the blessings that You have given to us. I don't presume to understand how or if we are to change what we have been taught is wrong, but I do know that Your love is bigger than any issue we humans have to try to understand. I ask for guidance and leadership in all parts of our lives. Bless Covenant as they go through this difficult time, and help Annie and the church members to seek Your will. In Your holy name I pray, Amen."

"Thank you so much, Harry. Take care of yourselves and again, let me know if I can help in any way."

I walked to my car and felt surprisingly happy about this conversation. You can't ask much more from church members than their willingness to study and pray about difficult issues, and whatever conclusion Harry and Earlene reached, they would have done that.

I did not feel nearly as good about my next visit. It was to be with Jake and Peggy Morton, and after everything that had happen with both of them, I had no idea how I would be received. I knocked on their front door and waited to see if they would answer. Their car was visible in their driveway, so I knew they were at home, but I still wasn't sure they would talk with me.

After a couple of minutes, the front door opened slowly, and Peggy looked at me through the screen door.

I smiled at her and said, "Peggy, I'm sorry for this drop-in visit, but I wondered if I might talk with you and Jake for just a few minutes."

"You need to go, Annie. Lucas talked with both of us this morning about his future in-laws, and Jake is livid. He is thinking about disowning Lucas if he marries Lisa, and this is not a good time for him to talk with you."

"I'm sorry, Peggy, I will go. Please know that I will be available to help in any way I can, and I will continue to pray for your family."

"Thank you, Annie. We need all the prayers we can get."

I walked back to my car, and I just sat there for a minute. How can this one issue, this issue of who someone loves, divide spouses and parents and their children, as well as church congregations so severely that some are willing to sever both family and church ties? I wonder if anyone has studied this issue in our society to determine where its power to destroy comes from.

I felt so depressed about the Morton family that I wasn't sure that I wanted to see Wayne and Anita Fleming, but I was determined to see each of the families that had voted no to the family event. I had never been to the Fleming home, but with the help of my GPS, I found it and saw two cars in their driveway, so they seemed to be home.

The Flemings lived in a really nice doublewide with trees and shrubs and flower gardens all around it. No flowers were blooming, but it was a well-kept yard. I was a little nervous about my unannounced visit, but I walked right up to the door and knocked.

Wayne answered the door and said, "Well Pastor Annie, this is a surprise. Come on it. I'll get Anita."

"Wait just a second, Wayne. I apologize for not calling you first to see if a visit was okay, but I was out doing some visiting, and I thought I might stop in to see you. Please don't bother Anita if this is a bad time."

"No, not at all. She'll be tickled pink to see you. Come on it and sit down while I get her."

I walked into the meticulous living room and kept standing, waiting to be sure this was a good time. Anita walked in with a big smile on her face and said, "Welcome, Pastor Annie. I'm sorry the place is such a mess but I am so glad you stopped by. Have a seat. Can I get you something to drink? I made some fresh sweet tea for lunch, and there is plenty left."

Feeling a little more comfortable, I said, "A glass of tea sounds wonderful, Anita. Thank you."

I sat on the sofa, an early American plaid, and tried to relax. Anita brought me the tea and a plate of homemade chocolate cookies along with it. The tea was delicious, and I could not resist the cookies. They were even better than the tea.

Wayne came back in the living room. His hair was wet and was freshly combed, and he took a seat in a recliner across from the couch.

I thanked them both first for the tea and cookies and then for their hospitality.

"I don't usually drop in on church members without calling first, but I am spending this afternoon trying to talk with the members who voted no on the family event that is coming up this Sunday. I just wanted to make sure that you guys know that even if we all don't agree on this issue, we can still worship God together. We want you to know that Covenant values your membership and your participation."

"Why, thank you, Annie for saying that. We never had any intention of leaving Covenant. We love our church and you as our pastor."

"Thank you very much. I guess the vote to have the event did not upset you then."

"Not at all. We don't have anything against gay people or illegals or ex-cons or anybody who is different from us. We can worship with anyone."

"May I ask why you voted against the event then?"

"We just don't think the church should be messing in all that business. It just gets everybody stirred up and mad at each other. The church should be preaching the gospel and winning souls to Christ and should just leave these other issues to somebody else," said Anita.

"Who do you think should take stands on these issues?"

Wayne said, "Anybody who wants to, I reckon, and we do believe the government should make sure everybody gets equal rights. Other than that, we think things will usually work out for the best if you just let people work it out themselves."

I knew I should keep my mouth shut, but I couldn't. "So you think African-Americans would have made gains toward equal rights without any input from churches or Christians back in the sixties?"

"Sure," said Anita. "It might have taken a little longer but eventually things would have worked out. Why do you think the church should be involved in all this, Annie? Don't you think they have enough to do just preaching the gospel?"

"I think a big part of the gospel of Jesus Christ is seeking justice for all of his children. A big part of his daily ministry was to reach out to those around him who were rejected by society or considered outcasts. I guess that's where I get my ideas about what the gospel includes. But I want you to know that just like we want to make sure everyone is welcome at Covenant, we also want everyone to know that we don't have to believe everything just alike. Even if we see the gospel a little bit differently, we can still serve God and worship together."

"We feel the same way, Annie. Just because we didn't vote to have this event doesn't mean we won't be at church on Sunday. That's our church, and that is where we worship God no matter who else is there."

"I am so happy to hear that, Wayne and Anita. I was worried that you might be upset with the church."

"Not at all, Annie."

"Great. I have enjoyed talking with you so much, but I have got to get back to the church. Will I see you guys tonight?"

"Definitely. We have dessert duty tonight."

I had a short prayer with them and feeling greatly relieved, I headed back to the church. I felt hopeful that at least for now, Covenant would stay intact and we would work together for God's purposes and not our own.

Chapter 54

I went into the office to gather my thoughts. I really did not have any responsibility for tonight's program except for picking up Damien and taking him back to the halfway house, but I felt as if I had the weight of the world on my shoulders. I knew what we were doing was important, but part of me wanted to run and hide from all the people who were going to be angry about our stand and our actions.

In most situations, the things that we do and say in church are pre-approved by me or one of the church leaders, but tonight, the panel was going to share their own stories in their own words, and not knowing what was going to be said was making me a little crazy.

I arrived at the halfway house to pick up Damien at 5:35. I rang the bell on a desk at the entrance, and an older gentleman appeared from a back room. "You must be here for Damien."

"I sure am."

"He's on his way from the kitchen. He was running a couple of minutes late because he had to shower after work and grab something to eat. I just want you to know that he is a fine young man. I know he's made some mistakes, but from what I have seen of him, he is someone who has learned his lesson and is now trying to make something of himself. So treat him well."

"I certainly will. His mother is a member of our church, and she is a lovely person."

"She's great, isn't she?" said a deep male voice from the doorway behind the desk. I looked up and saw a lean and muscled young man who had the darkest eyes I had ever seen. He was smiling at me, and although I was several years older than him, I was wowed. He was really handsome in a youthful and carefree way. He looked like a kid without a care in the world. He reached out his hand to me and said, "Pastor Annie, I presume? I am Damien LeBlanc."

"Hello, Damien. I am so happy to meet you. I have heard very good things about you from your mom."

"You have to remember that she's a little prejudiced when it comes to me, but I am trying my best to live up to her expectations."

He signed out in a book on the desk.

"Make us proud, Damien."

On the way to the church, I asked Damien if he had any questions about what to say to our group tonight, and he said, "No, I'm on top of it."

I could only hope that was true.

By the time we arrived at the church, the crowd was gathering, and I was already counting about forty people in the audience.

People who had shown up a little early were having coffee and one of the many desserts that had been provided for tonight, but I knew Edna was always one to start on time, so I encouraged church members to find their seats.

Five or six more people had come in since I had estimated the crowd numbers so we were very close to fifty. I knew what an incredible turnout that was for a Monday night.

Edna began with prayer, and then she introduced the panel members and explained briefly why we were having this panel discussion and how it would work.

"We are going to hear the stories of our panel members, and then we will take a short break to try to finish off the dessert and coffee, and then the panel has agreed to answer any questions you might have. We will start with Jesse and Lorraine Akin. I believe Lorraine is going to speak for them. Then we will move on down the panel after they finish, and each panel member will introduce themselves and tell their story."

Lorraine stood up and picked up the microphone, and I could tell she was in a very comfortable position, on stage in front of a crowd.

Lorraine introduced herself and Jesse, and then told essentially the same story I had heard the first time we met, ending with her own recollection of how they finally got together after she left pharmacy school.

"During our second year, I got a career opportunity that I couldn't pass up, and so I left school in the middle of the year, much to the horror of my parents, needless to say, but more importantly, much to the dismay of Jesse. He put on a brave front telling me that I should not pass up this opportunity. In fact, he put on such a good front that I was little hurt that my leaving was not bothering him at all. I cared for Jesse and had grown to depend upon his friendship. The career opportunity I had gotten was a small part in a couple of TV shows with primarily black casts. I was having an exciting and busy time, but I missed talking with Jesse, and I could not figure out why he didn't call me. On a break, I went to Chapel Hill instead of home, and when we saw each other, I ran into his arms, and he held me tight, and then he finally kissed me. We realized we were in love, and it worked out that we were able to marry before his third year of school, and we lived off of my earnings from the movies and a part-time job I had as a pharmacy tech.

She took a deep breath, and I could tell she was getting to the harder part of their story.

"None of our parents attended our wedding as they disapproved of the relationship," Lorraine continued. "A local pastor married us, and two friends from school agreed to be our witnesses. For the first five years, it was us against the world, and sometimes it was tough. Many people did a double take when they saw us together out in public. Most people did not say anything, but their reactions were clear in their faces and their body language. Some people said things, and they were hateful and frightening, and we had to learn to accept what we could not change and to embrace those people who accepted us as a couple. When we moved to Bakerstown, our relationship shocked a lot of people, but eventually because we lived there and people got to know us, we felt more accepted. It was only when we traveled together or went into Charlotte that some people felt it was their right to let us know they disapproved of our relationship. The years have been good to us, and attitudes about mixed-race couples have changed a lot, particularly among young people. Truly the only thing missing for us is anonymity, the ability to go out into the world and nobody notice. That would make us happy. Our love has grown deeper and stronger, and we know we can face adversity and survive, but we are happy for other couples in a relationship such as ours that Covenant is reaching out to them and saying, 'If you don't feel welcome in other churches, you will be here,' and I believe that to be true. Thank you for that."

Lorraine sat down to applause, and then the next panel member, Elizabeth Smith stood up to speak.

"I don't have a long speech to make tonight, but I just want to introduce myself to you. I am Elizabeth Smith, a single, never married mother of two children, ages one and three. I am a junior at UNCC majoring in education, and when I graduate, I hope to get a teaching position. Because I have two children and am not married, I have hesitated to go to church anywhere even though I was raised in the church, and I want my children to grow up in church. I was afraid that even if people were nice to my face, they would talk about me and my children behind my back, and I just couldn't face that, especially for my beautiful and innocent children. My parents have pretty much written me off because my choices have embarrassed them, and they don't even have any interest in their grandchildren. I do feel hurt and abandoned by their rejection, but more than that I feel unworthy of God's love and the support of a church. My grandmother, Lucille Smith, is a long-time member of Covenant, and occasionally she would invite me to attend with her, but to be honest, I could tell she did not want me to be talked about or scorned by church members, and she was not one hundred per cent sure that would not happen. Only recently when you all have scheduled this special event, and after Pastor Annie came and talked to me about the church have I felt brave enough to come to your church. What I hope will happen is that through your love and acceptance, I will again feel as if I am worthy of being in God's house. I am excited about bringing my children to Sunday school, and I hope you will grow to love them like I do. Thank you."

After Elizabeth spoke, there was a few seconds of silence, and during that time, there were also a few sniffles here and there. What she said touched the congregation.

The next panel member to speak was Elena, and she seemed very nervous and intimidated by the large group in the audience. She spoke very softly at first and said, "I am Elena Maria Alvarez Sanchez, and I am an American citizen. My parents came here from Mexico twenty-five years ago, and my brother and I were both born here after that time. It took seventeen years, but both my parents have become citizens as well. However, my mother's two older brothers who already had three children each when they came to America, have not been able to become citizens, nor have their children. They work hard at low-level jobs, they pay their taxes, and they stay out of trouble, but all of them worry about being deported from a country which they consider their own at this point. My cousins' children graduated from high school, and two of them paid their way through a mechanics program at the community college. They are families without a country, and it is very sad for them and their children, and there does not seem to be an easy solution to these problems. Having a church family would be very comforting to my cousins, and I have begun to tell them about Covenant. Not every Hispanic immigrant is Catholic, and yet that is the church which has been most welcoming to undocumented residents. I am hoping some of my cousins and their friends will believe they can come here and worship and be welcomed. Thank you for letting me speak."

Damien stood up next and took the microphone from Elena. Before he walked away, he leaned over to her and gave her a hug. Then he faced the audience and began to speak. "My name is Damien LeBlanc, and I have just recently been released from prison and am living in a halfway house. I was born in New Orleans and raised by my mother. My father was killed in an oil rig accident in the Gulf when I was five years old. My mother is a wonderful Christian, and we were active members of a large Baptist church in New Orleans. I was in middle school, I made good grades, and I had just discovered girls when Katrina hit. Our home was destroyed along with everything we owned, everything that was important to a thirteen-year-old boy. My mother and I made a bad decision, and we did not evacuate when we were told to, and eventually we ended up on the roof of our house begging God to send someone to come and rescue us. He did send someone, and we were two of the people that you saw being rescued by helicopter the day after Katrina hit. We were put on a bus and taken to Houston, Texas, where we stayed in a school gymnasium for two weeks. My mom and I were desperate to go home, but we saw pictures of our street, and everything was gone. One of the Red Cross volunteers was from Charlotte, NC, and she had taken an interest in my mom and me, and when she got ready to go home, she asked if we wanted to go to North Carolina. Her parents had a trailer near Bakerstown that was not being occupied at that time, and they offered it to us. It is the only time in my life that I screamed at my mother that I hated her because she wanted to take me away from everything I had ever known. My father's grave was in New Orleans, and I went there to talk to him about guy things all the time, and now I was going to lose that, too. We made the move to North Carolina, and I lived my life still filled with anger at my mom and God and the world in general. I graduated from high school, but just barely. Then I got tired of struggling financially, and I saw other guys making a lot of money selling drugs. I never in a million years thought I would ever do anything like that, but to be honest, I had lost my ability to care about anything, and when a guy I worked with asked me if I wanted to make some easy money, I said yes. That worked for about six weeks. First, I got caught and was charged with possession, and then I got caught transporting a big load of pot for my friend, and the next thing I knew I was going to prison for eighteen months. It was a bad time for me, but I did grow up during that time. I asked God to forgive me, and I quit blaming Him for letting Katrina ruin my life. I asked my mom to forgive me for being so stupid, and she did without any hesitation. I took some college courses while incarcerated, and I became pretty good at fixing mechanical things. I now have a job doing just that, and I will be enrolling at a community college in January taking the courses to prepare me for a four-year college. I want to be a mechanical engineer, and I believe I can make that happen. Covenant has been good to my mom, and I am hoping that I will be accepted here just like she has been. I want God in my life, and I want to be part of a church. I've got a lot to make up for, and I think Covenant will be the place to start. Thank you."

People all over the fellowship hall were openly crying, and of course, I was one of them. Hearing this panel share their pain was difficult for everyone there. Now there was just one person left to speak, and that was Dawn, Heather's partner.

Dawn stood up and reached for the microphone when, all of a sudden, Heather stood up beside her, said something to her, and then Dawn sat down and Heather took the microphone. I was as confused as anyone else in the audience, but then Heather said, "After hearing what everyone has had to say, I cannot be such a coward that I can't even speak to the members of the church where I spent my youth. I am Heather Artz, and this is my life partner Dawn Fisk. We have two children, and we live less than ten miles from this church. My mother Vivian is an active member here and has been telling us that she thought we would be welcome here for a couple of years. However, we have visited many traditional churches and have never felt completely welcome at any of them. It's like when we visit churches, we are not treated like a regular family coming to worship. People either fawn over us and welcome us a little too much, or they look the other way and pretend we are not there. We just want to be treated like everyone else. We work at our jobs, we struggle to pay our bills, we dote on our children and want them to have every opportunity available, we watch television and play games, and we love God and want to worship him in a safe and loving environment. We long to be able to go out to shop or to eat and not have anyone look at us and start whispering to their companions. We don't want to have to worry that our children will hear some of the hateful words said to us when we are out together in public. Like Lorraine said, we just want to be anonymous when we go out as a family. When I was a teenager, I dated young men, even one that many of you know, but I knew early on I was gay. I just did not know how to be okay with that, and I tried to change the way I felt for a long time. My mother knew about my struggle, and she insisted that I go to a counselor for some help. I thought she was sending me to someone to 'fix' me and to help me get rid of my feelings of being gay, but in my first visit when I said that to the counselor, she just looked at me and said, 'I am a gay woman, and your mother has asked me to help you accept yourself as you are with pride and without guilt or shame. She doesn't think you need to be fixed.'"

Heather had to pause for a moment in her talk, but then she composed herself and said, "My family would like to take a chance on Covenant being different and really accepting us as we are, as would all of these other panel members. It is very hard for us to do this as we have all been disappointed too many times in the past, yet here we are trying again to be accepted. Please don't hurt my children or Elizabeth's children or those of Elena's cousins, and don't hurt Damien and his mother or Jesse and Lorraine. We all represent a lot of hurting people who want to join you in worshipping God, and I pray that we can find a way to do that together."

Heather sat down, and there was a collective sigh in the room. We had all been touched again by her comments, and I think for the most part, we all wanted to assure that these people or anyone with a similar story would never be hurt by the actions of our church. It was a huge responsibility, but one that I believed that this congregation was ready to face.

Edna walked to the front of the room slowly and said to the panel members, "Thank you so much for sharing with us. Your words have touched me and many others in this room, and we are grateful for your courage."

She then turned to the rest of the congregation and said, "Let's take that ten-minute break for coffee and dessert, and then the panel will take some questions from you."

I sat in the back of the room and watched the interaction. At first, the panel members talked with each other. Lorraine and Elena had almost immediately gravitated to each other and were involved in an animated conversation. Damien and Elizabeth had moved toward each other slowly and were talking quietly. Heather and Dawn sat and looked out at the crowd. I wanted to run up to them and make conversation with them immediately, but I restrained myself and quietly prayed that someone from the congregation would move up to talk with them.

I had not had a chance to see who was at this meeting, but I continued to sit quietly in the back of the fellowship hall, I noticed Wayne and Anita Fleming walking up to where Dawn and Heather were sitting. They shook the women's hands and just started talking like they had known each other for years. Wayne must have said something funny because Heather and Dawn both burst out laughing. I could feel myself relaxing.

After a few minutes, Edna called everyone back together and asked for those with questions to raise their hands and to speak loudly and clearly. After a few long seconds of silence, Pete Stoudemire raised his hand and then stood and said his question was for Damien. He said, "Damien, I am proud of how far you have come, but I have a concern. From what I read in the papers, people who have gone to prison often repeat their crimes and end up there again. What can we as a church do to help you prevent that from happening to you?"

Damien stood up, took the microphone, and said, "Sir, I just want to thank you for asking that question. First of all, I will say that it is my responsibility to see that I don't make the same mistakes again that put me in prison before. However, it would mean everything to me if I knew there was someone besides my mom who cared about whether or not I was doing the right things and who might be available for me to talk to when I had a problem. If I get to know some of you better, then maybe that would be something you could do to help me."

Erin O'Reilly stood up and said, "My question if for Elena. Have your cousins and their children learned to speak English well? If they came to worship with us, would they need an interpreter?"

Elena stood and said, "They have all learned to speak English as do many immigrants. The children often learn first because they are in school, but then the parents want to learn as well. Sometimes it is kind of funny because the children teach their parents. My cousins and their families would not need an interpreter for worship."

Faye Emerson stood up next and said to Heather and Dawn, "Please forgive me if I don't say this the right way. Before tonight, I have never met or spoken to anyone that I knew was gay, so this is all new to me. My faith tells me that I should welcome you and your family to our church, and that I should celebrate the love you have for each other. But I am 68 years old, and all my life I have been taught that homosexuality was wrong and was sinful. I really don't think I believe that any more, but I don't know if I can change how I have felt my whole life. How do I start working on myself to make these changes in attitude that I really want to make? Is it possible to alter my belief system?"

Heather and Dawn looked at each other for a moment as if they were deciding who would take that question. Finally, Dawn stood up and said, "I'm pretty sure you just took the first step by being honest about your feelings and concerns. We know that for many loving and compassionate Christians, this is a major concern. You don't know how to talk to us, and you are afraid that you might say the wrong thing. All we can do is keep telling you and showing you that we really are regular people and that loving each other is 'normal' for us. I didn't decide to be gay nor did Heather. But why should we have to deny our true selves because society is still having a hard time accepting us? My hope and prayer is that if you are able to welcome gay couples into your church, that as you get to know us you won't even think about our sexual orientation or judge us by it, but instead as Martin Luther King said, we will be judged by the content of our character."

The next person who stood up was Elizabeth White who, of course, was part of the panel. She said, "I know I'm supposed to be to be answering questions instead of asking them, but I really want to know something. How and why is Covenant Baptist Church reaching out to so many people that other churches don't seem to want? What makes you guys different?"

Now there was a long silence, and the church members were looking at each other awkwardly and even laughing a little nervously. Then Edna walked to the front of the room, took the mike from Dawn and said, "If you read about the life of Jesus Christ and his time here on earth, you would have to note that he always pushed the limits of his society. He treated women as equals, he loved the unlovable, and he hung out with people who were ostracized by the society in which he lived. The bottom line is that he told us to love each other, and he didn't seem to make exceptions to that rule. Our church isn't the only group trying to figure out the right things to do in our current society. We are one of many. And we are just a small group of people who believe that what we are doing now is what God has called us to do, and because of that, we must act."

"Thank you for explaining that. It makes me even more interested in your church when I hear what you have to say."

Sarah Burnside stood up and said, "I really don't have a question, but want to say a few things. I have listened to what this panel has said tonight, and what I keep hearing over and over is 'I have been hurt by both people and events in my past, and I don't want that to happen again. I'm very afraid to take the risk of trusting others to not hurt me or my children or anyone in my family, but I want to move on. But please don't let me down. I don't want to be disappointed again.' I can tell you that I am in the same place that you are in, and it is scary as hell to reach out and ask to be loved and accepted just as we are, but if it works as planned, then it will be a glorious experience for all of us, and I think it is worth the risk."

Throughout the congregation, people were nodding their heads and affirming what Sarah had to say. Edna rose again and asked if anyone else had a question for the members of the panel. I feel sure there were questions that begged to be asked, but people were tired and already had lots of things to think about. No one responded, and Edna closed the meeting with prayer. Then she announced that there was more decaf coffee and desserts in the back if people were interested.

I expected people to rush out the door as it was a weeknight, but most of the crowd hung around, and several of them reached out to the panel participants for a little conversation. It was as if they wanted to practice what they had heard tonight to see if they were comfortable with it. We had no idea what Sunday would bring, but this night was certainly a beginning for new relationships.

Chapter 55

I slept like a baby until that horrid alarm clock went off at 6:00. It was time for another early morning prayer group. After two cups of coffee and a quick shower, I was functional, but tired. I wanted to get to the church a little earlier today so I could get the heat going, so after drying my hair, applying a minimum of make-up, and dressing in slacks and a sweater and a wool blazer, I jogged over to the church. I was about twenty minutes early so I quickly turned on the heat and a few lights, and then I turned on the music.

Now all I had to do was wait for everyone else to arrive, and as I did, I prayed for the courage to face the rest of the week and the strength to handle whatever came my way. I apologized to God for being such a coward and asked him to stay right beside me as I faced whatever happened. I was beginning to feel a little more relaxed and yet energized about the week when I heard the door to the church open. I turned around and saw Peggy Morton coming in.

I stood to greet her, but she immediately said she could not stay.

She said to me, "Annie, please pray for my family. It is broken. Jake has told Lucas he is no longer our son and he is not welcome in our home if he marries Lisa, and because of that, Ava has said we are no longer her parents, and she won't be coming to our home again. I can't bear this, Annie. Something has to give, and I don't know what it will be. Will I lose my children? Will I lose my husband? Or will I lose everyone I love? Please, Annie, help us to fix this. I don't know what to do."

I tried to respond to Peggy, but she turned and said she had to go. I was forced to stand and watch her run out of the back of the church, get into her car, and drive away. I hurt for her family and all families who let ideas or beliefs come between them and destroy their relationships

Other church members began to arrive, and we gathered near the front of the sanctuary. We had a few extras this morning, and this time of prayer seemed to be both meaningful and comforting. I prayed quietly for Peggy and her family, for love to conquer all for them, and for their reconciliation. This quiet time with God passed quickly, and as always happened to me, I again knew why this time was important, both for me and the church.

When I eventually got back to the church office, I checked the phone machine. There were already twenty-one messages from this morning. I looked at it and thought, "I just can't do this all day."

I called Edna and explained the problem and asked if there might be any money available to pay someone just for a week or so to respond to all of the messages and to answer the phone. She said she would make a few calls and would call me back.

While I was waiting, I started listening to the messages and making notes about them. There were again five hate-filled messages, and I was amazed how easily I deleted them. I returned four calls rather quickly and I knew if I absolutely had to, I could return all the phone calls. I just would not get anything else done. I had returned three more calls when Edna called me back.

She said, "Would having someone in the office about twenty hours this week and next work for you?"

"That would be amazing," I answered. "Thank you, Edna."

"Do you have anybody in mind to do this job?" Edna asked.

"Well, I was thinking if she could leave her children in day care for the whole day, Elizabeth White might be good. She is smart and well-spoken and seems to be able to handle a lot of responsibility."

"That's a great idea, Annie. Would you like me to call her for you?"

"Yes, please."

I didn't know whether to work out the final details of my sermon or the bulletin for Sunday or to return more phone calls or to try to visit Cliff. I returned a few more phone calls, but then when I decided to prioritize, I started finalizing my sermon.

I worked a couple of hours on my sermon, always stopping to answer the phone when it rang, but not yet responding to all the messages, when the phone rang again, and it was Edna. She told me Elizabeth would be in about 1:00 today, and then she and I could work out her hours for the rest of the week. I was so relieved that I would have some help for the next few days. That helped me believe I would survive this week, and because of that, when John called and asked me to go to lunch with him at noon, I said yes.

Lunch was casual and comfortable. We met at the local pizza place and had their buffet. I had a lot of salad and one big piece of pizza. John had a little salad and several big pieces of pizza. It was fun, not momentous. We laughed a lot, and it was a definite distraction from everything going on at the church. Before we left, I asked him what he was doing in Bakerstown in the middle of the day, and he said, "I am finally looking for office space in town. I think the time might be right to set up my own practice, and I'm just beginning to look around."

"Good for you, John."

As we parted, he said, "Good luck for the rest of your week. I hope everything goes beautifully for you and the church."

Chapter 56

Spending a little time with John gave me a new perspective. I was more relaxed and excited about the events coming up in the church.

I got back to the church a little before 1:00 and even though there were ten more messages on the phone machine, I did not let that get me down. Right at 1:00, Elizabeth came in. I gave her all the information I could think of about this Sunday and asked her to start on checking messages and returning calls. She jumped right in, and I did not hear from her for about an hour.

At 2:15, she knocked softly on my office door, and when I told her to come in, she said, "I hate to bother you, but there were a few questions I could not answer, and before I return those calls, I thought I better check with you."

She was very efficient and asked me between eight and ten questions that were easy to answer, and she made notes about what I was telling her. Then she gave me four messages that she believed I needed to answer myself, and she took off to return more messages and answer the phone again. Elizabeth was every bit as competent as I thought she would be.

We both left the church about 5:00 after we agreed on the times Elizabeth would work the rest of the week. She headed out to pick up her children and take them home, and I headed off to the VA hospital in Salisbury to see Cliff during evening visiting hours.

I had not visited Cliff since he had been admitted to the VA hospital, and I had to use my trusty GPS to find the hospital. Once I did, I thought I was going to have to use it again to find the building where Cliff would be, but the staff was excellent, and they pointed me in the right direction. I had told Sarah that I would like to visit him tonight, and she said since I would do that, she might stay at home with her kids, and that she would let Cliff know that I was coming.

I found the building I was looking for, and again, staff directed me where I could find Cliff. When I saw him, I knew he was in the right place. He looked rested and at peace as he sat at a table in a recreation room laughing at two guys trying to play ping pong. They were awful at that game, and Cliff was teasing them about their skills or the lack thereof. I watched him for a moment, and then he saw me, stood up, and gave me a hug.

"Annie, it's good to see you. Thank you for coming to visit."

"I'm glad to see you, too, Cliff. You look great. How are you doing?"

"I feel really good, Annie. I want to apologize for jumping all over you that day you and Vivian came to visit me. I was very low that day and I did not want to hear anyone tell me there was something wrong with me. But you were right, and now I have a whole different perspective. My depression about everything that happened to me is slowly going away. Some of it turned into anger, and when that happened, I was able to cope with it better. Anyway, being here and actually confronting everything that happened and everything I felt has helped me a lot. And the best part of being here is that I have been able to help some of the guys here that were in much worse shape than me. As I got better, I have brought them along with me, and that has made me feel useful again. I did not know how much I had missed that feeling since I was not teaching anymore."

"Cliff, I'm so happy you are feeling better. You sound like a man with a mission, and there is nothing better than that."

"I agree, Annie. Hey, let's go sit down in our lounge and talk."

We walked down a hall that looked like a hospital, but then we turned into a lounge area that had comfortable furniture, a coffee pot, soft music playing, and brightly-colored walls and window dressings. It looked like somebody's living room, and when I said that to Cliff, he agreed and said, "That's what makes it so special."

Then he said, "Let's go sit near the window in the back. It's my favorite place here because there are lots of squirrels running around in the trees outside. Don't ask me why I find them so fascinating, but I do."

I grinned at him and said, "It takes all kinds, Cliff."

He laughed out loud at that, and about that time, a couple of guys walked up to him and one of them said, "Talking to the squirrels again, Cliff. We really are going to have to report you."

Cliff grinned and said, "Nobody's gonna listen to you two crazy guys. I'm not worried."

They just looked at Cliff and laughed. Then they looked at me, and the youngest and the cutest of the two said, "Cliff, I hate to tell you this, but this is not your wife. Perhaps you are confused, or perhaps you are not?"

"Show some respect, Brandon. This is my pastor, Annie Adams."

"Whoa, like in a preacher? You got to be kidding. If I had a preacher that looked like you, I'd have perfect attendance for church."

"Um... thank you, I think," I said.

Cliff got a little more serious and said, "Really guys, she is my minister, and I need to talk with her. So get lost."

"No problem, man. No offense meant."

Cliff and I sat down by the window, and I said to him, "Cliff, you have an amazing rapport with those guys. Are you like that with the other patients as well?'

"Yeah, I guess so. A lot of them are younger than me, and I guess I am someone they look up to. Most of them have been through things so much worse than I have, and it has helped me get a perspective and a desire to help them in any way I can. I'm not trying to be something I'm not, but I can be a friend, and most of these guys don't have enough of them. Some of them have family close by, but a lot of them only see their family on the weekends, and it gets lonely in here for somebody to talk to. I have tried to do what I can without interfering with their treatment."

"I don't mean to say something I shouldn't, but has it ever occurred to you that you might have found another career for yourself? I don't know what additional education you might need to work with guys like this, but you are a smart man and you could certainly do whatever it took."

Cliff just stared at me, and I thought I had said the wrong thing to him. I started to say something to him, but he put up his hand and said, "Shhh, just a moment."

After a silence of forever, Cliff said to me, "Annie, I never thought of doing something with these guys as a profession, but I think I might like the idea. I have felt useful again in here for the first time in a long time, and I could continue that if I made helping these guys my calling. I don't know if I would train to do something medical or psychological or something else, but I could get very excited about this. I don't want to react too quickly, but you have certainly given me something to think about."

"Okay, Cliff, I hope this is a positive thing. I wouldn't want to do or say anything that would hurt your treatment since you seem to be doing so well."

"First of all, Annie, I am not nearly as fragile as I was for a while, and second, I really like the idea, and the least I can do is explore the possibilities. Thank you for that."

"It just seems as if you have found a place to serve, and I know from experience that can make people very happy. Now, I have not talked with Sarah a lot, so catch me up with what is going on with Robbie and Justin."

We spent a half hour catching up on his boys and also what was going on at the church. He said, "I wish I could be there Sunday to support what the church is doing, but I'm not going to do anything to mess up my own healing. I want to go home and be with my family as soon as I can, but you know I will be praying for you guys."

"Thank you, Cliff. That means a lot to us."

After a little while, I headed for home. It was a little bit of a drive, but I would not have missed this visit for anything. Cliff seemed to be headed in the right direction, and I had great hope that he would return to his family very soon.

I had missed a couple of calls while I was talking to Cliff or while I was driving home. One was from John just telling me he enjoyed talking to me at lunch today, and the other was from Greg wondering if I had any time to get together with him this week. I couldn't help but think about the saying, "When it rains, it pours."

I went into the office the next day, and the phone kept ringing. While I finished up the plans for Sunday worship, I answered the phone, typed the bulletin, and finished the sermon. I called the deacons individually and asked if there was any reason for us to meet tonight. I thought I would be more comfortable if we met and went over all the plans one last time before Sunday, but I was going to leave it up to them. They were to think about all the plans and then call me back with any concerns. I asked them to call me by 3:00, and we could decide. I also contacted William and asked if he would like to get together to go over the plans for worship, and he thought that was a great idea. I asked if he was available tonight and explained the deacon situation. He said tonight would be good and to let him know what time.

As I waited on these phone calls, I tried to keep busy. When I had too much time to think, I would work my way into a panic where I wondered what the heck we were doing. We had demonstrators at our door, people calling us with hate-filled speech, and members trying to decide whether or not to stay with Covenant. Was this ministry, or had I forgotten what that word meant?

Chapter 57

The deacons agreed that just to be safe we needed to meet again tonight and review what we had already done as well as what still needed to be done. We decided to meet at 6:30, and after I knew that, I called William and asked if 8:00 was too late for us to meet about the music for Sunday's service. He said that would be fine so my evening was all set up.

The deacons and I gathered, and there was palpable tension and excitement between us. Apparently, I wasn't the only one who was stressing over this event. I decided that we should address our feelings about what had been going on, the demonstrators, the media attention, the hateful phone messages.

I begin by asking, "What's new?"

In response to that, everyone laughed or just grinned, but immediately there was a spirit of camaraderie that was vital to our mission. Through the last few weeks, we had become a team, and that had to continue if this Sunday was going to work.

I then asked Edna to pray, and as always, she said what we all needed to hear. "Heavenly Father, we are scared to death of this can of worms we are opening, yet we know this is what must be done. We thank You for Your spirit being here with us tonight. We so wish that Your human form could be here with us so that we could actually hear You say the words, 'This is what I command you to do,' but our faith in Your presence and Your will must not falter. You told us to love our neighbor as ourselves, and that is all we are trying to do. Please continue to direct our actions and calm our fears. Help us to remain loving to all, even to those who do not love us. In Your name we pray, Amen."

I asked Edna if I could ask one more thing before the meeting got started, and she said, "Of course, Annie."

I asked the group if they would share their feelings about everything that had been happening. No one spoke for a bit, and then Charlotte said, "This may sound just awful, but I am proud to be a part of something that might make a difference in someone's life. If just one person who has not felt welcomed by our church or any church can be shown that we really do accept them and love them, then we have reached our goal. We are a small group of people, but we can be a mighty voice."

Alan said, "Now I really do feel bad about what I'm thinking. I am downright scared that somebody might get hurt. Heck, I'm even scared it might be me or Faye, but I don't want any violence at all, and I'm not sure how to make that happen. I feel a little bit helpless because I can't control what the 'crazies' might decide to do. I keep telling myself that the protesters are just people who believe differently from us, but they have been so hateful, I can't quit thinking about that."

"I'm scared, too," said Fred. "I believe in what we are doing, but it doesn't keep me from being afraid. We are a bunch of old people stirring up the pot when we should just be quietly enjoying our retirement. Sometimes I look in the mirror and say 'You idiot. What are you thinking?' Then to be honest, I answer myself. And I'm not crazy, you know, even if I answer myself. I just say 'Why not you, Fred? You claim you want to be a follower of Christ, but the first time in your life it gets hard, you want to turn tail and run.'" With a trembling voice, Fred then said, "That helps me get my courage back."

We all sat there quietly for a minute, and then Edna said, "We are all scared of what could happen on Sunday and we are all scared it might be a total disaster of a day, but we are all committed to doing what we believe is right and what we believe God is leading us to do. I do not sense any hesitation on the part of this committee nor on the part of the church as a whole, and I say 'We go forward.'"

"So say I," said Charlotte. Then everyone agreed, and we began to discuss the final arrangements for this family day.

After a somewhat brief discussion, we looked at each other, and Edward said what we were all thinking. "I think we are as ready as we can be, and the thing to remember is that we will be here Sunday to worship God just as we always are, and that is the most important part of the day. With God's help, we will handle what the day brings."

"I agree," I said to the group. "We have worked hard, and we are prepared for this event. You guys have been amazing, and this church will make a difference in this community because of what you have done."

Edna closed with prayer, and we all stood up but didn't move. I felt a little silly saying what I did, but it just seemed appropriate.

"Group hug?"

We laughed as we broke apart from our hug, and this time the group went on its way.

I sat for just a few minutes with Edna, and I asked her if she had heard about members who were opposed to what we were doing having meetings about leaving the church as a group.

She answered, "Yes, I have heard those rumors, and they cause me much pain. I'm hoping that most of that opposition died out after Jake's outburst, but we can't be sure. But, Annie, we have to do what is right even if problems result. I will say to you that I have also heard that these families have appreciated your willingness to talk with them and to assure them they are most welcome at Covenant even if they don't support everything we are doing. That is so much better than implying, 'If you don't like it, just leave.' I appreciate how you have handled that, and I can only hope and pray that these families will find a way to stay with us."

"I hope so, too, Edna. Every member of this church contributes in some way to its makeup, and we need them to remain a part of us."

My next meeting for the evening was with William about the music for Sunday. He always did such an outstanding job of choosing the right music for every occasion that I didn't really feel a need for this meeting, but it was something he always requested. He always asked for a few minutes each week to discuss his song choices and the reasons behind them. What I believe is that these few minutes gave us a reason to sit down and talk to each other on a regular basis, and that is how we have developed a pretty strong friendship.

I thought he would probably be practicing in the sanctuary, and I was right. I snuck in the back door and stood and listened. William was sitting in a chair on stage and was playing a guitar and singing "His Eye is on the Sparrow." I had never heard William sing a solo, and even though Charlotte had told me how talented he was, I was mesmerized. Not only did he have a beautiful voice, but the accompaniment on the guitar was heartrending. I became emotional just listening to him practice, and I knew this song would be perfect for Sunday's service. When he finished the song, he looked up and saw me. "Good song for Sunday, right?"

Blinking away tears, I just nodded my head.

He smiled and said, "Come on up, and I will tell you what else I have planned."

It was dark in the sanctuary with just a couple of lights on, and I suggested we go back to my office to talk, but he said, "No, it's nice here. Let's sit on the front pew."

He sat in the corner of the pew and leaned against the back and the end of the pew. I sat in the middle of the pew.

He said he was planning to sing the solo as the special music and that the hymns he wanted to use were "Savior, Like a Shepherd Lead Us" and "Amazing Grace". He said, "I picked 'Amazing Grace' just in case there were people there who had not gone to church in a long time. It seems that even non-believers know that song. One other thing. The hymn of commitment will be 'Just As I Am.' The title of the song and its lyrics seem to be perfect for this particular Sunday. What do you think?"

"I think it's all perfect, William. I don't know how you get it so right every Sunday. You really have a gift for that."

"Do you and the deacons have everything else put together?"

"I hope so. They are an amazing group of people. Anything they were asked to do, they did, and they did it well. What I think is we will have a great worship service. Whatever else happens, we have very little control over. God is in charge of all that."

"I think you are right about that."

William got very quiet, and yet I felt like he wasn't ready to go home.

Finally, I said, "What's on your mind, William?"

He put his music aside, and it seemed like he was breathing a little harder than usual. I waited patiently to see where this was going.

"Annie, you asked me a short time ago if I had ever come close to getting married, and I want to tell you about that. Annie, I'm an old man, and I've never been in love. In fact, I have never made love with anyone. I realized pretty early that I wasn't very interested in impressing all the little girls at school. By the time I was thirteen, I knew I was different from all the other guys that I played with. The only students I wanted to impress were the other boys. You won't remember these times because you are just too young, but nobody I knew talked openly about people who were 'different.' I had no idea what was wrong with me that I felt so different from my friends, but I started praying really hard that God would fix me, that he would take away all these strange feelings I was having toward other guys. I had heard the word 'queer' used in very derogatory terms, and in fact, I had probably used the word myself in a joke. I could not make a connection between that word and what I was feeling. I lived in continuous denial all the way through high school. I even asked a young lady to the Prom, and I even kissed her good night, several times. I would have died if anyone guessed my secret. One of the reasons I went in the army was to prove my manhood to everyone else. I thought if I could fight in Vietnam, no one would ever question my sexual orientation. When I got to college in the late sixties, there was still very little discussion about sexual 'deviants' as homosexuals were called. I studied all the time and practiced my music, so when I didn't date, everyone just thought I was a late bloomer who was obsessed with my music and my grades. There was a little truth to that, but I was still trying to cover up who I really was. One of my professors lived with a male friend, and I started to talk with him about my feelings, but I honestly didn't even know what questions to ask."

William took a deep breath, and as he continued, a tear ran down his face.

"When I finished college and came home and started teaching, I put my heart and soul into it and when I still didn't date, people again assumed that I just hadn't found anyone that was right for me. In a few years, after my brother and sisters had children, I became the favorite 'bachelor uncle,' and I was generous with my nieces and nephews at Christmas and on their birthdays. I really love those guys, and they are an important part of my family ties. I have spent my entire life covering up who I really am. You are the first person I have ever talked to like this. I am a gay man, and it took me sixty-seven years to be able to say that out loud."

We both continued to sit, still and quiet, in the semi-darkness of the sanctuary. My heart was broken for William and all the people like him who had been so ashamed of feelings that were normal for them. I felt grief for this kind, loving man who had never experienced the high of being in love or being loved in an adult relationship.

"William, thank you for sharing that with me. I can only imagine how difficult that was for you. I am sorry you have never been in love, but I hope you know how very much you are loved."

"Thank you, Annie. I do know that, and believe me, I appreciate it. I guess I was just born too soon for who I am. As much as I have grieved and moaned about all the changes in our society and in our churches, I'm beginning to understand that change for some people, including me, means freedom to be who you really are. How can I possibly be against that?"

"How can any Christian be against that, William? I will never understand how a person living his or her life as a gay man or woman is so threatening to so many people and why society thinks they have the right to condemn, persecute, discriminate against, and humiliate those who live and love differently from themselves."

"Go Annie! When you talk like that, it makes me feel like a regular person with regular rights."

"William, you are a regular person, and you certainly should have all the rights everybody else has. I can't promise you that will happen, but don't ever feel you are not worthy of them."

"I know, Annie. I think in the last few years when more and more people have become open about being gay, I slowly began to quit being so ashamed of myself. And what our church is doing not only affirms me as a gay Christian man, but also makes me believe that God really does love me just as I am."

He paused for just a few seconds and then said, “I don’t know that I’ll ever be okay telling anybody else I am gay, but at least I don’t hate myself anymore.”

“That’s worth a lot, William.”

‘It really is.”

“It’s been a long day, William, and I am so glad I ended my day with you. In my moments of doubt, I can remember our conversation and know that what we are doing here at Covenant means a lot to many people, and no matter what we have to face, it is worth the cost. The music choices for Sunday sounded perfect, and I will particularly be looking forward to hearing your solo.”

“Thank you, Annie, I’ll do my best. Look, you go on home. I’ll lock up.”

“That would be wonderful. I’ll see you Sunday.”

I went home extremely motivated to not only make this family day event successful but to also make inclusion an ongoing priority at Covenant Baptist.

Chapter 58

I woke up the next morning with my anxiety level sky high. I felt unfocused, like there were twenty things in my head that I needed to do, but I couldn't decide where to start. I thought maybe a run would help me get my head straight. It was cold but I enjoyed running in this type weather, so on went the sweat pants and a couple of layers of t-shirts and then a sweatshirt.

I ran-walked for forty minutes and tried not to think about anything except what I saw around me. The sky was a gorgeous, cloudless Carolina blue. It was 8:30 a.m., so most of the traffic on my running route was already at its destination. One school bus was still picking up students on my road. The scenery on my run was not particularly pretty today. Other than a few pine trees in yards that I passed, there was no green on any other trees. It wasn't quite as brown as in the dead of winter, but it was getting close to that. The houses along my route were a mixed variety. A couple of big brick houses along the route were very well cared for, and they were right next to small mobile homes. A majority of the homes were nice middle-class homes, nothing fancy but neat looking. There were also a lot of wooded areas along my route, and I normally enjoyed the sounds coming from the woods, primarily the birds. Today it was rather quiet, but that was fine with me. I wanted quiet today.

I spent the rest of the day in the office. Elizabeth came in at 1:00, and together we answered forty-six phone calls and eighteen messages. We finalized the church bulletin and printed and folded 230 copies of it, 150 more than usual. Both of us were feeling particularly optimistic.

On Friday, I was in the office again during the morning, but I had an appointment with Brian Stanley in the afternoon. My time with him had been invaluable to me as I had grown as a pastor. How he managed to be so helpful to me when he really wasn't sure I should even be a pastor was an amazing feat. I was looking forward to today's appointment.

Rev. Stanley's secretary Evelyn greeted me with a smile, and I asked her how her grandson was doing. He had had his tonsils and adenoids out last week. She said, "He has eaten more ice cream than even his father could eat. I believe he is taking advantage of his parents being overly concerned for him, but then as a grandmother, I can only approve of that."

"That makes sense to me," I said.

Then she said "He's on the phone, but he'll be done in a minute."

"No problem."

Thirty seconds later, Brian walked out and said, "How's the celebrity doing?"

I just looked at him without smiling, and he said "Sorry, I guess that is still a sore spot for you, huh?"

"Just a little." I had not seen him in two weeks, so lots had happened since that time.

"Come on in," he said, "let's talk."

My time with Brian had become extremely important to me in the last few weeks. I could present all my questions and concerns as a pastor to him without the fear of looking weak or stupid or incompetent. When I sat down in his big, overstuffed visitor's chair, I felt as if I could relax and let go of all my professional concerns. I felt like Brian was in charge, at least for this hour we spent together.

"Are you ready for Sunday?" he asked.

"I actually think I am. I'm a little worried about who might be there and what might happen, but I am ready for this Sunday's worship service, and that is about all I can control. Our deacons have done an amazing job with this event, as have many other church members. Our panel discussion went very well, and I think the congregation is as ready as they can be at this time. Obviously, getting to know people who are different from you takes longer than a two-hour meeting, but it was a great beginning."

"Any regrets?"

I couldn't speak for a minute as that question seemed to touch me in a very emotional way. Then I said, "Are you asking if I am sorry this thing has become bigger than life? Maybe. But if your question is am I sorry that we are having this event and focusing the church on the issue of inclusion, then the answer is no. Brian, I just can't see the church going any other way and saying that it actually follows the teachings and the actions of

Jesus. My faith has grown so much as I have observed the strength and courage of the Covenant congregation. I am honored to be their pastor, and I am going to try my best to live up to their standard of Christian behavior."

"Annie, I need to tell you something, and this is really kind of hard for me. You have grown so much as a person and as a pastor since you have been at Covenant. I still don't agree with everything you say and do, but I cannot argue with the fact that you are the right person to lead Covenant at this time. I have seen growth in your ability to communicate with your members as well in your capacity to care about them. You have loved your congregation as Jesus had directed you to, and they seem to love you in return. As much as you downplay your leadership at this church, it is clear to me that you have not hesitated to help them go where they are called to go."

"I need to hear that so much. Most of the time I feel very positive about my role with the church, but then I go into a tailspin and panic completely about what's happened in the last few days. I really don't want Sunday to be a circus, but I can't see that not happening, and so the question is, how do we manage to make the circus into a worship experience. Got any ideas?"

Brian sat there quietly for a full minute, and I could tell he was intensely thinking about my question. Finally, he said, "Annie, you have to be in charge. You cannot let your own insecurities or your nervousness stand in the way of your leadership. You have got to ignore distractions such as protesters or the media and remain totally focused on the worship service. I know you like to give your congregation a lot of credit for what they do, and that is a good thing, but on this Sunday, you have to step up and be the one that everyone listens to and focuses on. Your church has come a long way in this planning process, and you cannot let them down now. You must be the leader they need."

I stared back at him, and I knew he was right. I just hoped and prayed that I could be that.

We chatted a bit longer, but I knew Brian had already given me the direction that I needed, and all I had to do was, with God's help, to follow it.

Chapter 59

I woke up early on Sunday morning, and the first thing I did was to look outside. The weather was cold and clear, and there were no demonstrators yet. Good beginning.

The deacons and I and a few other members had agreed to meet about 9:00 at the church. That was an hour before Sunday school, and two hours before worship. Tables and chairs had been set up for the luncheon, and we had said if the sanctuary filled up, the overflow could sit in the same chairs. The nursery was ready with two paid workers and a list of possible volunteers. A table was set up in the narthex with name tags and sign-in sheets available. Our two security persons were coming at 9:00 also so they could help with parking but also be on alert for any other problems. Media would be allowed inside the sanctuary in the last two rows, but absolutely no cameras were allowed inside or outside on the church grounds. The media had been told this several times, and they were not happy, but we did not want our members or our guests to have their pictures or those of their families made public. Deacons and several church members had been asked to remove anyone from the church that they saw trying to take pictures. The two deputies would remove them from the premises if that happened.

I walked on over to the church about 8:30, and I saw right away I was not the only early bird. Coffee had been made, and I helped myself to a cup. Edna and Mary had fixed two trays of coffee, cream and sugar and were walking down the driveway. I looked out of the church, and I saw five or six demonstrators gathering at the end of our drive.

Everything seemed under control at this point in time, so I went into my office, closed the door, and sat down to think and to pray. I felt at peace and almost like I was in a zone where I felt completely in charge. At 9:00, I stepped out to meet those who were arriving, and they were a calm and confident group of people.

We did a final review of what needed to be done, and then Edna led us in a prayer for peace and for courage, asking God to help each one of us today as we completed our assigned duties.

At 9:50, several members arrived, particularly those who attended Sunday school classes, and we greeted each other with more affection than usual. It was a wonderful time of unity for our church. I looked down the driveway again, and the crowd of demonstrators had gotten a little larger, and now they were holding up signs as cars turned in toward the church. Some of the latest arrivals said the signs were hate-filled and condemning, both of the church and its members, and particularly of gay people.

I took a deep breath and went back to my office to look over the sermon one more time. At 10:30, I knew I was ready, and I walked out of my office to the front of the church where many of our members had gathered. When I looked down the driveway, there were again a few more demonstrators, about twenty altogether, but I also saw traffic backed up on the highway waiting to turn into the church driveway. There were at least ten cars waiting to turn in, and it appeared that the demonstrators were standing in the way. Danny O'Reilly, Jesse Akin, and Pete Stoudemire were jogging down the driveway along with the two deputies who had been helping with parking. As the rest of us stood and watched, the deputies took charge and moved the demonstrators back off the driveway and onto public property. While they did that, Danny and Jesse directed those cars waiting to turn in and head up the driveway. Pete started walking alongside the cars. There was a collective breath taken among the members gathered in front of the church, and Faye and Edna walked to those cars to welcome whoever was in them. Charlotte and Fred were waiting at the table just inside the church to greet visitors and introduce them to church members who would take care of them personally.

It was all coming together. I had no idea how many guests we would have, but whoever came would be welcomed and included in our church community.

I went to find William and when I did, I told him what was happening. He just looked at me and said, "This is a very good thing."

At 11:00 promptly, William started playing the prelude "To God Be the Glory," and I walked in and took my place on the stage. When I looked up after taking my seat, I couldn't believe what I saw. The sanctuary, which holds about 250 people, was packed. I did not see one empty seat. There were black faces and brown faces, something that had not been seen in this church in a long time. There were families seated together that had two men or two women next to several children. I saw Damien, and beside him was Al, the man who worked at the halfway house. Beside Al, there were four other young men who looked a little uncomfortable in their dress shirts and ties. I saw Jesse and Lorraine and another couple, the man Caucasian and the woman Asian, sitting on one of the back pews. I saw Lucille White sitting proudly beside her granddaughter, Elizabeth, my new friend. The church was full of young people and lots of children, all shapes, all sizes, and all colors. Intermingled with all these people were the members of Covenant, with all their gray hair, their traditional clothing, their deep Southern Baptist roots, and their loving and non-judgmental hearts. It was indeed a glorious sight to behold!

When William finished the prelude, he walked up to the pulpit and invited the congregation to sing our first hymn, "Amazing Grace." William had asked his sister to play the piano for the services today, and she was every bit as talented as he. Everyone stood, and we all sang a robust version of the hymn. It was obviously a hymn known by all, and the music was very inspiring.

At the end of this hymn, everyone sat down, and I rose and walked to the pulpit. I said to the crowd, "Before I welcome you officially, I want you to do one thing for me. I'd like you to look to your left. Yes go ahead and do that now." I paused and then I said, "Now look to your right." I paused again, and then I said, "Now one more thing. Turn a little and look behind you."

There was a little noise from people turning in their seats, and there was a little nervous laughter because the audience wasn't quite sure what they were looking for.

Then I said to them in a most vigorous voice, "My name is Rev. Annie Adams, and this is what heaven is going to look like. Enjoy your preview of it right now!"

There was joyous laughter, a few amens, and a scattering of applause. When everyone became quiet, I took the opportunity to welcome everyone there to Covenant Baptist Church for this special celebration of families. I told them they were all invited to lunch after the service, and I told them that our members wanted to get to know them, and that I hoped they would all stay.

Then I opened the time of worship with a prayer.

"Dearest Heavenly Father, what the heck are we doing here today? We have stirred up all kinds of hostility and resentment and probably a little hatred by inviting some new people to our church. And what are these guests of ours doing? They are acting as if they have a right to love You and to worship You with all of their hearts, their souls, and their minds. What is this world coming to? We pray that it is coming to a place where You want us to be, a place that You are leading us to where love is the primary emotion that Christians feel for each other. For far too long now, we Christians who are regular church-goers have felt so superior to the world around us, particularly to those people who are different from us, whether it be by skin color, ethnic origin, sexual orientation, marital status, or socioeconomic status. We have kind of always thought down deep inside that You love us best. Forgive us for ever letting that thought cross our mind. We are trying to change, but it is so hard. We keep falling back to our old ideas, and we are desperately afraid to change them. We worry about what might happen to our world if we do. Mainly, we worry about what might happen to our status if Christians lead the world to new ideas of equality. Today we are asking for courage and for insight about what You would have us do and for the faith that tells us that where You lead us is where You want us to be, and that You will be there with us. Thank You for joining us today, and I hope You enjoy this worship experience as much as we plan to. We love and honor You. Amen."

Our next hymn was "Savior, Like a Shepherd Lead Us," and then, as Baptists are known to do, we took up an offering. It was getting close to sermon time, and I made myself take a deep, cleansing breath and relax against the back of my chair. I was ready. Just before my sermon, William came up on the stage, sat in a chair, and played his guitar and sang "His Eye is on the Sparrow." It was a wonderful testimony of faith and acknowledgement that God loves each and every one of us in a personal way.

When he finished, he went to his seat in the front pew, and he turned to me and gave me a discreet "thumbs up." I smiled at him, took a deep breath, and went to preach the sermon of my life.

"The scripture I have chosen this morning is found in Romans 8: 31-39. I find this to be a very comforting scripture about our relationship with God.

> 'What then shall we say to this? If God is for us, who is against us? He who did not spare his own Son but gave him up for us all, will he not also give us all things with him? Who shall bring any charge against God's elect? It is God who justifies; who is to condemn? Is it Christ Jesus, who died, yes, who was raised from the dead, who is at the right hand of God, who indeed intercedes for us? Who shall separate us from the love of Christ? Shall tribulation, or distress, or persecution, or famine, or nakedness, or peril, or sword? As it is written, "For thy sake we are being killed all the day long; we are regarded as sheep to be slaughtered." No, in all these things we are more than conquerors through him who loved us. For I am sure that neither death, nor life, nor angels, nor principalities, nor things present, nor things to come, nor powers, nor height, nor depth, nor anything else in all creation, will be able to separate us from the love of God in Christ Jesus our Lord.'

"This scripture teaches us first of all that God proved his loyalty to his children as He sacrificed his only son for us. What greater proof of God's love could we possibly need? We are also told that because of Jesus' sacrifice for us, that perhaps He has the right to judge us, but instead he takes the path of interceding on our behalf before God. Then Paul tells us that nothing we can think of that is frightening or a result of evil in this world can separate us from the love of God which is in Jesus Christ. What a foundation for our faith, and what a comfort for our hearts. Loving God and knowing that He loves us is a primary component of our faith, and it shouldn't be that hard for us. Let me follow this up with another question, however. What can separate us from our fellow man, our fellow brothers and sisters in Christ? There seems to be a list of factors that can do this, and I want us to look at them. Can that superiority we feel because we are white, middle class, educated, and heterosexual keep us from loving our neighbors in the way God intended. Does that darker skin color or kinky hair or foreign language spoken or different lifestyle put up barriers between 'us' and 'them'? If it does, I think we can safely say that is not what God intended."

I took a deep breath and looked out over the audience.

"So how do we change that? I think we have to take God at his word when he told us to love our neighbor as ourselves. He didn't say just the ones who look like us and act like us and talk like us. He meant all our neighbors. No matter how hard we try, I don't believe we can do that without asking God to help us. Changing lifelong patterns of behavior that are part of our community and family culture, particularly those that have been reinforced by the churches we attend, might be the most difficult challenge of your life. It's not enough anymore to put up a front and say the right words about loving our neighbors. We actually have to do that. The very first step in that process is being willing to make changes in who we consider our neighbor and who we believe God has called us to love. We need to not be 'holier than thou' in our thoughts and in our private conversations with people we know who agree with us. Perhaps we should examine our conversation with our family and close friends in order to eliminate any words that make fun of or humiliate groups of people. Our society has come a long way in learning how to be 'politically correct', but if that change does not come from the heart, and we only act that way when it is expected by those around us, it means nothing to God. The change in us and how we view and love our neighbors has to be real to matter to God, and if that happens, our world will become a place where love for our neighbor means something."

I went on to suggest ways that we all might modify our behaviors, such as reading articles about people different from us, joining a group that supports various minority groups, and actually meeting and getting to know people who are different from us.

However, I continued to emphasize that any change starts with the desire to change and the willingness to look at the world and those in it through God's eyes and not our own.

It was not a long sermon but I did my best, and I tried to be kind and non-judgmental myself. How hypocritical it is to condemn and berate those who don't believe as you do by telling them to be more loving to their neighbors.

When I finished, I prayed for courage and enlightenment, for the process of change in our lives, and for love and acceptance for all God's children. Then I took my seat.

William announced that our closing hymn would be "Just As I Am," and then he said, "At Covenant, we don't focus on people walking down the aisle and making public pronouncements about their faith, although whenever someone feels led to do that, we certainly are open to it. Instead, our focus is that everyone here, every week, should affirm and re-commit their lives to Jesus Christ, His teachings, and Christian service. You can do that wherever you are sitting or standing right now. Let me also say that if any of you would like to talk with Pastor Annie, she will be available immediately after the service at the front of the church. Finally, please do something for me. Pay attention to the words of this song."

Just as I am, without one plea,
But that thy blood was shed for me,
And that thou bidd'st me come to thee,
O Lamb of God, I come, I come
Just as I am, tho tossed about,
With many a conflict, many a doubt.
Fightings within and fears without,
O Lamb of God I come, I come
Just as I am, thou wilt receive,
Wilt welcome, pardon, cleanse, relieve,
Because thy promise, I believe,
O Lamb of God I come, I come

"Just As I Am" was sung with great emotion and gusto. Many of us there identified strongly with the words of that song.

After we finished singing, lots of people were wiping their eyes, and then Edna came up to say grace.

Before she prayed for the blessing on the food, she said, "We are so happy that each of you has chosen to be here with us today to worship God. You are welcome any time to come and be a part of our community here."

Then she turned to me and said, "Pastor Annie, I thank you for your words. I believe we all have some things to think about and pray about, and I, for one, appreciate you bringing these ideas to my attention."

She blessed the food and pointed the crowd in the right direction. I could see our members who had volunteered to interact with the visitors walking over to their assigned family or individual and quietly talking with them as they walked to the fellowship hall. I hoped there was enough food. I couldn't seem to move. It was over. People came. They listened, and they worshipped. There were no disruptions. It was a wonderful service, and I was completely drained. But it was time to get up and try to meet as many of our visitors as I could and to make them feel welcome.

There were only a few stragglers in the sanctuary, and I shook hands with each of them and welcomed those who were visitors to our church. The really great thing about our plan was that it was not up to me to welcome all the visitors. They were being given personal attention by the members of the church, the people who really counted in making the visitors feel welcome.

As I walked into the fellowship hall, I paused for a moment and just looked around. Pete Stoudemire was helping two men with a toddler find a high chair, and then he sat down with them to have lunch. Faye Emerson was talking and laughing with Heather and Dawn and was holding their daughter's plate as she helped her find something to eat for lunch. Fred and Edith Miller and their daughter Belinda were guiding a Hispanic family consisting of two parents and four very young children to a table where they each sat by a child to help them with their lunch. Damien and Mary were sitting with Lucille Smith and Elizabeth and her children, and Wayne and Anita Fleming were bringing them tea and then sitting next to them. Jesse and Lorraine had each taken a visiting family, one a black couple and the other a man by himself with two school-aged children. It was a montage of Christ's church, and our congregation had painted it.

My heart was filled with love for this church and for how completely it represented God's presence here on earth. This group was courageous and daring and different, and they were just getting started. I was very proud to be a small part of this project. I walked farther into the room and started meeting our guests and welcoming them to God's house.

About 2:00, the last person had left except for the cleanup committee, and I went back to my office. The deacons had decided ahead of time that once we got through the day, we were all going to want to go home. We would need to process everything that happened for a few days, and then we would meet to evaluate the event and make plans for the future. I straightened up my office, and put everything away in my files, and I was thinking I could head home and crash. There was a soft knock on my door, and when I said, "Come in," Edna appeared.

"I thought you had already left," I said. "I know you must be exhausted."

"No, I had a little business to take care of first. First of all, I just want to say that I think everything went beautifully this morning, even better than I hoped for. Annie Adams, the deacons and the members of this church would like to extend you a permanent call to be the pastor of Covenant Baptist Church of Bakerstown, NC. We knew a little about where we wanted this church to go, but you have defined it more clearly for us and have started us toward our goal by this event today. You helped us bring it altogether, and we love you and are grateful to you. Please come be a part of us for a very long time."

As I looked at Edna with complete surprise and, of course, tears in my eyes, I felt an exquisite sense of joy and a complete feeling of accomplishment unlike anything I had ever experienced. I had a flashback of my college religion professor, my youth pastor at my home church, my Sunday school teachers, and most of my family, all of whom had said to me about being a pastor of a Southern Baptist church, "You can't be that." And I had the most beautiful revelation that not only could I be that, "I am that."

27670098R00190

Made in the USA
Charleston, SC
18 March 2014